Freedom to Survive

Other books by E Rae Harcum:

Psychology for Daily Living (Nelson-Hall, 1979)

A Psychology of Freedom and Dignity (Praeger, 1994)

God's Prescription for Mental Health and Religion (Hamilton Books, 2010)

Incidental Psychotherapy within Christian Relationships (Hamilton Books, 2011)

A Compatible Psychology for Christians (Hamilton Books, 2011)

Freedom
to
Survive

A VISIONARY NOVEL

E. RAE HARCUM

Blue Dolphin Publishing

Published by Blue Dolphin Publishing, Inc.
P.O. Box 8, Nevada City, CA 95959
Orders: 1-800-643-0765
Web: www.bluedolphinpublishing.com

ISBN: 978-1-57733-250-3 paperback
ISBN: 978-1-57733-414-9 e-book

Library of Congress Cataloging-in-Publication Data

Harcum, E. Rae (Eugene Rae), 1927-
    Freedom to survive : a visionary novel / E. Rae Harcum.
        p. cm.
    ISBN 978-1-57733-250-3 (pbk. : alk. paper) — ISBN 978-1-57733-414-9
(ebk.)
    1. Psychology teachers—Fiction. 2. Islands—Fiction. 3. Utopias—
Fiction. 4. Survival—Fiction. 5. Human beings—Philosophy—Fiction.
I. Title.
    PS3608.A72514F74 2011
    813'.6—dc22

                                                            2011019832

Printed in the United States of America

5   4   3   2   1

Dedication

To my sister, the late Lois Harcum Kriegh,
to her death a loving model
for the peoples of a much better world.

Those who devise wicked schemes are near,
But they are far from your law.
Yet you are near, O Lord,
And your commands are true.

Acknowledgments

M Y GREATEST DEBT IN WRITING THIS BOOK is to my late sister, Lois Kriegh, for her many helpful comments and wise advice, and for her inspiration and emotional support during the early stages in the preparation of this book. She was truly a testimonial to the reality, utility, vitality and beauty of the human spirit.

Many colleagues and students—notably Ellen Rosen and Louise Breyer—stimulated and broadened my thinking about the psychological and social issues in this book. I thank my good friends, Stase Michaels and Gwen Perkins, for reading an early version of the entire manuscript, for making extremely helpful suggestions concerning both content and style, and for offering gratifying encouragement. Stase was unstinting in sharing her considerable professional expertise in all phases of this project.

ONE

ONLY A RARE MORAL PHILOSOPHER would accord Florence Gorsuch the full responsibility for what was to happen on Kipua Island. To be sure, everyone knows that she was truly the major engineer for the particular train of events. But it is also true that other persons contributed specific actions, which undoubtedly could have greatly influenced the consequences.

And whether Flo should ultimately receive high praise or high blame for her actions depends entirely upon our views as evaluators. We must decide whether or not the personal comfort and physical welfare of a relatively few individuals should ever be sacrificed for even significant scientific gains. Would it matter if those gains could ultimately benefit thousands, or even millions, of other worthy human beings?

Your answer depends upon your convictions, of course. What do you think the world is like, and by what rules does it operate? Everyone has convictions. Convictions determine one's commitment to specific behaviors. A person always acts in accordance to his or her convictions. In fact, for a person of integrity, the behavior is a sure indication of the underlying convictions. And Flo was unquestionably a person of integrity.

Flo had been wrestling with the most basic, and most important, of psychological questions: Does a person truly possess some freedom of a will which can make him or her at least somewhat independent of life's circumstances, but which can thereby also make him or her somewhat uncontrollable by any moderating factors in that environment? Unfortunately, despite the importance of the question for social order, professional psychologists have not as yet settled upon an answer. Thus, we wonder.

1

Indeed, psychologists are still debating whether or not precise, absolutely exact answers to the puzzles of human behavior are even theoretically possible, particularly for behaviors that really matter. Despite enormous technological advances in behavioral science, must we nevertheless concede that there will always be a residual degree of unpredictability and lack of control—call it freedom—for human behaviors because of the very nature of our species? Depending upon their answers to this crucial question, different groups of psychologists have committed themselves to mutually exclusive psychological pathways for the improvement, and even the survival, of human society. Now, Flo actually believed that she had at her disposal the means to provide a solution to this greatest of psychological puzzles. Undoubtedly, the goal was worthy. She could not know that there would be disasters along the way.

Regardless of our moral judgments about the value of the end result, Flo's motives were always scrupulously the best. Everyone would also agree about that. At first, Flo herself had no significant doubts about the wisdom and value of her actions. Going back to the beginning, no one on the island had been fearful of a bad result. Should anyone involved have known better? Which of them could have known?

In fact, as the sequence of events was being set into motion on the island, Flo was filled with happy anticipation. She watched the old supply ship creep almost imperceptibly down from the horizon toward her beloved island. The arrival of the ship was a common event. To others it would not seem at all remarkable. But the scene had special meaning for Flo. On this very day, the *Cornucopia* was bringing a special human cargo to Kipua Island. Despite the painfully slow progress of the carrier, that precious cargo was almost upon the island at last. For Flo, the prospects were exciting and laced with the most optimistic hope for the future.

Flo strove to hide her strong emotion. To her, a person's feelings were private, not to be communicated, even casually, to just any bystander who happened to be curious and observant.

But, on this special day, she could not help betraying her true mood. An inquisitive and careful observer could notice high excitement in her tight clutch on the handle of her pretty pink parasol. She even wore a guileless grin across her face. At this happy moment, that revealing sign of satisfaction replaced the usual gentle smile of a confidently proper matron.

Flo's mood of high excitement was indeed altogether uncharacteristically childish. It was like that of an eager child awaiting the imminent arrival of Christmas. It reflected the same impatient anticipation of hungry children as they endured the reluctant drip of molasses down the side of an upturned jar, toward the craved stack of buttered pancakes on the breakfast platter. The sharp frustration of the delay in satisfaction was exacerbated by the high perceived value of the final reward.

Flo had not been so excited since the moment she started down the aisle on her wedding day. She had looked up to see Paul standing by the altar. His beautiful face that day was glowing with the happiest of smiles.

Now, without explanation, she suddenly felt a twinge of sadness. She had always regretted that she and Paul never had children. That would have been an even greater peak experience, she was sure.

But, suddenly again, her exalted mood returned. She reminded herself, "Today will be the start of something wonderful."

Flo's sheer eagerness for the arrival of the boat could not hasten its onward movement. In spite of her fervent attempts at psychokinesis, the progress of the squat boat never quickened. Notwithstanding the heat of the day, it seemed to be frozen immobile on the turquoise plain of the sea.

The *Cornucopia* was in fact intrinsically slow. Its functional design inhibited speed. The old ship had been built for maximum cargo capacity, as a breadbasket for the islands. It needed stability for coping with stormy seas in trying to keep to a fixed schedule. So, speed was not important in its job description. But the ship was characteristically reliable and punctual. That was the important thing. Thus, its arrival seemed reassuringly inevitable.

Whereas sleeker boats could knife cleanly through unresisting water, with hardly a ripple to mark their passage, the *Cornucopia* just shoved the opposing water roughly and indomitably out of her way. Now, the blunt bow and broad beam of the arriving ship constantly enraged the sea against its forward progress. The

resisting result was an immediate chaotic disruption of gently undulating waves into turbulent froth. A foamy wake, starting at the
bow, followed the ballooned side of the stubby ship, radiating out
from the stern like a lacy bridal train. Thus, there was momentary
ugliness closely surrounding the ship, but then symmetrical fans
of transient beauty in its wake.

The angry turbulence in the sea about the ship provided welcome proof to Flo that it was truly moving onward. Before long,
it would be moored on the island at the very dock on which she
was standing. Then, the execution of her cherished plan would
actually begin.

The panoramic scene from the dock indeed added a pleasant
tonic to her spirits. The weathered white hull of the steamboat
stood out beautifully in harmonious contrast to the blue sea-
scape. Indeed, the black smoke from *Cornucopia*'s single stack did
produce a brief ugly contrast to the rest of the pretty scene. This
contrast only emphasized the surrounding beauty, however. The
localized ugliness was soon dissipated into the vastness of the
South Pacific sky, scattered into nothingness by the prevailing
easterly breeze from the island. To Flo, such dispersion of man-
made impurities into the atmosphere by the natural breeze from
the island seemed to be metaphorical to the events of the day.
The purification of the air was like the triumph of good over evil.
It signalled the natural working of behavioral science to alleviate
man-made social ills from the planet earth. The healing process
was to begin this very day on her own island, and actually at her
instigation, at least partially under her control.

The bright sun and sparse clouds were parts of an apparently
perfect prospect. The air was clear and warm. The breeze aloft
pushed towering puffy clouds eastward toward the horizon.
White-capped waves splashed and disintegrated against pink
coral reefs. Indeed, it could be a dynamically painted scene for
a tourism catalog, commissioned by the most optimistic of travel
agents. Thus, the intrinsic beauty of the scene enhanced Flo's
feelings of joy this day.

Flo had seen the *Cornucopia* make many similar deliberate
approaches over the seventeen years that she had been on the

island. When Paul first brought her to Kipua, she had been thrilled at the novel scene. In her youth, the boats on Lake Michigan had not been as exciting to her. There always had been various kinds of boats on the lake, of course. There had been sleek sailing boats, motor racing boats trailing broad tailfeathers of spray, tugboats, garbage scows, sand barges, lake steamers, giant ocean-going ships. It was an interesting natural mix of commerce and pleasure. Flo regretted that, in those days, she had often been too busy with frivolous girlish pursuits to notice the multifarious meaningful activities on the lake.

Here, on the island, the widely-spaced arrivals of this floating general store were always special occasions for the people. Indeed, the regular appearance of the familiar boat was anticipated eagerly by all of the islanders. Its advent signaled important mail, as well as wrapped packages, and often special surprises. Indeed, frequently there were interesting new faces among the arriving passengers, as there would be today.

Flo enjoyed the scene for all of those good reasons. But, also, to her it represented part of a comfortable, reliable routine. The familiar event occurred at about the same hour on the fifteenth day of each month. To Flo, it was an assurance of physical human intervention, human consistency and control of events in a world that often seemed disturbingly beyond control. It helped to show some order in a world that was too often wantonly unordered. Indeed, the floating crate of cargo always seemed to be inching persistently ahead like the inevitable future. Sometimes, it arrived after an annoying dragging of perceived time. Nevertheless, it always arrived about when it was expected. The appearance of the ship on the horizon each month was like a cuckoo in its clock when the hour was at hand. Even the bubbling bustle on the dock was a fixed part of the expected periodic scenario.

Now, ever impatient for beneficial change, Flo sought some useful way to fill the damped time of waiting. She was never one to tolerate a waste of anything, if she could help it. Nor could she keep her nervous energy corked like a forgotten bottle of wine aging somewhere in the recesses of a cool cellar. Thus, having noted the general disarray on the dock, she closed and put down her flowered parasol, and began to coil some tangled piles of rope deftly into neat circles. She worked like an accomplished sailor, unmindful of the danger to her fancy flowered dress.

She called upon several scruffy men, who were idly loafing about the dock, to help in tidying the area. Her only authority on the dock came from the perceived air of command in her best school-teacher's voice, bolstered by the gray hairs on the head of a seasoned teacher and school principal. No one on the dock had the temerity even to think of ignoring her pointed request. In fact, with a steady stream of firm commands, Flo kept the former loiterers scrambling for several productive minutes.

By the time those on the dock could discriminate among the passengers along the rail of the *Cornucopia*, the dock was about as neat as one could reasonably expect from a functioning dock on a South Sea island. Flo examined the results critically, and was somewhat pleased. Nevertheless, she lavishly thanked her volunteer helpers, as if they had handsomely scrubbed a hospital surgery to perfection. She noted with satisfaction that indeed she had not even damaged the pretty flowers in her dress.

When Paul was alive, he always said that Flo was a sub-clinical practical compulsive personality. It was, of course, an entirely fictitious diagnostic category of personality disorder. He himself had fabricated the term in order to tease Flo. He certainly did not use it to be ugly. He merely meant that Flo had an almost uncontrollable need to discover things that needed to be done, and then to do them. And she always finished them as they should be done. That was the open secret of her success in everything that she tried.

Flo's mild compulsive tendencies gave her the drive for perfection in the truly important jobs that she routinely tackled. Thus, Paul's fanciful diagnosis also meant that her tendency toward neuroticism was not out of hand. The compulsive-like drive was actually an asset, not a harmful disorder, or a problem to be solved. For example, she could very effectively restrain herself from performing truly meaningless tasks. In fact, she considered any task to be a waste of time if you could not provide a good reason for performing it.

Flo still needed all of her skills these days in order to keep her life positive. Paul had died in a mysterious and tragic accident five years ago. Her life was sadly lonesome, to be sure, but she had been well trained in self-reliance. The best possible training was provided by her first teaching job in the inner city of Chicago. At first, the task had been horribly difficult for someone who had been reared in Evanston. It was her father who had insisted that she take the inner-city job. He claimed that she needed the broadening of experience. And, he was right. Indeed, the experience worked to perfection in Flo's case. She gained a certain mental toughness from the job, but she never lost her innate human sensitivity. This human quality survived, probably because she had never been far from the tender embraces of her home and family.

Eventually, in the school district she came to be known affectionately as "The Mighty Mite." The name recognized her small stature, of course. It also honored and acclaimed her persistent drive and spirit. Her power came from her dedication and energy. She was smart, active and fair. Thus, she provided a mighty tower of psychological strength to those who tried to do what was right. She was also a formidable adversary for those who would not satisfy themselves with doing the right thing. There were enough of that kind around to provide the necessary toughening experience.

Now, many years later, she still possessed basically the same taut body and mind. Her body was maturely trim, shaped by her preference for the essentially fruit and fish diet of the island, and by her frequent brisk walks along its main roads and trails. Long ago, she had actually bought an exercise bike for her bedroom. But, Flo preferred to conduct her serious workouts outside where she could meet people. She enjoyed the exchange of pleasantries with the islanders along the way as she faithfully walked her daily rounds. Thus, the sincere desire for exercise was never allowed to interfere with a chance to chat. So, her daily tour consisted of brisk dashes of exercise between frequent stops for social interludes. Clearly, the social benefits were more important to her psychologically than the gratuitous exercise was for delaying the effects of aging on her body. She loved to say that her friends kept her young.

Flo's mind was still sharp. It was honed now by the duties of principal of the lone island school, and by the multiple hassles of serving as mayor of the island government. She was a vast source of ideas for improvement. She was also a dynamo of personal power to implement those ideas. In fact, one of those creative ideas was just now about to blossom. Hopefully, the bloom of her idea would begin to unfold as soon as the boat docked.

Flo wondered how this familiar routine on the dock, obviously ordinary, of a ship arriving in port, could overlay such vital events. Truly, this arrival was crucial in the lives of so many people. Perhaps, it was vital to everyone in the world. The supply boat was, at last, bringing Professor Sculleigh Burnhouse, the world-class, internationally famous psychologist, to her beloved island. He was the prime reason for her excitement.

Charles Sculleigh Burnhouse had been a child intellectual prodigy. He had garnered one academic accolade and prize after another all of the way through school and college. Incredibly, he had actually been singled out for special recruitment by graduate schools. Burnhouse's scientific work had become internationally recognized even while he was still a graduate student in psychology at Stanford. Such precocious recognition was extremely unusual in the academic world.

After receiving his Ph.D. at the age of 22, Burnhouse had spent two years as a post-doctoral student at Harvard under the aegis of B. F. Skinner, the main proponent of the Behavioristic theory of psychology. This theoretical orientation argues that animals, including human beings, do not possess freedom of will or any other unobservable mental characteristic, and therefore the science of psychology should study only the observable characteristics of animals. For the Behaviorists, therefore, we can understand animal behavior by simply observing innate behavioral mechanisms and how animals respond to rewards and punishment. Burnhouse later took a teaching position back at Stanford, achieving the rank of professor seven years later. His rapid promotion to professor actually had set some sort of a modern-day record for the university.

Burnhouse was the critical cog in the master wheel of Flo's developmental plan for the island. Thus, one of the most published and widely heralded psychologists in the world was about to honor her small island. Burnhouse had planned, at her request, to conduct a major psychological research project on Kipua. His project would surely transform the island into a virtual paradise for islanders and tourists alike. Also, it would make Kipua famous throughout the entire civilized world.

For Kipua to be the host site for the prestigious Professor Burnhouse's bold social experiment was thus the culmination of a cherished dream for Flo. Today's event represented many years of extensive planning and dedicated and desperate persuasion. Today, every niche in her grand dream was filling nicely with appropriate golden pegs.

But, all of this was not perfect. There was a tiny nagging problem. The problem was tiny because it seemed inconsequential to Flo's conscious mind. It was nagging, however, because it did not seem inconsequential to some deeper unconscious level of Flo's brain. Indeed, it was minute, but it burned incessantly in the covert places of the unconscious.

So, despite the pregnant scene before her, happy with promise, there was deep within Flo's consciousness a definite pinprick of worry. Despite her great joy of anticipation at Burnhouse's arrival, Flo could still detect a persistent faint voice hassling her mind from somewhere deep within her private being. That unbidden voice was grinding out an apparent warning of dread consequences from the proposed research, even though the words themselves were not quite understandable.

Nevertheless, the sheer presence of the voice itself was disturbing. Flo fought to make out the exact words. Her best efforts to make sense of them had so far been abjectly unsuccessful. She would feel better if she just knew exactly what the words said, what the presumed warning was about. That would help her deal intelligently with them. The sounds were unmistakably distress calls, sounding an urgent alarm. That much she knew. That much was sure.

Often, on previous occasions, that same faint discordant voice had been correct, even though outward logic and conscious personal motivations had, as now, overpowered it at first. Foolish as the muted voice might be, or appear sensibly to be, it added to the stark white of her knuckles as she clutched anew the ornate handle of her dainty parasol.

Some would call Flo's faint inner voice a manifestation of "her better judgment." But, she wondered, how could such a weak voice represent a stronger, or better, basis for decision than her best intentional reasoning? The problem of the faint inner voice was that it did not present any strong logical arguments to her conscious mind to permit deliberate conscious debate. It just continued to sound those inarticulate alarms and warning bells.

So, Flo tried, this one more time, to guess at the nature of the warning so that she could consciously and deliberately dismiss it. She again conjured up possible objections. Then, she satisfactorily refuted each one in turn. Finally, she tried to pretend that the annoying nagging was simply a tangible fabrication of her personal insecurities.

But, even though the voice scolded Flo in the unintelligible language of hidden conflict, one truth was clear: she really had no such personal insecurities. Her self-confidence was displayed for all to see in the many tangible successes that she had enjoyed. Flo had been, among other things, teacher of the year in Chicago; assistant superintendent of the Cook County School District; and now, in semi-retirement, simultaneously school principal and mayor of Kipua Island. Therefore, she was used to success, despite the occasional faint clamor of these insistent inner voices. Or, perhaps, the presence of the faint voice was partially responsible for her successes. Flo desperately wanted to get control of it, or to have it go away.

Flo had understood completely that Burnhouse's experiment could raise ethical questions. It could also be decidedly dangerous. There could be trouble, if the results did not turn out as expected.

Psychology is not an exact science. That is especially true when one is trying to change important human behaviors. There is always a viable element of risk when scientists start messing with animal minds, especially human minds. Therefore, possibly the faint voice was only sounding a reasonable general warning to be cautious. Perhaps, it was just an instinctive protective mechanism to aid human survival.

On the other side, Flo's conscious mind had provided many strong logical arguments in favor of conducting the psychological research on her island. First, the research was aimed at verifying Burnhouse's scientifically sound ideas about the best way to improve the quality of human life, for everyone, everywhere. His research might even discover a way to prevent the total decline, or demise, of our troubled modern society.

Second, Burnhouse's superb reputation as a research scientist indicated that he knew what he was doing. Such a man was too responsible a person to tolerate an unreasonable risk.

Third, Burnhouse's project had been approved and funded by the prestigious Schoonover Foundation. Therefore, it had survived the toughest scrutiny from all of the high-powered staff and consultants that such a well-heeled institution could command. The conservative Schoonover board would surely not support a project that was ethically questionable, or seriously dangerous.

Finally, Flo came to the bottom line in her internal arguments. The project on Kipua was actually her baby, her brainstorm. On the basis of her own convictions, she herself had initiated the first contact with Burnhouse about bringing his proposed project to the island. She had even participated in the planning of his original research proposal to Schoonover. Therefore, she believed in his social plan because she believed in herself.

In the end, Flo felt that she had to trust the reasoned arguments of her conscious mind. What else could she truly trust more?

Flo had even fought her best fight against those on the island who had earlier opposed Burnhouse's ideas for social improvements. Some people had fiercely denounced his proposed experiment which had been designed to verify his psychological theories for beneficial social change. Flo had been successful in combatting their objections, and in gaining their approval at the end.

Despite Burnhouse's credentials and prestige, it had not been easy for Flo to convince the island council to invite him to bring his experiment to the island. In particular, Dan Crow, the Vice-mayor of the island and an influential member of the council, had initially strongly opposed the idea. As a former career marine, who retired as a Sergeant Major after twenty-six years in the Corps, and a patchwork quilt of ribbons on his uniform jacket, Crow felt that he had a pretty good idea of how a good organization worked. To his mind, the keys to success were honor, respect and discipline. They worked fabulously well in the Corps. They would indeed work well anywhere. Good people made good teams that could get a job done. Manipulating people by fancy psychological tricks would never work, he argued. Crow simply felt that the experiment, even if successful, would not improve the existing social organization of the island. He feared that instead it would create complete disorganization.

Flo had finally persuaded Crow and the rest of the island council to go along with the plan simply as an experiment. She had pointed out the valid scientific arguments. She recounted the laboratory and anecdotal evidence that the plan would be successful. Finally, she argued that the people who came as a part of the experiment would bring substantial revenues to the merchants of the island. For Crow, that argument finally tipped the scales in favor of Burnhouse. Crow was now a businessman and a committed leader in governance. He strongly felt his responsibilities to bring economic opportunities to the people of the island.

Flo herself was also not unmindful of the benefits to the island. To be sure, the bulk of Burnhouse's large budget would be spent right here on the island. And, because of Burnhouse's prominence in the higher circles of behavioral science, the name of the island would appear in major newspapers around the world. Undoubtedly, that would eventually bring still more tourist dollars to the island. Strangely, that particular economic thought brought a slight, but perceptible, increase in the sharpness of the tiny inner voice. She wondered if the possibility of abundant American dollars had unconsciously influenced her conscious decision.

But, truthfully, Flo still could not think consciously of any valid reason strong enough to make her consider stopping the experiment. The only danger would occur if the experiment would fail to produce the expected results. And that was not likely to happen. Too many good scientists had predicted a positive outcome.

Admittedly, Flo had some small practical basis for questioning whether or not she had acted wisely when she, as mayor, persuaded the island council to invite Burnhouse to try out his revolutionary psychological theory on the island population. She knew that psychological experiments could always be dangerous. The researchers were dealing with the minds of real people whose basic personalities were largely unknown to them. And no resident on the island had the least bit of experience with psychological experiments. The labs that they had taken in college were essentially only demonstrations. That kind of experience really did not count. No one here had hands-on experience with serious experiments in psychology. And this experiment was especially serious. It would have important implications for the welfare of all human beings.

Another disquieting fact was that Professor Burnhouse had the general reputation for being an uncompromising devotee of scientific rigor. Apparently, he did not have a particularly high regard for the immediate human implications, only the long-term ones. Flo was not sure about the details of the rumored charges against him. She did recall that Burnhouse had been criticized for the degree of realism that he had inserted in some of his experiments on personal stress. He actually had set up some conditions in which his research subjects had been led to believe that truly their own lives, and the lives of their close friends, were in imminent danger.

Such realism made it easier for him to argue that his research results were valid and relevant to true-life emergency situations, of course. That surely was a plus. But many psychologists questioned the ethics of treating the research subjects in such an unfeeling way. To be sure, these concerns were about subjective personal feelings. They did not involve actual physical dangers to the subjects.

Also, other psychologists had argued that the practical results of Burnhouse's studies made them sufficiently valuable to society to justify the risk. Therefore, the alleged harsh treatment of the subjects, even if true, was amply justified on scientific grounds. That was indeed important. Furthermore, as the canons of ethics of professional organizations demanded, Burnhouse had provided complete de-briefings for the subjects in order to explain the need and purposes of his research. He even provided psychotherapy for those particular subjects who needed it after the study was completed. The purpose was to insure that any possible harm that might have been done was fully rectified.

Flo asked herself whether or not this impersonal characteristic of Burnhouse, indicated by the preference of science over specific people, was necessarily a bad thing. She decided once again that it was certainly not a valid reason to cancel the proposed study.

Such scientific objectivity was no problem, if there were no unforeseen snags in the conduct of the research, of course. But suppose the experiment unleashed unexpected mental demons? There was no safety net in Burnhouse's plan in case the experiment failed. In fact, Burnhouse had been so confident of the correctness of his theory that he would not even consider possible failure. He had argued that the procedures which implemented his theory were in themselves a sort of psychological safety net.

Flo wondered, however, if his argument was based on scientific objectivity. Was it simply personal overconfidence? So, as the cliché advised, time would tell. Particularly, the results of the experiment would be manifested in future events that would provide the final empirical answer. And that result, she hoped, would quiet the small internal voice.

TWO

THE *CORNUCOPIA* finally forced its tortured way into the lagoon. Now in calmer water, it slowly eased itself with still-grumbling engines toward the dock. Two dark, half-naked men with mooring lines slung over their shoulders were standing fore and aft, ready to pitch the lines to similar waiting men on the dock. Such preparatory activity heightened the sense of anticipation for everyone. For a moment, the only sounds were the concerned voices of mothers sternly admonishing their children to be careful, and the rhythmic slap of the waves against the weathered pilings of the dock.

Flo was standing near the end of the pier next to Jake Blankenship. Jake was Flo's brother. He had come to Kipua to be near her. He was the proprietor of the only taxicab company on the island. In truth, he liked to joke about his proprietorship as constituting a company. Actually, the entire rolling stock of his transportation enterprise was limited to the one ancient, near-wreck behind him.

Jake Blakenship had been a supervisor in an automobile assembly plant in Dearborn, Michigan, when he was injured in an industrial accident. A drunken machinist had left a crescent wrench lying on an overhead crane. Someone saw the wrench falling and called out a warning. Jake had looked up just in time to receive the blow on the middle of his forehead. His head was deeply cut, and a circular piece of bone was punched in from his skull, pressing on his brain. Strangely, Jake never lost consciousness. With his finger, he could move the patch of bone, because it was separated from the rest of his skull. Each time he pushed it, he got a sick feeling in his stomach. The feeling was so strange

15

that he pushed the bone several times before the duty nurse made him stop.

Several volunteers carried Jake to the plant infirmary, where the doctor on duty insisted on summoning immediately the neurologist on call. In the thirty minutes it took the specialist to arrive, Jake had developed an excruciating headache. Subdural bleeding had caused pressure on the frontal lobe of his brain, and produced irreversible damage to it. The neurologist rushed him to the hospital for immediate surgery to reduce the swelling, and to re-attach the bone fragment.

Jake was left with a small indented place on his forehead, and, after several additional surgeries, only a portion of each frontal lobe of his brain. The further surgeries had been necessary to try to eliminate the occasional seizures which were the consequence of the injury.

Jake was forever changed from an organized and responsible worker into a person characterized by chaotic and irresponsible behavior. He could no longer hold his former job, and indeed no job that required planning, moderation and restraint. Because his employer was judged to be legally culpable, Jake received a full disability pension which was sufficient to meet his minimal needs.

Jake had come to Kipua at the urging of his older sister, who had moved to the island five years previously. Because Jake still had seizures when he became overly stressed or seriously upset, he could not hold an ordinary job. Flo wanted him to be where she could help watch over him.

A doctor in Hawaii had found the right combination of medications to control Jake's seizures. Therefore, it had been two years since he had an episode. Consequently, he was cleared medically to be able to drive an automobile safely.

But, in fact, Jake divided his time among a variety of activities. The least time-consuming activity, but most important, was signing the pension checks from his former career. The rest of his time was more or less evenly divided among such activities as driving the relic of a formerly prestigious vehicle, combing the beaches for treasures and hanging out at the Crow Bar on Main Street. The latter two were his favorites. For Jake, a treasure could be a pretty rock, or an appealing shell, as easily as it could be a commercial object containing gold or silver.

Jake's attire, as usual, was more appropriate for his various activities on the beaches than for chauffeuring visitors. The stubble on his face could be confused with a beard. But it was not a beard. Everyone knew that actual fact. A beard would not be shaved off every several weeks, or so, when a particular benign mood of social civilization came over him.

Jake maintained the dignity of his style of life by convincing everyone that he disdained money. At least, he disdained any more of it than was absolutely necessary to stay alive and happy. Mostly, that meant to support moderately excessive drinking and gambling habits. Jake was probably the best poker player on the island. His injury had not materially damaged his ability to make and execute short-term strategies that could cover a hand of poker very well.

Everyone knew about Jake's superior skill at poker. But, Jake wisely lost enough poker hands to be able to find people still willing to play with him. That required the finest degree of psychological finesse. He could judge with precision how much a person was willing to pay for a lesson in the finer techniques of poker.

Jake had not been in favor of the plan to bring Burnhouse to Kipua. His experience of managing people in industry had taught him that 99 out of 100 people were friendly, fair and reasonable, if that was the way that they themselves were treated. But, often the hundredth person was somehow different. That person did not respond to any reasonable overtures. The hundredth person could be a confirmed misanthrope, apparently delighting in anything mean and low. There was no way to work with such people, or to get along with them. In short, the hundredth person would wreck any hopes of a Utopia on any island. The hundredth person, appearing on several occasions in different bodies, had in fact caused Jake to turn sour on life in areas with large populations. Unfortunately, the hundredth persons tended to leave the strongest impressions, at least on Jake.

As he watched the *Cornucopia* plow toward the pier, Jake wondered at the type of man who thought that he could completely control everyone. In Jake's view, Sculleigh Burnhouse must be a fool. But, to be sure, Burnhouse must be a rich fool. Jake had to admire him for that. Jake did not care much for money himself, but ironically he admired people who knew how to get it, especially if their acquisition plans were clever.

The venerable supply ship eventually chugged and groaned its way up to the pier. It was promptly tied up by the two deck-hands on the ship, and by the assorted willing volunteers on the dock. Then, the deck hands quickly stretched the single gang-plank over to the pier.

Groups of eager passengers rushed ashore in the natural order of their degrees of impatience. First on the dock were some children and their mothers. These passengers were regular inhabitants of the island, happy to be home. They had been off on holidays, on buying trips or to complete various errands. Frequently, the islanders took the *Cornucopia* to Saipan in order to secure certain specialized medical and dental treatments that were not available on the island.

This first group to disembark was soon followed by two fat businessmen dressed in standard tourist uniforms of flowered shirts and white trousers. This portly pair worked as drummers for distributors of alcoholic beverages and restaurant supplies. Everyone on the island called them the "Booze Brothers". Hastily, these interesting gentlemen arduously schlepped their sample cases to a dolly waiting for them on the dock. Then, they began to roll their merchandise noisily down the dock toward the town, unmindful of damage to either the dolly or the dock. They acted like this was a rather routine trip for them, which indeed it was.

The Booze Brothers were in a hurry, as usual, because they had less than an hour to sell their wares and get back on board their mode of transportation off the island. As usual, the *Cornucopia* was scheduled to depart in one hour. Capt. Kebomba always departed on schedule.

On one occasion, a few years before, the boys down at the Bar Belle Saloon had tricked the gullible duo of drummers into drinking too much from their own sample kits. The locals had proclaimed loudly that the taste of the samples seemed a trifle odd.

The brothers kept trying, but naturally, they could never discern the alleged peculiar taste. Eventually, they became so toxically befuddled that they missed the departure of their only means of transportation off the island for the next month.

The jokesters at the Bar Belle did, however, pay dearly for their impulsive prank. The following month on the island was marked by misery and lamentation on Main Street. In a word, the extended presence of the Booze Brothers was a disaster for everyone who worked in the village. It seemed that the Brothers had no other visible means of recreation than to sell their product. Therefore, once their business had been completed, life on the island was abysmally boring for them. In desperation for something to do, they tried the game of poker. They had to give up the cards, however, when they had been relieved of all personal possessions of value. First to go was all of their cash. Then, they lost their sample cases, with complete contents. Next to go was whatever clothes off their backs that were not absolutely necessary. Finally, they exhausted all of the credit that they could squeeze out of the foolish and pitying inhabitants by their heart-wrenching pleas.

Then, the lost souls tried to amuse themselves by complaining to anyone who was compassionate, or unwise, enough to listen. In fact, the well-rounded salesmen raised the level of complaining to a fine art, appreciated by no one on the island. Their visit was nevertheless educational because they completely destroyed the myth that fat men were jolly.

Eventually, the Booze Brothers played out that annoying string of tactical complaints. They were just about to move on to the ultimate source of entertainment: being beaten to within an inch of their life by former captive audiences to their whining. The fortunate, timely arrival of the *Cornucopia* on its next regular trip prevented them from finding out just how their last attempt at self-entertainment was going to work out. Everyone was happy for their narrow escape. No one really disliked them.

Today, the last of the passengers to disembark from the moored boat was a striking couple. They stood out because he was so ordinary in physical appearance, and he was accompanied by a woman who was so remarkably beautiful. This pair was the long-anticipated Professor Sculleigh Burnhouse, and his esteemed research associate, Monika Luthsaar.

The couple's elaborate ritual of disembarkment seemed orchestrated like an overacted scene from a B movie. Burnhouse cavalierly assisted his associate ashore like she were European royalty, and he was a baronet assigned to be her escort. Monika moved and posed like she was about to break out in song at any moment.

Jake began to chuckle loudly, but was immediately shushed by Flo. In truth, however, Flo could hardly blame Jake. She knew that she herself had been amused. The little hidden voice inside her grew yet perceptibly louder.

Behind the sunglasses, Burnhouse seemed to have a pleasant face, more pretty than handsome. His large forehead was exaggerated by a slightly receding line of sandy hair, which was now tousled by the wind. He wore his hair full about the ears. It was obviously an expensive haircut.

Burnhouse was as overdressed as a Hollywood mogul on safari. His billed nautical cap, Navy blue blazer, with gold buttons, and white slacks were indeed highly fashionable, as were his white canvas shoes. But, his marbleized silk ascot, of vibrating purple and magenta colors, absolutely gave him away. He could not forego this touch of flamboyance, even on a basically professional excursion. His attention to such details for forming impressions indicated that Burnhouse nevertheless attempted to maintain the highest standards in everything, as best he knew how.

Indeed, Flo was not greatly impressed. The intensity of the inner voice gained yet another decibel. Now, it was loud enough for her to hear the question: Was this just a superficial flamboyance, an ill-advised affectation, or did it extend deeper into Burnhouse's character, even to professional aspects? Did this one eccentricity really matter in a scientist? Flo was not comfortable even asking the question.

Under the circumstances, however, no one was likely to spend much time contemplating Sculleigh Burnhouse. Not with Monika Luthsaar on the same dock.

Monika was indeed attractive, as Flo had been told. Flo decided that even the florid descriptions of Monika were flagrantly understated and inadequate. Monika's simple slack suit, in pale pink, could not completely mask a vibrant personality, matching that of Burnhouse.

The presence of the colorful personality took Flo by surprise. All prior descriptions had concentrated exclusively on Monika's physical appearance. The reason was obvious.

The spare description of Monika as attractive certainly could not cover her perfect physical endowments. With her ample blond hair, purposefully disheveled wildly in an image of wantonness, and the complementing magazine-cover figure, Monika commanded everyone's full attention. The collective gasps of amazement on the dock were like a trumpet fanfare as a queen entered a royal hall.

It occurred to Flo that, for the sake of safety, they should confiscate all of the sharp knives and other dangerous tools from the men on the dock. None of them could possibly be paying attention to any dangerous task that they may be supposed to be doing at the moment. They could easily inflict grievous bodily damage upon themselves.

Monika's face was not really remarkable—except that it was perfect. Some women are pretty because they have some particularly cute feature. Not Monika! The nose was straight, and just the right size for the exactly oval face. The blue of the eyes was augmented in a most pleasing way by the golden hair, which made those eyes the dazzling color of the bluest sky. The teeth were also perfect, often pleasantly revealed in a friendly smile. Thus, the overall picture was enhanced by an inner beauty which exceeded that of the formal features in static repose. The tasteful use of muted cosmetics on the face completed a picture as close to artistic perfection as a growing adolescent of the opposite gender could imagine, or dream about.

Truly, just as she stood, Monika could be the cover girl for any magazine, for men or for women. Indeed, on several occasions in her youth, she had been a model in fashion magazines. Flo thought that Monika could also benefit the swimsuit edition of several popular magazines for men.

Monika was not only beautiful, she was also fresh, open and appealing as a person. Flo immediately surprised herself by liking Monika.

Flo had heard that one of Monika's attractions for Burnhouse was her good looks. Such beauty, coupled with the pleasing personality, could secure the cooperation of anyone, male or female, for the conduct of his research. Flo could believe it.

Flo did note with a mild distaste that Monika's high heels produced a little extra strain on the taut fabric of the slacks stretched over her gluteus muscles. So, as far as Flo was concerned, Monika was admittedly young and fabulous, but really not perfect.

Monika obviously loved the full attention of the crowd. She played to the crowd, continuously striking delightful poses. She talked just a little louder than was necessary for the occasion, just in case the attention of anyone near the back of the crowd might be wandering.

Burnhouse hung in the background at first. He was well content to let Monika enjoy this special moment in the attentional spotlight. Obviously, this was a familiar routine for both of them. Both knew that later there would be a time for the prestigious professor to shine, by showing off his vaunted intellectual powers.

So, Sculleigh Burnhouse and Monika Luthsaar were certainly an interesting pair. Not knowing the truth, one would more likely guess that they were part of an advance film crew on location from Hollywood. They did not look like a pair of renowned researchers from a prestigious university a few miles up the road from Hollywood.

Flo greeted them in her friendliest manner. "Professor Burnhouse and Dr. Luthsaar, it is a pleasure to meet you both. I am Florence Gorsuch. Please call me Flo.

Burnhouse smiled, and gallantly kissed her hand. "Thanks, Flo. My friends call me Skull. That is a shortened form of my given name, and not a personal description, I hope. This vision of loveliness, as you surmised, is Monika Luthsaar."

"Welcome to our island, Monika," Flo said in her best deep mayor's voice. She immediately hated herself for trying to sound mayoral and masculine.

To Burnhouse, she said, now in a higher-pitched voice, more like her natural one, "Surely, Skull, I can see that the name is not descriptive. It certainly is distinctive, though. Did you two have a pleasant trip?"

"Yes, I think we did," answered Burnhouse, looking at Monika. She nodded agreement, and dashed off another dazzling smile.

Flo decided that it was necessary to begin the business of the day. "Look," she said, "I hate to start off on business so soon, but time is short. We will have time to get better acquainted later.

"This evening you are scheduled to speak at the Catholic church immediately after dinner. My brother, Jake Blankenship, here has his cab ready to take us directly to dinner at the manor house of the copra plantation, as guests of the dePuy family. Pierre dePuy is owner of the plantation, and he is also a member of the island council."

Jake and the visitors nodded pleasantly to each other. Jake shook hands first with Burnhouse and then with Monika. He was pleasantly surprised by the strength of her grip. She surely is not just a pretty face," he thought, "or a super figure."

Flo continued, "I have taken the liberty of arranging for a couple of the dock workers to deliver your luggage to the Crow Bar, where you will be staying. Your research equipment will be delivered to an empty room in the schoolhouse. That will be the base of operations for your research project, if that is satisfactory."

Burnhouse and Monika both nodded mildly interested assents to the plan. They eased themselves into the worn, but comfortable, seats of the old taxi for the short ride to the plantation house, and to dinner. To his credit, Burnhouse did not show in his actions that he had noticed that the decrepit vehicle was not a modern limousine. Flo saw that he had glanced about the cab, so she knew that Burnhouse was aware of its condition. She saw no need to apologize for it, though.

As they reached the end of the pier, and turned onto the one main street of the village, the visitors tried to take in as much of the scene as possible. Jake drove slowly to give them a better chance to see it all.

Burnhouse emitted a few inarticulate sounds of satisfaction. Then, he said "Exactly what I expected." Flo assumed that it was a favorable comment.

Along the main street there were several stores and shops, a sort of all-purpose department store, a storefront bank, two saloons and two churches. The churches were on opposite sides of the north end of the street. The one on the lagoon side of the street was substantially larger. It was the Catholic church because most of the islanders were Catholic. One saloon was halfway down the row of buildings from the pier, across the street from the bank. It was identified as the "Bar Belle" in large yellow letters on a rooftop sign that once was blue. Below these letters, smaller letters of about the same yellow color spelled out the message, "Everyone is welcome here."

The building itself was a simple box, like the others. The grain of the wood siding was deeply etched by the sands of many tropical storms which had left only faint traces of earlier paints. The sign itself had obviously been more recently re-painted. The railed porch running along the front of the box reminded Skull of a set for an old western movie. A faded painting of a young lady in a theatrical costume, skimpy by 1890 standards, decorated the wall beside the entrance. That was presumably the original belle of the bar. The Bar Belle was easily the most interesting sight in a thoroughly intriguing and captivating scene.

The second saloon, the Crow Bar, was almost a replica of the Bar Belle. One slight difference was the more abundant vestiges of paint. Someone could perhaps say that the building was recently painted. That was, of course, a relative term, meaning that it probably had been painted within the last ten years.

Another distinction from the Bar Belle was the large sign on the roof. The weathered sign faintly displayed the name of the establishment. Also, there was a large crowbar, obviously carved from a single tree trunk and crotch of a limb, hanging below the sign.

The village did not show strong vital signs of prosperity, but it was reasonably well-kept. The buildings did look to be in basically good condition, except for the paint, which the blowing sands had obviously also scoured mercilessly. "Sand blasting is an excellent way to remove paint," thought Flo.

"This will do nicely," Burnhouse said pleasantly. "It looks exactly like I hoped it would look. I am truly eager to get started."

Flo felt a quick surge of personal satisfaction at his words. She had invested so very much of herself in his project. She would take it as a personal failure, if Burnhouse's project did not succeed on the island. Perhaps, that was why she continued to worry so irrationally that Burnhouse would not succeed.

Soon, the old taxi had covered the short distance to the edge of town. This was, to be sure, a meager accomplishment. It was attributable to the size of the village, and not to any pretense of speed for the vehicle.

Then, the party headed westward through rows of tall, curving coconut palm trees. Burnhouse noted that the plantation had the look of mild prosperity and reasonable attention to maintenance and appearance.

"Please forgive me if I rattle off some more business," said Flo. "The dinner this evening has a second purpose. It will do more than sustain our bodies with necessary nourishment, and provide our souls with pleasant entertainment. The other purpose of the dinner is to provide an introductory meeting between you and key members of the island council in a relaxed social setting. Another member of the island council, Dan Crow, owner of the Crow Bar tavern in town, will also be present.

"Dan had not been sure that it was a good idea for you to come to Kipua. I believe that a great many of the potential problems of government can be prevented by first establishing good interpersonal relations among the various parties to negotiations. So, we will get started on that right away."

"Good idea," said Burnhouse, smiling. Monika smiled her agreement with him and nodded slightly.

"Thanks," said Flo. Then, she continued, "After dinner, as I said, there will be a town meeting at the Catholic Church for you to explain your proposals to the general island population. I know that it is unusual to schedule such a meeting so soon. But, news of your arrival will be all over the island by nightfall. Rumors about the purpose of your visit can quickly get out of hand. So, the people should be given the facts as soon as possible. I had understood from your prior correspondence that good communications and excellent cooperation with the island population were essential for the success of your experiment."

"Right. That's fine," said Burnhouse. "You understood me perfectly. It is a good idea. Let's get on with it."

The Catholic Church sanctuary had been rented for the purpose because it was the largest auditorium on the island. Burnhouse reflected on the irony of that situation. Likely, there would be strong opposition by the church to his research proposals. He hoped that the parish priest was not the excitable type. If the priest ignited flames of opposition in his flock, the plan would get off to a rather explosive start. Burnhouse told himself to be patient. He would have the answer to his question this evening. But, he worried faintly about it as the old automobile bounced steadily toward the plantation. Monika also looked a trifle serious. Burnhouse took her hand, and gave it a slight squeeze. The scientists liked to hide their nervousness at beginning a new level of boldness in social design.

Then, as the taxi rounded a bend in the twisting road, there was an almost blinding flash. It was in stark, stunning contrast to the brown dirt of the road and the saturated green vegetation of the palm trees and forest. The sight was truly startling for those who had been accustomed to seeing the natural colors of sea, sky and landscape. There, directly ahead of them, at the edge of a small clearing, was a white stuccoed plantation manor. The house was bordered by a ten-foot white stuccoed wall. All of the white surfaces were dazzling, shimmering in the bright sunlight.

Both Monika and Burnhouse let out involuntary gasps of surprise. Flo and Jake chuckled in concert. The visitors had given the universal startle response of all newcomers upon seeing the plantation house for the first time when they came around that bend in the road. A stand of bamboo along the road completely blocked the view of the white expanse until the sudden clash of brilliance drowned the unexpecting visitor.

There were no breaks in the solid surface of the high wall, except for the front entrance. Massive wooden gates, painted in unrelieved white, hung on huge ornamental iron hinges, also painted white. The gates now stood open to welcome the guests, exposing the continuing white of the house beyond. The huge expanse of continuous white gave the impression of a large imperial palace in the jungle.

The complex of house and walls was very functional. When closed, the thick gates could withstand the direct onslaughts of armies. All of the gates were stout, constructed of roughly hewn logs. Such strength had been needed to repel disgruntled or thieving natives during the early days when the plantation was just getting started. Small portholes, or firing ports, in the heavy gates allowed those inside to view—possibly to shoot—anyone approaching the compound. There was a smaller service entrance on the opposite side of the compound. It was also protected by similar sturdy gates, with similar firing ports.

While the walls had the appearance of a warlike fortress, the plantation house itself had the general aura of a luxurious home in the suburbs of a safe countryside. Everything was spacious. Wide verandas covered the front and the north sides of the house. A large swimming pool shimmered adjacent to the north veranda. To the south of the house, against the compound wall, the visitors could see servants' quarters, work sheds and plantation offices.

As the cab circled the drive to the main entrance, dePuy came down from the portico to greet them. He wore a starched dress shirt of finest linen, characteristic of the islands. His black tuxedo trousers and patent leather shoes completed a flawless and fashionable manner of dress. His urbane and friendly manner easily matched his elegant attire. One could be jealous of the successful dePuy, but one could not dislike him.

dePuy was known about the island as a decent man. He was unquestionably fair to his workers, and equally insistent on fair performance from them. He would not tolerate careless work. But, he was generous with sincere gratitude and high praise for good work. Despite his present wealth, he never forgot that his father and grandfather had worked in the earth with their hands. Thus, he was not ashamed to get his hands dirty when there was a messy job to be done, as an instructional device for his employees. He did such jobs willingly, as a tangible role model. His employees respected him for this sincere common-man approach.

Now, this evening, he was playing a different role. Tonight, he was a fine gentleman, and a gracious host. He effortlessly assumed those roles with the same attention to detail that made him a successful businessman.

"Hello, Flo. Hiya, Jake," dePuy sang out, in a most friendly manner. He reached out to help Flo up the veranda stairs. "Happy to have you with us, Professor Burnhouse and Dr. Luthsaar. I am Pierre dePuy. Please call me Pierre."

"My friends call me Skull. It is a nickname, in case you wondered," smiled Burnhouse.

"Splendid! Capitol! Of course, it is," laughed duPuy. But, he was actually giving his rapt attention to Monika. Most people spent a lot of time looking at Monika. Flo feared that dePuy might soon faint if he did not take a quick breath, or stumble if he did not watch his step.

Monika charmed him further with her best smile. "My friends call me Monika. They stay away from nicknames, if they want to be my friends," she purred. "I hate nicknames. I think that they rob a person of dignity."

Monika knew that she was beautiful, without question. She also knew that essentially every man on the planet would want to please her, to be her friend. No one called her anything that resembled a nickname, except that Burnhouse occasionally called her "Dr. M."

dePuy was surely no exception to the general rule. "Monika, why would anyone wish another name?" he asked, as he gallantly kissed her hand.

"I happen to think that nicknames are nice. Right, Jake?" said Burnhouse, with an ingratiating mock grimace.

"Yep," said Jake, with a wink. "They are found in the finest circles, Doc."

Then, returning to business, the sometimes taxi driver said, "I will be back in time to take you to the Catholic church for your meeting. See you later."

Jake jumped into his car, and ground it into gear. Then, he clanged and rattled it off down the dusty road toward town. As he waved and blew kisses to native girls with one hand, he drank from a bottle in a brown paper bag in the other hand. Burnhouse guessed that he was either steering with his knees, or the old car was following familiar ruts in the road.

"What a disreputable character!" commented dePuy, without real feeling because of his personal liking for the man. Everyone liked Jake. They all understood that his injury had damaged his brain and his abilities in certain areas, but it had not affected his basic good sense and his good heart.

Motioning for his guests to follow him, dePuy continued, "We have cold lemonade to drink on the veranda," he offered, "Or anything else that you might prefer."

"Lemonade is fine for me. I'm working tonight," said Burnhouse with a smile. It was one of his rare attempts at humor.

dePuy's wife, Blanche, his daughter, Rene, and Dan Crow, local bar owner and member of the island council, were already seated on the north veranda. Everyone rose to meet the new arrivals. After introductions, they seated themselves comfortably with their cold drinks, except that Dan Crow remained standing, and occasionally paced about.

Crow was dressed entirely in white—suit, shirt, shoes—except for a rose-colored tie. He was a large man—six feet and a few inches in height, and 250 pounds of muscle—a superb specimen of an athletic build. He had the black hair and dark skin of his American Indian heritage. His hair was cut short like a marine drill sergeant. Such a haircut was his custom. He was in fact a former marine drill sergeant.

Crow's outgoing style of warm interpersonal relationships masked the fact that he was highly experienced in guerrilla warfare. Few people knew that he had earned many combat decorations, although they did know that he was a combat veteran. Crow had retired to the quieter life of the island after years of service to his country. He had retired because his old wounds bothered him on rainy days in chilly climates.

Crow's proprietorship of the Crow Bar was rather uneventful. He never had trouble, because no one dared earn his ire. He would tolerate no misbehavior in his bar, or indeed at any time in his presence. Nevertheless, he was a good friend and responsible citizen.

Crow looked just uncomfortable enough in his clothing to suggest that it had been many months since he had wrapped a tie around his neck. He frequently stuck a finger inside his collar in a futile attempt to stretch a little more room for his thick neck.

Blanche dePuy was an attractive woman. Her greatest beauty lay in her pleasant smile and thoughtful attitude of service. She was content to run the family from a distant vantage point in the background. She was so efficient at such an endeavor that no one understood just how the family functioned. Everything simply seemed always to be in order and in place. Blanche was entirely happy with her role of service to others. When her family took time to think about it, they absolutely adored her.

Rene, in a contrast of styles with her mother, enjoyed, as an only child and beautiful daughter, a center-stage style of life. While she was pleasant to all, and not loath to serve others when needed, she nevertheless was the precious sparkling jewel in the family crown. She had taken full advantage of the family's wealth and position to develop the good qualities of an aristocrat, somehow without acquiring the bad ones.

Rene had just received a degree in business management at UCLA. As originally planned, she had returned to work in the family business with her father, whom she adored. Because she sincerely cared about the welfare of the plantation and its workers, dePuy was grooming her to be manager of the family copra business. Later, when he retired, she would be chief executive officer of the complete enterprise. As his sole offspring, she would also eventually become the owner of both the plantation and the business.

Today, the social group on the veranda was most congenial. The gathering at first engaged in small talk about the weather and the unusual boat trip. No one thought it appropriate to plunge into a discussion of the proposed business of social change. Burnhouse hated small talk. He was good at it, of course. He had been to a lot of places, and he had done a lot of different things. Thus, his mind generated abundant fodder for small talk.

As usual, Monika was the center of attention. No one, not even the vivacious Rene, bothered even to try to compete with her.

Soon, a maid announced that dinner was being served. dePuy ushered the others into a huge, ornate dining room, with several servers standing stiffly erect about the walls. Behind the servers were expensive paintings and tapestries. The table was set with the family's best silver and finest crystal, amid a profusion of tropical flowers and lit Italian candles.

During dinner, the conversation finally turned naturally to Burnhouse's plan for the experimental society. By some sort of prior tacit agreement, Monika relinquished the floor to him when it came his time to pontificate about his behavioral plans.

All of them knew something about the plan, of course. The members of the island council had actually participated in the drafting of Burnhouse's research proposal for financing to the Schoonover Foundation. dePuy had discussed the plan frequently with Rene and Blanche in their home.

Blanche supported the plan in terms of her general understanding. That is, she supported it in theory, but she really did not know much about the proposed details of its operation.

Although not outright oppositional, Rene was a bit skeptical about some parts of it. Those parts primarily concerned the specific details of the operation.

Rene was most interested in the project because she had taken several psychology courses in college as part of her major. Naturally, she was familiar with Burnhouse's reputation as a researcher and writer. She was, in fact, thoroughly thrilled to be in the same room with him, despite her reservations about his particular project on the island.

"Professor Burnhouse," she said, "I am familiar with your basic research on learning, of course, but not with its specific practical applications to universal social problems. The application to individual human problems seems rather straightforward, but the application to the global society seems to be a giant leap. How did you become interested in applying your formal laboratory research results to human society?"

"It is not a giant leap at all," quickly responded Burnhouse, defensively and more sharply than he would have liked. It was a knee-jerk reaction to a familiar annoying criticism. Then, he collected himself well enough to say more calmly, "Actually, we think that the practical applications do follow closely from our laboratory results. It is just that the unit of analysis becomes larger, effectively substituting the global society for a single human being. But, to answer your question, the practical application to society was almost inevitable."

Burnhouse now spoke slowly, with an air that he had answered this particular question many times before. "You see, I was a post-graduate fellow with Skinner. As you probably know, the possibility for social application was his major interest in his later years. As a part of the research for my fellowship, I visited a society in Oklahoma that lived according to his plan and ideas. I was hooked by their success on the idea of a Utopia based on psychological technology.

"And, by the way, please call me Skull. My title makes me feel too old, at least when I am away from the university."

Immensely pleased, Rene smiled, and murmured, "Thanks, Skull." She was not usually a name dropper with her friends. The opportunity to drop the name of Skull Burnhouse, however, would be sufficient to cause her to break the rule.

Blanche inquired, "If an experimental society along the lines Skinner proposed already existed years ago, why do you need another one here now? What is the problem with the earlier evidence?"

"Good question!" smiled Burnhouse, with spirit. "A very good question! That, in fact, was the major question that I had to answer for the Schoonover people. The reason has to do with the basic nature of scientific proof. True, there are actually several such societies in existence now, but none of them had originally been set up with the primary intention of providing hard scientific data. The founders were mostly interested in providing a better place to live for themselves, meaning a better local society. They thought that Skinner's plan would provide it. But, to be able to reach valid scientific conclusions, you must deliberately control conditions and record behaviors exactly, so that you can unambiguously relate causes and effects. You need to have sufficient control over the conditions of the experiment so that you can conclude precisely what variables in the total situation of the experiment were responsible for particular results."

"Excuse me for interrupting, Skull," said Blanche, "but, I do not know what you mean by 'variables in the total situation'. Could you explain it?"

"Surely," replied Burnhouse, affably. "A variable is any aspect of a physical environment that can change. For example, there could be changes in temperature, changes in the number of people present, changes in the number of hours since your last meal and changes in the array of responses that are available to you. The psychologist tries to discover what variables influence particular behaviors. Then, we try to produce the particular conditions of the variables that will produce those behaviors that we desire. Okay?"

"Yes, I understand. Thank you."

Burnhouse smiled, and continued. "So, our goal on Kipua is to adhere so rigorously to the Skinnerian plan that we can say positively that the good results on the island will be produced by the actual operation of that plan—or the variables established by that plan, if you prefer. That is the basic idea, anyway. We want to make sure that critics of our plan cannot find any valid basis to argue for some other possible cause for our success. Okay, so far?"

"Yes! I get it," smiled Blanche. "It makes sense to me."

"But, there is more." Burnhouse was now obviously enthusiastic. "What is especially crucial and exciting about our study is a new, bold extension of Skinner's idea. You see, Skinner's plan was basically to scrap certain so-called technical advances of modern society, like mechanical lawn mowers, and false notions of how behavior can be controlled. For example, he proposed that society abolish from its thinking the concept of free will, because that concept is a barrier to scientific thinking.

Rene interposed, quickly, "I do not think that such a thing can be accomplished. People are too much in love with the idea of free will."

"That is partly what we are here to find out," answered Burnhouse. "And, we will use a method that is different from the particular one that Skinner proposed.

"Skinner's plan was for committed communitarians to withdraw from the larger society into enclaves of believers. These communities would start anew without the burdens of incorrect and inefficient thinking from the outside society. They would believe in a technological-based society, and commit themselves to it and train their children to think similarly. As each such group prospered, and enjoyed the good life, converts would be gained and new colonies of believers would be established. Eventually, the Utopian societies would absorb more of the outside society until theoretically the entire country would be absorbed."

"I see where you are going," said Rene. "It has been over forty years since Skinner first published his plan, and there have been precious few takers. There have been, as you said, a few approximations of Skinner's proposal, but the idea surely has not been popular. So, you want to attempt a much more direct confrontation with modern society."

"Right!" smiled Burnhouse, as he waved his fist in the air. "People do not want to re-locate, or to make other drastic changes in their lifestyles, without a guarantee of success. Particularly, if they have been successful in the larger society, they are reluctant to give it up in order to share equally with a less talented neighbor."

"Or, less fortunate one," interjected Blanche.

"Correct. Or, a less fortunate one. But, in any case, the proposed change was just too drastic, and too unsettling. So, I propose to integrate, or infiltrate, the Utopian ideals into a selected region of the larger society. And, as you know, that region is Kipua. In other words, some changes will have to be made gradually, as the people develop a readiness to accept them. This part will entail the utmost skill in shaping the behaviors. It surely will be difficult, even for those of us who are experts in the process.

"Of course, other changes must be made immediately, in order to fulfill the concepts of the plan. For example, we cannot compromise on the free will issue. We must give a lot of thought to the kinds of compromises that we are willing to make. It will be tough, but the prize is worth it."

"I hope it works," said Rene. As she looked about the room, she could see that she spoke for them all.

Now, dePuy turned to Monika. "How about you, Monika?" he asked. "How did you get involved in all of this?"

Monika shrugged. "My research interests had always been in programmed learning. When I met Skull at a convention, I saw how the two interests came together. Indeed, it has been fun working with Skull on such an important idea." She gave Burnhouse one of her most bedazzling smiles. He winked back at her, and grinned an intimate grin.

The talk then turned to the food and flowers, and small details about the lives and habits of the diners. Burnhouse learned that the dePuy family members spent all of their lives on the plantation, except for extended trips to other continents for their education, and short trips for vacations. They were obviously quite well aware of world events.

The same conclusion could be reached for Flo and Dan Crow. They were extremely well informed, and interested in social policy and reform. Burnhouse had been quite surprised when Flo first mentioned her idea to him. He had not expected such progressive ideas on a tiny, far-away island in the Pacific Ocean.

After dessert and coffee, dePuy rose and announced to the diners that a porter had reported to him that Jake's cab and the dePuy automobile were waiting for them in front of the house. Everyone wanted to hear Burnhouse's presentation. They filed quickly out the front door toward the waiting vehicles.

Rene dePuy managed to slip into the front seat of the cab with Jake. Burnhouse and Monika climbed into the back seat of the old relic. Flo was happy to ride with Blanche in the back seat of the spacious Cadillac of the dePuys. Crow sat beside dePuy, as the plantation owner drove his own vehicle.

Flo was thrilled. She felt that the bold experiment had now truly begun.

THREE

THE CATHOLIC CHURCH was an engaging wooden structure, like a typical small-town church in rural U.S.A. There was a polished brass bell in the tower rising high above the entrance, and a small wooden cross crowning the tower. The front of the church was un-relieved white siding. The white wooden doors now were opened wide, revealing waves of dark-stained wooden pews.

Sea shells lined the crushed coral walkway that led to the front door. A simple sign proclaimed that the church was the Mary Immaculate Catholic Church of Kipua. It also gave the name of the rector as Fr. Jacques Schindler.

Jack Schindler met them at the front door of the church. He was short in build, almost stout, friendly in manner, albeit slightly reserved. His reserve was not characteristic, because he was not sure that he could welcome the Burnhouse experiment to Kipua Island. Nevertheless, he was too kind not to be hospitable.

Despite good opportunities for academic posts in the Catholic church, Father Jack had opted immediately to do missionary work in some underdeveloped area of the world. He had not really de-sired an overseas assignment. In fact, he would have preferred a post in a poorest inner-city section of the United States. But Father Jacques was just happy to serve anywhere. Now, he had learned to love the island and its people. He wanted never to leave the island.

The priest's upbeat style and love for everyone made him almost a saint to the members of his congregation. Regardless of denominational declarations, he considered everyone on the island—and indeed the world—to be his parishioner. Conse-quently, evil acts by any of them wounded his soul deeply.

Nevertheless, Jack blessed everyone with his cheerful pres-ence. Everywhere he went, he waved his omnipresent Bible as a

36

tangible token of his blessing. Often he would touch his Bible to the head or chest of the person who was the focus of his attention, or prayers, for the moment. It was like he was infusing the person with spiritual power from the book. No one resented this physical connection. It was really a blessing from the cleric. Every aspect of Father Jack's behavior expressed a massive desire to connect with his flock.

The church sanctuary was illuminated by indirect lighting overhead, supplemented by many candles. The floors were wooden, lightly stained by the body oils from many bare feet, and polished to a fine patina by years of footsteps. The creaking sound at each step tallied the age of the building. The functional wooden pews, without cushions, were situated so as to provide a center aisle and side aisles along the walls.

A large crucifix covered most of the back wall beyond the altar. A small electronic organ, a gift of the dePuy family in memory of Pierre's father, stood to the right, behind one lectern. Across from the organ was a small seating area for the choir, which was behind a raised pulpit.

The walls were plentifully supplied with translucent windows of deep purple. Daylight passing through the windows produced a royal purple ambient illumination. The same effect at night was achieved by the reflection of interior incandescent lights and candles off the stained glass. Undoubtedly, consistently day and night, the church provided a worshipful place for the saying of Mass.

Now, flickering candles produced a faint dynamic light show all about the room. Burnhouse decided that it was a beautiful sight. He did not believe in the worship of deities, but it was indeed beautiful.

Burnhouse was slightly sad that his scientific message would clash with such a pleasant setting. Science was also beautiful, but in a quite different way.

Turning to the business at hand, Burnhouse carefully examined the heterogeneous crowd inside the church. The gathering was large, as expected, overflowing the room. There seemed to be a reasonable cross-section of the different segments of the island population. There was a large representation of natives, along with their Chief, Launo, and the tribal shaman, Malevi. Burnhouse noted that the particular followers of each man formed separate groups on opposite sides of the sanctuary. dePuy had mentioned the conflicts and competition between the chief and the holy man. The two native leaders tended to be on the opposite sides of every issue. dePuy had reported that Malevi had supported the proposed social experiment, while Launo had opposed it.

Burnhouse liked the looks of the chief, despite the man's opposition to his views. Launo had an open, friendly quality about him. Paradoxically, he took an immediate dislike for the shaman. Malevi seemed to be forcing himself to present a pleasant appearance. He was failing, however. Burnhouse made a mental note to keep a watchful eye on Malevi, despite his presumed support for the experiment.

There was also a nearly equal mixture of townspeople and plantation personnel, both supervisors and workers. A few gang chieftains and gang members in their colorful club jackets could be perceived scattered about the room.

The meeting began with a flattering introduction of Burnhouse by Flo, pursuant to her official position as mayor. Then, Burnhouse set right to work with his presentation in his most beguiling fashion. He could be truly charming when he chose to be. To be sure, at the moment, such was his choice.

"Friends," he began, "this is a most exciting time for me. I have been hoping for many years for a chance to try out our plan for an Utopian society. Your island seems to be the perfect spot for it. Actually, the general plan that we are following was crafted by the great Behavioristic psychologist, B. F. Skinner. Your island government has now been kind enough to give me this excellent opportunity. I thank some of the people in this room for making my dream become a reality. You all know who these people are. They are your island council members. Let's give them a round of applause."

Burnhouse began clapping enthusiastically. The audience responded with a moderate level of polite applause.

"Thank you. And thanks to your representatives. These people brought us here to demonstrate a way to make a better life, not only for you, but, by forging an example, for all of the peoples of the world. It will be a magnificent enterprise. I hope that you will help us make it a success."

Here, he paused for effect, trying to look both benign and serious. He attempted to make eye contact with as many people as possible. Each time he was successful, he put on his most re-assuring smile.

Then, Burnhouse continued. "Your island council has asked us to conduct a revolutionary experiment that will make this island both influential and famous. But, more important, because of it, your island will become an idyllic place to live. We intend, first, to institute a scientifically-based plan for a beneficial social organization. Then, we will prove it to be effective by our research. When the proven plan is then implemented throughout the world, it will make every society that uses it a virtual Utopia. It is new hope for a troubled world.

"But, you have to know, and of this you should be proud, that Kipua will have been first. It will be an established model for all other societies of the world to imitate."

At this point, there was an angry shout from Chief Launo. He jumped to his feet, and exclaimed, "No, no, I am not proud of this. We will have no more of this foolishness. You say that you plan to come in here and impose a new social order on us. But, forget such plans. Hear me! We will object to any new plan imposed on us. We have our own culture, thank you. We are sick of colonials, neo-colonials, or whatever, coming in here and rescuing us poor natives from ourselves.

"We are happy now. My people are happy with me as chief. I was groomed by my father in the ways of my people. My family has been the cradle of chiefs for many, many generations. Why would you, then, callously reject the wisdom of a thousand years? What right do you think that you have to come in here, a white outsider, a pagan by our standards, and try to turn our way of life upside-down? We are a proud and responsible people. We choose to keep the responsibility for ourselves, and the credit to ourselves for our own achievements. You insult us by your ill-conceived suggestions."

There was a noisy murmur about the room, a mixture of surprise and indignation. No one had expected the normally reticent Launo to make such a strong protest, particularly so soon.

Burnhouse was not ruffled by the outburst, however. Obviously, he was used to such reactions. Maintaining his aristocratic composure, first he smiled a self-assured smile. Then, he said, "Well, there are actually two answers to your question, Chief Launo. The first is merely a legal one, and therefore it is not too important here. But, it is a true fact that we have secured from the U.S. government, and from your own local government as well, all of the legal documents that are necessary for us to begin our project on Kipua. In fact, it required a special act of the American congress, but we rightfully obtained it.

"But, in any case, that answer in legal terms is surely not the best one, let us admit quickly. Unfortunately, it does imply incorrectly that we are here to foist upon you something that you do not desire. But, that implication is definitely not true. In fact, nothing is further from the truth. Actually, our project will *never* work without the full cooperation of the entire population on Kipua. It is *our* job to convince *you* that our way is best for you, and for your families. Actually, we could not make you do anything without your cooperation, even if we wanted to—which we emphatically do not."

"Okay, Professor. I will take you at your word. I will tell you what I want. I wish you to go home right now," said Launo. "Listen to what I am telling you. If you are really serious about honoring our wishes, go home now. Just do it!"

There was again a surprised murmur about the room. The islanders were not accustomed to hearing Launo speak up to public groups with anger, particularly in such extremely audacious words.

"Well, now, it's not quite that simple," said Burnhouse, still smiling in a placating manner. "We feel that you should give us a fair opportunity to explain our program. Please, give us at least a chance to make it work. If we cannot convince you that our plan is a good idea after a reasonable period, then we will decide that our experiment has therefore failed. At that point, we will leave, quickly and quietly, with no finger pointing. That is a solemn promise. It seems fair to me. Can you allow me that much?"

"All right, I will listen for a while longer," agreed Launo. "But, I do not guarantee support, or even continued listening."

"Fair enough," smiled Burnhouse. He had not expected such strength of opposition so soon. But, he felt confident enough to continue. "Because I intend in the future to spend many hours and days describing the plan to you in detail, I will not go into much of the particulars at this time. What I want to emphasize now, as strongly as I can, is that this plan, and indeed no similar plan, will ever work without the full cooperation of the people involved. You have been carefully selected to be the kind of population that will permit a fair test of the plan. We are counting on your earnest cooperation to make it work. I say again that we must have such cooperation, if we are to have any chance at all to succeed in our experiment. Scientific success for our project does not mean necessarily that our plan works. Science merely requires that we find out definitely whether it works, or it does not work."

The room was now filled with shouts, most of them angry. Launo had many supporters. "And if it does not work, who suffers?" he shouted. "The answer is obvious. We are the ones who will suffer. You will just take your research notebooks and bank accounts back to your cozy home and fancy offices in a faraway land. Listen to yourself. Your plan actually gives all of the control to you from the very beginning. You are the ones who decide whether or not the plan is working. Then, you alone decide when it is time to leave.

"Why should we agree to such an unfair arrangement? I do not call it cooperation, but totalitarianism."

Burnhouse was still undaunted by the opposition. He tried to continue, but the rude and raucous noises of such a large crowd in the room rocking with reverberations prevented him from being heard. The meeting was dangerously close to being over. It was about over, finished business or not, for lack of crowd control.

Flo stood up to rescue the deteriorating situation. As mayor of the town, and thus mistress of these ceremonies, she called loudly for quiet. Finally, she was able to make herself heard. "Friends," she said, "this is not becoming of you. Professor Burnhouse is our guest. He came here in good faith. You gain nothing by abandoning civility and good manners. Please hear him out.

"What he is proposing is very important to our island and to the whole world. His proposal revolves around just a few main points. The first point is that our global society is in trouble. I will not waste time in giving you examples of that. You know what I mean. You read the newspapers. So, as a society, we must do something immediately to change things around. The change must necessarily be rather drastic. What Professor Burnhouse plans to do will be shocking because he plans to turn the existing society upside down. We must help him do it, however, because the methods that society has been using up to now are obviously not working. You know that. Read the newspaper! Listen to your radios! Professor Burnhouse wants to try something different. He wants to find out whether or not his plan will help us. It is an experiment to try out a plan to make life better. The situation is like a surgeon cutting out a cancerous tumor. There is immediate pain involved, but it is necessary for the cure. He is trying to make life better not only for us, and for all of the peoples in the rest of the world. Is that not a worthy goal?"

The room had gradually quieted as she spoke. The return of order and quiet was a mark of the respect that the people had for Flo. When sufficient quiet had returned, she motioned for Burnhouse to continue.

"Thank you, friends" said Burnhouse. "I will take just a few minutes to tell what we are about. Please hear with open minds what I am saying. I think that you will like it. Chief Launo has actually missed the point of what our plan is all about. It is a cooperative plan. It absolutely needs, it literally requires, your cooperation. And, it is intended for your benefit in the end. Please put aside your quick emotional responses, which I understand are entirely natural. Give yourselves time to see the fundamental sense of our plan. Our plan is based on scientific truth, not appeals to emotions, not to soft sentiments.

"In contrast to the emotional and unscientific appeals of the advocates of absolute virtue as a way out of the social problems of our day, my plan, as I said, is based on the scientific work and theories of the eminent psychologist, B. F. Skinner. Skinner described his scientific plan for a utopian society in his book, *Walden Two*, written in 1948. Basically, his plan was to replace the idea of human freedom to make voluntary choices, and also the subjective and moralistic concept of human dignity, which is based on such an idea. He proposed to replace them with certain well-established principles of science and mechanisms of behavioral technology."

His words were again met with scowls, gestures of rejection and angry shouts. The audience was not receptive to such talk. Indeed, the crowd was manifestly increasing the various unmistakable signs of hostility and aggression.

But, Burnhouse, though mindful of the hostility, was determined not to be intimidated or deterred. So, he pressed resolutely on with his proposal.

"This plan of Skinner's has been viewed with horror by many authors, as I know. I have learned to expect that. In fact, I see many of you reacting just that way tonight. It is natural. So, I truly expected that. But, I beg you, do not reject his plan outright before you learn more about it. Really know the plan before you consider rejecting it. Let me read to you what Skinner had to say about his plan in 1974."

He pulled a sheet of paper from his briefcase, and began to read:

> One would scarcely guess that the authors are talking about a world in which there is food, clothing, and shelter for all, where everyone chooses his own work and works on the average only four hours a day, where music and the arts flourish, where personal relationships develop under the most favorable circumstances, where education prepares every child for the social and intellectual life which lies before him, where—in short—people are truly happy, secure, productive, creative, and forward-looking.

"That sounds good, doesn't it? Which one of you would not like that kind of life? That is the promise made in the name of psychological technology. I am here to tell you that the science of behavior can truly achieve that good life for all."

"Your words, and Skinner's words, certainly do sound wonderful," said a native matron, sitting in the corner of the room. She was gently rocking a small baby in her arms. "I do not doubt that you both are sincere and genuine. But, how do I know that your plan will really work for me. Will it work for all of us whose ancestors were original inhabitants of this island? Can you guarantee me a better life?"

"No," said a solemn Burnhouse, in a most serious manner. "I cannot do that. There are no guarantees here. Be sure of that. I am talking straight with you. This will be an experiment, sure enough. But, tell me, where could you ever get guarantees for the good life? We do not have guarantees, but we do have solid evidence. We have valid empirical evidence that we are on the right path.

"Basically, we are trying to answer a tremendously important question. Thus, the vital issue for psychology, and for society, is laid clearly into view: is society to be saved by behavioral technology, derived from the processes of empirical science, or by vacuous emotional appeals to human virtues and values, whatever they may be, derived casually from folklore and hearsay?"

"Fine," said the lady, "such an answer would truly be important. But, I would like to know then why people object to Skinner's plan. How do you intend to prove its value on Kipua?"

"Precisely why I am here tonight," Burnhouse patiently reassured her. "I will answer both of your questions as I go along, if I may.

"First, after hearing Skinner's above description of his technocratic society, you may indeed ask why anyone would object to any plan so designed to achieve such marvelous goals? Skinner's answer to this question was extremely simple and straightforward: People objected to his optimistic plan only because it was deliberately and intelligently designed.

"Skinner argued that society had a strange idea about how cultures should be established. Oddly enough, society did not desire such ideal results if these results had to be achieved as a consequence of objective achievements in behavioral science from the disinterested labors of certain members of our species. In other words, the people were irrationally blocked from thoughtful acceptance of a proven plan by their blind negative emotions. Their fixed beliefs, rooted in such purely emotional baggage, was that anything having to do with rigorous empirical science, and thus devoid of subjective human values, was necessarliy bad for society. They felt that the use of behavioral science robbed people of some alleged, intangible characteristics that are supposed to be a valuable part of human beings, and therefore human society. For example, they referred to some alleged entity called 'human dignity.'"

"What? Are you denying that human beings have dignity, some worth as persons?" exploded Father Jacques. "Do you deny that God gave value to each person, to make them just below the angels?"

"Yes, that is exactly the point that I wish to make," responded Burnhouse quickly to the priest. "I say such humanistic and artistic use of language is just intellectual word salad, without true meaning. As a scientist, I question what such words mean in an objective sense. What do they refer to? How do you measure such things? You can't. And, that is the point. They refer to nothing tangible that we can deal with and understand. We are saying that science, sensible and rational, will save us. That is what science is all about. With science, we know what we are talking about, because we are talking about things that we can see, and feel, and measure."

The priest was horrified into a numb, speechless state. Everyone waited for him to respond, but he could not.

Finally, the silence was broken. But it was not the cleric who spoke.

"It works for me, Bro," said a young black man in a brown club jacket. It was Percy Hernandez, the chieftain of the gang called "Junkyard Dogs". "My gang and I are with you all the way, man. We want a hand in saying what is right and wrong. We are fed up with letting the fuzz and the plantation big shots have all of the say. It is about time that we all had some hand is what is going on. It would be cool if we all had a say."

There was a chorus of strong agreement, mostly from gang members. This was indeed support for Burnhouse's plan. But, it was not support from the group that Burnhouse had most desired.

Then, a loud voice cut through the raucous shouts of support for Burnhouse. It was as chilling as a leak in a raincoat during an icy rain storm.

"Do you mean that science can establish the goals for our people, actually tell us what is right or wrong," asked someone, in an incredulous, but somehow menacing, tone. It was Mary Murphy, a middle-aged lady dressed in a waitress uniform, standing about three rows from the back of the room.

Mary was employed by Dan Crow at the Crow Bar. Every resident on the island knew that she had a rather unhappy past. In recent years she had been a strong member and supporter of the Catholic Church on the island. Father Schindler had been a very powerful, positive influence on her life. Now, she was much respected and well-liked. Everyone knew that she could always be counted on to help someone who needed it. She was the very sort of person whose support Burnhouse needed.

Mary Murphy had seen hard times before Dan Crow had come into her life. She had grown up in poverty in Philadelphia. To escape the responsibilities of caring for four younger brothers, burdens that she had borne since she was thirteen, she had married her childhood sweetheart before they graduated from high school. Although the marriage had not been happy, for years she stuck with Dennie Murphy through one lost job after another. She was barely able to keep the marriage together. Courageously, she still managed to keep their debts small enough to maintain a positive credit rating. She was wise enough to make sure that there had been no children to add to their troubles, financial and otherwise.

Then, Dennie had gotten the job offer to work on the plantation on Kipua as a general mechanic. The way the job opportunity came about was some kind of a miracle. One of Dennie's brothers was bragging to an old army buddy about how his brother was a genius at fixing anything mechanical. The army buddy happened to be a foreman on the plantation. The plantation overseer was looking for someone with exactly the qualifications that Dennie possessed. Mary saw a possible solution to all of their problems. In addition to a steady income, Dennie would have a chance for a slower pace in his life style.

She coaxed Dennie into applying for the job. After a quick check of references, which Mary had still managed to keep respectable, Dennie was hired for more money per month than he ordinarily made in six months. So, they had come to Kipua. To them, at the time, the place was just a name on a map.

Things went well for a while. For six months Dennie seemed to enjoy the job. Mary thought that he was settling down into a peaceful routine. She was even beginning to think that it might be reasonable for them to adopt a child.

But, the regularity and responsibility was just too much for Dennie. One evening, after the *Cornucopia* had sailed off to other islands, Mary discovered a note where Dennie's belongings should have been. It merely said that he was sorry, but he could not take the routine of life on the island any longer. So, he was heading for adventure somewhere. He might try diamond mining in Africa, or lumbering in Brazil. In any case, there would be no use in trying to find him. His last words were classic: "It's been good to know you, Babe. Take care."

Mary was immediately thrown into a panic. She had no job skills, except as a waitress. There were no jobs for waitresses on Kipua. She had used the extra money from the new job to pay off some bills on the mainland. What cash they had about the house had, of course, vanished with her husband. She estimated that it would take about a thousand dollars for her to get back to the mainland, and then another thousand to get established. With her present prospects, the magic figure for escape might as well be two million dollars. For several sleepless days and nights, she anguished over her problem, without success in finding any kind of satisfactory solution.

Finally, she had to settle on a solution that she had rejected as unacceptable many times before. She would have to take a job as a hostess at the Bar Belle saloon. Because of her attractive appearance and personality, and pleasant singing voice, she had several times been offered a job by George Moredis, owner of the *Belle*.

The job entailed entertainment of the customers with a little singing, and providing them with a little companionship with their drinking. There was no salary, but the job provided free meals and a room upstairs. Also, she would get tips plus half of the price that they charged for the drinks that were bought for her by the paying customers. The drinks were actually tea served in shot glasses, but charged at the price for liquor.

Mary agreed to take the job, if the customers were informed that she was drinking tea, and not liquor. She did not want to participate in a lie. If the customers were willing to pay liquor prices in order to enjoy her companionship, that was their business.

Mary had no illusions that the job itself would merely provide an existence. It would not provide her with the means to get off the island. So, she took the job with the full realization that she would have to entertain men in her room for money in order to get the extra cash to escape the island. She could see no other avenue of escape.

Mary hated this solution to her problems. But, many times over the years she had been forced by circumstances to develop a practical and tough outlook on life. She could justify her decision, because there was absolutely no other decision possible. She did not consider herself a bad woman, because she did not choose to be bad. She absolutely could not bring herself to contemplate remaining forever as an entertainer at the Bar Belle.

She was successful as a prostitute, because she considered each encounter as a business transaction for which she was bound to give satisfactory service. But, there was not a lot of extra money on the island for pleasure. Almost everyone on the island respected her for her honesty and sense of fairness. Those who did not respect her were wise to keep their thoughts to themselves.

Mary was about half-way to her goal of two thousand dollars, when it happened that one evening Dan Crow became one of her casual customers. Dan was so taken with her that he immediately offered her a job in his own establishment. He would have to expand his business to do it, but he had been considering such a move for some time anyway. She would be a bartender, and a waitress. The pay would be sufficient so that she would not be forced to entertain customers after hours any longer. Indeed, such activities would be ruled out as part of the employment agreement with Crow.

This offer of Crow's would mean that Mary could stay on the island as a regular working member of the community. Because she liked the island itself, she decided to stay under the new circumstances. As a sort of commitment to a new life, she used her savings as a down payment to build a one-bedroom house on the edge of town. Joyfully, she settled down to the secure comfortable life that she had always craved.

Mary made Crow agree that there would be nothing of a sexual relationship between them. That would, she reasoned, merely represent a change in venue, or style, and not a basic change in her life situation. She felt that this was an important issue to validate that she was not a person of immoral character. A life of celibacy now meant that her former tactic was not chosen voluntarily. Therefore, the new life style meant to her that she was not a bad person.

Crow agreed to her terms, although he did not completely understand Mary's reasoning. He even offered to marry her. But she steadfastly turned him down. She was very fond of Crow, but the original circumstances of their relationship did not make marriage seem exactly right to her. Marriage now would somehow make her feel guilty about her former occupation.

So, Mary had settled down to a happier life than she had known before. She became active in Father Jack's congregation. She was in fact very loved and respected in the church.

Now, facing Burnhouse, Mary gave ample evidence for being disturbed. Her feet were spaced apart and her arms were akimbo. It was a decidedly hostile stance. She looked almost ready to leap forward for a physical attack on Burnhouse.

"Yes," said Burnhouse, calmly. "That is exactly what I am saying. Science will tell us what is right and what is wrong for us. Science will set the goals for our society. But, you must remember that science is only a tool for our use. Human beings will actually make the final selection of goals on the basis of the scientific information. That is better than selecting your goals of behavior on purely whimsical grounds. You see, your objections to our plan are purely emotional. That is bad. How could whimsically-based decisions be better than scientifically-based decisions? That is the basic point."

"Tell me that again," said Mary. "I am not sure that I fully understood what you are saying."

"Surely," agreed Burnhouse. "What I am saying is that Skinner believed that the conditions of a good life, as he described them, would be acceptable to modern society only if these conditions had evolved naturally without any such plan or deliberate design. That is, people would prefer if the organization of their society had evolved haphazardly, without any direction, except through emotional impulses, entirely without the use of science. Specifically, he believed that society opposed his plan simply because the plan obviates the cherished concepts of human freedom and human dignity, or worth. In fact, his plan actually requires the elimination of these concepts from our thinking."

Mary was obviously distressed by his words. But, before she could speak, Jake Blankenship spoke up: "We hear you. But, is it not true that even some psychologists believe that Skinner's interpretation is wrong? I have read what they have said. They have said that the true objection of those who oppose his plan is not what you said. They say that they have opposed the plan because they have predicted a different result from the happy state that he described for his plan in the passage that you read. They predict instead a most unhappy outcome. They say that his predictions are off the mark simply because his premises about people are wrong. They say that perhaps in the universe there is a planet inhabited by creatures for whom the technocratic plan will work. But, they contend the planet in question is definitely not the planet Earth."

Jake's words evoked an outcry of support. Many yelled out that they agreed with the opponents of Skinner's plan. Mary yelled, "No! No, to the technocrats!" Someone else was heard to bellow, "Not on my planet, you don't! Get your plan off my planet!"

Burnhouse was still not dismayed or deterred. He was still determined to finish his presentation. He was almost through. He continued to shout above the clamor, "Listen! Listen to me! Please let me finish. There are three main positive ideas to be implemented in our plan. The first, as I said, is that we must get rid of old, but false, ideas about human values. Our value judgments about what is right and wrong in behaviors have been passed down from parents to children, from generation to generation. Most of our society has not really questioned whether or not they are necessary or valuable for the benefit and survival of our society. They have persisted without consideration of the fact that they just have not worked. Skinner merely called our attention to that hard fact. But, it is obvious, when you think about it. For proof, just look at the mess our society is in.

"So, we must begin by abandoning the folklore of what is right and wrong in a moral context. Then, we can determine by scientific study and analysis which potential practices of this society are in fact the ones that are best for the survival of the society. That is the answer to the lady's second question. Society is in a terrible state now because it relies on subjective moralistic concepts. Our plan is to replace such subjective notions with objective technical procedures based on scientific research. If the society is thus improved, our plan will be validated. How can you object to that?"

Again, there were cries and shouts of protest. Again, Mary Murphy voiced the basic problem: "You mean that we should forget the teachings of the church, and the wisdom of our families? I can tell you that I will never cooperate with that part of your plan."

Burnhouse remained calm. "I know that some of these ideas may seem new and even startling to you. I am merely saying that we will actually retain only those ideas that are proved to work. But, at the same time, this means that we must get rid of the ones that do not work."

Jake was indignant now. "Professor, listen to what you are saying to us. You said that the goals and beliefs will be determined by scientific research. Then you start out by rejecting some of our favorite ideas on no evidence at all. What evidence do you present that the concepts of freedom and dignity are harmful to society?"

"First, there is the logical argument," responded Burnhouse, with exaggerated patience. "Science must be objective. It cannot work as it should, if it is negated by burdensome subjective emotional assumptions. Second, look at the sorry state of our society now. That is the real proof. Our society had been basking in the presumed light of the prevailing assumptions of freedom and dignity. Clearly, science has not been able to operate properly in such a climate of emotionalism and subjectivity. Let's give science a chance, at least."

"Nuts!" said Jake. "With all due respect, Doc, I think that the problem is that our society actually shows too little commitment to the ideas of freedom and dignity. That is where our social problems start. There is not enough commitment to those ideas, not too much commitment to them."

Others would have protested more, but Burnhouse pleaded: "Please, please, let me describe the complete plan tonight. You can discuss it among yourselves. Then, we will discuss it together later, if you wish. Please let me go on to the second idea."

The group quieted somewhat. In a few moments, Burnhouse was able to continue.

"The second idea," he said, "is that we must get rid of the mistaken notion that human behaviors are caused by acts of free will. We must understand and accept that people are controlled entirely by their heredity and environment. That simple fact means that they can be understood and controlled scientifically. It means that a behavioral technology can, and must, be used to shape the members of society toward performing those behaviors that will make them happier and more productive."

Again, there was a general outcry, but no one individual spoke up above the rest. Burnhouse raised his arms for quiet, but did not speak. Flo joined him with upraised arms, occasionally touching her lips with her fingers to request silence.

When the roar of angry sounds subsided, Burnhouse continued: "The third idea of our plan is that, once we have found out what social practices are beneficial to society, we commit ourselves to instilling those practices in our people. We will do this by using what we psychologists call positive reinforcement, or what you laypersons call rewards for good behaviors. All good behaviors will be rewarded in some way. They will not necessarily be rewarded for each instance of individual performance. But, eventually all good behaviors will be rewarded.

"Let me emphasize at this point that we do not advocate or condone punishment in our plan. We will give only desired rewards for good behaviors. We think that a major problem with modern living is that it relies too heavily on punishments. And punishment is bad. It causes all sorts of bad things. It causes animosity to those who mete out the punishment. It produces confusion about what behaviors are actually being punished. And, finally, it engenders harmful fears and anxieties about life in general for the person who has been punished."

For the first time, there were a few smiles and nods of agreement. Someone at the back yelled, "Amen." Someone else blurted in a loud voice, "Tell that to my old football coach." There was widespread laughter at that.

Seeing the mood of the audience to be in a transient change, Burnhouse hurriedly finished his presentation. "Friends, together these three ideas provide the basis for using psychological technology for designing a superior society. First, we use science to discover which behaviors are valuable to society. Then, we use established psychological principles to shape the behavior of our citizens toward performance of those behavioral goals. That is why we call the proposed society "TECHland." The first part of the name is an acronym standing for Technologically Evolved Classless Habitat. The name reflects the fact that the society has been developed through the use of scientifically derived principles that have been proved to work, and that therefore everyone will be treated equally, unconditionally, without class biases or discriminations. I do not see how anyone can honestly object to that.

"Well, that is the plan, almost in a nutshell. I hope that my presentation has been clear. I trust that you will find it in yourselves to be able to support the TECHland experiment. I understand that we are scheduled to take a short break now. After the break, I will answer your questions."

Flo Gorsuch rose to the podium. "As Professor Burnhouse said, we are scheduled to take a short break now. People with small children, and any others that need to, can leave.

"Stretch your legs, and relax a bit before we resume," she said. "Let us try to be settled back in our places in ten minutes. For those who have to leave, thank you for coming."

Flo stepped over to congratulate Burnhouse on his presentation. As Burnhouse took a sip of water, he also congratulated himself. So far, the opposition to the plan seemed manageable.

FOUR

FLO CALLED FOR THE PEOPLE who were still in attendance to take their seats. When they became sufficiently quiet, and in reasonable order, Burnhouse again ascended the podium.

"As I said," he announced, "I will now take your questions. But, before I do, I would like to call your attention to one significant point. Just now, Florence Gorsuch addressed my by the title of "Professor." I now respectfully ask her, and you, to refrain from such practice. The new society will not make use of such honorific titles. The idea is to maintain a sense of equality and fraternity among the people.

"Now, let us get to the questions. Please keep in mind that tonight we would like to hold the discussions to basic and simple issues. We can discuss the details later."

A young man sitting next to Chief Launo rose to speak. It was Niko Kipuani, the eldest son of the chief. Niko had graduated from the University of Oregon five years ago. He had become so Americanized that he was almost a caricature of the American college student. He favored faded T-shirts, jeans with ragged holes in the knees and beach sandals. He considered it very liberal of himself to be strongly in favor of the TECHland plan. He said, "Mr. Burnhouse, I understand that a point of your plan, in its very name, is a provision for eliminating social class. How can this be possible, given the vast differences in motivations, talents and abilities to be found in any society, even on such a small island as this?"

"The plan," answered Burnhouse, "includes a provision for each member to spend some part of his or her day performing physical labor. The goal is for duties to be assigned by the Managers in charge of different functions in the community. The only control by the Workers will be in terms of the credit-hours assigned to each task. Nevertheless, each person must daily perform tasks which require the use of his or her large muscles."

"Thanks," said Niko, "it makes sense to me."

Burnhouse noticed that Dan Crow, sitting down front, appeared uncomfortable, apparently undecided about whether or not to ask a question. Trying to be helpful, Burnhouse asked, "Dan, you look like you have a problem of some sort. Do you have a question for me?"

"Yeah. Lots of them," said Crow. "So many, that I hardly know what to ask. My biggest concern is the virtual abolition of punishment as a way of shaping good behaviors. As a former marine, I do not see how you can get away from punishing a guy's mistakes. There are always going to be foul-ups who do not get the word. Some recruits are all thumbs. Others are wise-acres who just think that they know more than you. How are you going to shape them up with just positive rewards? Some of those guys never do anything right. So, you never get a chance to reward them."

"You are making my point, Dan," responded Burnhouse enthusiastically, with a disarming smile. "With all due respect, you are showing what I call the punishment mentality. Unfortunately, most people on this planet have it. You tend to look for things to punish, rather than for things that you can reward. This is exactly what I mean by turning our thinking upside down. You must actively look for behaviors that you can reward. That is the guts, the very heart, of our plan.

"You need to realize that, if a person has made a mistake, you have asked him or her to do something that is beyond his or her ability or training. Or it may be something that he or she is not motivated to do. Actually, it is really your mistake in demanding a performance from that person that the person was not prepared to achieve. You have set your goal for the particular person too high, you see. Therefore, your pupil or trainee should not be punished for what in truth is your own mistake. If there were legitimate punishment, *you* would be one to get it. It is your job to train a person adequately to do what you want him or her to perform, before you even ask him or her to do it. And, then, when the task is performed correctly, you reward him or her for performing it. It is that simple."

"It's not that simple!" shot back Crow. "For example, there are some jobs that are just too tough for a particular guy to accomplish on the first attempt. What then?"

"No problem," said Burnhouse. "The standard solution in such a case is to use what we call shaping. That means to reward successive approximations to the behavior that is eventually desired. So, you reward the success on sub-goals along the way. There must be achievable goals for each person so that you can always use rewards. Successive sub-goals are set closer and closer to the performance level that you ultimately desire. That way the trainee always achieves success. Therefore, he or she never fails, and is thus always rewarded. That is what you want. It is better than continuously passing out punishments."

"That makes sense for most guys," agreed Crow. "But, what about the classic foul-up. And what about the guy who just wants to give you a hard time by not cooperating? Don't these guys simply deserve a kick in the slats to get them going?"

Burnhouse had a ready answer. "You have to train your people well enough so that this is not a problem. You should not give them the will, or a chance, to rebel. Again, it is your fault, if they do not comply."

Crow revealed in unmistakable body language that he was not convinced. He simply shrugged in resignation. He did not pursue the matter, given the lateness of the hour, plus his perception of an overwhelming probability that pushing his issue would do no good. He merely said softly, but with determination, "I'll get back to you later on that one, Doc."

Rene dePuy also saw a problem. "Mr. Burnhouse, it seems to me that you are asking for trouble by attacking morals. What will become of us if we stop worrying about what is right or wrong?"

"The answer to that, my dear," responded Burnhouse, "is that there is still right and wrong. Absolutely! The difference is in how the right and wrong behaviors are defined, in how the definitions of "right" and "wrong" are established. Instead of subjective definitions that have been passed down from generation to generation, the right behaviors will be those that science has proved will benefit human beings, in the sense of contributing to their survival. Therefore, the world will actually become better, because of the re-definition. Remember, we do not simply declare that there are no correct or incorrect behaviors. What we do assert is that there are no 'right' or 'wrong' behaviors in terms of some moral evaluation, or value judgment. Then, we merely change the way we establish which behaviors are correct and which of them are incorrect.

"The point is that the correctness or incorrectness of a behavior is established according to an objective empirical assessment through scientific investigation. It is not established in terms of someone's subjective value system, that in turn had been indoctrinated by someone else's hand-me-down system. The evaluation is in terms of what best achieves society's goals. So, we do not simply accept some notions of right and wrong, because of our natural emotional attachments to our parents, to other relatives, friends, God, country, or whatever. We determine what behaviors are desired or not desired on the basis of what we can prove scientifically actually will work for the betterment of all society. Thus, we do not have fixed presuppositions about what the best, or correct, behaviors will turn out to be. All of those decisions are the natural fall-out from the careful operations of objective science."

Rene gave an unconscious repeat of Dan Crow's performance of disbelief and rejection. But, she also said nothing more. She knew that there would be opportunity to continue the discussion later. She firmly intended to do just that.

Rene could not have known at the time that in just a few months she would have tragic reasons to regret the destruction of morality on the island. Then, she would fervently wish that she had immediately fought harder to preserve a firm adherence to basic human values on the island. But, the opportunity was missed.

Now, Burnhouse hurried to extend his point: "The basic premise of the plan is extremely simple. It assumes that society will progress most favorably if it commits itself to complete control by a psychological technology. Such technology will have been developed through the use of scientific methods. This commitment must be accomplished without interference from certain subjective feelings and personal emotions. Unfortunately, such subjective factors are now a common part of our human heritage. Although these emotional feelings are a traditional part of our human culture, they can nevertheless hold us back from a full use of our factual knowledge about how to interact together successfully as human animals."

At this point, Father Schindler rose. He reared like a bear on its chunky hind legs, ready to attack. The priest's agitated manner indicated a compelling desire to speak. His opposition to the anti-humanistic proposal had been clearly predictable. It was indeed amazing that he had not left the meeting. All eyes and ears in the room were intently fixed upon him, anticipating his words.

Anticipating the reaction of the priest, Burnhouse called upon Father Jack immediately. "Yes, Father, do you have a question?"

"Yes," responded the cleric. "Most certainly. I have been restraining my tongue, because I do support science, especially behavioral science. Science, like everything on this earth, is of God, a gift from God. So, perhaps, I can partially agree with you, depending upon the specific ideas that you consider to be hindrances to human development. I preach daily about the need to inhibit evil ideas, as a matter of fact.

"My question concerns the nature of the objectionable ideas. You implied earlier that some such harmful ideas could actually be part of our Christian heritage. You opposed the idea of the freedom of a human will, for example. That troubles me greatly, of course. But, that is not a new idea for us to counter. Perhaps, we could somehow live with it, while still maintaining our opposition to the idea. But, what about your other ideas? Would you give us some examples of what you consider to be other such interfering ideas and values that are a part of the fabric of our culture?"

"Surely, Father," said Burnhouse. "Unfortunately, I do not think that, as a priest, you will find them agreeable at first. In fact, a major question of my experiment is whether or not you, and others of similar thinking, can be convinced that our plan will work, or should work. Please give us a chance to convince you that we are correct."

Father Schindler was not mollified. He said, "Professor, I will continue to listen for a short while. I try to be reasonable and fair. But, I do not think that I like where you are going with this. So, let's hear more about the theory behind your plan. I cannot support any technology that denies the reality and the nature of Almighty God."

Burnhouse was agreeable. "Okay," he said, taking a deep breath and pausing, "Let's get the big picture. On the first point I think that we can all agree: Our society is in deep trouble. There are many problems that have resisted solutions."

"On that fact we surely do agree," nodded the priest. He was accompanied by a chorus of "amens," and other forms of agreement from various locations about the sanctuary.

"Thank you," said Burnhouse. Then, he continued, "Although there is surely no simple answer to these problems, a group of us psychologists who call ourselves Behaviorists, are convinced that we have identified the key problem for which the others are but symptoms. We should work together to solve all of those problems."

"I am all for cooperation, if that is possible, again without compromising my faith" said Jack. "Go on."

"Let's hope that we can work it out," said Burnhouse. "So, here is the plan. We Behaviorists believe that the basic threat to our society is posed by certain other psychological theories which assume that human beings possess the ability to make voluntary choices of their behaviors. Proponents of those theories say that, without such choices, virtue is impossible. They say that our society will be saved from the various psychological threats to its viability only by the actions of virtuous persons who believe in themselves and in human virtue itself. These virtuous persons are committed to the belief that people are at least partially free to choose their own actions, and therefore that they should be held responsible, with appropriate compassion, for the behaviors that they have selected. Undoubtedly, many of you in this room agree with them. Surely, the clergymen present, and their flocks, would accept that point of view now."

Now it was the turn of the Protestant clergy. Cal Prescott, the Presbyterian minister on the island, could keep silent no longer. He rose to his feet, demanding the floor. "I must speak," he said. "I can listen to no more of this!"

The Reverend Calvin Wesley Prescott, the son of a garbage collector in Atlanta, had graduated from Tuskegee Institute with honors. Then, he had attended seminary at Duke Divinity School, ultimately taking a master's degree there. He had served several churches in the rural south, before feeling the call to be a missionary. Prescott had been on the island for thirteen years. He had not chosen the specific assignment to the island, but he was delighted with it. He especially loved his cordial relationship with Father Jack.

Now, regaining his personal composure, Cal Prescott said firmly, "Amen. You are entirely correct about our view of God's gift to man of the ability to choose on the basis of virtue, Sir. And we have the blood of martyrs, who made the ultimate choice, to prove it to us. It is the backbone of our faith. You cannot attack it."

"Sorry, but I must," said Burnhouse, in a soft, determined voice. "I am here to tell you that such emotional thinking is not the way to a superior society. Such emotional adherence to cherished values and beliefs only causes the members of society who hold such beliefs to denigrate the very science that will save them. Therefore, they dismiss the knowledge gained from science as it pertains to human behavior. The values with which you have been indoctrinated by your society as part of your heritage of learning have no scientific basis. What is more, a blind adherence to those values then causes you foolishly to reject the valid results of scientific investigations. Obviously, the results established by vigorous science will be more useful to all of us than mere folklore passed down by our fathers and mothers."

At this point, the room was filled with a thunder of angry human sounds, mixed with sounds of pain. The room was, for a moment, chaos. The audience was infuriated at the callous trashing of cherished tradition. Even the best efforts of Flo could not quiet the crowd. Most members of the audience were on their feet, shouting and waving their arms. Some were behaving in threatening ways. A few mothers quickly ushered their children from the room, fearing for their very safety.

The roar of outrage was even greater this time than Burnhouse had anticipated. Involuntarily, he raised his arms in a defensive posture. The crowd was held under control by a microscopically thin thread of social decency that could easily break at any moment.

Finally, Jack Schindler's voice was heard above the rumbling human cacophony: "Stop!" He was obviously severely disturbed. The shock of the anger in his voice brought a stunned silence. Time seemed to stop for a moment. But, Jack could not at first speak further. It was not a deliberate dramatic pause. Nevertheless, a few seconds elapsed before he could compose himself well enough to continue. They all waited for the fiery torrent of words that would surely follow. Finally, he spoke. "Folklore! What you call folklore is our religious faith!" the young priest growled, scarcely able to contain his anger and disgust, showing a human part of himself that no one on Kipua had seen before. "Mister Burnhouse, what you are proposing is considered blasphemous to God by every Christian in this room. We will not tolerate it. I have heard enough! I will hear no more of this!

"Now, I call upon every decent person in this sanctuary to leave it immediately. I will lead the Godly ones out of here. Any member of my congregation who does not leave at once will be subject to the severest sanctions of the church. This issue is not open to any discussion. I speak to all of you. Turn your backs on this vile proposal. Go! Go now!"

Indeed, no one in the church had ever seen Father Jack so distraught and angry. Thoroughly cowed, if not convinced by his rage, his parishioners rushed to the exit at the back of the sanctuary. Only a few spoke to each other as they left, and then only in whispered voices. Their initial rage had now turned to dismay, disgust and depression.

The young priest waited, impatiently, still agitated, while his parishioners marched quickly out of the room. As the last few approached the exit, he turned again to face Burnhouse. Again, it took him a moment to compose himself for speech. No one dared to break the silence before he spoke.

Finally, he said, this time in more of a pleading tone than in anger: "Mister Burnhouse, I urge you in the strongest terms to cease and desist this ill-advised plan. It is in fact an attack on the holy church. I fear that, if anyone is foolish enough to listen to you, the results will be socially and spiritually disastrous for each one of us. No one on the island will be able to escape the fearsome consequences. Think about what you are doing. The church will do more than simply decline to assist you in this evil venture. The holy church will oppose you with all of the resources that it can bring to bear on this island, and at all other levels of your organization. I can assure you that this will happen as soon as I have filed a report.

"Because you have rented our holy sanctuary, I think that I cannot in good conscience order you to leave now. My first emotions tell me that I should find a whip and scourge you from this holy room. I will pray for wisdom to know what is proper behavior for me in this matter. Nevertheless, I must ask, at the very least, that you remove yourselves and your materials from this place just as soon as the agreed time of rental has expired. And, please do not return."

Then, he turned accusingly to Florence Gorsuch. His voice was low, but full of intensity.

"I must add, Madam Mayor," he said, probably for the first time that he had so addressed her, "that I am greatly disappointed by your actions to persuade the island council to bring this awful, evil plan to our island. You will surely hear from my superiors as soon as I can report this matter to them.

"I bid all of you good night. I will pray for all of you, and for us."

The priest then quickly rushed out of the room, following the last of his fleeing parishioners. He hurried as if the devil himself were grasping at his heels.

Cal Prescott had also risen to his feet as a result of Burnhouse's remarks. His deep anguish was also apparent on his normally serene face. He obviously had difficulty in waiting for

Father Jack to finish his passionate speech before he began one of his own.

"Sir," he said, "I cannot leave until I have added my voice to what the good priest has said. I support everything that Father Jack says. I only wish that I could say it stronger for me and for my people. My advice for you is to take your pagan experiment elsewhere, if you must persist in testing such ideas. Do not try to inflict them on our people. We are simple, trusting and peaceful. But, serious attempts actually to do this research will surely lead to total disaster on this island. Think seriously about what you are planning to do. The best thing is for you to call off the experiment altogether.

"I also call upon the members of my church to leave this unholy gathering at once. Do not listen to the voice of the devil. Do not cooperate with anything that this man tries to do in the conduct of such a vicious enterprise. I am leaving now. I call upon all who love the Lord to follow me at once. Do not look back."

With that, he walked resolutely toward the door at the back of the room. He exited quickly, without a further glance about the room. He too felt the tangible presence of the devil. All of his family and the complete flock of his parishioners were close behind him.

The few islanders who still remained in the room sat either in stunned silence, or rattled off messages of approval or disapproval for the actions of the clerics, the council members or the TECHland plan. Even among those who still remained, the majority of the comments were decidedly negative with respect to the Behavioristic plan.

Burnhouse merely shrugged, to no one in particular. "It was to be expected," he declared. "It is my job to bring them around."

"Fat chance!" said Jake Blankenship, smiling at first. Then his face assumed the same worried look seen on many other faces about the room.

The voice inside Flo Gorsuch was faint and unintelligible no longer. It said in clear and faultless diction, "This is what I have been trying to tell you! The people on this island will fight Burnhouse and his plan."

In the somber atmosphere that ensued, Flo suggested that Burnhouse make any statements that he desired to put on the record. Because there was now no concerted objection from the audience, Burnhouse continued, "Against such illogical and unsupported thinking, such as you yourselves have just witnessed, I offer the fruits of scientific inquiry. In fact, I can point out to you that some experimental societies based on Skinner's model have already been successful. But, they have not been accepted as proof by the opponents of science. These opponents used the golden ploy of questioning the conduct of the experiment and the nature of the experimental societies. They said that these previous social experiments were not conducted under sufficiently rigorous conditions. Therefore, they have not provided evidence that would be accepted as proof by everyone.

"So, that is exactly why we are planning to conduct our experiment. We want our experiment on this very island to provide a final answer. It is a desperately needed final, definitive answer, as you have seen. We want our research to resolve, once and for all, and for all people to see, which psychologists are right, and which are wrong. That is surely a worthy goal. I am sure that you will agree with me on that. Thank you for hearing me out."

Florence Gorsuch rose to speak. The inner voice was even louder now, trumpeting a clear message. But, nevertheless it was still not loud enough to neutralize her reasoned thought. She called out, "My friends, will you help us? We have a difference from our opponents in attitudes and predictions about Skinner's plan. Science advises us to stop arguing interminably over this difference merely on the basis of our accumulated biases. We must test our differences experimentally. That is all we plan to do here. We simply ask you to help us give our different views a fair test. Remember that we are merely asking you to help with an experiment.

"Before we leave, I will ask if there are any general comments or final questions at this time?"

Burnhouse rose again: "I will answer your remaining questions, if I can, in this forum. But, I may have to delay more technical questions for discussion in smaller groups."

There was a forest of waving hands. The groans of distress, and the angry hoots of derision, gave clear evidence of general unpopularity for Burnhouse's words, except for those gang members who had remained in the room. A few more people now stomped out of the room. Some were waving their arms in general gestures of rejection, or giving thumbs-down signals. Some were heard to mutter such words as "gross," "vile," "blasphemous," "stupid" and "disgusting."

Jake Blakenship seemed to be speaking for most of the audience. He said, "Wake up and smell the coffee, Man. You already have your answer about your so-called scientific plan. The answer for here and now was given to you tonight. Accept it! Your plan will never work here. Give it up! Someone could be hurt, if you continue."

"I don't agree," said Burnhouse. "I was prepared for such blind emotional opposition to the plan at first. I was actually expecting opposition. That is nothing new for us. We knew that it would be a problem to be overcome. The basic question of the experiment is, in fact, whether or not we can effectively overcome such emotional opposition."

Flo considered it best to end the meeting at that point. Speaking to a now nearly empty auditorium, she said, "Thank you, Mr. Burnhouse, for the interesting presentation. It appears that you will have your work cut out for you. I trust that your project will work out as planned. We will expect to hear more from you later.

"Thank you all for coming, and staying to the end. I declare the meeting adjourned."

The now-sparse audience slowly began to file out of the room. Some were standing and still talking excitedly in small groups. Flo turned to Burnhouse, apologetically. "I'm sorry that you were treated so roughly, Skull. But, Jake could be right. Do you think that we should consider abandoning the project? There was obviously a lot of strong opposition to it."

Burnhouse was aghast at the suggestion. "No, no," he said. "This was just the same initial reaction to our ideas that we always get. I can turn these people around, with your help. But, you must help. Nobody said it was going to be easy."

"Right!" said Monika Luthsaar, linking arms with Burnhouse.

That was a fair summary of the evening. Big trouble and more work were ahead. Each of them pondered these troubling thoughts as they sought the comfort and sanctuary of their beds. Many people on the island found that sleep retreated from their sleepy eyes that night. The strong emotions potentiated the disturbing thoughts.

* * * * * *

The satanic bell on the clock by his head jolted Skull Burnhouse into a new morning. Burnhouse hated the demanding nature of alarm clocks. They took over the absolute control of your life. For a few minutes at least they dictated what you must do. They were so necessary, yet their function was so hateful. Burnhouse hated for anything, or anybody, to tell him what to do. He understood, of course, that he himself had willfully programmed the clock to perform the despised intrusion. So, perhaps he was unreasonable to resent the mechanical device as it fulfilled the inevitable performance of its designed duty.

But, now he decided that his reverie on alarm clocks was just an unconscious dodge to insert a delay from the harshly enforced separation from his bed. Once he got past that hated hurdle, he would be eager enough to get on with the business of the day.

His sleep had been uneasy, full of disjointed dreams of dragons defeated and maidens rescued. It was easy for even a Behaviorist to interpret the meaning of that dream. To be sure, he truly felt that he was on the threshold of a great service to humanity. And he was eager to get started today. He was to launch the research program today at a breakfast with Monika, Dan Crow and Florence Gorsuch.

The mealtime conference was, in fact, a major concession for Burnhouse. He never ate breakfast. He usually just quickly threw down a glass of juice and a cup of coffee, and off to his planned operations. For him, a lavish dinner provided the usual welcome capstone to the performance of a good day. To his mind, a splendid meal should never be spoiled with talk of business. And, breakfast was merely a nuisance. Today it was an unnecessary delay of his further plans for the morning.

But, today was indeed special. This particular breakfast was strictly business in his opinion. Burnhouse understood personal human psychology well enough to know that other persons mellowed out over a meal. Persuasion of others to one's particular way of thinking was many times easier if the person were simultaneously enjoying a pleasant meal. This fact amazed him, but he understood it as an undeniable fact. For some, it worked even at an ordinary breakfast. He would use that principle to his advantage this morning.

Burnhouse quickly took care of the morning necessities, and selected an array of comfortable clothes. As usual, his clothes were more of a deliberate costume for an occasion than casual attire. With his white slacks, horizontally-striped blue and white T-shirt, white boat shoes and red handkerchief loosely knotted about his neck, he could easily be mistaken for a displaced apache dancer. Burnhouse was definitely not ordinary.

As he made for the stairs, Burnhouse could hear Crow's boisterous laughter long before that rough gentleman came into his view. He was delighted to hear the sound. He hoped that it was a good sign that Crow was not preparing for a battle at breakfast. That would be unbearable so early in the morning.

Crow and Flo were indeed enjoying a round of kidding. Crow was stoutly maintaining that educators could afford to sleep late. Flo alleged that Crow had to get up early to count his money. Burnhouse wondered if Flo was deliberately trying to set Crow up to be in a good mood for the opening discussions. If so, he was glad.

Monika was late, as usual. She was never *very* late, because that would be unprofessional. But, she apparently thought that she owed it to herself to create a little anticipation for her arrival. The group at breakfast did not provide much of an audience. It was just Burnhouse's party, with Mary Murphy to serve them, and a couple of plantation workers enjoying, for them, a mid-morning break of coffee and doughnuts. But, Monika didn't care as long as there was some audience.

Now, Monika arrived. As usual, all other activities ceased. Her planning had not been in vain. Everyone noticed her entrance, and everyone dutifully admired. The plantation workers were absolutely entranced by her poise and beauty.

Monika smiled sweetly to everyone, and softly murmured, "Sorry, that I am late."

Burnhouse just looked away, and rolled his eyes. He whispered, so that she could not hear him, "Sure, you are." Florence simply smiled, and nodded a friendly greeting to her. Crow softly said, "No problem, ma'am," in his best imitation of the accent of a Southern gentleman. He was, no doubt, sincere. No one ever became truly upset with Monika. At least, not for long.

For a few minutes, they were busy getting started on the meal. It was bountiful by any standard. Because this was Crow's regular morning for steak and eggs, he saw no reason to deviate from that pleasant routine, even for such a famous guest. He could eat and still give his full attention to the work at hand. Besides, he had worked out with the bar bells already this morning. A good breakfast was his just reward. The rest of them were appropriately content with fruits and juices.

As soon as he was able, without seeming to push, Burnhouse turned the conversation to the business of the morning. They all understood that the main problem of immediate concern was to discover how to make a smooth transition from the old form of island government to the new TECHland plan.

After a slow sip of coffee, Burnhouse began, "Friends, now we must move on to the really tough job of deciding just how to make the transition from the usual customs of the island to the TECHland system. I will tell you of my proposals, and then you can give me some feedback. Is that satisfactory?"

Seeing a round of nods in assent, Burnhouse continued, "The main concern is to keep one crucial principle inviolate. Without this principle, we will just be spinning our research wheels, because we will have missed the main point of Skinner's plan. The principle is that we must eliminate the concept of a voluntary will from our thinking, so that we can be effective in removing it from the culture. We must school ourselves to think in technical terms, not in terms of personal wishes and feelings. No one should take personal offense at anything that we undertake from now on. This first principle helps us to use the technology that is available. Is that agreed?"

Everyone nodded assent. Crow said, "Okay, Skull, but I hope that you know what you are doing."

Burnhouse smiled weakly, but said with assurance, "But, of course."

Then, he continued. "Second, we must agree that there can be no force or aversive situations set up to avoid, or to remove, resistance to our plan. There must be only rewards for good behaviors, and no punishments for undesired behaviors. Is everyone okay with that?"

Flo and Monika both nodded, and replied in the affirmative. Crow also nodded, but with obvious reluctance. He said, "I will go along with you on this, Skull, but I think that it is a mistake. I do understand that without those conditions, you really do not have a reasonable test of the TECHland idea. So, I go along. I hope that I will not be sorry."

"Me, too," responded Burnhouse with a smile of gratitude. "I appreciate your willingness to go along with me, Dan.

"Okay, let's go on. To implement the first principle, there is not really anything much that we can do, except to set good examples, to teach, and to confront any expression of a belief in free will. I will set up some seminars to discuss this issue with the leaders of the community first, and then with other interested citizens."

"But, who are the leaders, Skull?" asked Flo.

"That is actually the next problem that we have to tackle," answered Burnhouse. "We must establish a transitional government. It must be one that will implement the second principle—namely, the elimination of coercion and force."

"Good luck," said Dan Crow.

"Now, now, Dan," admonished Burnhouse. "We must keep a positive attitude. Okay?"

"Okay. Sorry," apologized Crow.

"No problem," said Burnhouse. "So, we are agreed among the group of us here. But, Dan, we must be alert to the possibility of making slips of the tongue that will undermine our cause with the people on the island. We must present a unified front."

"Right," agreed Crow. "I will try to be more careful. I am still on your team. Sorry, again."

"Good. Thanks." Burnhouse was relieved. Dan Crow could help, or hurt, his plan in many ways.

Forcing a cheery smile, Burnhouse continued. "So, moving on, let's talk about setting up a new government for the island. Skinner proposed a system of Planners, Managers, Scientists and Workers. As the titles suggest, the Planners are the leaders in terms of principles and philosophy. The Managers are the leaders in terms of seeing that the daily work of the community is done properly. The Scientists conduct research on ways to improve the operation of the community. The Workers perform most of the actual labor of the society."

At this point, Monika interrupted. "You should say, Skull, that none of this part of Skinner's plan is set in stone. It is not in any way crucial to his plan. This part was just a suggestion that could be modified according to the needs of each new society. So, we can follow these ideas, or change them as we see fit."

"Absolutely correct, dear," said Burnhouse. "As I said earlier, only the two principles—the abolition of thinking in terms of free will and any form of punishment—are crucial to the TECHland plan. The rest are just suggestions of things that might work. They can be changed if the experience warrants a change.

"Let me go on anyway to describe Skinner's system. Skinner's plan proposed a compact government composed entirely of a six-member Board of Planners. The Board was usually evenly divided according to gender. Each Planner served for no more than 10 years. The Planners established policy, supervised the Managers, served as judges and generally ran the community. They were compensated by the same credit system in use for all members of the community. Each member had to earn 1200 credits annually to pay for his or her keep in the community. The Planners were allotted 600 credits annually for their service on the Board, and therefore were required to earn an additional 600 credits by performing other activities, half of which were to involve physical labor.

"The Planners were chosen by the Board of Planners from names supplied by the Managers. The Managers were specialists in charge of the various functional divisions of the community. For example, there were managers of Food, Education, Play, Labor and many others. They were selected by the Planners on the basis of their success and motivation as Workers in their particular field of interest.

"The Scientists evaluated and developed the procedures and policies for the society on the basis of the greatest observed efficiency and economy. For example, they tried to improve practices with respect to such items as animal husbandry, child care, education and the use of raw materials.

"Great care was taken not to foster the development of a caste system in the division of labor. For example, everyone was required to perform some physical work for some of his or her credits. Although no task was considered demeaning, the community did recognize that some tasks, such as cleaning sewers, was not preferred. Thus, the Workers were allowed greater numbers of work credits for the performance of such tasks."

"But, there are certain differences between Kipua and the hypothetical Utopia that Skinner envisioned, are there not?" asked Flo. "I seem to remember that the citizens of Skinner's society signed some sort of agreement to abide by the rules of the community. Is that not correct?"

"Right you are," exclaimed Burnhouse. "But, that is not a real problem. The only point there could be that the signature indicated that the person understood the rules. Remember, there is no such thing as a voluntary commitment in the behavioral plan. So, all that we have to do is to make sure that the people on Kipua understand what we are trying to do. It is crucial that we do not try to force anything on anybody. So, whatever we do must be palatable to everyone, or almost everyone."

"That is surely important," advised Crow, "because we may be getting into some constitutional issues by the particular form of government that we start here."

"Like what? asked Monika.

"Well, I am no lawyer, of course," said Crow, "but I think that we could violate some of the provisions of the Bill of Rights. For example, in Skinner's plan, the people are not permitted to criticize the government, except directly to the government officials. That seems to violate freedom of speech. Then, Skinner's plan also takes away the right to vote. Of course, none of this is a problem if no one objects. Your problem is to change attitudes about freedom before anyone challenges you about the loss of freedom. That will really be tough. In fact, I hazard a guess that it will be impossible.

"It seems to me that you will have to run a gigantic bluff at first. You must pretend that you are not running roughshod over peoples' rights, until you have them convinced that they like the good life without those constitutional guarantees."

"Yes, that seems to be the only way," said Burnhouse. "So, let's get on with it. Is everyone agreed?"

There were universal nods of assent, but also some looks of concern.

"I propose that we begin by continuing the same governmental, social and economic order on the island as presently exists. The Island Council will fulfill very nicely the role envisioned for the Planners in Skinner's system. The owners of the various shops and businesses will take the jobs of Managers, except that the formal divisions will be more along the lines of proprietorship than function. We could not ask, for example, the owners of certain businesses simply to give them away to the community for all to share in equally, can we?"

"I would hope not," said Crow. "As cooperative as I feel, I would not be willing to give up what I have worked so long and so hard for, just because someone asked me to do it on the basis of some abstract principle. Surely, all other business and property owners would feel the same. I could not imagine the dePuy family simply donating their ranch and their business to your cause."

"Of course not," agreed Burnhouse. "So, that part of the TECHland plan is settled.

"The next step is to establish Monika and I as the Scientists for the community. We will have to do the studies, and make the observations, that will guide us about when the community is ready to move ahead with other parts of the plan. We will have to concentrate first on the educational part of the program, because that is the most crucial. Obviously, we will need to devise some sort of educational Blitzkrieg in order to gain converts before too much resistance develops.

"Okay. Now we arrive at the trickiest part. We must remove punishments and aversive conditioning from Kipua. And, that has to begin with the police. We have to hope that the Island Council will hold fast in instructing the police to avoid force in keeping the peace. We will be meeting with them and the chief of police later this morning in order to induce them to forego force henceforth on the island."

"God help you," said Dan Crow.

"Or, whatever," replied Burnhouse, with a shrug. "There is one more thing that I want to bring up before we leave this morning. Although it is not crucial to Skinner's plan, we should bend every effort to enhance a spirit of cooperation on the island. We should discourage all competition among individual persons. No one should triumph over another, and no one should be defeated by another. Such things build unwholesome resentments. They would be poison to our efforts. Any competition should be against lower standards of effort and achievement. That would be productive, not destructive. Okay?"

"Okay," said Flo.

"Okay," said Crow.

"Okay," said Monika.

"Good," said Burnhouse. "Let's get going."

* * * * * *

The Island Council was gathered in the game room of the Crow Bar. They could not meet in their usual meeting place in the Catholic Church because Father Jack would not have it. Now they were gathered, in a rather casual manner, around a netless ping pong table. Because the room had been reserved, there were no game players in the room. The arcade games were uncharacteristically silent. Mary Murphy had set up a coffee pot on a small table in the corner, with a stack of styrofoam cups. While the others were content with the coffee, or with soda drinks from an ancient machine, Burnhouse and Monika sipped from glasses of juice bought to them as a special service by Mary.

There were five members of the Council. In addition to Flo, Crow and dePuy, the membership included Niko Kipuanui and Maxine Boniface, the proprietor of the village department store.

Maxine had been persuaded, as had Dan Crow, that the social experiment would be of great financial benefit to the island. She was not very knowledgeable about the details of the TECHland plan, however.

Flo called the meeting to order at 10:30. Then, she said, "Because this is a special meeting of the Council, I propose that we dispense with the normal business of the council and restrict ourselves to a discussion of ways to implement the TECHland plan, which we have previously approved. Is that agreeable?"

Seeing general agreement, she proceeded, "You all know Skull Burnhouse and Monika Luthsaar who are our special guests for the discussion today. They will be our scientific advisors for this project. We must listen carefully to what they propose. But, please understand that we do not have to follow their suggestions. We are still the government on Kipua. But, keep in mind that every time we react contrary to their advice, we lessen the chances for a complete and valid test of the TECHland model."

"How so?" asked Maxine, obviously puzzled.

"Because any departure from the TECHland model means that literally the TECHland model would not be the model that was tested at this time and place. It would mean that our data would apply to the different model that we actually followed. That test would be of some value, I am sure, but it is not what we are setting out to accomplish. Our purpose is to test the TECHland model. Is that clear now? Do you see what I mean?"

"Sure," said Maxine. "Now, I understand. Thanks for the explanation."

"Good,' said Flo. "Now, Skull, I ask that you make your initial proposals to the Council. I ask the Council to remember that most of these proposals are tentative, and therefore can be changed at any time as conditions warrant."

"Thanks, Flo," said Burnhouse affably. "I should say that Monika and I have already undertaken preliminary discussions with Dan and Flo, and we are in agreement. By those discussions we just meant to expedite the process, to get the discussion started.

They were not meant to exclude anyone from the full discussion later. They involved Flo as the mayor, of course. We invited Dan because he was convenient, and because we suspected that he had the greatest reservations about the plan. Our meeting was merely to reach agreement on the proposals to bring to you. Now, it is entirely your prerogative and responsibility to make the final decision. Is everyone satisfied and comfortable with that?"

Because everyone seemed comfortable with the situation, Burnhouse continued, "As Flo said, much of what we propose is tentative. There is only one condition that is set in stone, so to speak. Without that condition, we would really have no test of the TECHland model. I merely remind you of this, because you have already agreed to that condition when you agreed to the experiment. But, I again emphasize its importance. Namely, we must eliminate the concept of any freedom of will—of voluntary choice—in our island society. We must assume that there is a joint genetic and environmental cause for each behavior, and therefore we can control it. It also means that no one ever voluntarily chooses to perform bad behaviors. We believe that something in his or her background caused that behavior to happen. Period. That's it! Therefore, we must not make value judgments about people which assume that the person was acting through choice.

"This way of thinking about the nature of people leads to a full commitment to use the best behavioral technology available to control behaviors. Therefore, we should not hold back on the use of effective technologies on the basis of some vague notions of alleged special characteristics of human beings. People should be treated and respected as complex systems of many intricate mechanisms. Nothing more. Their worth or value to the community does not extend beyond the behaviors that they are able to contribute to it."

"Does that mean that we do not have to be concerned about people's feelings?" asked Maxine, incredulously.

"No, no," objected Burnhouse. "We must surely be alert to preferences and resentments, for example, because they play a part in behavior. Our job is to train ourselves to avoid behaviors that cause resentments, and to train our people not to resent certain behaviors that previously might have provoked resentments. That is just good technology."

"That is theory, anyway." said Niko.

"Yes, that is theory. That is what we are here to test, to see if it works.

"A related matter concerns the exclusive use of positive rewards for good behavior. There will be no punishment for bad actions, that is, undesired behaviors. We must avoid the production of aversive conditions of any kind."

Crow interjected, "So, how do you deal with one of those so-called undesired behaviors?"

Burnhouse was ready for the question. "We are going to have to give you all training in the appropriate techniques. They are called 'behavior modification techniques.' All that I will say for now is just to ignore undesired behaviors. Then, try to discover some way to prevent that particular behavior from happening again. You see, the person did not choose, in a voluntary sense, to be bad. He or she was just responding as he or she had been trained, or had learned, to respond to the prevailing conditions at the time. When the person shows signs of doing the right thing, reward those signs. Try to catch the person being good, so that you can reward him or her for it. That is the plan in a nutshell."

Burnhouse went on to explain the mechanics of the proposed government as worked out at the earlier breakfast meeting. The Council accepted them unanimously. They authorized Flo to meet with Burnhouse, Monika and Chief Gupta of the island police force to work out ways to move toward elimination of physical and psychological force and other aversive situations on the island.

* * * * * *

Monika, Flo and Burnhouse met that afternoon with Chief Gupta, to explain their proposals. The meeting did not go well. Although Gupta was not insubordinate, he obviously did not agree on the abolition of punishment and force. The appropriate change in thinking would require a complete reversal of attitude.

Gupta stoutly maintained that he could not replace his pistol and billy club with M & M candies and warm embraces.

Nevertheless, he agreed to try this new system; that was truly all that could be asked of him. The rest was the re-educational responsibility of the scientific team.

* * * * * *

Percy Herandez was always one to test the limits. The word was out that the TECHland model was now in place on the island. Therefore, Chief Gupta was not only muzzled, he was toothless. He had even been seen around the village without his nightstick and pistol.

Percy marched into Maxine Boniface's department store, and slipped on a new pair of sneakers. With a cheery, "Thanks, Max," he then strode brazenly out of the store.

Understandably distraught, Maxine sent her clerk after Percy to demand payment. The clerk soon returned empty-handed, with the report that he had backed off in the face of Percy's folding knife.

Surprised, and still wearing his new shoes, Percy just grinned, and said, "This is going to be good!"

FIVE

IT HAD BEEN SIX MONTHS since Sculleigh Burnhouse had first brought his controversial social experiment to the island. The plan had seemed plausible to some of them at first. The experiment had intended to establish a beneficial utopian society through the committed use of behavioral technology. Burnhouse had hoped to avoid distractions from humanistic conceptions about the nature of human beings.

But, surely, the execution of such a plan must be tricky and difficult. The engineered community was to have become a model for a new benign society. Every personal need would be met and everyone would be happy. The key idea of the psychologist's plan was to deal with all human problems and needs scientifically.

It had been a seductive argument. Surely, the goal of happiness and well-being for the population was praiseworthy.

Now, they knew from sad personal experience that the supposed path to a superior society was littered instead with rampant evils. Horribly, the present result on Kipua was the literal reverse of what the optimistic founder and his backers had theorized and expected to happen. The empirical result was general vile excesses and terror. The island had quickly become a Hell, instead of gradually metamorphosing into a modern Utopia. The present tragic consequences were even worse than most of its opponents could have imagined. Only the most insightful and surest of critics could have anticipated such a worst result.

No one on Kipua had any basis for even a minimal hope to escape from the island. The large boats of the dePuy family, as well as Gupta's police boat, had been destroyed beyond any hope of repair by the junta that had taken control of the island. Similarly, all of the radio transmitters had been smashed long before. The junta stationed men on the dock to prevent anyone from leaving, or even communicating with the *Cornucopia's* crew, when the supply ship was in port. All outgoing packages were searched for messages that might give a hint of the events on the island.

The native fishermen had been warned of dreadful consequences if they even attempted to transport anyone across the open sea in their outrigger canoes. The same fate was promised to them if they accepted bribes to carry pleas for rescue. Apparently, only a few of them had even tried. In any case, few had made the attempt, and few had succeeded. Therefore, there was no consistent communication by the islanders to anyone in the outside world.

The situation on the island had deteriorated markedly since the last visit of the supply ship. Therefore, any description of conditions that may have been noticed and transmitted by the ship's crew to other ports did not describe adequately the current desperation of their situation. The conditions had now become worse than unbearable. They were, in fact, surely lethal in their implications. Logically, the next step, in a series of steps toward utter wantonness, would indeed be murder. The conscienceless scum of the island had shown no reluctance in the commission of the lesser crimes.

So, undoubtedly, there would eventually be murders on the island, if the conditions continued to deteriorate. That sad possibility now seemed entirely likely. Those of the inhabitants of Hell who were so inclined certainly had no significant fear of retaliation for murder. Retaliation was, of course, not in the existing plan of governance. Feelings of panic and frustration and moral confusion were mounting in the general population.

Held back by only the minimal practical rules, many of the former workers on the island had started to indulge their basic urges without reason or restraint. They acted like alligator-brained creatures. Cold-blooded and predatory without remorse, they had reverted to their primal state of birth. They were guided only by the pleasure principle, which is rooted in the physical heritage of the animal kingdom.

The spiritual and civic leaders of the island were steadily losing their influence to the advocates of personal satisfaction. In fact, the island priest, Jack Schindler, and the Baptist preacher, Cal Prescott, the only clergymen on the island, had both been viciously beaten on the orders of the junta leaders. Without regard to self, the clerics had spoken out courageously against the actions of the outlaw government. And it had cost them both physical and mental pain. The mental pain came from the realization that people whom they had long loved and served had subsequently betrayed them.

Flo Gorsuch had soon been converted away from the TECHland credo by the resulting evil that she saw around her. For weeks, she had seen that the basic result of the TECHland experiment had in reality been total disaster for her island. She had been constantly urging Burnhouse to abandon his experiment. She begged the island council to petition the government for martial law. Only her age and gender prevented the same treatment for her that the clerics had received. Despite that sure knowledge, she continued her efforts against TECHland.

The outlaw leaders simply ignored the fact that their tactics were in no way a part of the ideal TECHland plan which had originally been proposed by Sculleigh Burnhouse. It seemed that the primary tangible result of Burnhouse's experiment had been to open a Pandora's box of evil intentions and actions on the island. The present island leaders had perverted his plan into a license to practice whatever evil came to their minds.

Some of the decent individuals on the island had formed paramilitary squads, primarily in order to protect the clerics. But the sheer number of occasions that the clergymen were forced to take chances in the conduct of their pastorates was too great. There could never be a perfect level of success in protecting them. In fact, such efforts for protection had not been completely successful. Much of the religious work on the island had to be done in secret, because the force of numbers was so heavily on the side of the junta.

The responsible citizens of the island had formed a few safe enclaves for armed protection of their families. The rest of the island was controlled and patrolled by the coalitions of the junta. The areas of junta control were much larger, and these lawless areas increased in size almost daily. The boundaries of the enclaves were not well-defined. There were raids by small groups of the lawless ones from time to time. Excursions outside a safe enclave had to be well-protected by armed guards. Also, there had to be strict precautions not to alert the forces of the junta to the impending action.

There was an alarming steady file of defections from the ranks of lawful citizens to the ranks of the mob. To be sure, the shift in loyalties did not save anyone's goods or property. Nor did it save wives and daughters from the excesses of the mob. But the defectors, by definition, did not care. In fact, the abandonment of such caring was a critical part of the incipient defection process. Actually, the fact that the characteristic of caring had stopped functioning was the major sign of the impeding defections. In time, many of the wives and husbands, sons and daughters, did not care either.

Many islanders were caught up in the lure of the so-called good life, allegedly only possible when moral constraints had been removed. That is exactly what the TECHland plan had advocated. Now, the prevailing rule on Kipua was provided by the old cliché: If you can't beat them, join them.

In general, the rank and file of the defectors did not seem to anticipate that the good life would disappear when all of the "golden geese" were used up, or had disappeared. Nevertheless, a few strong persons of good conscience split with their families to join other so-called geese in the golden enclaves. These non-defectors were considered traitors by the ranks of the junta. They were therefore more likely to be targets for vengeful raids and sallies in search of revenge or booty.

So, life on Kipua had predictably become a hell for the golden geese.

But what about the lives of the faithful followers of the junta? If the reasoning of the Behaviorists had been at all consistent with the nature of human beings, then the quality of life should have been superlative for the insiders. The believers and followers of the plan should be uniformly happy. But, the fundamental truth was inescapable: the members of the mob were not happy. With the providers of goods and services dwindling daily, there was simply not enough of even the basic goods of life to go around. The available goods went to the strong, who were, of course, the leaders of the junta. No personal possession was safe. There was no greater penalty for stealing from one's cohort and neighbor than there was for stealing from an enemy goose inside an enclave.

In fact, everyone was a potential goose under the prevailing system. The only safety was in becoming a part of a smaller group that had banded together for mutual benefit. Therefore, the large enclave of the junta had become a collection of even smaller enclaves of gangs that were held together only by self interests. No one could experience quiet enjoyment of anything that he or she might hold in temporary custody. Thus, consumerism was rampant. A product was consumed, or an advantage exploited immediately, for fear that it would not be available for any enjoyment later.

There were no friendships. There were only alliances. There was no trust. There was only mutual interest. There was no personal security. There was scant hope for any measure of safety in the future. The only joy was in the desperate performance of excesses in the satisfaction of personal desires. These desires could never, however, reach a level beyond the most basic of physical needs.

Distinctly human qualities were masked or destroyed. The potential search for aesthetic, artistic and social goals was buried under the quest for the materials of survival and animal pleasures. The only meaning in life was obtained through a party mentality. Hedonism ruled. The big picture of life was no more than a *Playboy* centerfold.

TECHland had ironically become a stratified society. An undeniable social class system had developed. Caste was determined entirely by the relative possession of power. The best of everything was reserved for the members of the junta, of course. A small residue of the evil spoils did trickle down. But, it was never enough to satisfy the needs of the powerless people at the bottom of the pyramid.

* * * * * *

Rene was among a tragically unfortunate group of women who were paying a great price for the gross naivete of their former leaders. The new leaders were collecting the price.

Now, Rene's psychologically bruised brain was slowly losing awareness of the cruel rapes that she had been suffering for the past hour. Rene's inner being desperately begged for a quick end to the vandalic invasions now savaging her tortured body. She desperately searched her mind for a way to stop the torment.

Rene was surrounded in a dreary cattle shed by a mob of conscienceless brutes. Although the place had been hosed down, limed and covered with fresh straw, it was still a place for cattle. It was inhuman by its very nature. The nauseating smells of urine and manure still sifted through the deodorizing agents, mingling with the smells of stale human sweat and other vile odors.

Still, this ignoble setting was far more tolerable than the monstrous deeds being perpetuated in it. The animal house indeed was a fitting place for some of its inhabitants.

To be sure, Rene knew that, for the immediate future, escape from this place for her physical body was totally impossible. She was far outnumbered by vicious captors. Each one was capable of subduing her with vicious force, if challenged. So, her only hope for escape from her pain was through self-induced psychological oblivion. She must somehow achieve a complete comatose blanking of her mind. An extreme act of human striving would be required for her to reach such a blessed state of nothingness. Rene wondered if such a mindless state of unawareness could indeed be willed at all.

But, undoubtedly the mind cannot be ordered about like a mischievous schoolboy in the principal's office. A person cannot just simply will himself or herself to shut off a conscious awareness of excruciating stimulation. Seemingly, the harder she tried, the faster the mental blanking retreated from her. Perhaps, even such an escape was also impossible.

So, for now, Rene's traumatized mind was all too aware of her pain. Her circumstances were intolerable. But, she must tolerate.

Rene could also forecast the terrifying implications for her future. That dreadful forecast was at the same time totally unbearable and surely inevitable. Past cruel experience had made that horrible conclusion patently obvious.

Her present condition had not been unanticipated. Indeed, it had been surely predictable. Along with many others, she had been securely trapped on the island for weeks full of fear and pain and dread. The conditions on the island had steadily worsened. There had been no doubt about what was sure to happen, unless some major miraculous intervention changed the course of events.

So, Rene was praying for quick release. The beseeched blackout of mental capacity was the only way to escape the vile intentions of the ugly assortment of humans-turned-animals forming a long line before her. Each savage in the line was impatiently waiting for his turn at further wanton atrocities on her battered, helpless body and mind.

So, the future was predictable. Rene knew that as long as she was conscious there could be no respite from the relentless relays of rapists. Her only hope for relief came from a rule established by the mobsters who had now taken over control of the island. The rulers had ordered that all rapes be stopped when the so-called hosts lost consciousness. Therefore, to pass into unconsciousness not only stopped awareness of the rape, in fact it also stopped the bestial act itself.

Yes, there were still a few rules on the island of Kipua. There was some little restraint on the evil actions of the marauding bands of sociopaths now terrifying the other inhabitants. The leaders of the ill assortment of organized gangs and independent mobs had formed a loose junta to provide some order and a way to coordinate their mutual interests. The formation of the junta was a practical move. It prevented total anarchy and chaos on the island. Actually, it was necessary.

The people in control had established a firm rule on the island against raping unconscious victims. The rule could actually be trusted these days. Pitiably, little else on the depraved island could be trusted when you needed it. So, Rene knew that ironically the physical rapes would stop only when she could no longer be hideously aware of particular instances.

Such meager limits on licentiousness set by the junta had been joyfully welcomed by the victims. To be sure, the actual rules themselves had been established solely for the benefit of the oppressors. The rules were certainly not for the benefit of the oppressed; indeed they were not intended to be. The depraved minds of the leaders had nevertheless been sufficiently rational to understand that permanent physical damage or death to their victims did not play to the advantage of the junta. Victims of the crimes and atrocities had to be left in adequate condition for sufficient recovery. Then, they would be available to be raped, or robbed, again. As the leader of the junta, Sam Conaway, put it succinctly, "We do not want to kill the geese that lay the golden eggs." It was that philosophy which now provided Rene's only hope for an end to this particular ordeal.

Rene tried to distract her mind from her pain by focusing her anger at those scientists and academics and intellectual chauvinists who had brought this horror to the world, especially to her. She knew that this disastrous result had been predicted by many other thinking professionals in behavioral science when the behavioral technology plan was first suggested. These professionals argued that people were not machines. People could not psychologically handle being treated in such a manner. These psychologists argued that everyone should have known that the basic idea was ridiculous. You cannot improve society by abandoning the concept of personal control and responsibility. The most casual of observers of human behavior could have predicted the rapid erosion of prosocial behaviors under such conditions. The explosion of beastly behaviors would be extruded naturally and quickly from conscienceless minds.

Thus, the arrival of Professor Burnhouse and his hateful experiment had set into motion the mechanisms that had led inexorably to Rene's personal anguish and tragedy. Conditions on the island these days were always bad. At some times, they were worse. Now, they were worst.

So, now, was especially a time for the pain. Although Rene's anger blunted the pain somewhat, it really was small comfort to her. The whole situation was as senseless as it was horrible.

About two months ago, Rene had been one of the first to be raped. That priority was truly not surprising. She had been one of the most visible, and most enviable, women on the island. Her very happiness made her the primary target for the excesses of the new rulers.

Rene had survived the first ordeal with relatively little physical damage, because she had been fortunate enough to have fainted rather quickly. But, the psychological damage was most severe. For weeks, she had refused to come out of her room. She had allowed only Flo, outside of her immediate family, to see her. Because Flo had a little experience with counseling rape victims from her teaching jobs, she did her best to help Rene. But, it was an extremely difficult task. It was especially difficult because the danger was still endemic among them, even among the followers of the TECHland plan.

The present irony was that Rene had been captured on her first excursion outside of her house since the original trauma. She had thought that she would go crazy if she stayed in the plantation compound one more instant. She resolved to visit her friend, Launini, at the native village. Her father objected, but finally yielded on the condition that she would be escorted by two armed men. As it turned out, two bodyguards were not enough.

Now, through eyes whose vision was dim and blurred by her anguish, Rene saw Sam Conaway, as he once more forced his way to the head of a line. Mostly, he seemed to be content with watching the humiliation of the captives. Rene seemed to remember that he had been first with her today. He was a beast. He reveled in the discomfort and vulnerability of others.

* * * * * *

Sam Conaway was the type of man that authors have in mind when they write about people with closed minds. To be sure, for him there were always two ways of looking at every issue. One was, of course, his way. The other way was unquestionably the wrong one. It was fair to say that Conaway was basically immune to the antibodies of reason.

Conaway was the inevitable calamitous result of a series of unfortunate life experiences. The first negative circumstance was represented by a very weak mother, who never expressed an opinion. The second set of experiences was produced by a brutish father who never allowed a hint of dissent to any of his firm pontifications. The father, Big Steve Conaway, was rarely in the house. As the owner of his own truck for long-distance hauling, he was forced to be away for days, and sometimes weeks, at a time. Not that anyone minded. Big Steve's extended absences may, or may not, have been a boon to his family. He was always vicious and terrifying when present. He rigidly enforced tyrannical house rules whenever he returned.

The routine environment for Sam and his three younger brothers was laissez-fair chaos most of the time, when his mother was supposedly in charge. Then, there was storm trooper control at others, when Big Steve was there to be in charge. Only an extremely rare human mind could withstand such inconsistent stresses without becoming twisted. Conaway's mind, only slightly above average in intelligence, was not sufficient for the task. So, twisted he eventually became.

Big Steve's punishments were double-edged. There were demeaning diatribes for small offenses. There were severe physical beatings for perceived major crimes. Because Big Steve was often too drunk to make the discrimination, he compromised by indiscriminately meting out both types of pain, just to be sure. The arrogant bully justified his behavior to his drinking companions down at the convenient corner bar on the basis of trying to be a responsible father. As he often said, he was simply doing his solemn duty to society to rear peaceful, law-abiding sons.

After a round of especially harsh punishments on the boys, Big Steve was fond of quoting pieces of passages from the Bible that he had heard once somewhere. He could not recall how he had come to hear it. It said something about sparing the rod and spoiling the child.

When Big Steve was away, the brothers fought each other for whatever they wanted. There was, of course, no interference from their mother. But, they were always careful to stay within their father's stern rules. Big Steve on his return would always force their mother to tell him of any rule infractions. If she knew of no violations of the rules, she would have to make up enough to satisfy Big Steve. He always felt better after he had done his duty to correct the boys.

Sam Conaway was tougher and smarter than his brothers. He had at first only his father to deal with, but they had to cope with their oldest brother as well. Each succeeding sibling had to cope with an increasing number of carbon copies of the old man. Sam, as the oldest brother, was an especially faithful copy.

Sam finally did his brothers a good turn by leaving home at the age of thirteen. Once on the streets, Conaway supported himself by various devices, mostly illegal. He lived on the proceeds of professions such as prostitution, pimping, hustling and thievery. At the age of fifteen, he was able to sign on as a merchant seaman on a tramp steamer of Liberian registry, but doubtful ownership.

Life aboard the ship was hard. But, it was still easier than it had been with Big Steve. In fact, Conaway was tougher than anybody. That usually made living easy under the circumstances.

The two youngest brothers were in correctional facilities for emotionally disturbed juveniles. The third brother, second oldest, was in jail for aggravated assault. Except for his cleverness, Conaway would himself be in jail. He had indeed served jail time on several minor charges. But, he was exceedingly careful to avoid big-time offenses.

Conaway had found out about the job on Kipua from a chance meeting at a bar in Manila. He got the job because he knew how to control men. He had worked his way up to first mate on the ship by virtue of his uncompromising style, his quick fists and an artfully-used belaying pin. That meant that he could get good production from the deck hands without provoking open dissent or trouble. Apparently, such qualities were just the ones that the plantation manager was seeking in a foreman at the time. The reasoning was that Conaway could soon learn what he did not know about producing copra, and about plantation life itself. It was only important that he knew how to handle men, particularly native men.

No one on the plantation liked Conaway. His nickname among the workers was ordinarily "My-way Conaway," except when he had performed some particularly heinous offense. Then, he was simply "Sam Slime." The plantation workers were exceedingly careful not to use either name in Conaway's hearing, however. One unfortunate boy had been careless about such use. Conaway had beaten him unconscious on the spot. He would have killed the boy if other supervisors had not intervened to save his life. Fearing that his salvation from an enraged Conaway was only temporary, the poor boy had left the island, without telling anyone where he was going.

Everyone had to agree that Conaway produced fabulous results in terms of gross production, at least in the short run. Actually, there were some muffled rumors that his style would not wear well in the long run for the eventual benefit of the plantation. But, nevertheless, at the time Burnhouse arrived on the island, Conaway's future in copra management seemed golden with promise.

Conaway's hate-filled personality was a particularly bad match to the TECHland philosophy. The TECHland plan had no provision for rehabilitation for people like Conaway. He lived according to punishment, and aggravated fear of punishment. To him, rewards were personal advantages stolen or extorted from weaker enemies. He did not understand the concepts of love or friendship. For him, there were only practical alliances.

Conaway's greatest pleasure was in hurting or defeating someone. He particularly liked to defeat someone who was weak and defenseless. Such people, to his mind, were worthy of no respect. He felt remorse only when he had missed a good opportunity to hurt or to degrade someone who was helpless.

Now, Conaway was roaming the cattle shed. He ruled the site of Rene's horror, goading his minions to greater excesses of cruelty. He cheered and applauded like a football coach whose team was winning. He urged his players on to greater efforts as if time were running out on a game clock, trying to run up the score on an overpowered opponent. Afterwards, there would be a victory celebration. It would be a delicious time to brag about the enormity of the victory.

Occasionally, Conaway would get carried away with his own exhortations. Then, he would break into the head of the line, roughly cuffing aside anyone foolish enough to object. His hate for the dePuys was so great that he had already broken into Rene's line twice. But, nevertheless, his hate never diminished. It was always there. It was like an implanted pacemaker attached to the heart, foreclosing any possibility of respite from its awful actions.

* * * * * *

Rene prayed anew to find a means for escaping this daylight nightmare. There was no hope for her in feigning unconsciousness as a means to escape. The idea of faking a blackout had occurred to the women of the island as soon as the unconsciousness rule had been established. But it had also occurred to the junta. The leaders had forced the lone physician on the island, Dr. van Loon, to tell them how to detect fakes. He complied under the threat of a lifting of the rule. Because one of the tests for faking involved the degree of reactivity to severe pain, the women had decided that merely pretending to black out would not be reasonable. Despite the pain to be endured, the tactic simply would not be effective.

Thus, the few laws laid down by the virtually lawless leaders of the junta had basically the same purpose. For example, the leaders would not permit their followers to rob the shopkeepers of so much cash and goods that the shops would be forced immediately out of business. If all shops were forced to close, then there would be no one left to become a profitable victim. The various groups of mobsters had indeed begun to organize sufficiently so that a relatively formal arrangement had been worked out with the shopkeepers. Instead of enduring robberies at haphazard intervals, now the shopkeepers were being forced to pay fixed sums for tribute, or protection, on a regular basis.

The same was true for the owners of the copra plantation. The dePuy family was not exempt from the desires of the de facto rulers. The family still maintained armed control over the plantation compound and the surrounding outbuildings. But, they were nevertheless forced to pay a tribute to the mobs and gangs for quiet use of the coconut groves to produce their commercial crop, and for use of the docks in the town to ship the processed copra to their paying customers.

The island rules, minimal as they were, nevertheless meant that, for the time being, all of the islanders were permitted to survive. To be sure, for most of them the survival itself represented merely a hellish existence. Already a few natives and shopkeepers had committed suicide. Surely, more would follow if the horrid conditions did not change.

The natives who already barely survived by fishing in the lagoon and off the reefs were essentially left alone to earn their subsistence. Nevertheless, there was an occasional wildcat raid for some of their produce, and to kidnap women and girls for gang rapes such as was now taking place around Rene. The most recent raid had in fact netted by accident this most special prize: the only daughter of the plantation owner. Fortunately for Launini, this time she had escaped capture by hiding in a hay loft. Her escape was facilitated by the fact that the minions of the junta basically gave up further searches for new victims when they realized that Rene had fallen into their grasp.

Rene was not especially desired by the rapists for her physical appearance, attractive as it was. Indeed, she was not the most beautiful woman on the island. That honor, by consensus, belonged to either the exquisite Launini, or to Calia Prescott, the daughter of the Baptist minister on the island.

But the rapes were not about beauty. They were not even about sexual attraction. They were about power. In fact, the rapists took particular pleasure in assaulting Rene simply because she represented the privileges of the wealthy and previously powerful. Someone had even placed a sign on the wall today behind her place of terror. In crude lettering it said—"Rene the Queen." Apparently, the author thought that a rhyme was involved. Among the mobsters it was considered to be a distinction of high honor to "have been of service to the Queen." Hence, the queues before Rene were always the longest, always filled with the angriest men.

So, Rene understood that there was no scarcity of evil men who wanted to tear at her body. Her inner screams were even more desperate than the vestigial shrieks coming from her lungs. Neither was going to change the immediate course of events, however. The line before Rene never disappeared. It was never even shortened. For every man that finished with her, a new one joined from another victim. Some even got back in line like kids running back to get in line before a sliding board at a playground. Except that this was horrible.

* * * * * *

Flo was meeting with Dan Crow and Pierre dePuy at the school. The latest kidnapping of Rene and the other women had thrown them all into panic. Pierre was nearly out of his mind with worry, grief and anger. The civilized parts of his personality had been torn out by desperate despair and rage. He was primed for wanton aggression and revenge.

"We must stop this right now. We must make Burnhouse call off his experiment, write off his losses and get the hell off of this island," he ranted. "Enough is enough. You can see that it has gotten out of hand. We must do something. I want to kill Burnhouse with my bare hands! I want to kill him slowly. And, then I will start on Conaway and the others."

Neither of the other two was inclined to disagree with dePuy, or to speak up, if they indeed had disagreed. Crow was as disgusted as Flo with the way the experiment had turned out. "I agree with Pierre," he said. "Let's do something before more harm is done."

"Okay, let's do it," agreed Flo. "There is no use in waiting, or talking about it anymore. Pierre, it is better if you do not come with us. Spend your time looking for Rene. Dan and I will go to Burnhouse and try to talk some sense into him. I have pleaded with him before. It did not do any good, though. Perhaps, Dan and I together can persuade him to stop the experiment. He must realize that fact now, particularly because of this most recent horrible kidnapping."

"Thanks," said dePuy, slightly calmer. "I don't know where to look. But, I will look. It will give me something to do. Besides, I doubt that I could keep my cool with that monster, anyway." He crammed his crumpled hat on his head, and stalked out to mount

his horse in front of the building. Once mounted, he rode off recklessly toward the plantation.

Together, Flo and Crow walked the short distance down Main
Street toward the Crow Bar. They guessed that Burnhouse was
probably in his room. He had been spending most of his time these
days in that personal retreat. It was well-known that he spent
more time now sipping gin from a large bottle than administer-
ing rewards to other people. He himself had to know that he and
TECHland were defeated.

When Flo and Crow entered the saloon, Mary Murphy was
wiping the bar with a damp towel. She had been serving a cus-
tomer who was just leaving. She dropped a dollar bill in the cash
register, and slammed it shut. She turned to greet them with a
melancholy half-smile.

Mary was probably the only other woman on the island who
could function without the close proximity of an armed guard.
The reason was Dan Crow. When Burnhouse's experiment had
turned sour, Crow had let it be known on the island that he would
tolerate no hostile actions toward Mary. He had put out the word
that, if any harm or threat of harm came to her, he would surely
catch the perpetrator. Then, he would soon cause that individual
to die, slowly and painfully. Everyone was wise to believe him.
Given Crow's military background of covert operations, and his
numerous awards for excellence in the performance of those
skills, his threats worked perfectly. His general reputation for
speaking truthfully, without bragging, convinced all potential
purveyors of evil that Dan would do as he promised. So, no one
had given even a hint of a hostile act to Mary. She had also been
careful, to be sure. But, everyone knew that it was the threatening
promise of Crow that truly kept her safe.

"Mary, Honey," said Crow, "have you seen Burnhouse about?
Is he in his room? "

Mary shook her head. "Nope," she replied. "And, it is very
strange. I have not heard a peep out of him all afternoon. He usually has made a dozen demands by now. He did not even ask for
another bottle of the white stuff."

"He must have passed out," suggested her boss. "We will go up, and roust him out. What we have to do will not wait."

"I hope that you are planning to tell him to stop his damned experiment. And, tell him to get off this island." Mary was not one to mince words.

"Yeah," said Crow, with determination, as he and Flo proceeded up the stairs.

There was still no sign of Burnhouse. Crow banged on the door of Burnhouse's room. No answer. Further banging still did not produce a response.

Crow growled, "He must be really zonked." Pulling out his master key, he unlocked the door. He loudly called Burnhouse's name as he slowly pushed the door open.

Burnhouse was not there. Nor was he in the bathroom. Apparently, he was not any place on the premises. Burnhouse had disappeared! There was no sign of a struggle, or any other kind of foul play. Plenty of people hated Burnhouse, but there was no evidence that an enemy was responsible.

Crow ran to get Constable Gupta. They would have to add Burnhouse to the list of people that were missing. He must be included in the all-out search of the island. They would check first with Monika Luthsaar, to see if she knew anything.

* * * * * *

Rene could not tell how many rapes that she had endured this time. She did not know how long since this particular ordeal had begun. The last time this horror had happened to her she had remained fully conscious for only five minutes. On that occasion she had suffered 18 separate rapes from presumably as many men. She knew these totals because one of the vandals had been assigned to keep the statistics. Apparently, the purpose of keeping score was to be able to relish telling them to the victims later. Providing the information on the time and number of rapes was an innovative way of prolonging the pleasure which the junta and their followers had derived from the torture. Somehow the rape itself was apparently not sufficient for them. The horror had also to be fixed in the minds of the victims. The despicable de-briefings were simply a part of the display of unrestricted power, and total depravity.

She learned that she had been the first to pass out. She prayed that it would happen again.

Rene was still sufficiently alert to be aware that a native had arrived at the shed with exciting news. There was an immediate blast of cacophonic talking. Rene could finally make out from the shouts that Skull Burnhouse had disappeared. No one seemed to know what had happened to him. He had just disappeared from his room and from the island without leaving a trace.

Rene wondered what that event would mean to her. Would the cursed experiment now be over? Or, would it continue, because the mobsters truly loved it? But, right now, she didn't care about anything, except making her mind go blank.

Strangely, Rene wondered if the time to unconsciousness would get shorter as a woman had more experience with forcible rape. It surely would come sooner if a person could simply will themselves into becoming unconscious. She was coming more and more to doubt that such fruits of wishing were possible.

She knew that there were about a dozen women in the group that had been captured with her. She could tell by their alternating shrill screams and low moans that most of the women and girls were still conscious. It was a bad time and a bad place to be young and strong.

So, she had been praying, it seemed for hours, for an early mental blanking. It had not come. She knew that it must come eventually. The mental blanking had to be a psychological device with survival power. Otherwise, the capacity to faint would not have survived in the species. Although the mental shrieking of her mind was more fervent then the physical screams now originating in her lungs, there had been no relief. If she had the opportunity to kill herself, she would do so at once. She must end the agony. She could no longer wait for the blessed blanking of consciousness.

With disgusting grunts of joy, Sam Conaway was forcing himself into her. It was unbearable to have this trash of a man do this to her. She felt that she would drown with rage.

Suddenly, an excruciating knot of pain exploded within Rene. Then, at last, for Rene, for a while, sensation ceased.

One of the minions of the junta perfunctorily administered the tests for consciousness. He was sure that she was out. When she did not respond, he looked with disgust at the men forming the long line before her. Then, he shook his head in anger and frustration.

The animals in the queue were forced to accept their disappointment. They felt that the TECHland plan had failed them. Some muttered that the rule of the junta violated the TECHland code. Nevertheless, uttering disgusting oaths, reluctantly they scrambled to get into other lines.

SIX

WHOO-EE! WHOO-EE! The distinctive raucous call of the North Carolina highway patrol rasped through the morning quiet. Indeed, it was able to burst rudely through stubborn layers of resistance to grab Professor Harry Hawkey's attention. Its insistence absolutely demanded and commanded the stubborn consciousness of the pre-occupied college teacher. Harry's full attention had been rigidly glued elsewhere. It had been fixed on fears of dire events in another hemisphere.

Recent rapid-evolving events had focused Harry's thoughts on Kipua, far away in the South Pacific. The board of the prestigious Schoonover Foundation were considering him as a possible leader for a CRASH team for a rescue mission to that ill-fated island. He knew that CRASH was an acronym for something. But, he did not even know at first what that acronym represented. Later, they told him that it stood for Crisis Rescue And Salvage Help. That name made it sound both dangerous and important.

He discovered that the name was indeed appropriate to what the team would be asked to do. It would rescue people on the island who were in desperate need of help. From all appearance, that would include just about all of the inhabitants of the island. Thus, the team would be specially recruited and organized to save the people of Kipua. At least, someone optimistically assumed that such a rescue was at all possible.

Ironically, the people needed to be saved from a tragic misapplication of behavioral science. In fact, the potential catastrophe to human society on Kipua had been precipitated in the very name of social improvement for that island society. And the agent was that particular philanthropic foundation, the lofty Schoonover organization, itself.

Harry wondered what could have created the unusual conditions to make a global holocaust on Kipua even possible. But now such a catastrophe was actually probable. He could hardly believe it. Incredibly, he realized that he himself might ultimately be given the major responsibility for preventing an imminent hideous global disaster if the evils on Kipua were to spread.

In the midst of Harry's distress over the apparently gigantic scientific blunder on Kipua, the harsh intrusion by the local law was especially unwelcome. It was indeed paramountly annoying. The strident scream of the police siren had been like fingernails scraping a piercing screech across a chalkboard. It wrenched his attention agonizingly, reluctantly, from his pre-empting thoughts. The defocusing process was truly as painful mentally as the physical anguish from scraping a rough metal rasp across unprotected skin.

So, Harry was most annoyed. He thought angrily, "I am trying to think here." But, he cautioned himself not to say it.

"Now what?" Harry asked himself. He fully expected an unpleasant answer to the question. "What could I have done this time?" There were only a limited number of possible answers to his question. Running a red light? Missing a stop sign? He really had no idea of which law, or laws, he had broken.

This was not his first experience in such a situation. Harry was unfortunately familiar with his frequent lapses of concentration on his driving while he was behind the wheel of his automobile. He had the particular gift of being able to focus his attention on a task amid various distractions. This precious gift was very helpful to him in his academic pursuits. But, unfortunately, it was potentially deadly when he was behind the wheel of an automobile on the highway. In this case, the so-called distractions were the cues for effective driving. To ignore them was decidedly dangerous.

Harry knew that driving his automobile did not hold his attention the way it should. His problem was that driving an automobile on a North Carolina road was not nearly as fascinating as worrying about how he was going to save the world. But, he reminded himself soberly, sharply, you do not save the world by wrapping a car around a tree or flattening it against a culvert.

In fact, Harry truly had no recollection of the recent events surrounding him during his current distracted dash down the highway. How could he deal now with even this small extra problem? Whatever it was, the officer would surely consider it serious. But, right now, under the circumstances, answering to some presumably minor traffic violation had to be the least of his worries. Realistically, Harry knew that he had better concentrate enough on it to be able to deal with it before it became more than a distraction.

He reasoned that he must try to achieve some emotional calm. He would need it, if he were to get through this additional stressful situation with his dignity intact, and his driver's license viable. So, he began the process of re-aligning his thoughts toward coping with present reality. He tried forcing his mind grudgingly back to immediate awareness. He kept reminding himself that an intelligent mind was a flexible one. That idea usually helped in such situations.

Harry had been hurrying to an appointment with Beauregarde Bracken, Dean of the Division of Arts and Sciences at Ivey Southern University. Ivey Southern had been Harry's employer for the last 22 years. The appointment with Beau was at 10:00 a.m. Harry glanced at his watch and saw that it indicated 9:32. He had plenty of time, even without allowance for the extra two minutes to the true time that he routinely added on his watch. He was not really sure that the extra two minutes actually helped him to keep appointments on time. Nevertheless, its presence on the watch reassured him that his intentions to be prompt were sincere.

Harry needed Bracken's advice about whether or not to accept the leadership of such a dangerous salvage and rescue mission to Kipua. Perhaps, Bracken would agree that he could help to fix the situation that had been brought about by the grievous human error on that poor island. Dependent upon the advice from Bracken, Harry would also need the dean's permission for a leave of absence from his teaching duties. Realistically, without the leave, Harry could not accept the mission. Even if he wanted badly to go, he could not give up his job for it. Universities are usually quite liberal about granting unpaid leaves of absence. The replacement faculty member can add a different point of view to the department, and a special vitality. And, they can also usually be hired for less money than was paid to the regular faculty member.

Then, Harry was forced to remind himself that one could never be sure what Bracken would do. Bracken was surely bright enough to make good decisions, but Harry had concluded that Bracken's best decisions were reserved for his own field of expertise, which was physics. Bracken was likely to let irrelevant attitudes and biases enter into his decisions in other matters. The fact that annoyed Harry was that Bracken did not recognize this tendency in himself, and, therefore, felt that all of his decisions were as sound as those in matters of physics. This produced an arrogance about the near-infallibility of his actions as dean that Harry found insufferable. Harry could not completely respect a man who dealt with all complaints by patronizing the aggrieved party.

Actually, in fact, a denial of the leave could turn out to be a personal favor to Harry. A denial by Beau Bracken would neatly exempt Harry's active conscience from such an awesome responsibility. If he went, he would be responsible for saving the lives of many people on the island. Probably, also the denial of a leave might also save his conscience from the blood of innocent people in other areas. Many people in other lands were likely to be dependent as well upon the success of the CRASH mission. In fact, a denial of the leave would save Harry from having to lead a rescue operation that could undoubtedly also be extremely hazardous to his own physical health.

So, the bemused professor was mired in indecision. He pondered about how to resolve this terrible personal crisis. To be sure, he knew that he had actually helped to create this paralyzing dilemma for himself by his own actions. He had innocently backed into this very predicament of indecision. Ironically, he did it by actively trying to prevent the exact explosive situation on Kipua that had now come into being. That very situation now required a rescue. The eventual situation which he had tried to prevent was the one which eventually made the proposed rescue mission absolutely necessary.

Harry reminisced that such dilemmas seemed to be the main story of his life. He was always sacrificing his time and energy, not to say, stomach lining, in trying to help out where he sincerely thought his expertise was needed. Usually, it was without stopping to evaluate the personal cost to him as an individual. Never before now had he assessed the personal cost before he plunged ahead to offer his help.

Now, he was trying to be smart. He had to force himself to think seriously about such a commitment before he made it. To be sure, the present proposed enterprise was infinitely more important than anything he had undertaken before. The consequences for him could be costly indeed. He knew that he must take the costs into account this one time at least, because the risks were too great. He surely owed that much to his children, Harry Jr. and Beth.

"Well," he thought, somewhat ruefully, "why should I stop now?" The answer to that question, he knew, was clear. Undeniably, the mission involved immense personal and professional danger for anyone brave, or foolish, enough to attempt it. It also required interpersonal skills of leadership that he was not sure that he himself actually possessed. Perhaps, he could not even fully trust the opinions of others about his ability to get the job done.

He had reasons for doubts about his leadership skills. For example, he had not been successful originally in getting the people at Schoonover to listen thoughtfully to him. If they had listened, the debacle on Kipua would never have happened. He had tried his best to stop it.

Truthfully, it was not really fair of Schoonover now to ask him to lead the vital salvage and rescue operation. It was really too late after the project already had definitely gone very sour. It was surely their own heedless ardor for the extraordinary research that had made the rescue mission necessary in the first place. This fact was particularly important to his decision. He truly had no personal responsibility to put himself in harm's way.

On the other hand, he had to be concerned that the lives of other human beings were at stake. It truly did not matter that he, himself, was not to blame for their problems.

The people at Schoonover were undeniably desperate for his help. Finally, now, they appreciated the dreadful danger, if the situation at Kipua were not controlled. If the problem on Kipua were allowed to get totally out of hand, the foundation would be responsible for the loss of many lives, possibly a great many lives. Harry did not even want to think of the actual number of lives at risk. If the dangerous situation at Kipua spread to encompass other lands and other continents, the costs in human suffering would be immense.

The staff at Schoonover said that they considered Harry to be the person to have the best chance to save the people on Kipua. In view of the lives at stake, such a plea could not easily be rejected.

But, were they correct in such an assessment of the situation, and of his character? Harry wondered if he were truly the best person to lead the rescue mission. The frightening prospect was that the mission absolutely could not be allowed to fail. His active conscience would not allow him to refuse, if he thought that he could help in an effective way.

Such heavy thoughts had been filling Harry's conscious mind as he had hurtled recklessly down the highway. He had been wondering just how to explain to Bracken about this dangerous mission that he had been asked to consider leading. He was sure to receive patronizing treatment from Bracken because psychologists had created such a glorious mess.

Harry also had to explain to Bracken why the decision about Kipua involved a dilemma for him in particular. The reason for the dilemma was difficult even for him to understand. He asked himself again why he was seriously considering the job. Given the potential grave personal costs, the selfish answer was also undoubtedly the smart one.

The truth was that Harry realized in the vital core of his soul that he could not refuse to go, if he sincerely believed that he could be successful in leading the rescue mission. He simply had to go, if he felt that he could lead the team to a satisfactory achievement of its basic goals. Those goals included as the bottom line, and first of all, the immediate saving of lives. The decision about whether or not he was the best person to lead the team would ultimately be the responsibility of the high-paid experts at Schoonover. But, Harry reminded himself, he had to be convinced, too.

There was also a professional issue. The goals of the mission also encompassed the fundamental redemption of behavioral science. The experiment on Kipua apparently showed beyond any doubt that behavioral science had the capacity to create major social disasters. Harry doubted if indeed anyone had actually entertained such doubts. That proof could hardly be considered a vindication or endorsement for behavioral science. The major question now was whether or not behavioral science could also stop, contain and rectify the damage that had already been caused in its name. The world needed a best effort in order to be able to answer that question in the affirmative.

The success of the mission might also be crucial in the saving of human society itself from total destruction. That thought was indeed terrifying! Literally, society as we know it could be forfeited, if the rescue mission were not successfully engaged. The CRASH team would have to find a psychological antidote for the behavioral epidemic on Kipua. They absolutely must stop its spread. The philosophy of wanton excesses in personal satisfactions might find a prolific breeding ground in the depths of human physiology. It might explode like a bacterial culture in a warm and moist medium.

Harry had been professionally involved in debating the scientific issues that led to the Kipua experiment. Indeed, he had actively opposed the Behavioristic plan in several panel discussions at major scientific meetings. The main issue was whether or not a belief in a viable human will, capable of making voluntary choices, was an impediment to human social progress. Does such a belief prevent our society from taking full advantage of the behavioral technologies that we have invented and developed?

The attempt to resolve those serious issues through the Kipua experiment ultimately made the proposed damage control mission necessary. Would people actually be happier in a society that was committed to the belief that human beings did not have some freedom of will to make personal choices? The Kipua experiment seemed to have provided a clearly negative answer to this vitally important question.

To be sure, Harry had also personally opposed the specific field test on Kipua. Therefore, his professional concerns had made him a natural prime candidate to lead the rescue and salvage operation now that the experiment had disastrously failed. So, admittedly, he himself was partially to blame for putting himself into his present predicament. Actually, his interests and training had made him a natural selection to lead the CRASH team.

Harry had built a professional reputation for being a major researcher on the application of learning principles to social change. His research and theory indicated that beneficial social change was more likely to result from procedures which were based on a psychotherapeutic model. Such a model for change was vastly superior to a Behavioralistic model, which denied personal choice. The psychotherapeutic model placed responsibility for making social changes on the individual members of that society themselves. Thus, it did not place the blame on their leader or leaders. In contrast, the Behavioralistic model proposed that the leaders make and execute the decisions for the society.

Harry's thoughts were again harshly interrupted by unpleasant reality. It was the highway patrol.

"Sir, are you completely illiterate, or just unable to read speed signs? Or, are you hopelessly unconcerned?" asked the irate highway patrolman. This was the man who was responsible for the hateful intrusions into Harry's thoughts. His tone and manner were not at all pleasant. He warily approached Harry's car. "Let me see your license, please."

Harry always wondered about the purpose of the gratuitous "please" inserted at the end of such an authoritarian command. It was not as though the culprit was truly being asked nicely. He certainly did not believe that he had the choice to refuse, no matter how politely or impolitely he was asked.

But, the present process of stern law enforcement did have the beneficial effect of breaking his single-minded concentration on the concerns of Kipua. The full force of present reality now at last flooded over Harry. He knew that he must somehow deal with this crisis at once. He could be grateful that it could soak up his full attention. In fact, it occurred to him that, ironically, the policeman's intrusion provided a welcome break. Now, he had a brief respite from his anguish over the difficult decision that he must make. Later, he could get back to the deep worry over his really serious problems.

Thought Harry: "I must have run a red light," although of course he couldn't remember doing so. He said aloud, "I'm sorry Officer, I didn't see a red light." Of course, he didn't see it. Truly, he had been more absent-minded than usual. That is saying quite a bit for a tenured university professor. His almost unbearable problem concerning Kipua had preempted his conscious attention. It left only inadequate and unconscious automatic habits to be available for controlling his driving. Obviously, that level of remote awareness had not been sufficient in this particular case.

The knuckles on his fists were indeed white from their near-death grip on the steering wheel. His neck hurt from the strain of tense muscles. His eyeballs stung from staring at the road. He had stared without seeing or comprehension, it seemed. Every aspect of his posture spoke of the immense stress he felt.

The patrolman now took note Harry's distraught state. He was suddenly a little suspicious. "Are you all right, Sir? What is the matter? Are you hiding something?"

Harry was wearing his usual rumpled professor ensemble. The patched elbows on his old corduroy jacket, his ancient trench coat and mashed rain hat, fit the stereotype of someone who was generally too pre-occupied to make sensible choices of his apparel in the morning. Lottie had always seen to it that he had better clothes. But, now she was not present to tell him to put them on in the mornings.

So, there was not much about Harry's appearance to inspire confidence in him by the representative of the law. In fact, Harry's general demeanor gave all the appearance of a chicken lost in a den of foxes. He was truly scared, but not because of the encounter with the law. That was only a small part of his concerns. He had the look of a man who was considering a course of action that was necessary, personally challenging and undoubtedly also physically dangerous. In short, he looked like a frustrated, bewildered and cornered rat. Appearances were not deceiving. He truly felt like a beleaguered beast.

Getting hold of himself only with the utmost effort, Harry was now calmer. He whispered hoarsely, "I'm okay, officer. I am sorry if I ran a light. I had something on my mind."

"Well, get it off your mind, or get off my highway," snapped the officer. He was already flipping open his hated pad of citation forms. "You were traveling 70 miles an hour in a 55-mile zone. I guess you didn't know that. This invitation from the county will help you to pay attention and think a little bit when you are in an automobile." He preached in a loud monotone like it was a familiar sermon, preached to a juvenile audience.

"I see that your license does not indicate that you need glasses while driving. Why are you wearing them?" He was suddenly a little more suspicious. He thought that, if this man were in disguise, it was a marvelous one.

"I have reading glasses," murmured the academic. "I can see signs okay. I just didn't notice the speed. I simply forgot to take my glasses off. I was thinking about something else."

"You look different without the glasses in the picture. It says here that you are 5 feet 11 inches tall. Is that correct?"

Harry hesitated, and then only stammered, "Yes," like it contained two syllables. Actually, he liked to tell everyone that he was six feet tall.

As a matter of fact, Harry always felt just a little bit short, in a lot of ways, of what he wanted to be. He never felt quite as bright as most of his friends in graduate school. Many professors had told him that his perception was actually not accurate. It seemed true to Harry, however, because he tended to tackle the more difficult issues head on. Others tended to pick safer projects and thus had higher success rates. So, Harry tended to work harder than the others. And, he seemed to have less success in achieving his goals.

Another problem for Harry was that he remembered the disappointments better than the successes. For example, it was a considerable embarrassment to him that he never made the swimming team in college. It did not matter to him in assessing a personal failure against himself that the Ivey swim team had been nationally ranked at the time.

That sense of personal deficiency was why he was amazed at the Schoonover request for him to lead the mission to Kipua. Were not many others better qualified for such an important job, he wondered? Harry generally felt that other people tended to over-evaluate his achievements. He had been told often that he himself tended to under-evaluate them.

As the police officer thrust the ticket for the speeding violation through the window at Harry, he warned, "Sir, I advise you to keep your mind on your driving. I am fed up with you irresponsible scofflaws getting behind the wheel and endangering innocent people. Somebody could get killed. What you were thinking about can't be that important."

Harry was tempted to object to the unfair rebuke. He understood that, from the officer's perspective, the strong criticism of his actions was entirely justified. But, Harry's unlawful behavior was not the result of his personal irresponsibility. Quite the opposite! From a different perspective, Harry's behavior was not only caring, it was sacrificial. He reflected on the frequency with which we judge the behavior of others without knowing all of the pressures on them, and the information that only they possess. Without that knowledge, we may be overly harsh in our criticisms, or too sparing with our forgiveness. Nevertheless, the officer was just doing his job, based on the information available to him. So, Harry's simple answer was entirely sincere. "I'm sorry, Officer. I will surely think more about my driving from now on."

The officer finally smiled slightly. He saluted casually, and said, "That's better, Sir. You older college professors are not really our problem. Your intentions are good. If you can just keep your mind on business, you do all right. The young people are a worry, though, because they don't have the self-control. They are the real problem."

Then, suddenly all business again, he said, "Sir, now have a nice day, do ya' hear?" He stepped smartly into his cruiser and flipped off his blinker. Then, he kicked his cruiser crisply back onto the highway, amid a small shower of pebbles.

After the highway patrolman had driven off, Harry sat for a brief moment reflectively in his car. He was intently trying to calm, collect and re-direct himself. Silently, he thought, "Older, schmolder! Who is old?" He decided that such reminders of advancing years were not what he needed just now.

Then he reminisced rather sadly, "If you only knew what I had been thinking about when you blasted me, Officer, then you might not be so sure that it was so unimportant. I was not worrying about a few people killed in an automobile accident, tragic as that would be. But, if the Kipua rescue mission fails, there could be vast numbers of fatalities reaching holocaustic proportions. Many thousands could die before the tragedy could be contained—even if that could be achieved. I worry about all those things that could possibly happen. The Schoonover salvage operation must not be allowed to fail."

The cost of the traffic ticket did not really bother Harry. Admittedly, he surely could have used the money for preferred things. What annoyed him was the thought that he had done something stupid. And, he had to admit, driving without attention on what you are doing is stupid. He hated to do incredibly stupid things. College professors are not really stupid, of course. But they surely sometimes do incredibly stupid things. Especially stupid are the things like not paying attention to important events going on about them.

In his distracted state, Harry could have, of course, unconsciously driven right into a concrete wall. His late wife, Lottie, used to stay alert to remind him that he was driving, and where he intended to go. He was reminded once more of how much he needed Lottie, and missed her. He missed her for more than her monitoring of his driving.

Harry truly had not noticed his dangerous haste, because he was feeling such personal emotional distress. Such emotions were relatively unfamiliar to him. His job of teaching psychology to college students usually did not generate such feelings. He struggled to label the unfamiliar feelings. He wanted to understand what he felt. "It is mostly dread," he decided. It was indeed gut-knotting, stomach-burning, head-numbing depression, mixed with massive jolts of fear! There was plenty of fear! Quivers and chills pricked along the length and core of his backbone. What was happening at Kipua made him fearful for the future of the whole world. He really knew in his heart that he had to go. Really, he just needed Bracken and Old Schuh, his old mentor, to re-assure him that he was the best person for the job. Because failures distressed him so much, he could imagine how he would feel if he failed on Kipua.

"Keep calm!" he kept telling himself. "Time out! Take a deep breath, like you are trying for a foul shot to win the NBA championship!" But Harry knew that he was not a superstar of psychology, although he had obviously gained some prominence in his chosen field. "How is it that I stand at the foul line, so to speak, in possibly the biggest test of social organization for centuries?" he wondered.

He reassured himself that, to be sure, he would not be alone. He would be just a part of a team of experts in behavioral science. Everyone on the CRASH team would be picked to possess the courage and skill for success. They all would have a stout belief in what the team could accomplish. He told himself, "One missed foul shot by one player on the team this early in the game might not be too disastrous to correct, even if that player is the captain of the team. But, if we are to succeed, everyone else must do his or her assigned job with a full application of skill and with full commitment. Maybe I can pull it off. I absolutely must know what Beau and Old Schuh think."

After his talk with Beau Bracken, Harry was to meet with Old Schuh. Otto Schumacher had been Harry's mentor and friend during the younger man's undergraduate years at Ivey Southern. Almost everyone called him Old Schuh. They did it reverently, as you would refer to a Mother Superior. This title was a tribute to his unpretentious style. His style greatly belied a great spirit and an equally talented mind. Harry needed the wisdom of Old Schuh right now more than he needed advice from anyone else. He needed it more than he had ever needed it before.

Actually, Harry had little doubt that Bracken, in the end, would give formal permission for the leave of absence. More important was whether or not Bracken would agree concerning the wisdom of one of his faculty members committing to such a risky task, despite its extreme importance to human society. As a physicist, Bracken unquestionably understood science. Although he was not knowledgable about behavioral science, he was generally a thoughtful, intelligent man. Because of his known bias against behavioral science, he would be a good sounding board for the evaluation of the proposed mission. As a devil's advocate, he would essentially represent the consumers of the results of the research. Those were the ones whose lives could literally depend upon the success of the mission.

Harry now carefully eased his car back onto the highway. He tried to reassure himself that together, Beau Bracken and Old Schuh would help him know what he should do. True, in his gut, he already had a strong feeling that he had to accept the challenge. But, he needed strong reassurance from Bracken and Schuh that he was truly the right person for the job. The stakes were too high for the mission to fail. If he were capable of doing the job, it was his professional responsibility—and his Christian duty—to accept the leadership of the mission. With a sigh of distress, he drove on to his fate like a good soldier.

The incident with the highway patrolman had shaken Harry from his detached state back to a realization of the present exigencies of life. Now, he was more careful of his driving, aware that no further distractions would be tolerable, for him or for the patrolman. So, as a consequence, he arrived safely without further intrusive delays.

Harry noted that, because of his earlier excessive haste, and despite the interlude with the law, he was a bit early for his appointment. No matter. He would spend the extra time in composing his emotions, and his thoughts, in Bracken's comfortable waiting room. He did not mind waiting when he had something gainful to occupy his mind. Otherwise, his Type-A personality clicked in to carry him along the risky road to a potential heart attack.

Harry managed to find a parking space outside of the administration building without another embarrassing incident.

An empty parking space in front of the Ad Building was truly remarkable. Harry wondered if he had completed his full share of surprises for the day. He certainly hoped so.

When Harry arrived at the dean's office, Miss Rose Peach, Bracken's secretary, greeted him in her usual friendly way. One could always count on a warm smile from Peachie. Everyone knew that Peachie was the real mainstay of the School of Arts and Sciences. Bracken might be the brain of the school, but she was the heart and soul. Although she treated all faculty members with equal cordiality and respect, secretly Harry was actually her personal favorite. He was never grouchy or self-important. He truly respected the value of her contributions to the university.

Sometimes Harry wondered why Peachie had never married. She was surely attractive enough. Actually, how attractive do you have to be? She was a very nice person. Everyone would agree to that. She was physically attractive now, and presumably had been even more so in her younger days. She was short, and actually petite. Harry suspected that she dyed her hair, although he was not very experienced in making such trivial discriminations. Usually, he did not care. Peachie was always well-groomed, and well-dressed. Harry decided that Peachie had chosen to be married to the university, like nuns are married to Christ. She seemed happy with her choice.

Certainly, the university was happy. Peachie was so efficient that she could continue with her work while seeming to give her full attention to a guest of the Dean. She had been around the university a long time, and her loyalty to it was great. One almost expected to see a crown of university English ivy on her head.

Peachie informed Harry that the dean was still in conference, but would be out shortly. She shared the responsibility with the dean for arranging to keep his appointments on time. Harry didn't mind waiting when he was early. He very much hated to be kept waiting past the appointed hour, however. He doubted that he was unique in that respect. That was the reason for his dedication to promptness.

Soon, the dean's door opened. A faculty member from the English department emerged, closely followed by the dean. The

English professor, Henry Whitcomb, was a long-time friend of Harry. Henry routinely presented a serious manner, and many thought him to be totally colorless. Actually, Henry had a fine droll sense of humor that frequently caught his listeners by surprise. The effect was to enhance the comedy. Henry could absolutely incapacitate everyone in paroxysms of laughter. Henry would often come to Harry for help with psychological studies of character, or with help in understanding mental health metaphors.

Everyone exchanged warm greetings, and pleasant inquiries about the states of being. Then, Henry excused himself to run off to class. Bracken motioned for his new visitor to come into his office.

"Harry, I assume you will have the usual?" he said, looking at him over his spectacles. Harry nodded, with a smile of gratitude. Even though he did not much like Bracken personally, he always enjoyed visiting the dean's office because of Peachie, and because the dean was a gracious host. Even now, especially now, Harry was glad to be here. He expected to get answers to some of his important questions.

"Two usuals, please, Peachie," Bracken said to his secretary, with a smile. He was considerate to secretaries, at least. Then, as he softly closed the door behind them, the old clock on the mantle behind Peachie's desk intoned the hour of 10 o'clock. Harry smiled to himself in satisfaction.

The "usual" to which the administrator referred was the omnipresent tea in a pot next to Peachie's desk. The two men engaged outwardly in pleasant small talk until Peachie came in with the tea. Harry had learned to love tea with cream and sugar during his first visit to England. As the tea warmed his body, it also calmed his mind. Bracken was a master at making most people feel at ease. Unfortunately, he was not always 100% effective at this with Harry.

Peachie never objected to the waitress duties. She saw the sipping of tea with faculty members as an essential part of the dean's business. As Peachie softly closed the office door, Harry turned his mind to the business that brought him there.

SEVEN

BEAUREGARDE BRACKEN really had not wanted to be a dean. But, like a good member of the academic team, he had responded to the urging of his friends and colleagues to take the position when it became open. He tolerated his job by viewing it as a way for him to enable many faculty members to perform to the best of their abilities and skills. He often said that being dean gave him almost 250 heads and 500 hands to produce good works for the university and for society. He claimed that such production was far better than he could achieve working on his own. To Harry's mind, that was a perfect attitude for a dean. Teaching is not a job, it is an opportunity.

That Bracken's individual accomplishments would have been considerable was amply revealed by a brief glance at the walls of his office. The paneled surfaces were covered with plaques, awards, certificates and other tangible evidence of the professional achievements of the man.

Many of the books on the shelves around the room involved topics other than physics. In fact, Bracken thought that he had a broad common-sense perspective on life. It is unfortunate that his belief was not correct, because such an attitude would have been a valuable supplement to his academic skills. Bracken's problem was that he knew correctly that physics was the basic science for understanding the universe, but he consequently reached the false conclusion that, therefore, physicists knew more about everything than anyone else. This basis chauvinism about physics meant that Bracken considered a superficial study of social sciences, for example, provided for him a superior perspective on social sciences than one perspective held by the practitioners of social sciences. Bluntly, sometimes Bracken acted like an egotistical ass.

Bracken presented the physical appearance that represented an ideal prototype of an academic dean. First of all, he always looked like he had been dressed by a valet for the stars. He always wore expensive dark suits, and was never without the coat. He sometimes changed the color of his shirts, but he never departed from the bow tie. Although the color of his tie changed, it was always a bow tie. He claimed that he got in the habit of wearing a bow tie when he was continually hovering over the instruments for his research in graduate school. A conventional tie kept dropping into his measuring operations.

Bracken's handsome face was attractively adorned by wire-rimmed spectacles. A neat mustache completed a pleasing countenance.

The complete visual package presented by the dean was so appealing that he was continually being pestered by the publicity folks of the university to pose for pictures and posters for various promotional activities. More often than not, Bracken was glad to oblige. He loved the personal exposure. But, in all fairness, he was willing to help the university in any way that he could.

Harry settled back into the soft leather sofa. He suddenly noticed that his complete body had now finally started to relax a little. It seemed that the university was indeed a place of sense and sensibility. He could feel its strength. He could get solid help here, if he was able to discount the biases of Bracken.

The dean nodded expectantly for him to begin. "I hear you have a problem, Harry. Maybe I can help. Take your time, my man. Let's hear it all." Bracken was undoubtedly serious. He would at least try to help.

Taking a deep breath, Harry began. "I am going to give you the full background of the situation so that you can place my problem in a total context. Forgive me, if I repeat some things that you already know."

"Sure, Harry," said the dean. "Take your time. Do it any way that is comfortable to you. We will take whatever time it takes to do this thing right."

"Thanks, I appreciate your understanding, Beau." Harry actually felt better. He even felt somewhat encouraged, though not optimistic.

Despite Bracken's extremely busy schedule, he understood that time spent in encouraging and reassuring a member of his faculty often headed off greater problems later. He was sure that Harry could perform with distinction whatever task they had in mind for him. But, he also knew that Harry tended to underestimate his own ability. In fact, to Bracken's mind that trait was probably the only weakness that Harry revealed as a member of his faculty.

Harry began like he was lecturing to a class of students. He had rehearsed this presentation just as he typically rehearsed his classroom lectures, or indeed any important presentation.

"I have been seriously worried about the apparent downward spiral of morality in our society. My concern stems from my professional interests as a psychologist, and also from my social concerns as a member of the Christian church. I feel that in both of my roles, as a scientist and as a Christian, I am called to do what I can to improve conditions in society and for the individuals in that society."

Harry suddenly realized that he had indeed been lecturing—pontificating, really. It embarrassed him. He knew that Lottie always hated it when he did that. It made him seem so stiff and impersonal—like a textbook professor.

Bracken just smiled. He knew that Harry was appropriately serious about serious things.

Now Harry continued in a more conversational tone. "As a psychologist, I have concentrated more on the general social issues. That approach makes sense to me. The broader issues affect more individuals than I could reach by any small programs conducted for the benefit of a few individuals. That truly is, for me, the appeal of science."

Bracken nodded: "Yes, I think that makes sense. I do feel that way myself. While surely I do not disparage the work of those dedicated persons who work with individuals."

"Right," agreed Harry. "The problem is with society itself. The society needs a practical, beneficial orientation to human behavior which it does not now have. Our people are pushed and pulled by psychologists and others, all who should know better, into different competing orientations. They tend to emphasize points of disagreement, instead of bands of similarities. So, an integrated position on behavioral science has not been achieved."

The dean nodded in agreement again. He had much to say on that topic, but decided that now was not the time for a full discussion. Wisely, he remained respectfully silent, waiting for the psychologist to continue.

Hearing no comment, but noting Bracken's agreement, Harry pushed on: "I agree with B.F. Skinner, one of our foremost psychologists, when he pointed out the imminent danger of self-destruction by our society. Skinner argued that human existence must somehow be brought under some kind of control by the dedicated application of psychological principles to the solution of social problems. I want to read to you Skinner's very severe warning of social disintegration to us that was written some 15 years ago. It was written in 1975. I have it right here in my briefcase." Harry pulled out a piece of paper, which was well-worn from many readings. He began to read in a serious tone from the document:

> And no Calvin ever had better reason to fear his hell, for I am proceeding on the assumption that nothing less than a vast improvement in our understanding of human behavior will prevent the destruction of our way of life or of mankind.

Harry sighed: "I surely do agree with him on that. But, I definitely do not agree with the particular solution for behavioral science that he then proposed. Skinner thought that the cause of our social problems is our dogged adherence to the idea that behavior can be caused by an act of a voluntary will. This common belief, he said, prevents us from committing ourselves fully to a very simple solution that had been available for years: the use of behavioral technology."

Bracken was surprised. "You mean that this expert on behavioral science, Skinner, does *not* believe that human beings have any freedom of a personal will? That is nonsense! Why do you psychologists pay any attention to him?"

118 E. Rae Harcum

Harry fought to stay calm. "You put me into an awkward position, Beau. I do not agree with Skinner, but the view is legitimate metaphysically. But, the answer to your first question is 'Yes', and many psychologists agree with him.

"Strange as it seems to a layperson, it is true. But, Beau, I need to explain some terms. For example, the meaning of the term 'free will' must be clarified, because the term is so often misused. Actually, as a psychologist, I argue that human beings do *not* have a *completely free* will. That precise sense of the term would imply absolutely zero influence of environment and heredity on human behaviors. Of course, that idea is ridiculous. Actually, in such a case, there could be no science of psychology and no psychologists. That would mean that there could be no understanding, prediction or control of behavior. Then, the only cause of a behavior would be an inscrutable free will, which was observable and controllable only by the possessor of that will. There would be nothing for a scientist to use as a basis for studying the mind—whatever that may be—that causes behavior. Under those conditions, the cause of a given behavior would be entirely whimsical. In short, psychology as a field of scientific study would be completely wiped out."

"Wow!" said the dean. "I never thought of it that way. But, I can see that you are absolutely correct. This is another of the cases in which the weakness of language adds to our confusion. No wonder so many arguments are purely semantic. That is a pet peeve of mine. But, excuse me, Harry. Go on. Tell me where such an idea came from? Is there any empirical research to indicate that it might work? There must be, or otherwise good scientists would not support it."

Harry replied, "Of course, there is. You are right. But, more about that later. First, I want to describe the theory. The idea of a superb new human society based on behavioral technology, without tender concerns for the humanistic nature of human beings, was advocated by Skinner in his novel *Walden Two*, published in 1948. The idea came from his experiments on certain principles of learning. Skinner envisioned that such a society would produce happy, safe, healthy and fulfilled individuals.

"My own speculative projection of Skinner's blueprint for the better society lies in sharp contrast. My view is partly based also on principles of learning, but also based on broader views of human cognitions and motivation. My view conjures up some unwelcome images of holocaustic proportions if his plan were implemented. Such concerns are consistent with the real fears of many experts. My pessimistic speculations about the fate of any society that would be so beguiled as to follow Skinner's proposals faithfully now seem to have been frightfully fulfilled. Skinner's plan was tried as an experiment on Kipua, an island in the South Pacific. Given the suffering now in progress on the island, I hardly know whether to hope that I am right, or far wrong."

"I see what you mean," said the older man. "If you are right, the people on Kipua are indeed sorely in danger. Go on."

Harry obliged: "In contrast to Skinner, the group of psychologists who call themselves Humanists—of which I am one, I might add—merely assert that there is *some* element of personal choice in the selection of behaviors. That element of choice inserts a creativity and an unpredictability in responding, independent of environmental and genetic influences. Again, I emphasize, this does *not* say that environment and heredity do not have an influence on the selection of behaviors, only that such causal effects are not complete."

"Right. Only a fool would deny effects of heredity and environment," agreed Bracken. "I hope that no psychologist would suggest such a thing."

Harry forged ahead: "Sure, although some of us are often falsely placed into such a stupid straw-man position. That, too, is inexcusable. There is an intermediate view, which I support. One psychologist called it "choices within limits." I like that description because it says that heredity and environment provide the person with a repertoire of available possible responses in a given situation, and he or she can make a free choice from among those available responses.

"According to that view, we scientists can achieve some ability to understand the causation of behavior. Consequently, we can have some success in predicting and controlling it, even though we concede early on that our understanding and control will never be complete. But, we emphatically contend that prediction of human behavior can never be absolutely perfect.

"This view is in fact entirely consistent with the opinion of the vast majority of men and women who form the laity of psychology. They are the so-called common man or woman in the street. I have conducted research to prove that most of these people believe that behavior is undoubtedly determined in part by heredity and environment, but only in part. Therefore, they believe also that behavior can be influenced by a voluntary act of human will, which is sometimes partially independent of such heredity and environment. In a word, most people believe in a limited free will, as confusing as that oxymoronic term sounds."

"I am sure that you are right," agreed Bracken. "That has been my experience. And that is surely what I myself believe."

Now, Harry was persuasive: "The fact that our understanding will never be perfect is, of course, no reason or requirement to give up the quest. We must not abandon the science of behavior. Obviously, the more we understand about the genetic and environmental causation of behaviors, the better we can help people. We can understand most of it, even if we do not understand all of it. It is analogous to the theory of chaos in physics. You can predict that a given event will fall within a given domain of values, but not the specific value at any given time."

"It works for me!" said Bracken, enthusiastically. "Again, I say that I am surprised that anyone, especially a professional psychologist, supports a different view.

"But, excuse my interruption, Harry. I got completely carried away. Please go on. Tell me how the Behaviorists think that society could even operate without the conception of some freedom of will."

Harry proceeded with the standard answer to the familiar question: "Well, they argue that the behavioral technology must be based on the scientific management of human behavior through selectively giving rewards for some behaviors and not for others. In other words, learning is the key. We must teach the citizens always to respond correctly."

The dean was now uncharacteristically agitated. "But how do we know which responses will work, which ones are correct?" he asked insistently. "How do I know *what* to reward, if I am arbitrarily to preempt you of your personal choice?"

Harry smiled. "You have it! That is the very point," he said. "The plan says that the science itself will tell the technologist what to reward. The results of the scientific research will indicate which responses are best for society, and thus should be rewarded. Then, the technologist will implement what he or she learns, backed by the leaders of the government. The individual citizens will have no final say. But, to be sure, it is their behaviors alone that will provide the basis for the answers crafted by the community leaders. You see, the subsequent overt behaviors effectively become a substitute for prior choices in goal selection."

The physicist shook his head in disbelief. He made strange, disturbed sounds with his mouth and tongue. For a moment, Harry thought that he was going to choke. But, Bracken finally recovered his voice. "Go on," he said sadly.

Harry plunged ahead, "Behaviorists contend that there is no need, as well as no room, in psychological technology for the concept of a human will. More than that, Skinner contended that the human loyalty to such a concept causes the members of society to shy away from the frank use of the established effective behavioral technologies. Therefore, he argued, for the sake of the sheer survival of our society, the concept of a viable human will—human freedom or ability to choose voluntarily—must be absolutely eliminated from our thinking."

Now the physicist was truly aghast: "I ask again: Is there any empirical evidence for this idea? It seems to me that you could resolve this issue by a straightforward psychological research study. Has this been done?"

"Well," said Harry, actually a little sheepishly, "it depends upon whom you ask. It seems that the prior empirical evidence has been interpreted by each side in ways that simply confirm their own original biases.

"First, look at the larger society. Despite all of our technological advances in psychology, our society is a mess. Some of us conclude that it is caused by the failure of our vaunted technology. But, Skinner concluded that our social problems are not caused by the previous failed attempts to manage behaviors by technological means. Actually, he claims the reverse. He says that the problems are caused by our lamentable failure to employ such methods of behavior modification universally and wisely, and with full commitment.

"We Humanists think that he had it all backwards, of course. We argue that the use of behavior modification should be placed in the hands of virtuous people, who then decide which behaviors are to be rewarded."

Bracken nodded vigorously. "Amen to that," he said.

Harry continued. "Yes. In my view, a better society would glorify freedom of will and personal responsibility. It would honor a human dignity that was based on the concept of praiseworthy personal choices. Also, a viable society would believe in the intrinsic, unconditional worth of each human being. These are the vital characteristics that seem to be indigenous to any of the experimental societies that have been successful. And, in my view, that is precisely why they have been successful."

"But surely there are other psychologists who agree with Skinner, are there not?" asked Bracken, with a sincerely puzzled look.

"Sure," said Harry. "Of course, there are also strong believers in the promise of Skinner's proposals. Despite all of the negative responses of others, some psychologists really think that Skinner's ideas are great, as welcome as sliced bread and refrigeration. And Sculleigh Burnhouse, a psychology professor from Stanford, is—or was—one of them. Admittedly, too, these Skinnerians are not far-out eggheads or wool-gatherers, but scientists of good reputation. In a sense, that is really what makes them so dangerous."

"Right," said Bracken. "You are saying that they are good people and good scientists. But, the Behaviorists' and the Humanists' views pose a true dilemma. My question remains: Has there not been any direct research aimed at the problem?"

"Of course, there has," answered Harry. "Several experimental societies were ostensibly set up in accordance with Skinner's plan. The trouble is that none of the leaders were quite willing to go whole hog with the plan, to play out all of the string, so to speak. Each of them made what they concluded were necessary concessions to ordinary humanistic thinking in order to keep their community going.

"The success of the communities was taken by Behaviorists as validation of the basic plan. But, the apparent importation of humanistic ideas was taken as proof by the Humanists that the behavioral technology was insufficient—that it could not stand alone and still be successful.

"So, which corps of experts is correct? That truly is the question. A definitive empirical answer to it should be possible, as you suggest. That is why Burnhouse submitted a proposal to the Schoonover Foundation to do precisely what you have asked for. He wanted to test the Skinner plan empirically by instituting an experimental society on Kipua Island based on a precise form of the Skinner plan. So, you see, that is where the Kipua study comes in. The idea was for the society on Kipua to adhere strictly to the Behavioristic plan, without deviation, so that we would obtain definitive evidence for its success or its failure. Hopefully, definitive evidence would settle the issue and stifle the arguments."

"Good," said Bracken. "But, precisely why did he go to Kipua?"

"Because it possessed certain desired characteristics. This particular island in the Marianas group in the southwest Pacific Ocean was relatively insulated from other societies. To be fair, some degree of isolation from the general society was necessary. Nevertheless, the island was still a representative combination of modern and traditional cultures. Therefore, the results should apply to most modern societies. Indeed, it was carefully selected by Burnhouse for his experiment. He reasoned that it would provide a fair and appropriate laboratory for his experiment in the real world.

"Burnhouse's new society was imposingly called TECHland, which is based on an acronym for his behavioral plan: a society which would provide a Technologically Evolved Classless Habitat in its own land. Incidentally, some of the staffers at Schoonover had fun with their own names for the plan. Spencer Del Cristo, their fiscal officer—who, by the way, will actually monitor our finances—called it SANTAland, for STARGAZING AND NEBULAR THINKING ACADEMY. Some of the others preferred to substitute "Asylum" for the last word in this tongue-in-cheek version."

Harry and Beau both chuckled briefly at the humor. Then Harry continued: "This modification was intended in jest, of course. But, I think that this attempt at humor betrays a basic contempt for the project by the non-experts. Such scoffing is in fact the typical response to Skinner's deterministic ideal by most people who are not professional psychologists. Some of the professionals think that the idea is brilliant. But, almost universally, lay observers think that it is silly. That does not bode well for the possibility of wide acceptance for his ideas by the general population."

The dean was again in agreement, "That's right. And neither of us agrees with the Behaviorists on the idea of control by technology. From what you say, there is no reason for someone of humanistic persuasion to forego the use of psychological technologies. One does not have to give up the advantage to be gained from science just because he or she believes that all of the answers about life cannot be achieved by scientific means. The intelligent human being must control the technology, not the reverse."

Harry was exhilarated by Bracken's uncharacteristic understanding and agreement. Thus, encouraged, he was very strong on the next point: "Beau, you have hit the issue on dead center. Skinner's argument here has always struck me as making about as much sense as saying that we should try to put out a gasoline fire by smothering it with more gasoline."

Bracken chuckled softly at the image. Then, he turned solemn as the full implication of the idea became apparent to him. "Damn," he said, uncharacteristically at a loss for more appropriate words.

Harry nodded. "Scary, isn't it?" he asked. "But, there is more. There is the danger of turning the believers in a human will away from the pursuit of science. For example, if you somehow convince a devout Christian or Jew that science is incompatible with religion, then he or she will turn away from science, with unfortunate consequences."

"Oh, God," said Bracken. "You are right. I had never thought of it that way. It is not good to force such a discrete choice."

"Right," said Harry. "And there is no need for it. But there is a worse problem. That problem should be obvious to everyone: the elimination of the concept of voluntary choice necessarily also eliminates the concept of personal responsibility and guilt. If a person's behaviors are entirely the result of circumstances beyond his or her ability to control them, the person therefore cannot logically hold himself or herself responsible for them as an individual.

"Similarly, society cannot logically hold the person responsible for his or her behaviors, if there is no freedom of will. There can be no blame—no sin—if a person is not basically free to choose his or her own behaviors. Thus, the legal concepts of premeditation and intention would be wiped out. Indeed, they are even invalidated by the Behavioristic assumptions of complete determinism, that behaviors are entirely determined by the interaction of environmental factors with the individual's heredity. How can you hold a person responsible when you believe that he or she did not personally choose to respond in the antisocial way? That seems to be a major legal point. For example, we do not exact legal accountability or punishment for someone who is not personally responsible for his or her actions. Accordingly, we do not punish very young children, or mentally disordered or retarded adults, for crimes that they were incompetent to comprehend or to control. But, we did say at Nuremburg that those murderers who are judged legally to be sane, and thus are considered to have personal control of their actions, do have a choice. Therefore, they are held responsible for their crimes."

The older man finished the argument for him. "I see where you are going, Harry. Any thinking person should view the idea of general, universal personal irresponsibility as truly the blueprint for a real holocaust. Just think of the consequences of telling potential muggers and murderers that they are not responsible for their actions. It would be a disaster to tell them that they are simply the unfortunate product of poor parenting, poor teaching, poor environmental conditions and so on! You cannot reasonably tell them that they are not responsible, that the basic fault lies with mom and dad, aided and abetted by the rest of society. That gives them a ticket, a free pass, to do whatever they desire, no matter how heinous!"

"You got it," said Harry. "As my old commanding officer in the Navy used to say, personal environments can obviously provide extenuating circumstances, which definitely should be taken into account. But, they certainly do not provide excuses in every case."

By the time he had finished his pronouncements, Harry was practically shouting his convictions. He was in fact a man of numerous strong convictions.

Before Bracken could speak further, Harry rushed on, now just a little bit calmer: "I am not the only professional person who thinks that the Skinner plan is a disaster waiting to happen. For example, soon after Skinner's *Walden Two* was published in 1948, Negley and Patrick in 1952 wrote some pretty strong negative things about it." He solemnly read from a document that he had pulled from his brief case.

> Halfway through this contemporary utopia, the reader may feel sure, as we did, that this is a beautifully ironic satire on what has been called "behavioral engineering." The longer one stays in this better world of the psychologist, however, the plainer it becomes that the inspiration is not satiric, but messianic. This is indeed the behavioral engineered society, and while it was to be expected that sooner or later the principle of psychological conditioning would be made the basis of a serious construction of utopia—Brown anticipated it in *Limanora*—yet not even the effective satire of Huxley is adequate preparation for the shocking horror of the idea when positively presented. Of all the dictatorships espoused by utopists, this is the most profound, and incipient dictators might well find in this utopia a guidebook of political practice.... It is ironic to conclude our survey of utopian speculation in the pessimistic mood engendered by *Walden Two*. We have descended from the heights of confidence in man's capacities and noble aspiration for his progressive betterment to a nadir of ignominy in which he is placed on a par with pigeons.

Harry paused, as they both contemplated the full impact of the powerful wording in the quotation. His sigh was more of a moan. He said, "You see that these authors had a very dim view of the Skinner plan. They obviously thought it best for us if they did not mince words.

"But there were more negative opinions of the Skinner plan. Let me read you just one more response to Skinner's further elaboration of his ideas in *Beyond Freedom and Dignity* in 1971. Rubenstein reacted with even stronger language that same year." Again Harry read from a document, pulled from his briefcase:

> *Beyond Freedom and Dignity* deserves the widest possible audience because, unless there is a radical reversal of current trends, Skinner's utopia prophecies do in fact anticipate the kind of world we are entering. We are all in Skinner's debt—for having warned us.... In spite of Skinner's assurances to the contrary, his utopian projection is less likely to be a blueprint for the Golden Age than for the theory and practice of hell.

Harry put down the paper, sighed again, even louder, and shrugged. "What more can I say?" he added. "This particular idea for a Utopia has set the stage for a disaster waiting to happen from the very beginning. Most social observers knew it, and said it. Many of them said so emphatically, as I just read to you."

"Okay, okay, I yield. I agree, Harry," said the dean, nodding vigorously, placing his outstretched palms defensively outward in a calming manner. "I am sure that your thinking is right on the money about this. I agree with you strongly, without any doubts."

Emboldened by Bracken's approval, Harry plunged ahead. "Although such thinking in a society is an undeniable design for disaster, some scientists have actually tried Skinner's idea on Kipua, as I said. The flaming result of Skinner's plan, it seems, is now manifest on that unfortunate island. Apparently, more frightful chain explosions will follow."

The dean now spoke with some emotion also. "Why could not these trained behavioral scientists have foreseen such an unwelcome result? The disaster could have been predicted by simple common sense, it seems to me. Everyone would certainly agree that a person who did not believe that his or her antisocial

behaviors were chosen by an act of a personal will would consequently not feel personal guilt from such performance. He or she
would feel justified in performing whatever behavior he or she
desired."

"Yes, it would certainly seem so," agreed the younger man.
"But the contention of these blind believers in rewards is that the
antisocial behaviors can be prevented from ever even happening
in the first place. If the society fully commits itself to controlling
the environments and rewards of each citizen, through society, it
can insure that he or she will *never* make the undesired antisocial
responses. Therefore, a utopian kind of society will result, they
think, because it will not be held back by considerations of voluntary choice."

"But, wait a minute, Harry!" exclaimed Bracken. "I am sure
that most people, like me, would totally resent the implication
that I, like some lower animal, or incapacitated human, did not
have freedom of will. I would not cooperate with a plan based on
such an idea."

"Yes, that is the case in this present society," said Harry. "But,
you must realize that the rules are changed in the Behavioristic
plan. In that plan, the indoctrinated citizens will not even resent
the invasive encroachment on their personal freedom to act. The
simple reason for this is that the very concept of such freedom has
been obliterated from their thinking, from their complete society.
Because they will not know the concept of freedom, they will not
know the absence of freedom. Therefore, they will not know to
protest the absence of freedom. What a dreadful prospect!"

Harry lapsed into despondent silence. His thoughts were too
heavy to communicate at that moment.

The dean was now very serious. "I agree with your view,
totally and emphatically. Skinner's arguments are simply wishful thinking, in a practical sense, and also logically dangerous at
that. Sure, it would be nice if our behavioral technology were so
beautifully refined and effective that we could keep everyone
happy. Who could object to that? But how did Skinner think that
he could pull off such a feat?"

By now, Harry had regained his composure. "You have again
seen the true problem, Beau. Skinner argued that we already have

the behavioral technology to accomplish his vision, if we would but use it to its fullest capacity without contradicting it with the idea of a functional human will. As I said, plenty of the experts in behavioral science do not agree with that.

"But, even Skinner would have to agree that we have not as yet achieved anything like the high level of behavioral technology that he envisioned eventually. Therefore, it is foolhardy to try to impose his ideas on people who have not already been intellectually—and amorally—developed through the use of presumed perfect behavioral technologies. We agree that the last thing that you want to tell some criminal or thug is that he or she is not personally responsible for the evil deeds which he or she has perpetrated. You cannot tell him or her that some official in charge is actually the one responsible.

"At least, you cannot do this without dreadful consequences. Nevertheless, we see such sickening arguments from defense lawyers and some social service professionals every day in the newspapers. And we hear such trash constantly on the broadcasts of the television news. It is indeed impossible to avoid it, if you watch the news at all."

Harry was feeling mentally confident now. He added, with conviction, "The Behavioristic plan will not work on a planet inhabited by real people. The truth of that statement is currently being tragically demonstrated on the ill-fated island in the South Pacific. I am afraid that we do not know as yet the full extent of the horror on Kipua. And it will get worse until someone takes some action to contain it.

"But, Beau, I have to tell you truthfully that I, at least, was surprised and shocked at the incredibly short time that it took Burnhouse to accomplish this negative miracle. It is a satanic miracle of social disintegration. I wonder if the conditions were just uniquely right for a holocaust on that particular island. Or, are we human beings so tenuously perched on our civilization? Is our humanistic part just a flimsy cloak, or a paper shell?"

"In any case, we must find out what has happened. So, the Schoonover Foundation, which financed Burnhouse's experiment, has asked me to lead a team to Kipua to get the answers. I do not know, of course, what I will encounter, and therefore I do not know how long it will take. So, I am asking you to understand, and give me permission to go for as long as it takes."

Bracken shook his head sadly. His answer was not long in coming. "Given the circumstances, Harry, my friend, you must give it your best efforts. I agree that the danger to our society is real. And I think that you have the best chance to save it.

"The concept of wanton, conscienceless behavior could be spread by the converts on Kipua to other islands and other lands. Ironically, these scientists may have unleashed a Pandora's box of primal human motivations that can now never be governed. We must denounce and discredit these infectious ideas before this mental disease spreads beyond control."

Harry emitted a long sigh of relief. To be sure, Bracken's words were basically what he had expected. Now, it appeared that, for the next several months at least, the direction of his fate was fixed. Whatever it may turn out to be, it was going to happen.

And so it was. The dean now said in an official voice, "Harry, I now grant your request for a leave, happily and enthusiastically. My decision will have to be endorsed by the Provost of the university, of course. But, I am sure that his approval will be just a formality.

"As a scientist, educator and private citizen, I strongly urge you to go. You have the best chance of success."

Then he added, in a somber tone, "But, I do fear for you, Harry. As a friend, I wonder if I would actually advise you to take such a dangerous mission. I urge you to think it over carefully before you agree to do it. Once you are there on the island, you will be subject to the same dangers as the current residents. No one can guarantee your safety.

"And, if you decide to go, try not to rush the job. Take as long as you need. We will do what is necessary to cover for you here. If there is anything that the university can do at this end, just ask. Now take care."

Harry could only say an emotional, "Thanks, Beau. I appreciate the concern and confidence. If I go, I will surely do my best."

As the two bade solemn good-byes, Harry hoped that it was not for the last time. He had been deeply gratified by the dean's understanding. He felt a warmth and kinship for the dean that he had not felt before.

As he strode quickly to his car, Harry thought, "One down, and one to go." He wondered if he were just one step closer to a terrible conclusion to his productive career, or possibly even to his life.

EIGHT

HARRY NOTICED IN HIS REAR-VIEW MIRROR that a police cruiser was rapidly overtaking him. He experienced the usual citizen's sour feeling of guilt in his gut. His first thought was the usual: "Not again!" Although his distressing problems had once again dominated his attention, his preoccupation had not been so complete this time. Checking his speed and seeing that it was just slightly over the limit, he quickly adjusted it sufficiently downward. Warily, he kept his eyes and attention moving rapidly from the road to the speedometer, to the cruiser, and back again. As the police car slowly eased by, Harry recognized the officer who earlier had given him the ticket.

This time the driver simply smiled, and gave him the thumbs-up signal. Relieved, Harry smiled back and returned the salute of approval. He really did intend to be a law-abiding citizen.

As the officer accelerated down the highway, Harry returned to his anxious thoughts. Soon he would be meeting with Schuh. He tried to anticipate how Schuh would react to his crucial questions about Kipua and the CRASH team. He decided that, almost certainly, Schuh would advise him to accept the mission. But, he was also sure that Schuh had more confidence in him than he had in himself.

Harry regarded Schuh with great respect and affection. He would be inclined to follow Schuh's advice on just about anything. So, he would feel immensely better if Schuh strongly advised him to undertake the mission. Harry knew that he could bring himself to accept the physical risk, and even the risk of a failed mission, if only he were confident that he would actually do a good job in leading the team. He needed to feel that the CRASH team would have the best chance for success with him as leader. Despite Beau

Bracken's assurances, Harry was still not convinced that he was an appropriate choice for the job. Harry feared, in fact, that it would be arrogant for him to presume that he was even a good choice for such a complex, difficult and important job. He always had a major problem in defining for himself the thin line between strong self-confidence and a touch of arrogance.

Harry managed to stay sufficiently alert to his surroundings so that he found Old Schuh's house on the first attempt. To many people that would not appear much of a feat, given Harry's familiarity with the neighborhood. Nevertheless, it was actually noteworthy, given his concentration on the taxing mental cost of the problems facing him at the time. But, for once, he had succeeded in overcoming his habit of narrowly focusing his attention on certain of his significant problems to the exclusion of other considerations.

As he turned into the driveway of the old ante bellum house, Harry saw Schuh sitting contentedly in an ancient weathered swing on his high front porch. The old man's lofty swinging perch allowed him a clear view up and down the neighborhood. Schuh liked alternately to doze and to wave cheerfully to each person passing by. Everyone was his friend. That included even those passers-by that he had never actually met.

Schuh had lived in that same house since he was a young professor. His children had been born in it. His beloved wife, Elsa, had died in it three years ago. That was about the same time that Harry's wife Lottie had died. They had been drawn even closer by their concurrent common grief.

Harry felt better just from seeing once again the familiar sight of Schuh on the porch. Old Schuh had always been there for him. In fact, Schuh was there for everybody. The ancient house in the heart of town was an oasis of ordered structure and tranquillity in the middle of frequently a desert of chaos and stress for younger minds.

Even when he was sitting on the unpretentious porch, every aspect of Old Schuh's appearance and bearing inspired confidence and respect. But for the lack of academic robe, he could easily be mistaken for a headmaster of a public school in the British Isles,

134 E. Rae Harcum

or a dean at a university on the continent. His appearance was a prototype—almost a caricature—of a true academic. He looked like a man committed to learning and to the use of judgment in applying that learning with positive effect. His bushy crown of disheveled white hair was suited to the most stereotypic of concert halls. But, if one were to be brutally honest, his worn tweed suit, resembling pajamas after a night of restless sleep, and cheap polyester tie, were more appropriate to a soup kitchen. Harry happened to know that the particular tie had been a Christmas gift from the youngest great grandchild. The tie was deeply and thoroughly cherished by the old man.

Schuh's individualistic attire was completed by a pair of leather moccasins sewn lovingly for him by another of his great grandchildren. For most men, that would have spoiled the perfect academic image. For Old Schuh, the footwear seemed entirely natural and in character with his general habit of focusing on important things.

Horn-rimmed spectacles were low on his nose. The omnipresent book was perched like a bird comfortably in the bend of his elbow. A book was an integral part of Schuh's person. Harry mused that probably someday Old Schuh would be buried with a book clutched thus lovingly under his arm.

Schuh was sucking energetically on several sticks of gum, rolled together, which had for years replaced his beloved pipe. Characteristically, he had wisely given up the pleasure of his pipe when the Surgeon General's report indicated that tobacco was hazardous to a person's health. To ensure that he would never smoke it again, he had decided to have the old pipe bronzed and mounted on a stand which he kept in his study. He often could be found just gazing at it sadly, lovingly.

Sometimes Schuh would remove his roll of gum and hold it like a pipe when he spoke. At other times, he would just mutter around this gross impediment to speech. That process was much like he had always done with his pipe. Everyone readily forgave him this eccentricity. They knew how difficult it had been for him to give up his beloved pipe.

Schuh walked arthritically down the front steps to the front yard, where the two friends embraced. After a further exchange of greetings, they made a trip to the kitchen for mugs of de-caffi-nated coffee. Schuh could not find any clean mugs, so he had to scrub two of them before they could be used. "I guess that I have had a lot of company lately," he said, apologetically.

Harry was sure what the old man said was true. He said, simply, "I know what you mean."

Then, they settled in the den, before the beloved bronzed pipe. The spot was like a shrine. But, Schuh did not stop to meditate.

Schuh began immediately. "You are a bit early, Harry. I assume that means things went well with Beau?"

"Yes, I know I'm early," said Harry. "I guess I had a heavy metal on the pedal, or whatever, in my eagerness to get this thing resolved. I wasn't paying attention and got another ticket for speeding or whatever."

Schuh just shook his head and smiled, saying nothing. He himself had been there before. All of the egg-heads were infected with the same disease. Their problem was not attention deficit, but attention surfeit. The practical problem came from the fact that the attention was likely to be directed at inward and abstract thoughts, rather than at the concrete events in that environment.

"Anyway," said the younger man, smiling with some embar-rassment, "I guess that everything went well with Beau. In any case, he granted me the leave, and encouraged me to believe that I could do the job. That was supportive and flattering. But, con-sidering the danger, he was not sure that a friend would actually advise me to go."

"His point is well taken. He is right to be concerned," said Schuh. "The danger is something that you should consider very carefully. But I am sure that you will consider the physical danger to you to be a secondary matter to other considerations.

"The main point is that now you are here to discover Old Schuh's opinion about the situation on Kipua, and what you might do about that situation. The matter seems to be troubling you deeply. And you have extremely good reason to be concerned, my boy. I have read about Burnhouse's problems in the newspa-per." He sighed sadly, and paused reflectively for a moment.

Then, Schuh continued, "I know that you did not approve of Burnhouse's experiment from the beginning. You said so publicly and emphatically. So, what has happened to create this problem for you? How did you get involved in their planning?"

Harry admitted, "Yes, I am upset. And, as you know, that is not the right condition for making really important decisions. Let me back off a few steps to take stock of the situation, like they say in the problem-solving manuals. I need to remember my training. Perhaps, I can calm down and re-gain my perspective in this thing with your help."

"Right on, Harry," agreed Schuh. "Take it nice and easy now. There is no hurry. We are not going anywhere today. Let's do this thing right. Start from the beginning."

Harry took a deep breath, and let it out slowly. Then, deliberately he began, "I have been asked to accept a mission to rescue some people in danger on an island, named Kipua, in the southern Pacific Ocean. Kipua is a small island in the Marianas group. As you know, Skull Burnhouse went there about six months, or so, ago to set up an experimental society following strict Behavioristic principles. It was to be a scientifically engineered utopia based on behavioral technology, instead of subjective human values, which were to be eliminated from their thinking. Specifically, their plan presumed that human beings do not have freedom to make voluntary choices of their behaviors, and that people do not possess any peculiar value by virtue of being human. The society was to be governed entirely by the appropriate administration of rewards.

"Apparently the experiment has produced some terrible results in terms of human suffering. We really do not know exactly how bad the situation is because the sponsoring agency, the Schoonover Foundation, has not heard from Skull for three weeks. In fact, no one on the island has seen him recently, or knows where he is."

Old Schuh made some clucking sounds of concern and sympathy. He merely said, "I am sorry to hear that. Knowing Skull's reputation for responsibility and thoroughness, it sounds ominous. It sounds really bad."

Harry nodded. "Yes, it does sound bad. It also means that I do not know what I will encounter if I accept the mission. The consequences could be nasty indeed for everyone involved. But, the mission is important to science and to the survival of human culture. There is no doubt of that. It will also be hazardous to the health of everyone involved, for sure.

"Actually, I myself do not worry so much about personal physical danger as I do about the doomsday social consequences for everyone if I should fail. That is selfish, I know. The failure of the mission would undoubtedly be catastrophic news to all peoples of the world. Everyone on this planet should be counting on the CRASH rescue team, whether they indeed know it or not."

"Excuse me, my boy," interrupted Schuh. "I do not know about this CRASH team. What does it do?"

"Sorry," said Harry. "I am trying to go too fast. The CRASH in the description refers to an acronym derived from the real title of Crisis Rescue And Salvage Help team. It is a team of scientists and a Schoonover representative who will mount a rescue and salvage operation on Kipua. There will be five members of a blue-chip group to undertake rescue, damage control and evaluation operations as each is necessary on Kipua."

Schuh nodded: "That seems like a good idea. That kind of help will surely be needed. Good for Schoonover! Go on."

Harry continued: "I will have to trust that the staff at Schoonover knew what they were doing when they nominated me to lead the team that they are sending to cope with this imminent disaster. Of course, they themselves bought and paid for the full length and breadth of the very disaster that the team will try to avert.

"The situation on Kipua reminds me of some of the old World War II movies in which bomb disposal squads tried to disarm unexploded bombs. The brave soul trying to disarm the bomb would talk into a microphone attached to a tape recorder which was in a bombproof bunker a safe distance away, for obvious reasons. So, if the bomb was exploded in some way, there was a record of the last wrong move he made. Others would know not to make that particular fatal move."

Pursuing that thought, Harry digressed from his story for a moment. "If I accept the job, I will have to take along some bound notebooks for recording everything that happens. Then, there will be a record in case things go down the tube and I am not around to explain what went wrong. Actually, I, myself, was thinking about using a tape recorder. I gave it up because I want to have hard copies of documentation to keep together in one place. I do not want an errant magnet or whatever to wipe out the whole record of our efforts so that other scientists will not have it available to study. Oh, well, that is a detail. I should get back to the main point.

"Unfortunately, Schuh, the goodness of the bomb analogy is not really very comforting at this particular time. As you can see, the bomb disposal analogy is so very frighteningly appropriate. Actually, the fuse to a social bomb has already been ignited on Kipua. We are truly discussing a potentially devastating bomb. It could go off at any time. The bomb in this case is, of course, the metaphysical idea that human beings are simply marvelous machines without freedom to make voluntary choices, and also without a dignity or personal value that sets them apart from other marvelous machines. The main goal was to assess the consequences of such thinking. Burnhouse argued that such a scientifically oriented society would make better use of modern technology than a society that believed in our conventional moral and social values.

"In my view, if this idea were to gain acceptance by the peoples of the world, the trouble on Kipua would be like a match to an unrestrained forest fire. There would be no basis for holding a person responsible for maintaining decent behaviors."

Schuh nodded, and said, "That is the way it seems to me, also. So, what will you do?"

Harry explained: "The job of the CRASH team at first would be some sort of desperate damage control, to stop or to delay the spread of its effects. Then, we would have to discover what went wrong to have lit the fuse in the first place.

"We will have to find out what caused a potentially helpful human technology to become a terrible social bomb. Was some key part missing that could have turned the whole shameful process, the one that actually occurred, into a helpful blend? Or was some extra particularly harmful ingredient inadvertently inserted into the mix? If our science can answer those questions, perhaps then that same science can work out some steps to prevent future damage."

Schuh nodded in agreement. "Surely, it appears that we must thoroughly eradicate the strict Behaviorist credo from our thinking," he said. "I agree with Koestler, who said back in 1967 that the strict Behavioristic ideas never seem to die—or to stay dead. They bounce back each time that they have been slain by data and reason. Consequently, the constant resurrection of this restricted view must be vigilantly and creatively opposed."

Harry nodded in emphatic affirmation. "You are right, Schuh. If the result on Kipua is truly horrendous, ironically it will help promulgate, by such a vivid and horrible counter-example, a better plan for a better world. If it does turn out to show, as now seems probable, definitively and finally that Skinner's idea absolutely will not work, it will suggest that a different one must be tried. The different one, based on the very opposite assumptions about human nature, should also be given a most thorough and dedicated trial."

Schuh interposed, "But, I read that the plan definitely went sour. I even heard about Burnhouse's current problems on Kipua from the television news and from front-page reports in the local newspapers. And then the news stopped. That is a very, very bad sign. You would think that the network news would find a way to get the story.

"I was not at all surprised that there was big trouble, but I really had not expected it to be so monstrous and so soon. I thought that perhaps, given Burnhouse's prominence in behavioral science, the media had prematurely trumpeted a fanfare over simply the loose ends to be found in any project. They could have been publicizing the failure merely for the sake of copy. But now I see that I was wrong."

"My feelings exactly," said Harry. "My understanding is that Schoonover has persuaded the networks that it would be both dangerous and unproductive to send a reporter to Kipua. It is infinitely better to allow the professionals in psychology on the CRASH team to do their work first. To be sure, the press cannot be held off for long. So, time is important.

"You are right about my opposition to Burnhouse's plan. Long ago, when I first heard of Burnhouse's plans for Kipua, I wrote a protest to our mutual friend, Joe Higgs, Executive Director of the Board for the Schoonover Foundation. As you know, the Schoonover Foundation is a private philanthropic organization dedicated to research in a large number of health-related areas. Well, Schoonover was considering the funding for Burnhouse's project. They have big bucks and are second only to the Feds in dollar amounts for sponsoring behavioral research. In my letter, I questioned their wisdom—maybe even their sanity—in financing his plan. In my letter to Higgy, I said that Burnhouse's proposal to establish a TECHland community in the South Pacific was ill-advised and even seriously dangerous. Whatever the particular outcome, it would not be good for the people of Kipua, or for anyone actually.

"In my letter, I even illustrated my concerns with a little hy-pothetical story about what the outcome might be in one realistic situation. I thought that surely the lesson in the story would be obvious. I have a copy here of what I wrote, if you want to hear it."

"Of course, Harry," said Schuh. "But, let's break to get a little lunch first. We have rambled on into the lunch hour. I don't get very hungry, but my doctor tells me that it is very important for us old folks to eat. I have to go by the clock. Unfortunately, I forget to eat, if I wait until I am really hungry."

"Sure," said Harry. "I was so busy talking that I didn't keep track of time. I'm sorry. Why don't you let me take you out for a bite?"

"Oh, no," responded Schuh. "It is too much trouble to go out. I have plenty of soup, coffee and cookies, if that will satisfy you."

"That's fine," agreed Harry, as he turned to the familiar cup-board to get out the soup bowls. They were the same blue and white bowls that Elsa had always used for the soup. She had purchased them on a trip to the Netherlands. They were highly prized by the old man. But, he would not put them safely away in a china cabinet. It seemed to comfort him to be able to use them, as he had always done with Elsa. Everyone knew to be very care-ful with them.

"How does tomato sound to you, my boy?" asked Schuh, pulling out a can of Campbell's tomato soup from another cupboard, which was totally filled with similar cans. Obviously, Schuh was a great fan of tomato soup. And, he made no secret of his preferences.

Tomato soup with wheat-stoned crackers was also one of Harry's favorite meals. He ate the crackers plain when he was having soup, but he spread a little butter on them when he was just having a snack of crackers. Lottie always scolded him about the butter.

"Tomato soup sounds the best, Schuh," said Harry. He loved the familiar routine with his old friend. The mood was completed as he heard the pregnant whining of the ancient can opener on the kitchen counter.

Harry and Schuh enjoyed the leisurely lunch, happily regaling each other with familiar lies about former exploits and reminiscing about old friends. The business at hand was deliberately delayed, Schuh did not like to spoil lunch with business talk, any more than he liked to spoil business talk with lunches. In fact, Harry thoroughly appreciated the break from the heavy concentration on serious business.

After lunch, they re-charged their coffee mugs, and settled comfortably again in front of the Shrine of the Tobacco Pipe. Schuh had to worship quietly for a moment before they renewed the discussion. His new ritual of homage now replaced his old ritual of lighting the pipe. Somehow, Schuh felt more satisfied when the ceremony was over.

When Schuh was ready, Harry pulled out a few sheets of paper from his briefcase. He reminded Schuh that it was a copy of his letter to Higgy. Harry began to read from the papers:

> Higgy, I feel so strongly that Skull Burnhouse's proposed project on Kipua will be disastrous that I have written a little story that I think will show in a common-sense way how it is sheer folly.
>
> Suppose you are a Peace Corps volunteer sent to an underdeveloped part of the world to help an isolated tribe whose survival is threatened by local strife, famine and environmental pollution. On the basis of your technical knowledge and skills, and your study of the tribe, you become convinced that many of the customs and be-

liefs of the tribe are counterproductive. In fact, you consider them to be actual threats to its very survival. Therefore, this system of beliefs and practices must be eliminated in favor of a more productive social organization. Assume, also, that you have some firm ideas about the general nature of what that new social plan should be, although no solid proof that it will work for these people. Nevertheless, you are convinced that your ideas are correct.

Many other scientists disagree with your plan, however, actually arguing that a proper adherence and full commitment to the traditional tribal beliefs will ultimately lead to the survival of the tribe. These opposing scientists have also sent emissaries to the tribe, arguing that the principles which you propose are part of the problem, because your proposals have contributed to the erosion of the traditional beliefs. Obviously, you do not have the authority, or power—or, to be sure, even the desire—to coerce the tribe into making those changes which you judge would be beneficial.

You tell the natives that you have made a scientific discovery which can solve their problems. Your idea calls for them to turn their present culture inside-out, because a major change in thinking is needed. If they want to survive, they must renounce their irrational beliefs in certain traditional gods, cherished and worshipped for generations, and adopt your rational and laboratory-proven ideas. In public council meetings, you denounce their hallowed beliefs, using an adversarial and uncompromising style.

Those natives who are not for you are considered to be against you. You suggest that disbelievers resist your ideas because of their personal psychological problems. These problems have allegedly blinded them to the truth which you have revealed to them.

Because your behavior is equivalent to desecrating a religious symbol, national flag or other cherished icon, you should not be surprised if you are treated as a curiosity, or ignored, or even despised by the tribe. You could be chased from the village, or worse. The psychological principles affecting the natives' response are so obvious that they might be likened to common sense.

If you are not killed, you will probably be considered possessed by some renegade spirit, and perhaps even honored as a curiosity. You might even be allowed to keep your podium, perform for the amusement of the populace and receive maintenance grants of fish and rice from the meager stores of the Tribal Institute of Health. You could become rich by village standards, if you were actually entertaining enough. You might actually gain a few converts to your cause, who would therefore become totally alienated from the rest of the tribe.

Most likely, however, your opposition would actually strength-en the natives' belief in their own gods. Your mission would fail. You might be lucky to escape with your very life.

The tribe would not be helped, and maybe it would be harmed by your efforts, because some did listen to you. The next volunteer to try to help would, of course, encounter a residual resistance to any plan he or she might propose in the name of science. So, no one would actually benefit from your effort.

Schuh shook his head enthusiastically. "Your parable is right on, my boy," he said, forcing his words around a roll of several sticks of gum, which he had pushed into his mouth as soon as his coffee was finished. He had held the pack out to Harry as he read, but the younger man had shaken his head, "No."

Schuh continued: "Even if the natives were pleased with a description of life without the tribal gods—and that is not at all likely—they would then have to be convinced that a better soci-ety could indeed be achieved if the gods were eliminated, that some renegade tribal god had truly been responsible for their problems. Thus, the strategy of advocation would be crucial, to induce the tribe at least to listen seriously with an open mind to the arguments."

"Right. That is the next point," said Harry. "There is a clear parallel between the volunteer in this hypothetical story and the current practices of the Crusading Behaviorists. The Peace Corps volunteer was guilty of imitating the tactics and style—the behav-ioral proposal—of Skinner and his followers. I would argue that precisely the same scenario would be repeated exactly that way on Kipua, with the same tragic results. And, as you see, I would have been right."

"What did Higgy have to say in response to all this?" asked Old Schuh.

"Higgy's response was quite reasonable, as usual, I have to ad-mit," said Harry. "He too was more than a bit anxious about Skull's project. Even the Board of Directors of Schoonover themselves felt the same serious concerns. But they also believed that we really do need the scientific data that would come from Skull's project. Higgy reminded me that scientists may think that we know what the outcome will be, but as scientists we know that we cannot really conclude that we have the truth until the empirical results have been obtained and analyzed. He pointed out that sometimes a few risks are necessary to fuel progress.

"So, the Board eventually decided to fund Skull's project. It was undeniably a calculated risk. Then, Higgy wisely advised us all to say a prayer for Skull."

Schuh agreed, "Surely, the scientific argument was undeniably valid. But that is more than I can say for the ethics of it. Obviously, some people thought that it was okay ethically. But, I strongly disagree. The study was not ethical. You see, the real risks were placed on the people of the island without individual personal consent by the people of Kipua. The government should not have made the decision for them. Absolutely not! There should at least have been some sort of referendum, to allow the people to vote. I wonder what the victims on Kipua are saying now?"

They both understood that this was a textbook example of a rhetorical question. They remained silent for a moment as they gloomily pondered the answer. Neither could verbalize it. There was an oppressive and depressing silence.

Finally, in an effort to lift the shroud of gloom, Old Schuh abruptly changed to a new subject: "By the way, how is Higgy getting along these days?" He had been close to Higgy also.

"Higgy is fine, otherwise," responded Harry. "He said some nice things about Lottie in a personal note. I have not seen him since she died. Good old Higgy! He even asked about the dog. Old Trooper is staying with my daughter, Beth, and her Aunt Kay while I am gone.

"I have never seen another dog as good with children. Beth could tear his leg off and that would not bother old Troop in the slightest, considering who was doing the damage. But, nobody else could get away with that. Not even I could do it."

The old professor smiled at the recollection. "Yes," he said, "that sounds like Old Trooper. And it sounds like Higgy, too. Higgy is a fine, caring person. It is too bad that this mess has to reflect badly on him."

Then, he decided that it was now time to return to the business at hand. "You know, Higgy actually does have a valid point about the project on Kipua. Even the gradual progress of science often does entail some risks. It is a judgment call, of course. If Burnhouse's experiment had turned out to surprise us by confirming his proposal, a possible way to a better society would be opened to further study at least. If he has truly failed, as you predicted, we will know for sure that Skinner's proposal does not work, at least under the conditions in Kipua. If we conclude that the implementation of the plan was appropriate and adequate, we can discard the Behaviorists' technological plan once and for all. That would be a major plus for our behavioral science, in fact.

"This powerful argument really cannot be discounted, you know. Actually, Harry, that is the way science is supposed to go forth, as you well know. Consider this: maybe you non-Behaviorists were just too arrogant to be so positive about the result."

"True," agreed Harry. "You never can be sure, of course, no matter how confident you were."

"Yes," said Schuh. "Nevertheless, as it has turned out, it appears that you were horribly right to fear the worst-case scenario. Let us hope that it has not come to that."

Old Schuh was sad, but he spoke with confidence and reason. Harry knew that he was correct. He really had known it all along at some deeply embedded level of consciousness within his being.

So, Harry stated what they both knew: "In any case, Skull was undeniably determined to do it. After I talked to Higgy, I ran into Skull at a professional convention. I was venturous enough—or desperate enough—to try to dissuade him from his plan. He was scrupulously polite, but absolutely adamant in his refusal. He argued that the situation on Kipua was ripe for the institution of Skinner's plan. He insisted on instituting a large version of a token economy for the island along the lines of *Walden Two*. He obviously thought that it was an exciting prospect to validate the principles advocated by Skinner. Nothing that I could say would weaken his determination. He even suggested that I was afraid that his plan might work. So, I doubt that any words would have reached him.

"Anyway, I personally was sure of a disastrous outcome for Burnhouse at Kipua. But, I agree that, hopefully, the world will benefit from whatever knowledge is gained. I pray that it will not be at too great a cost for the global community, even if the specific outcome itself ultimately proves to be a disaster for Kipua."

"You are certain the problem is with the theory?" asked Schuh.

"Yes," said Harry, "I am sure. Most of my confidence comes from the fact that I predicted the debacle on theoretical grounds. That fact does point to faulty premises as the cause of the failure, rather than simply poor execution. And, that simple fact, of a valid prediction, is scientifically most important."

Old Schuh nodded again in agreement. He did not speak. He was a man who reflected on his thoughts before he spoke. Therefore, when he spoke, his words were especially significant.

Harry rushed on to make one more point. "You know," he said, "that I am not alone in my opinion. In fact, one author has said that Skinner's plan is "a blueprint for Hell." That is surely an unambiguous assessment."

"Um-hmm," murmured Schuh. "And I agree that he is right. No doubt about it."

Harry was reassured. So, now he waited anxiously for Old Schuh to respond to his vital question. It was not likely that he would accept the assignment without Schuh's approval. He was sure that Schuh would approve, but he wished to hear it all the same.

When Schuh spoke, the words came slowly. They came firmly, having the tone and finality of a conclusion from a scientific report. "Harry, my boy, you must accept the mission. I agree with everything you have said about the status of the mission. I also foresee the cataclysmic effects if Burnhouse's experiment—or its aftermath, if you prefer—is not stopped. And I also emphatically agree with Higgy and the folks at Schoonover that you are indeed the best person for the job.

"You absolutely must accept the assignment, Harry. Surely, your Methodist conscience will give you no peace, if you do not. And neither will I. You simply must go!"

Harry felt that Schuh's words had worked like an air-lock for him. They closed one door behind him, and opened another door ahead of him. Therefore, he must go forward!

He eagerly listened to the rest of what Schuh had to say. He was sure that he would need to keep it all in mind.

Old Schuh continued with his advice: "The CRASH team must try to neutralize the damage that has already been done, if that is possible. Then, it must discover some way to prevent the problem from reaching a critical mass for a catastrophic explosion. The difference is, if this kind of bomb goes off, it could destroy not just city blocks or whole cities. It could annihilate our very civilization itself. It would be like a behavioral epidemic, devouring all behavioral engineering antibodies as it spreads. We—the whole scientific community—must stop it before it becomes unstoppable, if indeed it has not already reached a hopeless state.

"Truly, we just do not know what will happen. The result could be like a fire in an isolated building. It could burn itself out, so that the only damage is the total destruction of the building itself and its contents. Similarly, the peril of Kipua could simply devastate the island, and then terminate itself at the shoreline. Perhaps, the horror on Kipua would merely be a lesson to the peoples in other lands. Or, perhaps, the contamination simply would not catch on elsewhere. That is probably the least damaging prospect, but, I think, the least likely.

"But, that best scenario is surely not probable. And we both know it. We must work on the worst-case hypothesis. More likely, if something is not done, sooner or later, some people of the island will escape to spread the behavioral pestilence to other islands and to other lands. They will scatter like panicked rats leaving a doomed ship. They will carry the disease with them on any available vehicle of transportation. Even martial law could not be expected to keep every infected person on the island.

"Others will leave in a cynical attempt to enjoy the fruits of leadership in a similar plan on other shores. They will gather to themselves the substances of the new society until it is suffocated. Then, they will move to yet new societies. Inevitably, they will run out of new societies to destroy."

"I agree," said Harry. "I think that it would be some kind of miracle if the news has not somehow gotten off the island already. If so, heaven help us. I do not know, then, how we could contain it. It is the very idea itself that constitutes the danger. To contain the idea would never be possible, given the undisciplined nature of human beings. So, a world-wide epidemic of this one devastating idea could get started. Just as with the explosion of the first atomic bomb, we cannot be sure that a chain reaction, once started, will not consume the world. The job of the CRASH team is to prevent such a tragedy. God help us all!"

"Right again!" added Schuh. "Sooner or later, bombs must be exploded or de-fused. They cannot just be left around. Some accident or fanatic lunatic will surely set them off. So, some strong action must be taken. This applies to bombs of social crises as well as to real dynamite, atomic bombs or whatever. The group of CRASH trouble shooters will be the bomb squad of record for this particular behavioral bomb.

"So, Harry, you fear for good reason. I am sure of it. I believe that the events on Kipua will determine whether we humans can solve our social problems well enough to exist on this planet, or sink further into a morass of immorality that will snuff us out like a campfire in a flood. The survival of humanity depends upon the success of your mission to Kipua. If it is not stopped now, it will never be stopped."

Having rendered his decision, Old Schuh paused for breath. For him, it had been an extremely long speech. Sensing there might be even more, Harry remained respectfully silent.

Old Schuh then continued in the same serious tone: "True, our civilization might be able to recover. The human animal has in fact proven itself to be wonderfully adaptive, successful enough to survive some enormous disasters which it alone created, as well as a bunch of nasty natural ones. I pray that we human animals who have evolved marvelously from the alligators and apes can do it this one more time. We must!

"Actually, your mission to Kipua is truly a part of that very human process of attempted social adaptation. Through such initiative, our culture is taking steps, trying hard to bounce back, to adapt. It is trying to correct by science a mistake which was made by that culture in the very name of science. You are part of this correction process. The essence of your mission is a fight against the distorted and misguided science that has caused this impending catastrophe. Your job is to counter the bad science with science practiced as it should be. We scientists must be the instruments for making God's plan for the world work now, before there is further calamity from human frailty and corruption.

"I can only hope. We do have a chance for salvation. The damage-control process will be horrible. But we must have confidence that there is a 'vein of goodness' in God's people, and that with courage and dedication we can make use of this vein in order to make science work as it should. This vein of goodness lives in the parts of our brains that give us our capacity to reason. We have brains that are well adapted for learning and reasoning, although admittedly still with the capacity to enjoy the pleasures of the sub-human animals. This beneficial vein is mostly overlooked by the Behaviorists, who prefer to emphasize the amoral animal motivations.

"What makes your task so very scary is that we must make His plan work. If you fail, humanity may continue down the steep slippery slope to total oblivion. The adaptation of human culture may be set back hundreds or thousands of years. Human society may become like a colony of apes or baboons, or worse. Could we become like alligators and other predators, except that—worse— we prey upon one another? Considering the large gains of the last several centuries, accelerating rapidly in the last several decades by greater concerns for human rights and freedom, that would indeed be an enormous setback. If the insights of great scientists can cause giant leaps in science, scientific mistakes can set it back the same amount."

He ended with a subdued, self-conscious smile and a shrug. That was probably the longest speech that Old Schuh ever made outside of a lecture hall.

Harry had confidently expected everything that Schuh had said, except the strong conclusion that he was the right person to lead the mission. Nevertheless, because of his respect and admiration for Old Schuh, Harry finally gave up his doubts. He decided that he could do it. He was hooked. He must go!

Once convinced, he was eager to get started. He thanked Schuh for his help, and bade him an emotional good-bye.

The sad thought occurred to Harry, as he warmly embraced Old Schuh in parting, that this might be the last time that be would see his aged friend alive. Then, a startling idea intruded. He thought that perhaps this will be the last time that his aged friend would see *him* alive. After all, he was the one who was about to embark on a dangerous mission of unknown dimensions with basically his own wits as his only protection.

NINE

ARRY ENTERED THE NEW YORK HALLS of the Schoonover Foundation feeling very much like a small minnow in a giant stream of swift flowing, but cloudy, water. It was vastly different from his familiar milieu at Ivey Southern. The major difference was in the apparent cost of everything.

The semi-lavish decor and the spacious offices made his functionally adequate office at Ivey Southern seem like the work place of a poor relative. But he quickly reassured himself that the true value of the final output ultimately determined the real value of an institution. Harry was proud of his own work in general, and also of the educational standards and products of his university. Both in terms of successful students and significant scientific research, Ivey Southern was among the best for its size.

Granted, he also knew that Schoonover had sponsored many worthy projects. The elegance of their offices surely did not mean that their work was characteristically weak and superficial. In fairness, their board should not be pilloried for their one bad mistake on Kipua. And perhaps he would still be wrong in the assumption that indeed the Kipua experiment would turn out to be a mistake in the final analysis. Unfortunately, however, his original assumption appeared to be all too correct at the moment.

In any case, Schoonover's present proposal of a joint venture for rescue and evaluation surely was a worthy one. A safety net is a good idea, even if it is never needed. If the Schoonover board did approve of him as the leader for their team, he was determined that he would be a good representative of his school and of his profession.

Harry still was amazed at how he had come to this place. To himself he seemed at first glance like an unlikely choice. But, he did know, of course, how he had been selected. He had been thrust to the front of the long line of potential leaders for the CRASH team by his own expressed interest in the general issues of the case. Ironically, he had in truth actually involved himself in the TECHland experiment precisely by his unsuccessful attempts to halt the project before it even got started.

In fact, Harry's own personal bias was a good reason for his *not* becoming personally involved now. He had said so to Higgy when the Schoonover executive first approached him about taking on the dangerous assignment. But, Higgy was not impressed by Harry's argument. They both knew that, to be honest, biases were inevitable, even in science. Moreover, there would be other members of the investigative team with strong biases opposite to those that Harry himself embraced. Hopefully, any important final effects of individual biases in the research would cancel out at the end. That is, of course, the way science is supposed to work.

"Besides," Harry thought to himself, "I have had to answer this important question of bias about myself many times as an evaluator of student papers, research submissions to professional journals and so forth. I asked: Could I be objective enough to evaluate this project, paper or person in a fair manner, despite whatever biases I might have? As they say, only my analyst would know for sure. Nevertheless, I have always been able to answer this question satisfactorily in the affirmative—especially to myself. That is what really counts. That is what personal integrity is all about. I give myself high marks in that respect." Harry was just being honest at this point, not arrogant.

Harry truly believed that a person had, first of all, to trust himself or herself to be fair. A person must be confident enough that he or she was sufficiently healthy as a personality to be fair, despite the cries of all those to whom he or she had to oppose, or to give bad news. Without that basic personal confidence, a true evaluation from that particular individual was not at all possible. Harry had many insecurities about himself in various respects, but never with respect to his personal integrity. He knew that he would not consciously be unfair to anyone.

The critics had their own biases, too, of course. That point was trite, to be sure. Nevertheless, it must always be kept in mind. A criticism could itself be nothing more than a mere reflection of the bias of the critic. To defend yourself against a charge of being biased is like trying to defend yourself against an allegation of being gay. How many fair evaluations do you have to present as evidence that you are not biased?

So, Harry concluded one more time, perhaps the millionth time, that he was able to be fair. He had so re-assured Higgy in a positive way. Maybe that was why the Schoonover Board asked him to consider such an important job. It could have put him ahead of all those famous experts who might otherwise seem better qualified for the sort of thing to be done on Kipua.

Maybe the big operators were so sure of themselves because they were simply acting out their personal biases. Therefore, they were not truly making discriminations and decisions. Perhaps, that was in fact exactly what it took to be a big operator. Harry decided that he had to think more about that proposition sometime. It was an interesting idea that probably had some truth to it.

Harry fervently hoped that Schoonover had simply considered him to be the best person to make the system work. He really did not think that nominating him for leading the mission was just a good-ol'-boy thing, passed his way because Higgy and he were graduate school buddies at Berkeley. Higgy had assured him that such was not the case. In any case, he was gratified that the people at Schoonover trusted him so much.

In fact, Harry had to admit to himself that he *did* have good credentials. He had gotten his doctorate from a very good place. He had enjoyed good success in publishing his research as a psychology professor at Ivey Southern. To be sure, Ivey Southern was not one of the so-called high-impact research universities. No matter! Harry believed that his colleagues in the psychology department were undeniably first class, worthy of even the best institutions. His colleagues at Ivey Southern simply preferred the pace, intellectual balance and closer student contact of the smaller university. So did Harry.

Harry's teaching position had also given him opportunities for some rewarding extended contacts with several well-known professors at prestigious institutions. This experience had come about by virtue of a couple of sabbatical stints at so-called "big time" universities in the U.S. and Great Britain.

So, Harry knew what the major players in psychology could do. And, he also knew that he could serve competently as a member of the team. But, nevertheless, he was not absolutely sure that he could be an effective emotional leader for such a high-powered group. Despite the repeated reassurances of Beau Bracken and Otto Schumacher, some small doubts had crept back.

Well, Higgy and the board had convinced him that Schoonover truly wanted to get the straight facts. They had said to Harry that the foundation did not want to skewer anyone, or to whitewash anyone either. In fact, they did not want to pre-ordain any conclusion. In the last analysis, he reminded himself, the task was simply science. And Harry did feel nicely comfortable with his scientific credentials.

Schoonover also wanted to undo as much of the damage as possible that had been caused by their project. Harry was sure that they did have a tremendous ethical responsibility on that point. In fact, he felt some small degrees of responsibility also because he himself had failed in his best efforts to prevent the TECHland experiment. Harry realized that such a failure should not engender much guilt.

The bottom line was that Harry truly cared about people. Harry had few peers in that respect among psychologists.

As Harry marched resolutely down the thickly carpeted halls of Schoonover, he was frequently directed by uniformed attendants who were stationed at strategic locations. He must have looked fairly legitimate. No one asked him to identify himself. Nevertheless, he wished in a juvenilely guilty way that he had a hall pass. Ultimately, one of the hall monitors pointed him toward a massive door. The door was completely devoid of identification. The monitor grandly opened it for him as if it were a throne room. Despite Harry's grandiose expectations, it was only a reception room.

Harry introduced himself to the receptionist in the hallowed center of the spacious and ornate receiving room which was the beginning of the Schoonover inner sanctum. She informed him that she was Eleanor Fitz, and that Dr. Higgs would be right out to meet him. The board was already in emergency session, she said. Harry was encouraged by the fact that the board obviously felt the need for quick action concerning Kipua.

The ceiling of the reception room was a full fifteen feet high. In fact, the room itself was as big as the average classroom at Ivey Southern, which usually held about thirty-five students. The walls of the wooden cavern were undoubtedly some kind of rare hardwood, stained and polished to a rich, dark brown. There were carvings, or castings—Harry could not tell which—along the edge between walls and ceiling. He decided that they must be carvings, because everything else was authentic and top of the line. He felt casually that the money would have been better spent on behavioral research. He thought that he himself could have used a couple of those bucks along the way for his own research.

Large oil paintings of ancient and presumably generous benefactors lined the walls. The paintings alternated with luxurious tapestries. The rug was well-worn, apparently of Oriental design. Presumably, it had been broken in for the casual look by less prestigious users. The chairs and couches were over-stuffed and flanked by numerous tables to provide easy resting places for beverages or corporate papers.

The centerpiece of the room was the huge desk of the receptionist. Although the desk could have held the full contents of Harry's office at the university, it was neatly stocked with just the necessities for secretarial labor: calendar, stapler, vat of paper clips, Scotch tape, pen holder. At one side, there was a separate work center for the computer and assorted equipment. On the other side, there was a fax machine and a duplicating machine. There were several other large pieces of mysterious and exotic equipment whose functions were unknown to Harry.

The receptionist herself was an extremely pleasant and attractive middle-aged woman. Her nameplate read, "Eleanor Fitz-gibbons."

Eleanor Fitz smiled: "Welcome to Schoonover, Dr. Hawkey. May I get you some coffee?"

Harry rarely refused coffee. "Sure," he said. "Black. No sugar. Thanks." He was usually a little less laconic, but he was still cataloging these fascinating new surroundings.

Eleanor disappeared into a side room and soon returned with a china teacup of coffee, perched on the edge of a large china plate. The plate also provided the space for a couple of sugar cookies.

Then, the secretary returned to briskly sorting papers. She seemed extraordinarily efficient at what she did. She was friendly and respectful, but still remained focussed on her regular work. Harry quickly judged that Eleanor was exactly perfect for the job. He was incidentally encouraged to feel that Schoonover took the trouble to match the right person to their jobs.

Harry seated himself in a comfortable chair, which rested behind a large coffee table. The coffee was too hot to drink, so he placed the saucer and cup on the table to cool. As he slowly nibbled the cookies, he pulled a sheaf of papers from his briefcase for review while he was waiting for Higgy. He had been over them before, but he needed to get a new start. Psychologists call it a process of "taking stock." Besides, he needed to capture a scientific mind set, if he were to present and evaluate this material in an objective way. Also, he always liked to have something to work on while he was waiting. Moreover, because he was a little nervous, it gave him something to do with his hands.

He read that in 1985, Burnhouse had visited several utopian-style communities. The experience had a profound effect on the man. In fact, Burnhouse became fully committed to a program of research and study on social improvement modeled along the lines proposed by Skinner. Burnhouse's visits to the utopian communities convinced him to apply his prior commitment to objective science for application to the betterment of humanity.

Ordinarily, Harry would applaud such a commitment. But, in the case of Burnhouse, he was not at all sure that the end result would be so beneficial to society. First, Harry did not agree with Burnhouse's theories. Second, he questioned Burnhouse's scientific objectivity in dealing with data related to issues dealing with personal choice. Harry feared that Burnhouse had difficulty in keeping his personal biases from influencing his judgments about such personally relevant scientific matters.

Harry had heard Burnhouse describe in a convention presentation his gradual, but complete, conversion to Skinnerian thinking. Burnhouse described how he sought more and more rigor in his scientific studies. He described also how he gradually came to feel more and more uncomfortable with the inherent ambiguities in theorizing as a part of the pursuit of scientific knowledge. Finally, Burnhouse was comfortable only when he denied the existence of anything that could not be weighed or measured with some mechanical or electronic instrument. Consequently, he discontinued theorizing entirely. Thus, he attempted to confine his research merely to describing functional relationships among the variables represented by measurements with his mechanical and electronic equipment. He became what is known in the field as a "brass instrument psychologist." That label is honored, or despised, depending upon the preference of the individual psychologist.

To Harry's mind, Skull Burnhouse's methodological rigor sterilized his science, rendering it essentially barren. Burnhouse's science was like the legendary gooney bird that flew faster and faster in circles of ever-decreasing radius until it flew into one of it own body orifices and disappeared.

Harry himself was completely committed to the idea that theory is vitally important to science. True, science is minimally possible without theory. In some areas, the simple description of physical events makes sufficient sense. But, to build a science devoid of theory would be like constructing an ocean liner without a helm and rudder. The passengers will surely arrive somewhere, even if it is only their starting point. And, they might not see anything of interest along the way. Without the guidance of theory, a scientist does not have a map of where he or she wants to go. Therefore, he or she has no way of determining when, or if, he or she has arrived, or what it means to have arrived wherever he or she has landed.

Burnhouse's whole-hearted embrace of strict Behaviorism was like a religious conversion, but with a difference. It was more of a conversion to a cult, characterized by fanaticism rather than by faith. Harry understood that it was difficult to describe this important difference. It had to do with the nature of faith. Harry considered that he believed in a faith in God that was not subject to doubt on the basis of any empirical evidence that could be provided. But, matters of scientific theory and facts about the world could be, and must be, in his view, tested by all available empirical evidence. The scientist relies on empirical testing when he or she can do so. That is what science is all about. Any proposition can at least be empirically tested in terms of its alleged practical value. If it can be used to understand and to predict the behaviors of people, it is valuable.

Thus, in Harry's judgment, Burnhouse was too narrow in the type of evidence that he would accept. Sometimes Harry even entertained a suspicion that Burnhouse's acceptance of evidence depended on whether it was favorable, or unfavorable, to Behavioristic views about the causation of behavior. Such a practice is a scientific no-no, of course, even if it is not done intentionally. Harry would never mention such unproved suspicions to anyone, of course.

The whole story of the TECHland experiment up to now was in the bulging boxes of documentation that Harry had already sent along to the airport. Whoever became the leader of the team would need them, and he or she was welcome to them.

The story of his own personal involvement started with the phone call from Higgy at Schoonover. Higgy said that he wanted Harry to do a job for him. Harry knew right away what Higgy was talking about. He had been reading about Burnhouse in the newspapers, and seeing him on television. Higgy really had not known too much about what had happened recently. Except, it looked very bad. Burnhouse's disappearance was ominous, to say the least, given the controversial nature of his ideas. Obviously, everyone feared for the very safety of Burnhouse, and, by extension, of every person on the island.

Therefore, at this point, Schoonover was not so much concerned for the conduct of the project as they were for Burnhouse's whereabouts and safety, and for the welfare of the people on Kipua. The natives had, of course, been civilized for many years through the early efforts of missionaries. Still, it could be true that

Burnhouse had succeeded in wiping out fragile social consciences with his revolutionary ideas. That was actually the very goal that he had originally set out to achieve. Could these unsophisticated people really cope with such radical technocratic ideas? Or, had such shocking ideas caused them to revert to earlier savage ways? What about the other plantation workers and shopkeepers? In a larger sense, the same question could truly be asked about the entire human species. Was the taming of our species sufficiently secure that we could trust it to prevail when all feelings of guilt for serious social transgressions were eliminated? Could human society survive if it deliberately stopped moral development at a selfish childlike level that was concerned only with happiness and pleasure? Could civilized culture be effectively controlled simply by impersonal rewards?

Harry greatly feared that it could not. It looked to him like the human species itself had actually faced a real empirical test on Kipua. Potentially, the dilemma would be a real challenge even to the survival of the human species.

Schoonover's board of directors was understandably very upset. They wanted a team of blue-chip scientists sent to the island in order to get an immediate handle on things before the situation got irreparably worse. Schoonover needed to straighten out the situation from a social and scientific standpoint—not to say even a business basis.

They felt major moral responsibility, of course. The citizens on Kipua, through no fault of their own, had suffered terribly from the fallout of the TECHland experiment. Multiple rapes and robberies, and several suicidal deaths, had been attributed directly to Burnhouse's experiment. Everyone feared that the situation would get lethally worse.

Schoonover was also worried about legal problems as well, if the early reports of human catastrophe were substantiated. Because Harry's worst predictions of dire results had come true, he could envision long lines of victims in front of the offices of personal-injury lawyers all across the South Pacific.

The result was that Schoonover wanted Harry to rush to the Schoonover national headquarters in New York to talk about heading the investigative team. Higgy had pleaded with him, on the basis of their long friendship, not to decline until he had heard their proposal. Schoonover had wanted Harry to be on the next flight to New York, and be prepared to leave immediately for Kipua if he agreed to take the job.

In an instantaneous flashback, Harry recalled the multiple reasons for why he should not accept the task. After all, he was a scientist and not a tracer of lost persons. He was certainly not an adventurer, or an anthropologist, or even a thrill seeker. Actually, he did not even like to try exotic new foods. That was especially true if the ingredients had been buried in the ground in an earth-enware crock for a couple of months, or hung from a tree for weeks in a monkey skin bag. He really had no experience with this type of field research.

Higgy had explained how Schoonover desperately needed someone that they could fully trust to be in charge of the investiga-tion. He laid it on super heavy about how he trusted Harry and his integrity above all people on the basis of their long friendship. He said that personally he would feel secure from confusing second-hand reports only if Harry would take on the job.

After that, Harry really could not turn down Higgy's request to visit Schoonover in New York City. In Harry's opinion, Higgy was a great guy, and the best of friends. Besides, Harry under-stood that he himself had been more or less at loose ends since Lot-tie's death. Also, a major consideration was that he was intensely interested in the outcome of the project. And, although he did not know Burnhouse well, he certainly wished no personal harm to come to the rash scientific pioneer.

Soon, Higgy burst out of the conference room to greet Harry enthusiastically. "Hello, old chum," he said with a broad smile. "It is good to see you finally. You are looking great, except a trifle fat. How was your flight?"

Higgy had always jogged and worked out in the gym. He was proud of his trim body. He never missed a chance to tease Harry about the professor's stubborn refusal to exercise in a gym. Harry liked sports and yard work, and that kept him in fairly good shape. But not in as good shape as Higgy, with all of the directed exercises in Schoonover's undoubtedly fabulous gymnasium.

Jonas Stockworth Higgs III, a handsome, well-built man, was the scion of a family which had inherited a fortune from his grand-father. The family wealth came from the proceeds of numerous real estate investments in Detroit. Instead of living a superficial life of ease, Higgy's father had pursued higher education with such diligence that he had become a professor of psychology at the University of Michigan. Therefore, Higgy had grown up in a genteel academic atmosphere, spending the school year in Ann Arbor and the summers at the family cabin in the Upper Peninsula of Michigan. Frequently, he took time off from a summer in the cabin to travel to various spots about the world. His classmates in school appropriately caller him "Maiden's prayer."

Higgy had taken his undergraduate degree at the University of Michigan, but felt that he needed a change of academic milieu for his graduate studies. It had been an agonizing decision to make. He finally decided on Berkeley. Berkeley had one of the best graduate programs in psychology in the world. It also offered a California view of the world, including the multiple delights of nearby San Francisco.

Higgy and Harry had met at the first orientation meeting for graduate students at Berkeley. They happened to have selected adjacent seats. Their first polite conversations blossomed into serious discussions, and finally into the easy banter of friend-ship. Higgy made friends easily with persons of any cultural background. He had many of them. But, he seemed especially drawn to Harry. He identified in Harry a totally empathic person with strong integrity and loyalty. Harry's devotion to Higgy was closely akin to hero worship.

Now, Harry was delighted to have the chance to exchange jokes with Higgy. He faked a posture of shame, and allowed as to how it was not wise for middle-aged men to get too skinny. Higgy was a few months older than Harry.

Then, Harry assured Higgy that: 1.) the flight was smooth; 2.) that the rest of the trip was also uneventful; and 3.) gym exercise was colossally boring. The amenities over, along with the friendly teasing, Harry announced that he was prepared and eager to go forth to work.

"Good," said Higgy. "I am sorry that we do not have time to chat more now because all of the key members of the board relative to TECHland are waiting for us in the conference room. Some of them have early planes to catch. We will get caught up over dinner later."

Higgy ushered Harry into a huge room, not surprisingly even larger than the reception room. It was flanked on one side by a glass wall overlooking the Hudson River, and on the others by magnificent walnut paneling. The paneling was partially hidden by oil paintings, presumably also of dead benefactors. Harry wondered how a person got his or her portrait into the conference room, instead of the reception room. Did you have to be the first to die, or the one to give the most money?

At one end of the room was a wet bar, and at the other a movie screen, revealed by partially opened walnut doors. Overstuffed easy chairs and ornate tables lined the walls of the room. At its center was a massive table, obviously hewn from some very exotic wood. Seemingly, it was about half a football field in length. On the table were various accouterments of the Madison-Avenue soldier: individual microphones, briefcases, note pads, water glasses and pitchers, a few lap-top computers and the like. The inhabitants of the room had obviously come to work.

Those inhabitants were scattered around the table. Most wore conservative business suits. Some wore uniforms of different military services. A few board members were dressed like they were prepared to fix the plumbing, if that turned out to be a problem. Harry thought idly that they must be young academics whose stars were on the rise. Everyone stared expectantly at Harry as he was offered a seat at the middle of the long edge of the table, facing the river. For some reason, he thought of what he had read about Aztec human sacrifices, who were treated royally before their hearts were cut out.

The meeting was relatively pleasant, or at least not too unpleasant, considering the great variety of conflicting opinions scattered about the room. Some members of the board thought firmly that it was not appropriate to send a mere scientist on such a mission. They said so without ambiguity or reservation. Harry was not offended. He could appreciate their concerns. He already knew that this mission would require some skills that were foreign to a scientist, and more suitable for a detective—or a military man, for that matter. But, still, it was truly more of a scientific investigation than a criminal investigation or an armed conflict. Or, at least he firmly hoped that was the case!

The strongest objections to Harry's selection came from a strange coalition: a professional psychologist; a best-selling author; and a former military officer. The objections of these three different dissenters were not the same, of course. Actually, their different objections were at cross-purposes to one another.

The psychologist, Ron Reeding, was on the faculty of the University of Sussex, in southern England. He had an aristocratic air about him. Harry considered that he appeared to be self-confident to a fault. His sandy hair was cut short, with no hair out of place. His rimless glasses were situated too far down his nose, forcing him constantly to give the impression that he was looking down his nose at his companions. He appeared to have been dressed by a valet, so impeccable was his attire. It was a dark business suit with vest. The shirt was white, and it seemed to Harry that there must be starch in it. The tasteful gray tie was anchored by a pin attached to a large diamond.

Reeding had been trained in the Behavioristic approach to psychology, and therefore he strongly supported the concept of the TECHland experiment. He proposed that the evaluation team should be led by someone who was more sympathetic to Behavioristic psychology, and specifically trained in it. He also argued that the leader should be someone with proven leadership credentials, and greater stature in the scientific community than Harry. Throughout his speech, he continuously assured Harry that there was nothing personal in his objections. Harry more or less believed him. The bias was blatant, but it seemed to be only professional.

Harry responded merely that he thought that he could be fair and objective, and that the Board would have to decide for themselves on his personal credentials and qualifications. Higgy jumped in with an unqualified endorsement of Harry's skills and abilities. He pointed to several significant slices of evidence in Harry's file before them. In the end, there was little support for Reeding's proposal.

The best-selling author was a superior-acting chap by the name of Peter Gaines. Gaines was one of the participants who was apparently dressed for a garage cleaning. His denim shirt was open at the neck, with sleeves pushed up past the forearms, revealing arms covered by a white turtle-necked sweater. The tail of his shirt hung over his denim jeans, partially hiding the thread-bare edges of the pockets. The frayed ends of his trouser legs cov-ered the tops of his scuffed western boots, which were adorned with the usual silver inlays in the high heels. Harry judged the boots were an affectation, because the man lived somewhere in eastern Massachusetts.

An abundant golden mane of unbrushed dirty hair reached to the top of the collar of Gaine's shirt. The image of a casual sa-vant was completed by a pair of horn-rimmed glasses, sometimes pushed down toward the tip of his nose, sometimes abandoned to the top of his head.

Gaines had the air of one who was used to personal ponti-fications, and total reverence by others to their substance. Each sentence was spoken as if there were no possibility for rebuttal. He agreed with Ron Reeding that the mission required a more substantial presence than could be provided by a faculty mem-ber from a relatively small university in the south of the United States. But, he argued that the person should not be a professional psychologist, but a person of broader perspective. In fact, he pro-posed that the person should not even be a scientist, but from a different profession altogether. He suggested that the leader should be a prominent public figure from a background such as government, literature or the arts.

Harry had retained no respect for this shallow man since he had tried to read one of his best-sellers a few months before. The author's colossal sense of personal superiority had come across in his book. In fact, he revealed contempt for anyone who was not in the mold of Peter Gaines. Gaines leading character had only disparaging things to say about anyone who was old, poor, uneducated, uncertain of himself or herself and generally maltreated by life. Gaines was similarly harsh on those who had been shaped in the conventional image of success: who had developed impressive signatures, who wore coats and ties and who had committed themselves to firm beliefs in something more than the pursuit of adoration and wealth. In short, Gained hated stuffed-shirts, unless they resembled scruffy turtle-necked sweaters.

Gaines arguments did not play well with the Schoonover Board. Apparently, too many of them were committed to the Society of Appropriate Dress, which he disdained. Also, they had a more normal conception of what was politically correct. In any case, there was no support from anyone else for his proposal. The job was not for a dilettante.

Harry was not sure whether the board acted out of a personal dislike and mistrust of Gaines, or from a reasoned judgment against his proposal. In any case, Harry was pleased with the substance of the board's response to Gaines.

The military men in general did not like Harry's open-minded, non-aggressive style or his general academic appearance. General Bright, an ex-marine, was the third major opponent. He had in fact originally proposed that they immediately send in a marine task force. That proposal received no support.

There was nothing particularly distinguishing in Bright's appearance, except the short haircut and erect bearing of a career officer. He wore an ordinary business suit with a Marine Corps pin on his lapel. His face seemed permanently sunburned, or windburned, from close contact with the elements. Apparently, he hadn't been retired for a long time.

Bright's proposed option would involve landing an assault force in company strength on the beach inside the lagoon. The board concluded however that there was little justification for such an extreme overt military action at this time. Besides, as Higgy argued, the ensuing publicity from such an aggressive action would be very detrimental to the scientific and academic image of Schoonover. He wisely said, "Why advertise our mistakes?" Although the welfare of the population on Kipua was now their main concern, of course, still the board did want to protect its image as much as possible. They knew that they still had good work to do.

Moreover, Bright had to acknowledge that someone could be hurt in a military assault. That possibility had stalled the military option for possible later consideration.

Nevertheless, the board did agree to alert the headquarters of the marine detachment on Saipan. The marines should know about the situation in case their help was needed in a hurry. The marines could be prepared to drop specially trained paratroopers on Kipua within an hour of receiving such orders. The problem would be, of course, to find a way for communication with them. The CRASH team would carry a portable radio to Kipua for this purpose.

Harry was concerned that the military people did not really understand the theoretical issues in psychology. General Bright, for example, asked Harry to explain the major theoretical issues between the Behaviorists and the Humanists in the context of the TECHland experiment. His question was in fact rather blunt: "Tell me, Professor Hawkey, what you two opposing sides are really arguing about. Is it some obscure point that is important only to some psychologists and philosophers, or some issue that is going to make a real difference to the survival of our nation? Will some answer come out of this thing that will be definite enough that we can hang our scientific hats on it, so to speak? Can we justify the great expense of your so-called rescue expedition? I am looking for a brief answer here, one that us military types can understand. Can you answer my question in twenty-five words, more or less?"

"Absolutely, General," said Harry. "Stripped of all the technical language, and ignoring a lot of the professional stuff, the answer to your question is simple. The issue is whether or not our human society will progress most beneficially if we orient ourselves to the exclusive use of behavioral technology, thereby ignoring any of the possible unique characteristics of human beings. That is what the Behaviorists propose. The alternative is that we orient ourselves to developing virtuous people, glorifying certain unique characteristics of human beings. That is the Humanistic view. So, the behaviorists want to begin the rehabilitation of society by the judicious use of differential rewards for good behaviors, whereas the Humanists want to rehabilitate society by teaching people to cultivate such human virtues as loving one another, caring for one another, having true concern for the welfare of others."

"That sounds like religion," interjected a surprised board member. "We promote science here, not religion. That is what it says in our charter."

"Yes, it does sound like religion. But, it really is not, although it is certainly compatible with religion. Nevertheless, it is truly a psychological approach," replied Harry. "The idea is to find some ideas that work in a practical sense."

"Are there any other questions for Professor Hawkey?" asked Higgy, now striving for closure.

"Yes," said the same member of the board. "Do you mean to imply that the Humanists want to do away with all of the techno-logical advances, particularly of the last several decades? I warn you that we at Schoonover have actually been responsible for financing many of those same technical advances in behavioral science."

Harry was emphatic. "Not at all," he responded. "That is a question that we have to answer all of the time. People do not seem to want to accept our answer. The Behaviorists keep trying to burden us with that particular straw-man argument. But, it is nonsense! We Humanists are open to exhaustive use of behavioral technology. In fact, we Humanists are the open ones, the agree-able ones, the enablers. Only the Behaviorists have promulgated restrictive ideas about what assumptions and methods can be used in behavioral science. Admittedly, a few extremists among the Humanists do oppose rigorous science. Actually, they feed off the strict, uncompromising Behaviorist view. But, again, most Humanists are wholeheartedly committed to science. The point is, however, that they want an enlightened version of science that does not restrict or censor information that can truly help our society.

"In my personal view, we can make full use of all technical advances. The point is that such use must not dominate our thinking. It must be a tool in the service of virtuous people. People must not be subservient to the technology. I hope that point is clear. There has been a lot of confusion about it in the past. I am sorry if I came across too strong, but it is an important issue for me.

"Now, are there any more questions for me?"

"I do not have a question, but I do wish to lodge for the record a strong exception to your interpretation of the Behavioristic/Humanistic debate," blurted Ron Reeding. "I say that the Humanistic view would dismantle science. But, I do not think that we should argue about it now."

"I agree," said Harry. "I will discuss the point with you at some later time when it is convenient and appropriate."

"I have a question, Professor Hawkey," said General Bright. "I want to know how you can be sure that the loving responses, and so forth, that you propose will be more effective than the so-called good behaviors coveted, and thus rewarded, by the Behaviorists? And how are either of these superior to a well-led company of well-trained marines?"

"First, I have to say that there is no way to be sure about anything so important," Harry admitted. "I hasten to admit that specific hard fact up-front. But, there are nevertheless lines of evidence to suggest that the Humanistic way is superior. One line of evidence is that the only social programs that seem to be effective in the long run have a spiritual basis. I do not mean necessarily religious. I mean spiritual in the sense that they are based on human values, such as love, freedom and human dignity. That means that they are conducted by people who show the love and caring for their clients that we have been talking about.

"The second line of empirical evidence is the very data of the TECHland experiment that you yourself have sponsored. From what we can tell to this point, the result of trying to implement a rigorously strict version of the Behavioristic plan is chaos and disaster. Of course, the final conclusion on that point will have to wait for a report from the CRASH team after the team gathers all of the data on the spot at Kipua, and then fully analyzes it."

"But, Sir, you have not answered my question about how your ideas are superior to the firepower of a company of marines," persisted the general.

Harry responded: "When firepower is needed and appropriate, it should be used. There is surely no better source of it than a first-class company of marines. But, I believe that even the marines prefer to work out peaceable solutions when that is possible. They are reluctant to use their awesome firepower unless it is absolutely necessary. Right?"

Bright nodded, and smiled his agreement.

Harry continued: "Right. Therefore, we want to apply behavioral science so that we do not have to use military might, or military science, if you prefer. But, to be sure, the marines will be our ace in the hole."

"Right on! Good answer!" exclaimed the general, pumping his fist in the air. "We do aim to keep the peace."

"All of this means, as I am sure that you can see," said Harry, "that the stakes are high, very high. You need to send the very best team and the very best leader that you can get. Whether or not I would be the best leader is for you to decide. I can only promise to do my best if I am selected."

"We really cannot ask for more than that," said General Bright. "That is all I ever asked of my field commanders. You will do."

In the end, the board yielded to the pleas of Higgy to try to solve their problems at a professional level of science and academics. Higgy argued that, at first, the softer measures would create less conflict and publicity. And, in truth, the Schoonover board did not actually know the exact situation on Kipua—whether or not it was sufficiently out of control to require armed interventions.

Higgy argued that the CRASH team could advise them within a relatively short time whether or not more powerful measures were necessary. Unfortunately, radio communication with the island had been silenced in some way. They would not know anything more for a while until the authorities on the island could communicate with them through some kind of surface transportation. Apparently, at the moment, that sort of emergency would probably require a native to paddle by canoe to a neighboring island.

There were still some objections from some of the members who had formerly served in military careers. Those who objected made it clear that there was no problem with Harry's credentials and abilities as an educator and scientist. They simply thought that the task itself did not require an educator and scientist, but a military commander, or at least a policeman. In their view, a combat veteran or a streetwise cop was needed to cope with the immediate crisis. But, now General Bright was an ally. He strongly supported Harry, saying that this was an academic that he could trust to have sense.

In any case, Harry was given the commission and a generous budget to solve whatever problems that then existed on Kipua. The board was particularly interested in any problems on the island that could reasonably be considered as direct consequences of the TECHland experiment because of their personal responsibility. They did not want the mission to fail because corners were cut in an attempt to save a few nickels.

TEN

A s he finished packing his bags for the long trip to Kipua, Harry admitted to himself that truthfully he never thought that he would become involved with the TECHland experiment on Kipua in person and on the spot. They had dangled the well-baited hook in front of him. Harry could not in any way resist the lure of such attractive bait as it turned out to be.

So, Schoonover made Harry an offer that he could hardly refuse. They would pay double his university salary for as long as it took. They would also square it with Ivey Southern for a replacement professor, if it appeared that the project would run into the fall semester. Higgy also agreed to let Harry pick his own three-member team of professional psychologists from anywhere in the world. That part of the deal assumed, of course, that Harry could get these prestigious psychologists to agree to serve. He was sure that he had the contacts to pull it off.

It was all so fast, Harry really had little time for second thoughts. He had been primed to accept their offer anyway, for humanitarian reasons. So, when the lucrative offer was made, he swallowed it whole. Thus, the hook had been set.

Once Harry had made the decision to go, the succeeding events were mostly out of his hands. The people at Schoonover asked him to name the proposed members of his rescue team, and arranged immediate telephone calls. Harry had no problem in gaining acceptance from his nominees: Patience Patrick, from the University of New South Wales in Australia; Rudy Freibauer, from SUNY in New York; and Deron Williams, from the Loosened Fetters League in Cleveland. Each of these volunteers understood the world-class implications of the project.

Then, the Schoonover people took over all details of the arrangements. The travel plans and other provisions for the trip had to be made with absolute dispatch. Indeed, the Schoonover people were models of efficiency.

So, there Harry was. He certainly never thought that the speed and scope of the disaster would be so great, and thus merit such haste to begin the rescue. Apparently, no one else had anticipated the worst-case scenario either.

Nevertheless, still he was afraid for the team members. There was no doubt about that! Harry understood that his state of fear needed to be analyzed to discover its real nature, its scope, its causes. He conceded to himself that to be afraid was actually sensible at times. He wondered to what extent his fear was the result of legitimate perils that would make any thinking person sweat. The stakes were so high that it would be arrogant—not to say, foolish—to be sure of success here, or in fact in any research endeavor. He knew that he would surely be a fool if he were not afraid. And he was sure that his Momma did not raise a fool!

If he did not have some substantial degree of conviction that he could handle the job, ethically he would have to withdraw at once. It was never too late to resign. But, he knew that he would hate himself if he gave up. "No!" Harry practically said it out loud, "I do not quit; I can handle it. Fundamentally, it is research, and research is what I do." Hopefully, it was the last time that he would have to make such an affirmation to himself.

Harry also knew that time was important here. It would take too much precious time for Schoonover to replace him. He owed it to Higgy to see this thing through. "So," he thought, "on with the game!"

Harry had been selected for the job because, to be sure, he was an experimental psychologist—which the job obviously required. So, he told himself to act like a professional, to call on what he knew about problem-solving and the interpretation of data. He must think of this as just another problem-solving task. It was too important for him to make any foolish mistakes though, although he knew that anyone was capable of those. Perhaps he could avoid them by warning himself against them. "So," he whispered to himself with determination, "do not make simple mistakes by simply being careless! Think about what you are doing."

The most unnecessary mistake of all was not to write things down. Anyone could write the data down for the record. Harry was determined to get everything on paper. He had packed several bound notebooks for the purpose. Once everything was recorded, he would be able to come back to the recorded data, to go over and over it from different angles. Eventually, he might be able to make some sense of it. He reassured himself that usually he could do that rather well.

So, he knew that he must set down the facts so that they could be studied later by others with cool heads, open minds and skills at understanding such things. If disasters must happen, society must learn what it can from them. They needed to salvage any good that was possible. The global cultures must be enabled to profit from what is happening there, in any case. From the ashes, society must develop the ability to draft new and improved plans for a better world than had been revealed recently.

As was his habit, Harry carefully warned himself against reaching premature conclusions. His team must guard against simply seeing and hearing what some members were fully convinced that they would see and hear. The diversity of views by other members of the team would help with that problem. The hope was that the different biases would wash out, mutually cancel effects, so that collectively the team would be able to see the truth.

The biggest problem was objectivity, as was always true in science. The team must discipline itself to view this fact-finding trip as a scientific project. It was science, of course! The detective work was just science in the real world without the comfort of fine laboratory controls. So, it was tougher than research in a comfortable, controlled laboratory.

But, Harry reminded himself that it would be a team effort. He did not have to carry the full responsibility alone. The experienced scientists with him would provide a good example of science ideally in action. He would have to handle them right. They must focus on science, and not personality or ideological cloaks. There should be no winners or losers. Actually, they would all be winners, or indeed they would all be dead losers.

Harry also reminded himself that he must caution the team about Groupthink. Groupthink is the feeling of group togetherness that causes pressures toward conformity and consensus on the members of a problem-solving group, despite good reasons for dissent. Thus, everyone must speak his or her mind without holding back because of counterproductive fears about causing dissension within the group. Unrestrained freedom of speech was essential for any good team, scientific or otherwise. It was needed for any group that could be expected to achieve a good solution for the problems it faced. A reasonable level of disagreement and tension was actually good. Of course, too high a level of argument could be counterproductive.

Harry really did not believe that there would be too much to worry about on that score, though. Really, there would not be too much of a danger from agreement and harmony. The reason in a few words was that Patience Patrick would be along as a member of the team. That should do it! If anyone were ever misnamed, she was the one! Her given name was the result of the Australian habit of designating things by their opposites. Because the members of her family were noted for their impulsive styles, and in fact she herself had been born prematurely, the choice of her name had not been difficult. So, Patience could be very impatient with those who disagreed with her. One reason was obvious: She was usually right.

Indeed, Harry was glad that she would be along because she was a good, bright and experienced researcher. She always spoke her mind, and the team would need to know what that excellent mind had to offer. Open contributions were what counted here. What did it matter if the group did argue a lot, as long as the arguments got the group to some useful place scientifically? "So, on to work!" he said softly to himself.

Harry had always liked Patience. He was not sure how she felt about him. The reason was her habit of telling things the way she saw them. Harry had a feeling, however, that she held back a bit in verbalizing his good qualities, if indeed she perceived any.

Patience and Harry came from quite different theoretical orientations. While he was a Humanist, she was a Behaviorist. That meant that there was little room for agreements between them about theoretical issues in psychology.

"Well," thought Harry, "I am committed now. So, Harry, my boy, look ahead."

He finished his packing and took all of the bags down to the front hall while he waited for his cab. The cabbie would have to help him with all of the stuff that he was taking. As he settled down on the sofa in the living room, his thoughts returned to Kipua.

The situation on the island appeared undeniably bad. He took no joy in that, although it was direct empirical justification for what he had been saying—even screaming in a civilized way—as a professional for years. He wished that he did not have to be a witness, though. Truthfully, the actual events seemed almost unbelievable. But, nevertheless, they did happen on that very island with hundreds of witnesses.

The task for the team would not be to assess whether or not the TECHland experiment failed. That would apparently not be necessary, because early reports indicated clearly that the experiment was a resounding failure. The question actually was: Was the failure caused by inappropriate personalities and bad execution, or by a failure of the original scientific and methodological premises.

Harry told himself that, for now, he must try to relax. There would be plenty of time later to psych himself and the team for the big push. Relaxation required that he entertain pleasant thoughts. That, as usual for him, meant to think about Lottie and the kids. It was funny for him to still be calling them kids. They were both grown up, and Harry Jr. had gone off to college. Harry's thoughts went back, as always, to Lottie. He really missed her still.

* * * * * *

Harry was asleep when the cab arrived. The insistent honking of the horn jerked him to consciousness. His life would be run by responsibilities for the next several weeks or months. He was not happy about the prospect.

So, finally, he and the cabbie schlepped all of his belongings to the cab. The thought occurred to him that a researcher often assumed the characteristics of a pack mule. Such duties were never in his contract.

Well, now he was off on his mission. He sincerely hoped that he would not be sorry for his decision to go.

* * * * * *

The flight attendant was methodically working her way down the aisle with the coffee urn. Harry followed her frustratingly slow progress with eager anticipation. He felt a burning hole where his stomach should have been. In his state of need, the delivery procedure for the coffee seemed painfully mechanical, repetitive and creeping. Actually, the process was entirely efficient, and as speedy as personal service could be accomplished. And, the service was as personal as a pretty woman could make it. There was the same sweet smile, the identical question and only a little variation in the response, depending on the request of the passengers. The attendant had replaced her uniform jacket with a functional apron. The effect was not quite homey, but it was pleasant.

Harry wondered idly how a person could abide such repetition on the job. Strangely, the repetitive aspect of teaching the same university courses year after year had never bothered him. But, there was, of course, always an interval of at least a semester between the repetition. And, the students were always new. They always revealed widely different personality characteristics. Also, the material for the course itself was always under continuous revision.

The key to freshness was to see the students as persons, and not as just other faceless, nameless space holders taking the course another year. You had to see the course material as evolving and exciting. Harry guessed the flight attendants must have the same interest in their work that he had in his. But, it must be difficult to see each passenger on each flight as an individual person. There is really not much chance to get acquainted.

Harry interrupted his reverie to note how odd it was for such a minor event as the serving of a beverage to be so important when a body was helplessly incarcerated on an airplane for a long flight. He had felt the same way about chow time in the Navy after he had been at sea for a few days. He had heard that prisoners in jail had the same feelings. Everybody craves a novel break in the routines of life.

Then, the professor part of Harry's mind took over. He concluded that his idle thinking was probably simply avoidance behavior. It was obviously designed to distract his burdened mind from his serious problems. He was really anxious about the future. He had to admit it to himself. He needed to relax. So, he needed a coffee fix, to help him relax, now as much as he ever had before in his life.

Lottie used to say that it was wrong for him to refer to his cherished cup of coffee as a fix, because it seemed to be making light of serious addictions. As usual, she was right. There was no doubt about that. But, nevertheless, coffee really was an addiction for him. That, unfortunately, was the literal truth, stripped of false rationalizations.

Harry recognized that his usual tendency to commit himself fully to any task, any that he was at all willing to undertake, was often a problem for him. Sometimes, it meant that he clung to a project like a bulldog clamped its jaws on an enemy, when he should let go for a while—or perhaps even permanently. You cannot take care of other pressing matters with your jaws clenched firmly on some different problem. Fortunately for him, Lottie had usually stepped in to bail him out of the troubles that this habit had so often produced for him.

At last, the coffee cart arrived at Harry's row of seats. He could finally relax over the hot brew. The coffee relaxed him the same way that some people relaxed over booze and cigarettes. Coffee was, of course, a lesser evil than the other two. He could, therefore, by this reasoning, dampen his conscience a little bit over his unbridled craving for it.

It had been an exhausting several days, with a long journey at the end. First was the flight to New York for the meeting at Schoonover. Then came the tiring transcontinental flight to San Francisco. He had insisted that he stop there overnight. Among other things, it gave him a chance to renew his acquaintance with the walk-away shrimp cocktail at Fisherman's Wharf.

But, it was lonely, even with friends. The last time he had been there, he and Lottie had such a good time. They met some friends later for dinner in Chinatown. For him, that was one of the best of the good old days.

Today, they had taken an early morning flight to Hawaii. After lunch, they took off for Saipan, stopping briefly for re-fueling at Wake Island. Harry thought how the days were really long when you were heading west. He felt chased by a sun which never went down. It really messed up the body's circadian rhythm. It made the body, as well as the mind, so very tired. Lately, longer days were the last thing he needed. "But," he thought ruefully, "for what is ahead, the days will probably not be long enough."

The plane was about to land on Saipan. Harry hoped that Higgy's man would be there to meet them. They needed him to help get them on the shuttle boat to Kipua. The group did not have much time to get on board before the boat shoved off. If they missed this trip they would be in big trouble. The boat did not come back again for a month. If that happened, the team would have to find a seaplane, or some other alternative means of travel.

Harry was really not looking forward to the boat trip. He always got seasick. "Oh, well," he thought, "it is only for twenty-four hours. I can stand on my head for that long."

The plan was for Patience to meet them at the airport on Saipan. She was to come straight from Sydney to the Saipan airport. Together, they would motor across town to the docks.

Harry was looking forward to seeing Patience. He had not seen her since the last convention in L. A., maybe three years ago. Lottie had recently died then, and Patience did her best to help him over the difficult time. At times, he had even enjoyed himself. Patience uniformly insisted that everyone around her have a corking good time.

Harry knew that Patience would be a tower of strength on this mission. She had a good combination of professional and personal skills. And Patience always said exactly what she thought, whether you wanted to hear it or not. She was a lot like Lottie in that respect. On this trip the team would want to hear everything that Patience had to say.

In a sense, Patience was added to the team as a sort of devil's advocate. She had received her doctorate under Skinner at Harvard in 1979. Since then, she had been a very strong proponent of Skinnerian views. Harry considered her to be strongly doctrinaire, which was a common characteristic of Skinnerians. He believed, however, that she did eventually respond to reasoned argument. She was also very bright. That was critical. A person could not just dismiss her arguments as biased Skinnerian doctrine, and settle into one's thinking as usual. You had to listen carefully to her. Otherwise, you might be very sorry.

Harry also knew from personal experience that Patience could also overpower you with her personality when her argument was weak. You had to be alert all of the time about where she was coming from in each discussion. If you stayed alert to the difference between logical argument and the force of personality, it was no problem. Harry was sure that she had other skills to more than compensate for her biases. His job was to see to it that she was a directed dynamo on the team, and not the proverbial loose cannon. He said softly to himself, "I guess that is why I am being paid the big bucks. Right!"

Rudy Freibauer, sitting next to Harry, gave balance to the team as a general counterweight to Patience. In Harry's opinion, he was probably even more intelligent than Patience. And he was a totally different personality. He was quiet and outwardly relaxed, a kind of human security blanket. In Harry's judgment, however, Rudy frequently shut up when he should resolutely have spoken up. Almost invariably, Rudy knew more about the subject than the expert speaker. Harry thought that Rudy really needed a little assertiveness training. But, to be sure, he as the team leader considered that particular failing in a personality to be far better for a working team member than the tendency of some people to speak up when they should very well shut up.

Rudy was one of the widest-read people that Harry had ever known. His range of interests and knowledge truly astonished everyone when he did speak up. Harry was, in fact, absolutely sure that Rudy knew something about everything.

Rudy sincerely liked Patience, as he tended to like everyone. But, most of the time he did not quite know how to take her. Despite his grand sense of humor, he always was serious about his science. He would never suggest an idea that he had not thought about a great deal. When Patience came out with some off-the-wall opinion, he would take it seriously, as usual. Then he would be totally flabbergasted when he discovered that Patience was just having fun by trying to beguile or confuse him to see what would happen.

Nevertheless, Patience had a lot of respect for Rudy's academic intelligence, if not for his personal style. Patience was a frequent world traveler. Rudy was more at home with a delicatessen pickle in Manhattan than with tea and cakes at tea time somewhere on the continent.

As one might expect from someone whose grandparents did not survive the Holocaust, Rudy was vitally concerned with issues of freedom, dignity, justice and such. Harry did not consider him bitter about what happened to his family. But, nevertheless, Rudy was totally committed to human welfare, particularly for minorities. To be sure, the emphasis on one particular group did sound a bit inconsistent. Nevertheless, Rudy was genuinely concerned about all others. He proved it by his willingness to work sacrificially on their behalf.

Rudy had been selected for the team because he was an experimentalist and very eclectic theoretically. He was easily conversant with any theory that Harry could name. Once a theory was mentioned, Rudy would immediately set himself to thinking about how the theory could be tested. If he had a specific theoretical preference, he was still able to keep it quite a secret. At least, no one had been able to find out what it was.

Also, Harry considered Rudy to have just about the best sense of humor of anyone around. He really liked Rudy.

Across the aisle, on the other side of Rudy, was the fourth member of the team, Joseph Deron Williams—"Posh" to his friends. Harry was extremely happy to include himself among that large number. Posh was the only black member of the team. He certainly had not been selected just for racial balance, however. The record would show that Posh was a very talented and productive person.

Posh had been a premier running back in Big 10 football. He gave up the promising chance for a lucrative career in the National Football League to take a job with the Loosened Fetters League. The LFL was a private philanthropic organization dedicated to improving the lives of African-American youths. Posh traveled about the country as a sort of professional agitator. He lectured to various groups, and counseled them on relevant issues. He always spoke out when he saw conditions that particularly needed attention and, therefore, publicity. Probably, his greatest value to all youth was to serve as a quintessential role model of human possibilities.

Personally, Harry thought that Posh's job was very important for anyone to do. Nevertheless, many conservative critics thought that the job was just trouble-making at its worst. Harry ordinarily did not like people who were looking for trouble. The critical difference for him was that Posh was truly trying to make life better for the kids from minority segments of the population. He was not simply trying to make life miserable for those who did not care, who had much and would not help. Posh vastly preferred peace. He made trouble only when friendly persuasion failed after a sincere effort in a righteous cause. He was, of course, highly successful, whichever method he used.

Posh would have succeeded in the other league, too—the football one. He was the type of person who would surely succeed in any league that he tried. He was the kind of guy that a person like Harry would love to hate because he was so multi-talented. Every decent person found out, however, that they had to love him instead. He was genuine to a core of precious metal.

Posh got his nickname in Junior High School when his father became Assistant Principal of his school in a poor section of Cleveland. The name called attention to the fact that Posh was so much better off financially and socially than his classmates. In Harry's opinion, it apparently was never meant in a mean spirit. Then, as today, everyone liked and respected Posh. His nickname actually reflected the fact that everyone viewed him as a really first-class person. He truly was an excellent role model for everyone, and not just for the black youth to whom he had dedicated his life. In addition to being a star athlete and good student, he had always been very popular with fellow students and co-workers, regardless of race, creed and so forth.

Posh's intelligence and drive enabled him to receive his Master's degree in social work from Ohio State while he was fulfilling his duties full time at LFL. Naturally, he did well at both tasks. He had been accepted for doctoral study at several prestigious universities, but had decided to take a brief break from graduate work in order to concentrate on his social mission. When he resumed graduate study, he would probably still stay on at the LFL. No one doubted his ability to carry out both demanding tasks at once.

Harry sincerely felt that, whatever your fight in life, you wanted somebody like Posh on your side. He felt more comfortable just thinking that Posh was here.

Sitting with Posh was the on-site representative of Schoonover, strong and efficient Kate Okanarski. She was the fifth and final member of the team. It would be difficult for anyone to know how to describe Kate's exact job with the CRASH team in a way that would be officially accurate and still adequate to do it justice. She was certainly much more than a research administrator, which was her official title of record. Also, she was simultaneously a recording and corresponding secretary, a purchasing agent, office manager, resource person, advisor, confidant, confessor and, to Harry's mind, altogether the only truly indispensable member of the team.

Kate had never married. Harry suspected that her unconscious air of efficiency and self-sufficiency had put off many worthy suitors. He himself was certainly not put off by Kate's capability. But, he did have to admit secretly to himself that he was a little bit threatened by it. Harry always had a tendency to compare himself to the best. But, surely, Kate was attractive enough in both appearance and personality to have received many offers of marriage. Probably, there were simply many men who could not measure up to what she was seeking, and had a perfect right to expect. It was not his business, of course, but Harry thought that Kate could make some lucky man very happy.

Although Kate was not a professional psychologist, she was very knowledgeable about psychology. But, more than that, she was a mature thinker. Therefore, she made an excellent lay representative on the team, a sort of consumer representative. If it turned out that the team could not achieve a consensus on an issue before it, she would then cast a vote equal to that of anyone else. Harry was indeed glad to have her along.

Harry was extremely proud of his team. He was also proud of himself that he had succeeded in putting it together. If any team could be successful on Kipua, he was confident that his team could do it.

* * * * * *

Posh was ten years old when he had his first serious fist fight. He was not accustomed to fighting, because it was not his nature to be angry. He just wanted to be friends, to get along. Usually the other kids could say pretty much what they wanted to, or about, Posh, and he would laugh it off. He knew that the bad things were not true, anyway. But, this day, Derek Holloway had gone too far. Derek had made some nasty remarks about the new clothes that Posh's mom had bought lovingly for him. Posh was very proud of the new outfit. It was a brown windbreaker, and matching slacks. Best of all, it was brand new, not one of the hand-me-downs that Posh so often inherited from his older brothers.

Derek had said, in a snotty tone, that his dumb outfit looked like it had been soaked in moose poop. Somehow, this triggered a demon in Posh. He beat up on Derek all of the way to his own doorstep. But, he never really satisfied his need to punish Derek for the affront. That sense of dissatisfaction always confused and troubled Posh.

Derek's father had called the principal, of course. The incident had occurred on the way home from school, and that made it a school offense. The rules were that fighting was a school issue until you had crossed the threshold of your front door. Then, you could come outside again, and really pound somebody, with only your parents, and theirs, to worry about.

Posh's father, Josiah, sat him down for a long talk. He explained that Derek was probably jealous of not only the new clothes, but also of the attention from Posh's mother. Josiah pointed out that Derek had to fend for himself pretty much. Derek was often alone because his parents were away constantly, trying to find enough food for their children.

His father taught Posh a lesson in compassion that day. Posh never forgot it. Posh made sure that later Derek Holloway became his best friend. Derek was still his best friend.

* * * * * *

The meeting with Dean Zlotnik was proceeding about as Patience had anticipated. Zlotnick was a large man. The loosely knit sweater that he wore made him appear absolutely gigantic. A full beard added to the impression of his size. His bushy eyebrows almost met the beard and the thick mass of hair above in a way that obscured most of his face, except for the darting eyes. The eyes, like the rest of him, were in constant motion. Even his horn-rimmed glasses were large. Now he was swinging them around by one ear support as he concentrated on the problem at hand. Occasionally, he would put them on his nose so that he could gaze intently at Patience as she spoke. He continuously paced up and down behind his desk as he spoke. Patience often thought that the Dean would be speechless if he were confined to a chair.

Boris Zlotnik was noted for his conservative attitudes and pedestrian approach to life. He had been imported from the University of Leningrad to be the chairman of the chemistry department at Royal University in New South Wales. Although his massive build and gross features gave the first impression of a longshoreman or lumberjack, he was quite astute and clever in dealing with people, particularly in the academic setting. He had quickly displayed the appropriate lobbying skills to assume a leadership position on the faculty. When the deanship position became open, he jumped to apply quickly.

Zlotnik had been selected for the job, although there were many better qualified people on the campus. To be sure, Zlotnick had better skills at securing a job than he had in performing it once it had been secured. There were surely many better qualified women, including Patience herself. Her friends had urged her to apply for the job. She had not felt ready emotionally for full-time administrative duties at the time. She still wanted to be fully active in research and writing. Later, she might try her hand at higher administration.

In truth, she was also afraid that the responsibilities of deanship might curtail her long-term habit of deciding, on a moment's whim, to take off on an adventure to some exotic place. Actually, depending upon the particular whim, it could also be some pedestrian place. But, Patience liked to feel free. It now occurred to her that it was a strange feeling for a Behaviorist to have.

Now, the dean was worried that her somewhat hasty departure from the premises just at this time would throw the psychology department into chaos. She was the hard-working chair, and master negotiator, that had made it work for the last two years.

Patience now contained her anger at Zlotnick with some difficulty. She explained, more or less patiently, that such dithering with the status quo was often a beneficial impetus to vitality in an organization. She was sure that the former chair, Nigel Faircloth, could step in and take over without losing a beat.

Then, Patience artfully played her ace in the hole. It was the hole card that would surely bring any college administrator into line. She said, "Boris, you know that the world is watching what is happening on Kipua. If this university has a part in saving the situation, it will reflect well on this entire administration. It will add to the prestige of Royal University. If you refuse to help, everyone will be wondering why. They will think that we do not have the expertise here, or that we don't care. You must let me go. I promise that I will make you proud."

It worked, of course. Boris smiled broadly like he had just received an early Christmas present. The glasses twisted a bit more rapidly. "Okay," he said. "I see your point. We all must make some sacrifices in such dire crises. I too will do my part to make it work. I grant your request for a leave. Make plans to leave immediately.

"Do not worry about us. Nigel and I will take care of things here. So, go, and be careful. I wish you the best of luck, and good sailing."

As they shook hands in parting, Patience was elated. She loved adventure, and she was looking forward to meeting the challenges with old friends. She had always liked Harry Hawkey, even though he was way off in his theoretical thinking. Personally, she thought that he was about as exciting as a picnic at your grandmother's house. He was bright enough, but he let his emotions get in the way of his scientific judgment. She would have to work on him, she was sure, to help him solve the problems on Kipua.

Patience hurried to the sporty convertible parked in the dean's space in front of the administration building. She jumped in, and sped, as usual, toward her apartment. Most of the faculty had purchased homes in town. Patience did not like all of the trials of ownership—yard work and such—preferring to spend her evenings in the lab, and in writing, or in just being convivial with friends. The apartment let her feel free to travel when the notion struck, as it often did.

Back at her apartment, Patience packed with the skill of one who has exercised the routine often. She thought that she did not have to worry on this trip about getting wrinkles in ball gowns. Then, she chuckled at her own joke. After a few chuckles, she laughed out loud. Was the joke that funny, or was she just excited?

As usual, Patience made sure that she had a sufficient assortment of hats for all occasions. She had a basic arsenal of about a dozen hats. With a box full of many extra bows, artificial flowers and whatnots, she could produce an infinite number of individual creations. Some of her friends thought that perhaps she was prouder of her creativity in hats than she was of her numerous scientific achievements. That wasn't entirely true, but Patience never disputed it.

Following her usual routine, Patience was on her way to the airport within two hours. Her philosophy about traveling was that she would make do without anything that she had forgotten. She knew that the brain that she carried along would be the only truly essential piece of equipment for any trip anywhere, but especially this one.

ELEVEN

PATIENCE WAS WAITING AT THE AIRPORT, as full of vitality and enthusi-asm as ever. Harry was surprised at how glad he was to see her. But, truly he should not have been surprised. He always liked and admired Patience. There was never a dull moment around her. They always had fun together, although she was always urging him to loosen up.

As usual, Patience was wearing a wild hat, with floppy brim, and cascade of flowers. Her white T-shirt, designer jeans and open sandals made her look to Harry like she was off to the Riviera for a fun vacation. But, he did not worry. He knew that she would be appropriately serious when the need for that arrived.

Harry reflected that Patience was actually quite pretty. In keeping with modern philosophy, she usually did nothing me-chanically heroic to emphasize her physical beauty. She was fond of functional, rather than flashy, clothing, except for the hats. Ap-parently, the functional aspect was determined primarily by her capricious desire of the moment. Usually, the result was rather pleasing in Harry's undeveloped opinion. Of course, Harry had decided long ago that, when a woman had a good figure, as did Patience, she would usually look good in just about anything she wore.

The one thing that Patience did to enhance her physical beauty was to smile often. When she smiled, her eyes narrowed in an appealing way. Her smile produced creases about her eyes that created a truly attractive effect in Harry's opinion. Some people smile with just their mouth. Patience smiled with her whole face.

So, all in all, Harry had lots of reasons to be delighted that Patience would be a part of his team. But, he could only recognize the professional ones.

Harry was thankful that Higgy's man—actually, it was a woman, Myoshi Kenobi—met the team at the Saipan airport without any problems. Myoshi had arranged for several cabs, and had them lined up before the terminal. Patience's gear had already been loaded. The entire entourage hastily crammed themselves into the cabs. Harry was not prepared for the wild dash to the docks through streets that were far too narrow for such speeds. Harry could only imagine what Schoonover had promised the cabbies to achieve such dedication to quick service.

Anyway, they made it to the docks actually with time to spare. As appropriate to the person in charge, the ship's captain, Captain Kebomba, a native of the islands, was intently studying his watch as their group screeched up to the moored ship. Obviously, they could not have counted on Kebomba to wait for them for long.

The transportation to Kipua, which was the second island down from Saipan in the archipelago, would be provided by the island shuttle boat, *Cornucopia*. The *Cornucopia* was about 100 feet long, and seemingly about as wide. That was an exaggeration, Harry knew, but it suggested how the ship was built for stability and large cargoes, instead of speed. Captain Kebomba told Harry that the top speed fully loaded was about five knots per hour. Harry was not sure whether the slow speed of the ship was reason to keep a punctual schedule, or to forget factors of time altogether.

The slow speed of the ship suited Harry fine, in some way. He could not shake the dread of Kipua. Surely, he knew speed was important to the mission. But, a deep part of him never really wanted to arrive on the ill-fated island.

Saipan was the largest island in a chain, located slightly below the center of a north-south string of islands, with each of the ends swinging slightly off to the west. The Schoonover file copy of Burnhouse's map showed that Kipua was about midway between Saipan and the island of Guam, which was the southernmost island in the archipelago.

The trip should take about a day, because Schoonover had arranged with the steamer company to re-arrange the *Cornucopia's* schedule. They would by-pass the closer islands in order to reach Kipua at the earliest time. Harry thought, "Perhaps, my dread

190 E. RAE HARCUM

will stop when I start working. We have so much to do in so little time."

Every view that they had seen so far had been just beautiful, except for the clothing manufacturing sheds near the airport on Saipan. Those sheds were absolutely a throwback to the last century. In Harry's view, the hot and humid climate of the islands really gave new gritty meaning to the word, "sweatshop."

The weather now was great, with just a few towering plumes of clouds. The dark blue of the ocean was a magnificent match to the pure light blue of the morning sky. It was difficult for Harry to think of strife and death and onerous work in such a calm setting. Under other conditions, it would be the perfect place to just let the cares of the world drop away. He would have to remember this perfection and this location, if he ever took another vacation.

Harry could not shake the feeling of dread and horror for what they would find on Kipua. He prayed that their communal fears would prove to be much exaggerated.

But, work they must, and worry they must, it seemed. As soon as they had dropped their luggage in their cabins, Harry called the CRASH team together for a brief meeting. The idea was to start them off by getting their heads into the task ahead. It was basically a psychological warm-up for the brain, just like the warm-up for the muscles before an athletic contest.

In order to keep the first meeting relaxed and informal, Harry had asked for the group to gather around the hatch on the main deck behind the pilot house and cabins. It was too breezy on deck to examine any documents; that would come later. The boxes that they were sitting on were not too comfortable, so they would not meet for long this first time.

Everyone settled down on his or her box, or on the hatch cover. They looked at Harry intently, as if they expected a classic speech. The collective force of their gazes was actually unsettling to him. He didn't know why, really. He had faced intense looks many times before. The stakes were higher in this particular game, though.

Fortunately, Harry had rehearsed his opening lines: "Well, guys and gals, this is the first official meeting of the team. First, I want to thank you all again for agreeing to serve. I really appreciate it."

There was an affirming chorus of, "De nada. No problem. Sure," and the like from the group. Harry warmed to the group. They were a nice bunch. Of course, they would make an excellent team.

Harry, nodding his gratitude, moved on. "Next, I want to get us started on thinking about what we want to accomplish. You all know one another, and that is a plus. You will get to know each other a lot better before we are through with this business." He had not meant for this pronouncement to sound so ominous. He knew that he had overdone it when Rudy gave an exaggerated mocking pantomime of total despair. The group laughter indicated that the team was still loose.

Harry looked about the horizon, and up at the sky, as if to plead for guidance in the next thing that he was about to say. It was also a come-back to Rudy. In any case, Harry wanted to say the next thought just right. The tenor of the mission—perhaps its very success—hung on whether or not they would accept his next utterance. He also wanted to build a pregnant pause so that the group would be fully concentrating on what he said.

But, there were no messages of wisdom in the clouds above, or in the waves below. He was left with only the devices of his own verbal skills and basic sincerity to gain acceptance for his next proposal. So he plunged resolutely on.

"The first thing to say is that if we are to be successful in this project, we must trust and respect each other enough to disagree, if that is the way we feel. We must even fight with each other, in a genteel way, of course, if that is necessary to be productive. I hope you will understand what I mean. We do not want to disagree simply for the sake of disagreement. That is not the point. But, actually, that would surely be better than just to agree simply for the sake of agreement. If we disagree, we want to be comfortable with it.

"The need for that kind of dedication, to accept disagreement, is one of the reasons we picked people who knew one another. You can get along without letting personal matters get in the way of your judgment. We are all professionals. That means something. It means that nothing we say in the course of our deliberations should ever be taken personally. We do not want any personal feelings or need for group solidarity, or a sense of team spirit, to cause anyone to give his or her approval to something that he or she does not truly believe and accept."

"Don't worry about that, Big Bwana," laughed Patience. "When you are stupid, I will tell you so."

Everyone joined in the laughter. It seemed to come easily, not forced. Harry was relieved. Hopefully, they would still be friends when this chore is over.

Harry faked a huge smile at Patience. Then, he said in exaggerated seriousness, "Would you believe that I wasn't worried in the slightest about your speaking your mind, O Warrior Queen of the Outback? I was worried that you wouldn't let anyone else talk."

Patience said nothing. She merely thumbed her nose at him. But, he could tell that her smile was genuine because there was the telltale crease about the eyes.

"Ignoring the rude communication from Dr. Patience," said Harry, "I will continue." Now, he too, was laughing.

Harry knew that the group would be appropriately serious when the need for it was upon them. For now, he appreciated the fun. The levity now merely reflected the fact that they knew what he was getting at.

"Go ahead. Have your fun, while you can," he said. "But, I must get this said before we go farther. Then I will not say it again.

"You are a member of the team because we want to have your views—I emphasize, *your* views—on the table for discussion, along with all of the others. The team as a group may override you when you disagree. That is okay. Don't worry about it. Intelligent people do disagree at times. But, we need to know that we are in fact overriding someone's point of view, if indeed that is what we are doing. We do not want to be making another choice, perhaps a weaker one, just because of ignorance about your views. We are not going to be stopped in our work just because one person does not agree. So, don't worry about destroying unanimity, or injecting dissent in the group. I assume that you all know about Groupthink. Is that right? That is what I am talking about here."

All of the psychologists, except Patience, nodded. Kate slowly shook her head.

"The rest of you bear with me a second while I explain to Patience and Kate. Okay?"

Turning to them, he explained, "Groupthink is a concept in social psychology. It refers to the tendency for people in group discussions to strive for consensus of opinion, even though the consensus may come at the expense of productivity for the group. Groupthink is in fact always a factor whenever there is a group discussion aimed at making a group decision. There are a number of plans for combating it, because, when it occurs, it means that there are some extraneous factors, other than the relevant facts, that are contributing to the group decision."

"But, I always thought that brainstorming was productive," objected Patience. "I thought that the advantage was that two heads were better than one."

"Well, they can be," responded Harry, "but only if you are careful to avoid the kinds of things that I have been talking about. You see, the two heads can be more worried, or concerned, about reaching agreement, than on finding the best answer.

"This means that we must vigilantly avoid the insidious traps of Groupthink. The danger of even having a team like this for solving problems is the general tendency for the team members to begin to think alike. Good teamwork in our case requires that we are totally candid about our views, despite what the other members of the team may think and say. I say again that good teamwork does *not* imply that you go along with what others are saying. If you agree, fine. But, if you do not agree, good teamwork means that you will seriously voice your disagreement. That is what I was talking about earlier.

"This is crucially important, and I hope that you believe me when I say that I really mean it. If we all thought alike, we would only need one member on the team. I am not trying to whip up continuous controversy just for the sake of arguments. And I hope that any controversy will be handled among us like ladies and gentlemen. So, disagree when you must, but do it with respect and good will toward one another. I must insist on that."

Harry looked about the circle of intent faces. Each face now appeared to be entirely serious. He concluded that there were no bewildered looks. He looked at Kate specifically. She smiled, and nodded affirmatively. Harry was strongly encouraged. Then, he was a bit apologetic. "You have been selected so that what I am talking about is not likely to be a problem. I feel apologetic for bringing it up. But the warning had to be made. Does anyone have a problem with this?"

As he looked again about the circle, Harry was happy to see that everyone nodded quickly, without any apparent confusion or reluctance. He really did not think that there would be a problem about this. The real problem with such a high-powered bunch might actually be the reverse. He might not be able to stop the dissident from trying too hard to correct everyone else. Harry had to admit that he himself would probably be the biggest offender in this, as a matter of fact. Despite general insecurities, he could be very positive about specific issues that he felt confident about.

Lottie used to chide him for expecting everyone to accept all of his pronouncements and pontifications as God's truth. She said that he was used to Godlike reverence from his students. He sincerely doubted that, to be sure. He demanded respect from the students. If he ever got reverence, he was never aware of it.

Anyway, he was pleased that this group seemed to understand. "Great! I hope that we will not have to discuss this again, because apparently we all agree," he concluded.

"Okay, now let us move on to some housekeeping matters. We have to decide how we are going to conduct our meetings. I hope that we will not have problems in deciding on how to reach decisions. We can use Robert's Rules, if you insist, but personally I hope that such formality will not be necessary. So, unless we have to resort to formal rules, let's try to decide everything by consensus, even though achieving a consensus is not necessary. Everyone will have a chance to say what is on his or her mind. We will continue the discussions until we find a solution that we can all accept. You may not agree in detail with a plan, but you can decide that it is the closest to what you want. If you can live with it, then let it pass. But, do let us know your reservations. If I try to cut off discussion before you have expressed your views, please, for heaven's sake, stop me."

"Alright, already, Daddio," said Patience impatiently. "Enough already."

Harry could now perceive that he had belabored the point beyond their patience. "I get your drift, Patience," he said, as contritely as possible. "So sorry. I will never mention it again, as long as you keep disagreeing with me."

Patience just made a face at him, and said nothing.

"Okay, let's move on," said Harry. "Next, if anyone has any administrative or scientific problems, please bring them to me or to Kate immediately. I want to make it easy for you to work and to think. Don't worry about finding an opportune time because, as far as I am concerned, this is not a clock-punching operation. We want to be as task-oriented as possible. Go to Kate first, because she is more likely to be able to help you if you need basic information or supplies. If we don't know the answer to a question, we will surely try to find out if such an answer exists, and who might have it.

"You all have copies of the files. See Kate if there is anything missing that was included on your checklist. Please study all of these documents so that we can hit the ground running when we get to Kipua. If things are as hairy there as I fear, we will not have much time to get organized. I will ask for proposals about priorities of efforts and the divisions of responsibilities at our next meeting. Are there any quick questions at this time?"

Each of the team members signaled that there were no questions. Everyone seemed ready to continue. Posh looked around, and then gave a thumbs-up sign.

"Okay," said Harry. "So be it. Now, this is what we have to do. The people at Schoonover have given us three major objectives: 1) to find out what happened to Burnhouse, and where he is if he is still alive; 2) to assess what actions should be taken to stabilize the situation on Kipua; and 3) to assess the scientific impact and meaning of the recent events on Kipua. The first two we must say are urgent, because Skull Burnhouse may be in real physical danger right now. We must do our best to save him, if that is the case.

"Let's each one of us start a list of hypotheses about possible causes for his disappearance, so that we can consider ways to check them out when we meet again. I think that we should start with the worst-case scenarios first. Those would be the ones that would present the most danger to Burnhouse."

Again, each member nodded agreement.

Harry continued, "Now, let us turn to just a little housekeeping before we break up. Posh, Rudy and I will be staying at the one hotel on the island. It goes under the interesting name of 'Crow's Nest,' which is the residential area of a place called the 'Crow Bar.' I gather that the names come from the owner, rather than that our lodgings are in the penthouse of a skyscraper.

"We have made arrangements for Patience and Kate to stay with the principal of the island school, Florence Gorsuch. Florence is also the mayor and a member of the town council. She is largely responsible for Burnhouse coming to the island, and now for our being here. Under those circumstances, she ought to treat us well. She has a three-bedroom cottage. That means that you each can have your own room. You will have to share one bathroom, but that is part of the vicissitudes of research in the field."

"No problem," said Patience.

"Minor problem," said Kate.

"Thanks," said Harry. "I guess that is all that we can do for now. Any questions, comments or suggestions at this time?

There were none.

"Okay, hearing none, I declare the meeting closed. See you all at lunch."

Kate and Posh stayed to lounge and chat on the hatch cover. Rudy and Patience moved slowly off below deck toward their cabins.

Harry made his way to the forecastle to watch the sea birds and flying fish. He was mesmerized by the stubby bow plowing painfully through the transparent water. He used to like to do this in his youth whenever he was on the water in any boat. When the sea is peaceful and calm, it provides an ideal setting for serious contemplation. Surely, now was an excellent time for such an activity.

It was not that he was doing very much deep contemplation now. Mostly it was pure worry. He just could not shake a feeling of apprehension about the situation on Kipua. Personally, he felt a heavy burden of concern for the safety and tranquility of the team—not to say the people on Kipua. The felt presence of Lottie was a comfort, as always.

* * * * * *

Harry had pulled a tenderfoot trick by falling asleep on the foc'sle of the old ship. It was a sure way to achieve a horrible sunburn. The sun was hot. But, he was lucky. The metal locker upon which he was leaning was hard, and also heated like a frying pan. These conditions had not permitted him to sleep for long. Checking his watch, he saw that he had not slept more than about five minutes.

So, he was now five minutes closer to Kipua. Like it or not, the ancient bucket of bolts was making steady grudging progress through the soft swells. The team would get to Kipua soon enough.

Harry decided that he had better get in a few more minutes on his homework before lunch. He made his way back toward his cabin. He would re-read Burnhouse's reports of the progress of the TECHland research on Kipua.

Even at a leisurely pace, it did not take long to reach his cabin. It was right at the foot of the ladder from the open deck. The sea breeze kept his room reasonably cool as he searched for the papers.

Ah! Yes! There was the box with the Schoonover reports. On top was the first of the splendid documents that Burnhouse had produced, and spread about the world. Harry wondered how Burnhouse was able to get such a fine cover on these things. He must have actually had them printed in New York City.

First Quarterly Report:
An Investigation of the TECHland Model
on the Protectorate of Kipua
from June 6, 1990 to September 6, 1990
(Research supported by a grant from
the Grover Keswig Schoonover Foundation,
Grant No. GKSF 90-153.)
Prepared by Charles Sculleigh Burnhouse, PhD,
Professor of Social Psychology, University of Chicago;
September 11, 1990

This report comprises the first quarterly summary of the research initiated on Kipua Island from the period beginning June 6, 1990, through September 6, 1990. It consists primarily of a narrative account of the events on the island surrounding the attempts of the grant staff, C. S. Burnhouse, Principal Investigator, and Monika Luthsaar, Research Associate, to inaugurate a model society based on a reward-contingency model.

Physical Description

Kipua Island is about midway between Saipan and Guam in the Marianas Archipelago of islands in Micronesia. The largest island, Saipan, is at the center of the archipelago, which runs generally to the north and south. The other islands curve off in northeasterly and southeasterly directions, decreasing in size the farther from Saipan. Guam forms the southern tip of the archipelago. In size, Kipua Island is also midway between Saipan and Guam, running about 15 miles north and south, and 11 miles east and west. Therefore, the total land area is about 155 square miles.

The island is bounded on the western coast by a mountain, Mt. Kipuana, with a strip of forest running along the base of the mountain and merging toward the east with the coconut trees of a large copra plantation, owned and managed by Mr. Jean Vincent dePuy. The plantation runs the north-south length of the island, and stretches across in places to the beaches on the eastern coast. Off the beach further to the east is the lagoon, formed by the ever-present coral reefs. A break in the reefs provides an excellent boat harbor. The anchorage in the lagoon is supplemented by several docks at about the middle of the beaches on the east coast.

The population of Kipua consists of about 500 natives and 50 Europeans and other nationalities, serving the copra plantation and the shops in the small town opposite the docks. Some of the natives still subsist by fishing and gardening, but most of the younger ones work on the plantation.

The production of copra is very labor intensive. Copra is the dried meat of the coconut. The native worker first rips off the husk using the sharp point of a pole embedded at the other end in the ground. Then, he cracks open the nut itself with a club. Next, the meat of the nut is laid out in the tropical sun to dry. It is very hard work, especially the process of removing the fibrous husk.

The island was selected for the site of the research because of its size, primarily in terms of population, and its character as a model of the merger of traditional native culture and new Western technology. It provides a microcosm of the world, with all of the major human problems, but insulated to some extent from the overpowering influences of the outside world.

Description of Natives

The natives are quite attractive physical specimens. They are surprisingly rather large, probably because of natural selection from the traditionally physically demanding life on the sea. They are brown-skinned because of the influx of coloration from the people of the Samoan and Marquesan Islands. The natives are open and pleasant, but they can be very fierce if their personal dignity is threatened by hostile or cavalier handling.

The life support for the village came primarily from the sea until the copra plantation was established at the turn of the century by French colonists, ancestors of the present owner. The social system is rather feudal, maintained by the power of the company store.

The existing social beliefs and organization will provide a great challenge to the initiation of the TECHLAND program. My study of the tribe's social organization has identified as the key barrier to their survival in modern society their belief concerning causality of events in their environment. They worship three gods, each represented by an idol in the center of their tribal compound. The first of these is Ru Tai, the God of the Unknowable Universe, who is thought to cause all natural phenomena which were not understandable or controllable by human beings. Ru Tai is considered to be responsible for, for example, making the grain sprout and grow, the rivers flood, the volcanoes erupt and the women get pregnant. Of course, all good things are attributed to the pleasure of Ru Tai, and all catastrophes are caused by his anger.

Although Ru Tai is temperamental and capricious at times, the villagers have built up a large body of customs according to what they conclude in fact appeases or displeases him. Most of these customs are actually beneficial to the tribe because of the natural reward-contingencies. That is, productive behaviors entailed rewarding consequences. But some very detrimental practices have been established through coincidental rewards, so that those connections are purely superstitious. These superstitions threaten the survival of the tribe because of the precarious ecological situation, with a scarcity of some natural resources and with multiple environmental hazards.

The other two gods are Lao Dut, the God of Happiness, and Jekuwa, the God of Goodness. They are the primary gods because they are associated with human behaviors. These two gods are responsible for all behaviors of man and animals, and are only indirectly affected by Ru Tai. Thus, all overt behaviors are the result of a conflict between the spirits of Lao Dut and Jekuwa within the body of the individual animal or person.

Lao Dut represents selfishness, self-preservation and vulnerability to external control by environmental forces, including other people. He advocates acquiescence to power, the yielding to control by agents in the environment as a means of survival and hopefully personal improvement. He is hated by the villagers, because he represents weakness and lack of personal control. For example, the men, particularly the young warriors, hate his advocacy of safety first, subservience over defeat and slavery over death.

The opposing god, Jekuwa, represents the actualization of the highest personal ideals of man, such as unselfishness, independence and strength. Jekuwa is invulnerable to threats, and uncontrolled by bribes or offerings. Jekuwa is loved by the villagers because he is the source of self-motivated achievement, creativity and personal glory in battle, all of which could be actually achieved if the internal force from Jekuwa overcame that from Lao Dut.

According to tribal belief, children are born with strong indwellings of Lao Dut, but little of Jekuwa. Therefore, they are selfish, with all of the other manifestations of Lao Dut. As they grow older, the force of Jekuwa strengthens. Finally, there is not a clear dominance of one over the other. Hence their behavior is much more erratic and unpredictable, sometimes reflecting momentary ascendance of one or the other god. As the child grows older, he or she begins to show the results of the internal battle, sometimes with an emerging clear superiority of one or the other, sometimes not. Typically, a more stable, predictable relationship between them is developed.

The tribesmen who become dominated by Jekuwa become the respected leaders of the village, honored for their concern and service for their people. The tribesmen dominated by Lao Dut become the cowards and servants within the society. They are despised by all.

These beliefs in Lao Dut and Jekuwa result in some detrimental behaviors by the tribesmen. The first of these is that a rigid caste system is in place. Helping behaviors are discouraged because a person who needs help is thought to be weak in the influence of Jekuwa and the potential helper is crassly demonstrating his strength of Jekuwa. Thus, offers of help are often resented, and therefore tend to be withheld.

The conflict, and resulting behaviors, will best be resolved, in my view, by destroying the belief in Jekuwa. Without the concept of Jekuwa, the villagers will be more open to beneficial cooperative efforts to improve the living conditions. False notions of self-esteem would not form barriers to the acceptance of help and the giving of it. The tribe would start working for collective goals, and be willing to subsume personal ambitions for the common good. Most important, they would be able to accept direction from their leaders, and to abide by mutual covenants among the members of the community.

The major problem is to discover some way to induce the villagers to give up the concept of Jekuwa in favor of Lao Dut. This will be difficult because of the entrenched nature of the belief. How can I, an admitted outsider with no authority other than my superior knowledge and skills in behavioral technology, go about advocating those changes in customs which I deem vitally necessary for the survival of the tribe? I must persuade them to give me a chance to try my system by demonstrating its effectiveness in practical, real situations.

The island council, under the urging of the mayor, Florence Gorsuch, has agreed to cooperate. In fact, we would not have chosen Kipua for our experiment without their invitation. I suspect that Ms. Gorsuch is not so much committed to my proposal as she is to the acquisition of some Schoonover dollars for her town. Other influential members of the council, Daniel M. Crow, the owner of a local saloon and hotel, and Vincent dePuy, the owner of the plantation, are divided on the issue. Crow is adamantly opposed to the idea, but dePuy favors it because he believes that a proposal should not be rejected until it is given a fair trial. None of them are very optimistic about my chances for success, however.

The support of the owner of the copra plantation, Jean Vincent dePuy, is crucial. He is very forward-looking about all categories of technology, including behavioral technology. He will be a rigorous evaluator and critic of our efforts, and will continue to support us only if we deliver a superior product—which to him means greater efficiency in running the plantation and greater productivity from the natives.

The natives themselves provide the biggest problems. They cherish their old tribal beliefs, and will fight to preserve them. The chief, Launo, is hostile, but he will respond to reason. His shaman, Malevi, is nearly out of control already. As would be expected of someone whose life work is threatened, he is going to do everything and anything to thwart my program. It is not that he has any moral or theoretical reservations about my agenda. He is simply upset by the potential loss of his personal power and prestige. I have tried to talk to him in order to win him over, just to giving me a chance, but he appears to be barely able to refrain from attacking me physically. That is no small concern because he is powerfully built, and he carries, as a symbol of office, a ceremonial mace that could crush your skull without much effort. Malevi is a formidable foe. My only power to control him comes from Launo, because no one else in the village or town has any influence over him.

The Methodology

I have rented space at the school in order to print some information about my program for the people. My main effort, however, will be to seize every opportunity to speak to groups of people to get my message across, and to demonstrate the beneficial effects of positive reinforcement on every occasion that is presented. The use of force to gain control is unthinkable in the TECHLAND model, of course.

Summary

In summary, I have encountered the expected initial opposition to my attempts to inaugurate a TECHLAND community on Kipua. But, the opposition is no stronger than expected. The toleration that I have received from several sources leads to optimism that the proposed program will succeed.

Respectfully submitted,
C. Sculleigh Burnhouse, PhD.
Principal Investigator

Harry had always thought that only a rash and unthinking person would proceed in such a manner. Burnhouse had secured the local equivalent of a soapbox or pulpit. He used it to preach against tribal gods openly and aggressively in the village equivalent of Hyde Park. He also had published pamphlets with uncompromising attacks against those same gods. There had to be little guesswork in predicting the outcome of that approach to the problem. Hawkey had been assured of that fact by those of his anthropologist friends who were knowledgeable and experienced in such things.

The only real question was whether or not the tribesmen were civilized enough not to have killed Burnhouse. Harry had read that the favorite weapon of the islanders was a war club carved out of solid hardwood. They were also partial to a kind of sword made of shark's teeth set around the edge of a wooden paddle. The shark's teeth could therefore lay open the flesh in several places at once, and thus produce death in a few seconds. Of course, the club could be even faster, if the warrior were both strong and skillful in selecting a lethal point of impact for the knobbed head.

Harry surely hoped that Skull Burnhouse did not suffer such an awful end. Burnhouse was the sort of person that Harry could accept as a casual friend. He could not see Burnhouse as his close friend. The truth was that Harry was consistently irritated by Burnhouse's persistent tendency to criticize others. Each occasion was a rather small thing, but, after a while, the general habit grated harshly on Harry's peace of mind.

Burnhouse seemed to consider that his own life was a superb model for others. He portrayed the role of what is commonly called "a beautiful person." He didn't drink coffee; he drank cappuccino. He jogged down Main Street, not Back Street. He wore the correct attire for each and every occasion. He liked to surf, and ski, and rollerblade. He never ordered the house wine.

There was nothing wrong about any of this, Harry conceded. It was just that he thought that a genuine person would sometimes have a politically incorrect impulse.

To Harry, the single most irritating quality of Skull Burnhouse was his intellectual chauvinism. Burnhouse presumed that everyone he met was his intellectual inferior. If the person was a blue-collar worker, Burnhouse was positive of his own intellectual superiority. Burnhouse was indeed a brilliant person, but his brilliance was dimmed somewhat by a generally closed mind.

TWELVE

AFTER DINNER IN THE MESSROOM aboard the *Cornucopia*, Harry convened the team over coffee. Capt. Kebomba had joined the first mate on the bridge to take care of some ship's business. The cook/steward, Palu, had cleared the tables, and was noisily washing his culinary tools in the adjoining galley. Palu was obviously advanced in years. His age was betrayed by a wrinkled and weathered body and face, and by the sparse halo of white hair around the crown of his head. But, his wiry muscles, abundant energy and quick mind suggested a young man. When the captain was busy elsewhere on the ship, Palu often took off his white coat, exposing a panoramically tattooed upper body. Kebomba was well aware of this insubordination, but tolerated it because Palu was indispensable.

Palu's name was a shortened form of a much longer Tahitian name that none of the team members could remotely pronounce. He had been doing his best to make the team comfortable and to facilitate its work. Harry thought that he must remember to give Palu a good tip when they landed at Kipua, because Palu had 13 children to feed.

The passage on the old ship was really not too bad. The accommodations were actually relatively comfortable. The food was okay, considering that it was not a cruise ship. Harry loved to eat fish anyway. The steward did a decent job of keeping the room neat and clean. He kept the laundry done. What more could you ask? Harry wondered how the old man did it. Maybe he had a washer-dryer combo hidden somewhere on board.

Everyone had settled down. Some were lingering over coffee. Harry began: "Let's get right to work. I trust that you all have examined your packet of documents. What do you think?"

As usual, Patience was first. "I think that Skull has met with some accident. For example, he likes to rock climb. He must have fallen somehow. He was not as good a climber as he thought he was. I know for a fact that he sometimes took foolish chances."

Rudy agreed: "Yes, an accident is always a possibility. Skull also liked to explore caves. There are many caves in the mountains on islands such as this. If he fell in a crevice, or was trapped in a cave, we may never find out what happened to him."

Posh joined in: "There is also a possibility of a swimming accident, because those beaches can be dangerous. He could have stepped on a sharp spike of coral, or have been trapped by a giant clam. Also, occasionally, a shark will find its way into a lagoon. That is not likely, but it could happen. There, again, we might never know."

"Right," said Harry. "Those are all reasonable possibilities. Write them down.

"So, clearly, we should check these possibilities as best we can by hiring natives to search the island thoroughly for physical evidence. I know that the police have already searched, but I mean to do another search that is as exhaustive as we can make it."

Harry, noting that everyone had nodded in agreement, said "Okay. Good." To Kate, he said, "Please get all that down. The main idea is to conduct as thorough a search of the island as we can, with the help of the locals."

Posh added another idea, "Really, I think that the team should also investigate the possibility of foul play. Skull was turning a lot of lives upside-down. Someone might have decided to do something about it. Surely, some of the natives have the skill and temperament to do him in, if they took the notion."

Harry nodded. He said, "Yes, I am mindful of the war clubs and shark-tooth paddles."

Because everyone nodded assent to each suggestion, Harry instructed Kate to write down the further possibilities as suggested. There clearly was no shortage of foreboding hypotheses to check out.

Kate had another idea: "Suppose Skull just plain quit, and ran off to another island. I know that it doesn't seem in character for him to do that. But, as you said, we must consider all of the possibilities. We can interview the natives to find out if any of them took him by canoe to a neighboring island. Some of them would have been happy to do that in exchange for a few bucks, I am sure. And, he could have given them a few more bucks to keep quiet about it. Skull is a proud man, and the failure of his great plan might have been more than he could bear. He might be in hiding on a neighboring island. Let's interview Monika Luthsaar and the natives to find out if they know anything."

At this, Patience practically screamed. "How can you even think of such an outrageous thing," she roared. "Skull Burnhouse was a truly dedicated researcher. Without a doubt, he would have played out the string until the project was over. He would not have given up until all of the data were in. Sure, he understood that the going would be rough at first. He had prepared for it. You are impugning his integrity, as well as his competence!"

"Just hold your horses, Patience," Harry tried to say calmly. "You remember that we talked about this very thing. We cannot, as scientists, allow personal feelings or even perceived personal attacks get us side-tracked on personal issues. I am sure that Kate did not mean any implications about Skull's character. Remember that we are all supposed to think of any and all possible hypotheses to account for Skull's disappearance. That is exactly what Kate was doing. We must give everyone the benefit of assuming that they are working on the task, and not grinding some personal ax. We cannot waste time in always making disclaimers about such things.

"So, you are out of line with such thoughts. You have no more evidence to go on than the simple statement of an hypothesis that any of us could, and should, have come up with, if we were thinking seriously. We absolutely cannot have members of our team holding back on ideas simply because they are worried that someone might be offended or insulted by them. You owe Kate an apology. What do you say?"

"Okay. Okay. You are right," Patience admitted. "I apologize, Kate. Sorry that I blew my cool. Forget what I said."

"No problem, Patience," soothed Kate. She was too good a trooper to let this bad start get the mission off track. Nevertheless,

Harry felt warned of a potential problem. A conflict of two strong women would be difficult indeed to deal with.

"Thank you both," said the relieved leader, content to have heard the deadly bullet of dissension zing past his ear this time. Fortunately, it hit nothing. At least, it apparently hit nothing mortal. "Let's get on with business," he said, trying to be upbeat and casual.

"I will say, however, that I doubt that Skull could have gotten a native to paddle him to another island. From what we can gather, they have not even been able to get many communications from the island. But, in any case, we must still check it out.

"Any other ideas about what might have happened to Skull?"

"I hate to push this, but he may have committed suicide. The shame of failure might have been too great," guessed Kate, looking a bit anxiously at Patience. "You have to remember that we are talking about his life work, his dream, here. He was very personally involved."

Harry quickly agreed: "We must list such a possibility, even though we do not think it likely."

He glanced at Patience. She did not seem pleased. But apparently she had decided to let it pass without re-iterating her objection.

"As psychologists, we should certainly also consider the possibility that he has become mentally disordered by the strain and terror," Rudy advised. "He could be wandering dazed about the jungle. Therefore, he could be in danger of succumbing to all sorts of calamities. There are wild boars on these islands, and lots of snakes, many varieties of them poisonous."

"Yes, and then, there is the chance of physical illness," added Posh. He could have contracted some kind of exotic fever, and so forth. He might have passed out in the jungle. As much as we might not like it, we should also be looking for a dead body, as well as for a live one."

Harry nodded. He motioned silently to Kate to write it all down. That instruction was not necessary because Kate had been writing feverishly all the time.

Patience had one more idea. "It could be," she said, "that Skull has been held prisoner by someone, or some group. As was said, many people did not like what he has been doing here. A lot of them would want him out of the picture. He could even have been killed."

"But, exactly who would want to do that? That would be pretty drastic." Kate was disdainful of the idea.

Patience replied, "Actually, I can think of two groups right away. How about the natives? Many of them are not fond of the way that he was systematically attacking their gods. He even said that he feared the witch doctor, what's his name."

"Malevi," said Rudy.

"Thanks. And then there are the police. They could have him in protective custody, or some such thing. Whatever they might call it. They may be keeping it a secret for Skull's safety. For that matter, someone else could even be hiding him at his own request. Perhaps, he fears for his own safety. That is equally likely as it is for someone actually to kill him."

"Well, in any case, we have to put these ideas on our list to check out," Harry said, reluctantly. "Personally, I cannot think of any more possibilities.

"How about the rest of you? Any more ideas?" Hearing none, he continued. "Okay, we will move on. If any new ideas come up, let me know. We will add them because we want a complete list."

All of the possible fates for Burnhouse raised calamitous possibilities. The mood in the room was solemn depression.

Now, Harry was eager to finish. "Now, let's get to the business of assigning duties to the team members. Kate will be the coordinator. She will help the local constable organize and manage the search. She will record all information, and see that the people who need certain information will get it. Please give her your results and conclusions in some legible form as soon as you can after you have put it together. We do not want to wait for you to gather all of your stuff in some complete and polished final report before we can find out what is happening. We will meet every day or so to compare notes.

"I will work closely with Monika Luthsaar to go through Burnhouse's papers and effects. He may have left a note as a clue for us."

Rudy quipped, "It's a dirty job, but somebody has to do it."

Harry pretended to ignore the general teasing laughter. Everyone was fully aware of Monika's absolutely gorgeous physical appearance and winning ways. Harry wondered if he was actually blushing? Perhaps, Rudy was not just making a good guess about his main motive for working with Monika. But, Harry knew that amorous designs on Monika would be foolish, given her obvious commitment to Burnhouse.

Shaking off the distraction, Harry turned sharply to Rudy. "Get serious!" he barked. "I'm too busy for romance!"

"No comment from here, Big Bwana," smiled Patience, obviously enjoying Harry's telling embarrassment.

To save his dignity, Harry forged ahead, perhaps too quickly. "Maybe Burnhouse left some clue that will help us find him, if indeed he knew where he was going, or what might happen. We can at least get some idea about whether or not he was depressed. We will also need to secure the full cooperation of dePuy and Mayor Gorsuch. Our job will be much easier if they are working with us, not against us.

"Posh, you can work with the natives at the village. Without getting in the way of the search for Skull, try to win their confidence. Find out if they know anything. According to Burnhouse's report, the chief seems to be a reasonable sort. So, start there. But, be careful of the shaman, Malevi. He is bad news."

"Okay, Big Bwana," said Posh, grotesquely imitating Patience. "You know, us natives gots to stick together, you know. And, you know, all that stuff."

Harry again ignored the nearly successful attempt at humor. Nevertheless, the others laughed as if it were funny. Harry was not often so ill at ease, and they were making the most of it.

"Rudy, let the plantation be your beat. Let that include the native workers and their supervisors. Give particular attention to the foreman and the household staff. We do not want to leave out anyone for full attention in our investigation. We must consider that at this point everyone must be under suspicion. Do not forget to investigate fully the foreman, Sam Conaway. His name has been mentioned frequently as a bad apple."

"Right," said Rudy. "Us blue-collar guys gots, you know, to stick together. Especially, if, you know, there are not enough Monikas to go around."

Harry groaned, and then smiled. He realized that he too should be enjoying the moment. "Enough already, you guys. This is serious business here." But, he was not angry.

Then, he continued. "Patience, that leaves the townies to you, including the school staff and the kids at school. Check out specifically the adults in the community who had a lot to lose if the new TECHLAND philosophy had really taken hold. That includes the shop owners and the recreational establishments. I am afraid that means spending a lot of time at the bars. But, as Rudy said, someone has to do it. If I have to make sacrifices, so does everybody."

Patience asked in mock seriousness, "Do I get an allowance for that? You know that booze can get very expensive."

Harry replied, "Nah. It's not necessary. You still have your looks and winning personality. Heck, I might even buy you a drink myself."

"In your dreams, you jerk," snorted Patience. Harry was not terribly sure just how serious she was.

Then, back to the task at hand. "Everyone, try to collect information on the most important hypotheses first," he instructed. "That means to concentrate on the hypotheses that assume Burnhouse is alive. That might require some interventions on our part. We surely do want to keep him alive, if it is not too late."

Harry paused. He did not like to bring up the next subject.

"Before we break for the evening, there is one more important issue that I would like to discuss with you. I have already discussed it with the people at Schoonover. They have agreed to let us make a decision about it based on our first-hand information in the situation. It concerns this ship, and whether or not it should evacuate any of the citizens on Kipua.

"I think that you can see the ethical problem. It is a very serious one. There probably are some people on Kipua right now who would like to escape the oppressive conditions. Others might like to take the TECHland plan to new shores. If we let either group book passage off Kipua, then we will risk losing the chance to contain and correct the problems on the island. We will also run the risk of spreading the TECHland idea to other shores."

The faces about him had turned solemn. Some were aghast. Some of the team members shook their heads in disagreement, even to a discussion of it. This would not be a universally popular action, whatever the decision.

Kate was sincerely worried: "On the other hand, we could be refusing to help people escape a situation that is aversive to them. Possibly, it would even be dangerous. If something were to happen to them, we would have it on our consciences. And, of course, we could get sued from here to eternity and back."

"Of course, you are right," agreed Harry. "We must keep lawsuits in mind. But, that cannot be the only factor under consideration here. My view is that we should try to keep them on Kipua. If they leave, we lose control of them. We have a responsibility to help them through this crisis. What do you say?"

Rudy and Kate leaned toward permitting open passage for anyone who wanted to leave. The others tended to agree with Harry. After heated discussion, Rudy and Kate agreed to defer to Harry's judgment. So, it was agreed that they would do their best to keep everyone on Kipua.

Harry agreed to tackle the difficult task of speaking to Kebomba. Schoonover would immediately buy all of his available space on board for the trip from Kipua. There would be no available tickets for other passengers off the island. It was an authoritarian and drastic action, but Harry was sure that it was absolutely necessary.

"That about does it for getting started," said Harry, with resignation and total emotional exhaustion. "Any other questions, problems or comments?" he asked. He fervently hoped not.

"Yes, Boss Man," said Patience. "I think that now it is about time that we back up a little bit. We need to talk about the psychological theories that were being tested by TECHland. We need that background in order to evaluate the experiment itself, and then to find out what went wrong."

"Okay," said Harry. "That is a good idea. But everyone is tired, and it could take a while. With your permission we will take it up first thing in the morning. Let's meet at 8:00 a.m. here in this spot. Is everyone agreeable?"

Apparently no one had any objections. They also were tired and drained.

"Okay," said Harry. "That is enough for tonight. I declare the meeting adjourned. Let's get some sleep so that we can do a job tomorrow. Good night."

With that, they all headed to their bunks. Each internally debated his or her own conflicting thoughts. In general, Harry's thoughts were racing ahead. This was going to be a research project like he had never been part of before—or had even seen.

"Oh, Lottie," he murmured to himself in the darkness, "I wish you were here with me now. I need your wisdom and comfort."

* * * * * *

As they settled down for the discussion of theories, Harry could see that Patience had a full rack of armed bombs. Somehow he felt that his body, in particular, was on the cross-hairs of her bomb sights. Harry had never before seen her so serious. Undoubtedly, she was going to confront him directly with the classical Skinner argument. Harry moaned softly to himself, "This is not going to be pretty."

He doubted that it was just an accident that Patience was wearing a Harvard T-shirt. "Really subtle, Patience," he said silently to himself. He concluded again that sometimes the smartest people are most transparent in revealing the causation of their behaviors.

Why had he not packed his Ivey Southern T-shirt, he asked himself, impulsively? It was a nice fantasy, but it did not suggest smart behavior under the circumstances.

"There was a good reason for not wearing the shirt," he reassured himself. The reason was that he did not want to appeal to authority in the discussion on Kipua. The relative merits of the graduate schools attended by the discussants was not at all relevant. Moreover, he feared that such tactics would incur the same resentment from the others that he now felt faintly toward

Patience. He never before thought that there was any detectable vein of insecurity in her. But, now he could detect a slight trace, he thought. Perhaps, Burnhouse's debacle on Kipua had truly threatened her professional stance on life.

Patience began, "Okay, Harry, you are the one making the charges. You should go first. Then I will destroy you with my rebuttal. Fair enough?"

Because she said it with a slight smile, Harry let himself hope a little that the debate would not be too unpleasant after all. He reminded himself that Patience was really a nice person. They had always gotten along quite well together before this mission.

Harry nodded, "Yes," and returned her smile with as much sincerity as he could muster. "Okay," he said, "here goes. Destroy away if you can."

He decided to get his theoretical cards on the table emphatically. Casting a cautious eye toward Patience, he asserted: "The issue between Skinner and me concerns utility, not metaphysical truth. Skinner asserted that he was talking science, and not metaphysics. I vehemently disagree with that contention. Our argument is actually about whether society would be, or would not be, better off without the concepts of human freedom and human dignity. We define dignity as the value, or worth, that a person has for society. Skinner's metaphysical argument reflects the assumption that human beings are simply marvelous machines. They, therefore, in his view, have no ability to make voluntary choices, and no intrinsic value beyond being such marvelous machines. So, being machines, human beings merely respond to the absolute dictates of their inherited capacities as developed by learning experiences."

Kate was distressed: "You mean that Skinner claims there is no value in a human life? That would be weird. It would imply that the taking of a human life would be okay. That argument even sounds like it should be against the law."

"Oh, no," Harry jumped in. "It is not that a person doesn't have value. But, the source of the value is basically the same as the reason for valuing a computer, a bulldozer or a microwave oven. The value comes from the function performed by the machine, not because of some intangible essence inherent in computers, bulldozers and microwave ovens. In the case of the human being the value does not come from some subjective notion of some kind of non-material essence that gives the person the ability to choose his or her behaviors.

"Skinner argued that, because our behavioral technology is based on this environmental control of behavior, the members of society hold back from using behavioral technology to its fullest advantage. He argued that a complete commitment to such use leaves no room for our cherished concepts of human choice and human dignity. His full reasoning is rather complicated and need not concern us at this point. The bottom line is that, he said, people think that the use of behavioral technology implies that people have no personal freedom or special value as human beings. So, in order to protect the concepts of freedom and dignity, the members of society then feel that they must avoid the full use of a behavioral technology. That is bad because such technology undoubtedly benefits our society."

Harry stopped, and looked quizzically at Patience. "Right, Patience?"

"Right," said Patience, giving a thumbs-up sign. "So far, so good. Jolly good!"

Harry continued: "My view is that Skinner's ideas are not reasonable in our experience. They are not even logical for a planet inhabited by theoretical people, much less one inhabited by real human beings. Skinner's theory is unrealistic for real human beings, because his research with rats and pigeons did not give him an adequate understanding of the nature of the human animal."

"How so?" asked Patience, belligerently. "We need more than your simple assertion for that, Doctor." She was definitely not happy.

"It's simple," responded Harry. "The key factor in the laboratory research in problem solving with lower animals is that the selection of the correct response to solve the problem for the rat or the pigeon is deliberately arbitrary."

"What do you mean by arbitrary in this connection?" Patience asked, more moderately, and with interest. But, still the question was asked in a confrontational style.

"I mean that the researcher makes a virtually whimsical decision about what response of the animal will be rewarded. Consider an animal placed in a puzzle box. Call it a Skinner box, if you prefer. The animal, which has been made hungry by some method—food deprivation, for example—must perform some response that will be instrumental in securing food to satisfy its physiological need. Obviously, that response must be one that the animal can accomplish. And, also obviously, the animal must have the physical and mental capacity to produce that particular response. Beyond that, the only guiding principle for selecting the instrumental response by the researcher concerns the desired level of difficulty of the problem for the animal. True?"

"Okay, okay," agreed Patience. "Go on, Professor. So far, your presentation has been rather elementary."

Harry searched for sarcasm in her voice. He was not sure whether or not he found any. Surely, she must know that he was not trying to be profound to this point.

Without comment on her evaluation, he forged ahead. "What all of this means is that there is absolutely no way that the hungry animal in a laboratory puzzle box can use reason to decide which response to make. The animal cannot deduce from the situation which of its potential responses will successfully achieve a bit of food or drink, or whatever else will satisfy its current needs. For example, the pigeon doesn't know that it must peck on a colored disk, or ruffle its feathers, or twirl around in place. It is for the experimenter to know and for the hungry animal to find out. The animal can discover which response is desired by the experimenter only by differential experience. It has to learn which response is rewarded as correct by the experimenter. That is why we call the process 'trial and error learning.'

"In summary, the only way for the animal to know what response is correct is for it to try some available response to find out whether or not that particular response is successful. Correctness is simply defined as the response which will secure the reward. The unsuccessful, unrewarded response is therefore only an error in a practical sense. That means that it is not the particular tangible response that the experimenter has arbitrarily selected as the one that he or she will reward. Even a so-called incorrect response will be useful in informing the animal that it is one of the possible responses that will not work. Therefore, it really is not possible for the animal to make a truly stupid response. Possibly, the only stupid response is to keep repeating an unrewarded response, or to do nothing. A so-called non-response is also technically a kind of a response."

"That's more then I can say for some humans," interjected Patience, this time in a clearly sarcastic tone. "But, where do you get off telling us about reasoning in animals. Are you a reader of animals' minds?"

"Ah! Ha!" exclaimed Harry, still ignoring the sarcasm. "That is where I want to go with this. You have helped me to make my point! The whole situation is different for humans. But, let me go on with the first point before I lose track of it."

"Sure, you need all of the help that you can get," cracked Patience.

Harry winced, but continued: "The same analysis that applies to the puzzle box is true for a rat in an alley maze. The rat must learn to take the series of alleys that leads to the reward. It must learn to avoid the blind alleys that lead to dead ends. Typically, in simple studies of learning, there is no way that the rat can deduce on the first attempt at a given choice point whether the correct turn—that is, the one that will ultimately lead to the reward—will be a right or left turn. The rat must make a try, and see how it turns out. Again, the only way that the rat can show any intelligence is by not repeating on subsequent trials the so-called errors as built into the maze by the experimenter. The task itself does not allow the animal to use any powers of reasoning that it may have."

"How do you define 'reasoning'?" asked Kate. "How do you distinguish it from so-called 'learning'?"

"The difference is in the trial and error part," responded Harry. "With learning the organism initially makes a response to an environmental stimulus for some habitual or whimsical reason. If the outcome turns out to be satisfactory—that is, it is rewarded—then the organism is likely to make some kind of a mental association or connection between the two, however you define 'mental.' Therefore, the learner will make the same or a similar response when that same stimulus, or a very similar one, is repeated. The nature of the association depends upon whose theory you support.

"With reasoning, the trial and error part is absent, at least in the overt behavior. The organism is able to infer or deduce from the current situation, and other similar past experiences, what the correct response will be. That is, the animal can guess with some degree of accuracy what response will be likely to achieve the reward. This association of stimulus and correct response is achieved in the absence of specific previous experience of having made that response to that particular stimulus. You see, reasoning requires a creativity—a creation of a novel connection—that is not present in learning. Is the difference clear?"

"Yep," said Kate, with a nod. "Now I think that I understand what you are getting at."

"Good," said Harry.

Patience interjected, "Okay on the definition. But, I deny that the phenomenon occurs."

"I know," said Harry. "That is a point of disagreement between us.

"Now, let's look at the comparable situation for a human being. Actually, basically the same situation would be true for a human subject put in a Skinner box or an alley maze. Of course, the human being would have at least one distinct advantage over the rat or pigeon. Being human, he or she would be able to think more like the human experimenter. Therefore, he or she could make a better (i.e., educated) guess about what response the experimenter would be more likely to select as the correct one. We do this routinely, probably every day of our lives. For example, the cook tries to anticipate what will please his or her family for supper. The buyer for the department store makes an educated guess about what goods and styles will be popular this year. Or, the defensive coach of a team tries to select a defensive scheme that will *not* be desired by the offensive coach of the opposing team.

"You see, the selection of which response will be rewarded by the experimenter is arbitrary, but not random. Animals, including humans, have preferences—for turns, for places, for all sorts of things. So, the human would have the advantage of establishing priorities of responses according to what he or she himself or herself would arbitrarily select as the correct response. This mental process is arguably getting very close to reasoning in the human."

"Hold on, now," interjected Patience. "Let's be clear about one thing. You can define reasoning and learning as you have done in an operational sense. That does not mean that the actual psychological mechanisms at play in the two objective situations are different. Let me remind you that Skinner assumed similar mechanisms in most cases. The only exception occurs when the learned habits show a spontaneous change, or behavioral mutation. The point is that there is no hidden personal agent which is making an inference or a deduction as you described it. Burnhouse agreed with Skinner on that point. The TECHland model is based on it."

"The difference that you have pointed out is quite true," agreed Harry. "The key issue between us concerns the very nature of creativity in responding. The Behaviorists give it minimal credit in their theorizing. They surely deny that it is related to any such thing as voluntary effort. As you know, certainly, not every behavioral scientist agrees with Skinner and Burnhouse on that interpretation. In fact, there have been many forceful critics of Skinner's proposal for designing a better society, which he promulgated in his two classic books, *Walden Two* in 1948 and *Beyond Freedom and Dignity* in 1971. That in itself does not mean too much, of course. After all, there have been many persons who have sincerely doubted the existence of God. We cannot prove that there is a voluntary agent within human beings that can create novel ideas and responses."

"You are right," agreed Rudy. "If I understand you correctly, though, the issue does not concern who is correct metaphysically, but who is correct in a practical sense. Which of the assumptions, correct or incorrect, will work for us in crafting a better society? So, what is wrong with a commitment to Skinner's views?"

Harry warmed to the task. Now, he thought that he was getting somewhere. "I have often been asked what I have against Skinner's ideas. In brief, I do not think that they will work in solving important problems in our society. You see, problem solving involves the generation of novel responses, because the habitual responses have, by definition, not been working. In Skinner's view, the novel response must be generated by mindless environmental factors according to impersonal physical laws. One could almost say that novel responses occur by accident, because there is no sentient agent responsible. So, the problem with Skinner's view is that his advice for designing a better society was based on his strict deterministic assumption about the causation of human behavior. Incredible as it seems to most of us, he actually attributed human behavior entirely to nothing other than fortuitous interactions between the person's learning experiences and that person's genetic inheritance. Therefore, whatever behavior a person makes in a given situation, according to Skinner's view, is completely determined by the joint effects of that person's biological inheritance in relation to the opportunities that he or she has had for learning in that or similar situations. This means that Skinner literally and expressly denied any possibility, under any circumstances, for human beings to choose any of their behaviors by a voluntary act of will.

"My problem is that this is a very pessimistic, indeed an absolutely fatalistic, view of life. The person in trouble must consider himself or herself powerless to control the circumstances surrounding the problem. If the correct, unguided, behavioral mutation occurs, the person is fortunate. But, there was nothing that he or she could have done to facilitate the appearance of the correct behavior."

Posh joined in: "This does not seem right to most of us, of course. We think that surely we are making voluntary choices. It is a deeply ingrained belief that has persisted for centuries. It has persisted because of its practical value. For example, I use it every day when I am working in a ghetto with disadvantaged kids. I tell them that, sure, they have a tough time, but that they have the freedom to make choices that will affect their futures. They can chase the easy dollars in drugs and crime, and surely end up in jail, or likely dead. But, they can choose to work, and to study in school. They can improve their chances for a successful and happy life. Actually, the real job is to convince them that they do have choices. When we do, it works.

"So, Skinner's view works against what we are trying to do. What is the problem with our success? What did Skinner say?"

"Skinner's counter-argument," answered Harry, "was that we human beings typically *think* that we are voluntarily choosing our behaviors. But, in his view, we actually could not have chosen another behavior, even if we had wanted. He argues that our belief in such intentional choice is simply an illusion, a product of our imaginations. To Skinner's mind, the mere existence of such a belief does not prove anything. He contended that we foster this illusion of causality because it makes us feel better about ourselves. We simply feel better, if we think that we are in control of our lives."

"But, does it not indeed make us feel good about ourselves?" asked Kate. "I sure like to feel that I am not some robot that cannot choose my behaviors. I want to, at least, feel that I have some effect on what I do."

"Sure, it does," replied Harry. "The problem according to Skinner is that these good feelings cause us to object to the use of science in dealing with people. But, he fails to see a gap between our perceptions of causality in real-life situations, and in formal laboratory experiments with lower animals. Because he could control animal behavior without concerns for their feelings of freedom, he concluded that such feelings of freedom interfere with the full use of behavioral principles in controlling human behavior.

"I definitely cannot agree with his simple assertion. In fact, that idea is so completely foreign to my own thinking, I cannot even adequately describe how much I object to it. The best description of my reaction is some mixture of disgust, rage and fear. The disgust and rage came from my belief that Skinner and his followers deliberately chose to ignore so much valuable data about people."

"He means me," observed Patience. "I plead guilty. If that is a crime, shoot me."

"Don't tempt me," laughed Harry. "But, let's finish the description of Skinner's ideas.

"Despite all of the evidence that it would not work, Skinner still chose, as a professed scientist, to advocate a view of people as qualitatively nothing more than elaborated forms of rats or pigeons. His monumental fantasy was that he could induce others in society to accept that view of themselves and others. He was able to promote such a view because of his strict ideas about what constituted acceptable scientific data. Skinner said that we should overlook data in the form of literary works and news accounts, not to say the personal testimony of many people. I think that he was callously cavalier in such an argument. Of course, people sometimes lie or mis-represent their true feelings and beliefs. But, that is not sufficient reason to disregard everything that they have said or written."

Harry paused to let his message sink in before he continued. "The fear concerns, in my view, the social consequences that we are now facing in Kipua. We are probably facing it elsewhere on this globe, as well. It concerns the argument over practicality. The argument is practical, because no one has found a philosophical or empirical way to prove Skinner's view either right or wrong. The same is true for the opposite view, of course. Therefore, as I have said, the issue boils down to which view is more useful to society. Or, perhaps I should say, which view is literally less dangerous.

"Well, I have done my best as a professional to counteract Skinner's influence on social thinking. I have written books and journal articles attacking his views. I have admitted, in agreement with Skinner, that you cannot prove his metaphysical position to be either right or wrong by any known method of direct proof. So, you cannot resolve the issue of a viable human will by empirical science. And perhaps it cannot even be accomplished by philosophical analysis. Otherwise, the philosophers would probably have done so by now."

"So," interposed Patience, "we know what practical arguments Skinner proposed. We have yet to hear what you have to offer."

At this verbal jab, Harry began hastily, "My arguments against Skinner's views have been entirely practical, as I said. I argue that there definitely is practical value for a belief in some freedom of will. I contend also that there is a great practical barrier to the preservation of social organization by the denial of freedom of will. My argument reduces to this: If all of your potential behaviors are beyond your personal control, you cannot change your life by a personal act of courage and resolve. A Horatio Alger would just not be possible. Therefore, this denial of a viable will is, in a word, just too fatalistic. My case rests."

At this, Patience jumped to her feet. She began to pace rapidly back and forth before the group. She presented the awesome presence of a prosecuting attorney preparing to present a summary argument for a death sentence. Her Harvard T-shirt heaved with her emotion. For once, she was wearing just a baseball cap on her head. Her blond hair was tied back in a pony tail, twitching back and forth like it were chasing flies.

They all remained respectfully silent for her to speak. Nothing was heard, except the sounds of the sea birds, the wash of the waves, the creaking of the old ship and the thump, thump of her sneakers on the wooden deck. Harry felt like he was in the eye of a hurricane, and the approach of the back side was imminent.

Strangely, Harry thought back to the last time he had seen Patience at a convention. It was in Los Angeles. By chance, they had arrived for breakfast at the same time, but discovered that all of the single tables were full. So, they arranged with a couple of graduate students from U.C.L.A. to sit together at a table for four.

The breakfast conversation had turned to practical applications of psychology. Surprisingly, to Harry, Patience had been very patient in explaining Behavioristic views with respect to the design of societies. Such mild behavior was in sharp contrast to her present demeanor. Apparently, she could be patient with the students. That admirable restraint did not carry over to professionals who she thought should know better.

Harry braced himself for the inevitable tornado. Surely, such preparation was not going to be wasted effort.

THIRTEEN

AT LAST PATIENCE SPOKE. Her voice as she began somehow reminded Harry of his second-grade teacher, Mrs. Harris. Mrs. Harris' speech always seemed to convey a mixture of the authoritative words of the Pope, and the insistent demand of a high-school football coach. Harry braced anew for the storm of her fury.

"This wooden-brained, cigar-store Indian, this wooly-headed slug," she began, lustily, "has the limitless gall to malign the most celebrated, the most respected behavioral scientist who ever lived."

Harry had to chuckle at the personal metaphor. At least, he assumed that she was referring to him. Patience *did* have a way with words. He called out, cheerily, "Don't hold back, Patience. Remember, I said that we wanted to know exactly what was on your mind."

Pretending to ignore him, with a toss of her pony tail, Patience continued her tirade: "This inconsequential worm is trying to promote his balderdash in place of the wisdom of a *world-renowned scholar*." The last three words were literally shouted, with slight pauses for emphasis between pairs of words.

Then, she looked at Harry with scorn: "*His* books were best-sellers and widely acclaimed by experts in psychology. How about yours, Professor?"

Harry winced, but could only murmur something about a "low blow." He shrugged his shoulders to indicate that none of his books had come within a light year of any best-seller list, except within the Hawkey family. But, the personal attack on his professional expertise did not bother him. He was completely familiar with the tactic from the wrath of many reviewers and editors. It was still strange and ironic to him that the alleged champions of rigorous science could bring themselves to use such tactics.

Patience sniffed triumphantly: "I thought so. But, Skinner's books sold because he had an optimistic plan. The philosophy of determinism is not fatalistic, it is optimistic. Skinner wanted to free you from unscientific, humanistic concerns that hold you, and the rest of society, back from the full use of our developed technologies to provide a better world. The fact that behaviors are determined means that they can be molded to promote human welfare. You cannot deny, if you have any sense or decency, that behavioral technology can make beneficial changes in this world.

"You offer, in place of such proven scientific evidence, a hodgepodge of fanciful ideas and wishful thinking without a shred of proof. You would destroy the whole scientific background of our society, its very underpinnings, with your ideas of personal ghosts which control our world. You cannot point to what you are talking about, or measure it. In short, in terms of science, you are talking about absolutely nothing. I rest my case."

With that, she marched stiffly to the hatch cover, looking neither to the right nor left, and sat down again. Then, she relaxed enough to glare triumphantly at Harry.

"Okay, sure," Harry said in a soothing voice. "I actually agree with you about the need for the intelligent use of technology. I have said that repeatedly. Why do you not believe me when I say it? But, I *also* say that the concept of a will can be added as a plus to provide other benefits. It does not have to interfere with our use of science. It only interferes if you make it interfere. We can use science and technology to carry us as far as they can. We can reap their numerous benefits. But, why stop there? Other ideas can also be useful to us.

"Skinner was partially correct, but ironically he went too far by stopping short. His total denial of personal choice is bad enough. But, it led him also to argue against a concept of human dignity or worth which is contingent on the notion of a freedom to choose praiseworthy behavior. He claimed that the concepts of freedom and dignity hinder the progress of a legitimate and effective behavioral science.

"I think that now we are ready to get into the meat of those arguments. Skinner's argument went like this: Because society values its members only to the extent that individual persons are perceived as voluntarily performing prosocial behaviors, therefore there can be no personal worth without the concept of voluntary behavior. This means that a person must earn any positive evaluation that he or she receives from fellow human beings. Allegedly, this positive perception of worth, or dignity, is achieved only when the person is perceived by others as voluntarily performing some praiseworthy behavior. If this were true, a person without voluntary choice could not earn dignity. Therefore, he or she would have absolutely none. This conclusion, to most of us, is a repugnant idea. Right, guys?"

He looked confidently about the deck. He received a general round of signs indicating approval. Patience was a glaring exception. Her response was a scowl. She started to speak, but then held back.

Harry continued: "The problem, Skinner thought, is that this way of thinking by the members of society causes them to cling to the false and competing idea of a viable human will, which they need in order to retain reasonably the cherished concept of human dignity. So, he said that an effective plan for behaviorally engineering a better society must begin with renouncing all traces of humanistic thinking. Particularly, that means to renounce the ideas of both human freedom and dignity. Having freed itself from this excess humanistic baggage—actual shackles to science, in his view—society would then turn to shaping beneficial prosocial behaviors by offering rewards to individual persons contingent upon their desirable performances. Thus, Skinner proposed to replace the concept of a viable, functional will with the concept of determined behavior, which says that all responses are merely the result of joint effects of heredity and environment alone. Therefore, our behaviors could be improved merely by appropriate manipulation of our external environments."

"And this proposal definitely meets with your objections," prompted Posh with a smile. Harry already knew that Posh agreed with his objection.

He shot back, "Right! This proposal really turns me off! In fact, I think that the social plan resulting from this kind of thinking is causing the devastation on Kipua right now. And it also raises the fear that it could spread to other islands and other continents.

"In the first place, Skinner's overall argument is just plain wrong. He was right in particular about earning dignity by performing beneficial social acts, of course. That is entirely consistent with common observation. We do admire people who we think have voluntarily done beneficial things to other people, particularly if they have done this service at significant personal cost, or sacrifice. But, *all* dignity of a person does not have to be earned in this way. As has been fully documented by countless social observers, our society in general also accords an intrinsic dignity to each and every one of its members. That type of dignity does not have to be earned at all. Everyone has it just as the birthright of being human. This intrinsic human dignity can obviously be augmented by the voluntary performance of prosocial behaviors, of course. I absolutely do not see how any knowledegable adult can deny that fact. A person can know it just from observing the people about himself or herself in the real world.

"But, there is also plenty of written evidence from what Skinner called the literature of freedom and dignity for the belief in intrinsic dignity. Unfortunately, as we said, Skinner cavalierly dismissed that evidence as not scientific, and therefore not worthy of consideration. Thus, he figuratively left his opponents in science to slowly twist in the wind. By one pontifical stroke he supposedly wiped out the heart of their evidence. And, in my view, all of those people who will therefore eventually be treated as if they have no dignity as a result of Skinner's argument will end up suffering as the people on Kipua are suffering right now."

Patience protested: "But, I am not impressed by such casual data. It is folklore and hearsay. You will have to do better then that!"

"Okay, if you insist," smiled Harry. He had to admit that he had sandbagged her, set her up for the scientific kill.

"There is absolutely irrefutable data on this point from the laboratory of two researchers in Virginia. Using several methods, they showed in their laboratory research that people believe in an intrinsic dignity for all people, a dignity that does not have to be earned." Hawkey emphasized the point about laboratory research as if he were a pastor quoting the Bible. "These people used the best methodologies in a valiant attempt to control for everything from subject bias, to social desirability and demand characteristics of the research situation. Their studies can only be criticized by trite objections that can be made about all laboratory research."

"Okay, okay," Patience admitted. "So, Skinner was wrong in his reasoning about why people oppose science. Probably most people are not that logical anyway. But, the fact remains that people do oppose the unconditional use of science. And, undoubtedly they do it on emotional grounds."

Posh spoke up. "You know, Skinner may be right after all," he said. "His view of science makes science totally inconsistent with religion. That is a problem. In my view, to accept his argument would eliminate the good works done by all of the churches in the world, now and for the future. And there is plenty of empirical evidence for positive social effects of the churches."

"I would not want to deny the good works done by churches and synagogues," said Rudy, "but is that really relevant to the present discussion?"

"I guess it really isn't from a philosophical point of view," agreed Harry. "But, again, arguing from a practical standpoint, as we have been arguing all along, it is undeniably relevant. Why should the behavioral technologists, of all people, try to squeeze out of the overall mix of ideas the beneficial beliefs in religions? It almost seems as if they are making a value judgment here, one based on something more than practicality. If a belief in God induces some people to help other people, what's the beef?"

"The beef," said Patience, impatiently, "is what we Behaviorists have been trying to tell you. The beef is that, because a belief in God is incompatible with science, it causes people to discount science."

"Hold it!" said Harry, more impatient himself than he wanted to show. "That is a major issue. If your argument is true, and surely it is for some people, we must try to change the way people understand science and religion. The two endeavors are not incompatible. As a Christian, I believe that God made *all* things. And that definitely must include the laws of science.

"Moreover, I think that most believers in the Judeo-Christian religions believe that there is no incompatibility between science and religion. I myself have always seen science and religion as simply two different avenues for gaining an understanding of God's world. Because I am convinced that everything is of God, then I believe that science is of God. Almighty God gave us brains to reason and to understand, even though there are some things that the human brain will never fully understand."

"Let's not get bogged down now on the supposed benefits of religion," suggested Rudy. "Such a debate would be fun at some time, but it will get us nowhere right now."

Harry looked around the circle. Everyone, including Patience, gave general signs of agreement with Rudy.

"You are right, Rudy," agreed Harry. "Let's save it for later."

"So, getting back to the main point, I contend that Skinner's view is certainly not correct according to my understanding of epistemology, which permits a much more liberal view of the nature of proof. A scientist cannot just declare that some thing, some entity, does not exist, simply on the basis of his or her own biases. Such biases are obviously based on the scientist's own limited experiences. Such a procedure is chauvinistic beyond words. Therefore, there surely does not have to be a conflict between science and religion.

"Apparently, Skinner thought that he had some special knowledge from some unknown source of what is, or is not, scientific. That kind of personal bias itself is not scientific. And, you cannot hide the bias behind some trite claims of some general deficits that can be leveled at any research.

"In my view, any aspect of life, any basis of personal experience, is scientific. The fact is that we simply trust some sources of evidence, and some researchers, more than others. And well we should."

"You have convinced me of that," said Kate. "But, I want to know more about the issue of fatalism. Which view is more optimistic, and which is more fatalistic? I take it that you and Patience disagree on this point."

Patience nodded in agreement. "Bloody well right!" she said, with decided emphasis on each word.

"Good point," said Harry. "This is a crucial issue. Along with many other critics of Skinner, I emphasize in my thinking the fatalistic aspect of his views simply because they presume no voluntary personal influence on the control of behavior. Without voluntary control, how then would society be able to select the desired behaviors to be rewarded? The selection of desired goals would itself be determined by the rewards for past selections of responses. The selection would not be the result of some reasoning processes which could and would judge the relative merits of the various goals. Therefore, if the persons who were selecting goals had been rewarded differently, they would select responses toward different goals.

"Moreover, who is to say which leaders, or gurus, or other individuals, should be selecting the goals for the whole society anyway? The selection must be made by the people themselves. As a democrat, I believe that. As a scientist, I believe that we must provide the best data and interpretation of that data to help the citizens make the correct decisions in selecting goals for themselves."

Kate nodded: "So, if Skinner were right, the individual person could not even select his or her personal goals. Those goals would actually be determined by the person who controlled the rewards. In fact, in this sense, there would be no basis for even talking about personal goals."

"Right on, Kate," said Harry. "Skinner's proposals, despite the good intent, were not the best for our young people to hear.

"Skinner did have the perfect right to promulgate his views on behavioral science, of course. And, to be sure, he was more or less on solid ground when he was performing laboratory research on rats and pigeons. Those were relatively simple non-verbal subjects. But, when Skinner attempted to extend his ideas to the social attitudes and behaviors of human beings, he erred in not expanding the arena of relevant data. Stripped of the scientific language, he was arguing that a person's verbal report provided no clue about what that person was thinking or intending to do. Despite all of the appropriate disclaimers about the problems of trusting verbal reports, that assertion is patent nonsense."

Patience was indignant. "Well, who died and made you the expert on scientific data? Who are you to call the assertions of a man such as Skinner nonsense? Skinner was easily twice as bright as you are. He was certainly much better known and respected in the profession. You do not know what you are talking about. You do not understand Skinner. You should know that the leaders do *not* themselves choose the target behaviors. They merely insure that the target behaviors selected by the scientists, on the basis of scientific evidence, are in fact carried out. The ultimate leaders are the scientists who interpret the data."

Harry was stung by the comparison between him and Skinner. It was not the first time that he had heard it. He understood that the track record of a scientist was an important consideration in judging which one to believe, but it was not the only factor.

"This is not a question of innate intelligence, or even global intelligence, but of functioning intelligence," he shot back. "Sometimes a person's biases overpower his or her basic intelligence. I think this is what happened to Skinner. I have three points to make that I think Skinner overlooked. First, the science of human behavior has not advanced far enough to let it completely control our lives. Second, science requires the interpretation of data. Where are you going to find completely unbiased men and women to interpret the data? For example, look at us today. We all have access to the same scientific data, but we still have divergent views even on which general direction to take. Skinner said this disagreement among scientists was no problem, because he was correct. Pardon me, Patience, but I think that is about the most naive that a professional psychologist can get."

At that, Patience nearly choked in exasperation. She struggled to speak, but Harry stopped her with a hand signal.

"Hold it a second, Patience! Please," he begged. "Just let me finish with the third point. Finally, if voluntary choice actually does exist, it will continually confound the scientists. They will be looking to discover behavioral mechanisms that do not even exist.

"Okay, Patience, did you have something to say before I go on?"

"Only that I am amazed at your chutzpah for even questioning one of the greatest psychologists that ever lived."

"I am not questioning the greatness of Skinner, but the notion of his infallibility. How can a scientist simply assume that he is correct on an issue without allowing the possibility that he could be wrong? This is fundamental in science. I teach my undergraduate students to accept the possibility of error."

Patience was silent. Her silence and her manner indicated to Harry that his point had been well taken.

He continued his argument. "Let us consider Point 2 a moment, in a bit more detail. I cannot believe that Skinner did not trust verbal report just a little in his own personal life. In any case, here is a major issue in behavioral science for which there is no agreement.

"Verbal reports would have given him a clue about human thinking. That is why I think it was so crazy for Burnhouse to set up a behavioristically based community on Kipua. Plenty of the recognized experts thought the idea was ridiculous, too. Schoonover was surely warned of disaster. Some critics in fact used pretty strong language in opposition to Skinner's views. Skinner was not the only modern prophet and, it seems, not the best one at that.

"The critical words of experts in psychology and political science have been echoed by other professionals and by students as well. Some of my students, friends and colleagues have described Skinner's plan for a better society as seductively neat and appealing. So it is! These assessments support my personal view that Skinner's vision of an Utopian society based entirely on rewards for desired behaviors is too idealistic. It is not consistent with the empirical facts of laboratory research, or even common observation of daily life."

"Now you really have gone too far," objected Patience. "Skinner's plan is based directly on empirical research from many laboratories. And you see his principles of learning demonstrated every day outside of the laboratories. Give us some examples of what you are trying to say."

"That's easy," responded Harry confidently. "I can give many, many examples of laboratory results that have been corroborated by casual observation in daily life.

"For a first example, let us consider the problem of incentive value. An incentive, as you know, is anything that the person will perform some task to achieve. That is, by definition, a person will work for an incentive. Conversely, a particular person may not work at all for something that has been proven to have incentive value for most people. For example, I know of a teacher who retired after thirty-three years of service in one job, but still happily goes to his office almost every work day. His colleagues have accused him of such things as being crazy, having no imagination or having suffered from a series of mini-strokes. But, keep in mind that this man is not simply continuing to do the exact same job that he did for thirty-three years. He is doing the parts of it that he enjoys, and not doing the parts that he did not enjoy—such as grading student papers and projects, and attending meetings. Therefore, some parts had greater, or less, positive incentive value, and some even had negative incentive value. Thus, the perceived value of the incentive is indicated by how hard the person will work to achieve it. In general, we would say that the greater the incentive, the harder the person will work for it. This is the premise of Skinner's system: Everyone gets the same level of reward (i.e., amount of an incentive) for the equivalent amount of work."

"Yes, that is the idea," agreed Patience. "That seems entirely fair and democratic to me. So, what is your problem?"

"My problem is methodological. There are large individual differences in incentive values for the same amount of physical reward, depending upon the reward history of the person, the motivations of the person, the perceptions of the person and many other variables. How does the Behaviorist know the mind of the subject person? Only by the overt actions of that person. Get serious! To be sure, the Behaviorists have not worried about the discrepancies between beliefs and behaviors. But, that fact does not mean that other psychologists have not dedicated careers to studying such discrepancies. At least, the more humanistic psychologists have tried to develop a methodology to get at an understanding of a person's beliefs and feelings. A selfish person would have unmitigated success in playing a cat-and-mouse game with a Behaviorist who was trying to discover his true feelings about the level of pleasure in performing given tasks.

"Let me give an example of what I mean. If the person has been led to expect a certain amount of reward for a certain amount of work, then he or she is frustrated and distressed if the actual amount of reward is less than expected. The person may actually *feel* punished, and will not work as hard next time." Incidentally, that is a real conundrum for the Behaviorist who avoids punishment as a means for controlling behaviors. He or she cannot stop a client from *feeling* punished.

"The effect is reversed if the person is overpaid. Therefore, the transient internal cognition of the person determines the incentive value of a reward at any given time. The complex interactions of such a multitude of variables would totally incapacitate the scientist who was trying to make exact predictions of behaviors."

Posh interjected: "So, let me see if I understand this. The amount of the reward, psychologically and not physically, is determined by the reward history of the worker. That means, as I see it, that the same physical amount of reward could be perceived as having different incentive values by two different workers. Right?"

"Right," said Harry. "Consider the retired teacher mentioned above. He liked certain concepts of his job, so he continues to perform those functions. His colleagues, who promise that they will never be seen at the office once they retire, presumably percieved far less incentive value in the performance of those functions.

"But, let us go on. There is more. Then, there is the problem of matching the amount of reward to the perceived amount of work. A person required to perform a task that is onerous to him or her will expect a greater reward than another person who enjoys performing that particular task. A technician would be chasing a will-o-the-wisp in trying to match the amount of work involved, because only the workers themselves know exactly how onerous the task is for them."

"Paradoxically, the technician would literally have to be a mind reader," observed Rudy. "But, Skinner doesn't even think that the worker has a mind."

"Right on, good buddy," chirped Harry jovially. Then, he turned solemn as he saw that Patience was again about to reach critical mass for an explosion.

Now he continued more·dispassionately: "Let me go on. Another related example of Skinner's problems with empirical data are the results from repeating rewards a large number of times. Continued rewards for a task tend to decrease the intrinsic liking for the performance of that task. We say that extrinsic rewards tend to replace intrinsic rewards. Therefore, as the cycles of performance and reward continue, the same amount of reward that was satisfactory earlier now becomes unsatisfactory. Thus, greater and greater amounts of reward are necessary to maintain the same level of performance. Again, the technician faces virtually an impossible task in trying to equalize the work loads and rewards of all of the workers."

Seeing that Patience was about to interrupt him, Harry stopped her by saying, "Just a minute, Patience. I am almost done."

"Okay, Okay," said Patience, holding up her hands defensively. "Go ahead, Mr. Fuzzy Wuzzy Brain."

"Thanks," said Harry. "The last thing that I want to say is that there are problems with Skinner's theoretical basis. I myself have strongly criticized Skinner's plan on theoretical grounds, as well as the empirical ones. These arguments against Skinner's proposal consisted of straightforward extrapolations from laboratory research. These are in contrast to Skinner's original feckless proposal for social applications, which is itself ostensibly based on empirical laboratory data. Several disparities between Skinner's prediction and laboratory data have been noted, however. It is ironic that Skinner's social proposal is so alien to empirical behavioral research, given his earlier commitment to hard data and his claims to an empirical base for his social proposal."

"How can you say that about Skinner, a man who is undeniably dedicated to empirical science?" complained Patience. "It is grossly unfair to say that!"

"It is not at all unfair," said Harry, "because Skinner's major book on the subject, *Beyond Freedom and Dignity*, included no data to back up his claims. But, it was loaded with lots of appeals to authority. Check it out. But, you will have your chance to refute me later.

"Moving on, I want to say that my own views also are based on casual observations of social behavior. But, in addition they are based on the literature of freedom and dignity, which Skinner denigrated and hoped to discount entirely. I have finally concluded that Skinner's proposal will not work at all on this particular planet, even for some small insulated portion of the animals and societies.

"Well, now I have said my piece. I think that I have good reasons to disagree with Skinner and Burnhouse. What do you say, Patience?"

Patience snorted sarcastically under her breath. Then, taking a deep breath, she began: "I say bullfeathers, because there are ladies present. I wonder what planet you yourself have been on, Dr. Hawkey, sir. You do not understand Skinner at all, really. Don't you know about interactions among variables? As every psychologist should know, the effects of one variable often depend upon the level of another—possibly fringe or tangential—variable.

"In the first place, let's consider the tired old complaint that the research of the Behaviorists is not relevant to human behavior. As a Behaviorist, I am sick of hearing this one. The answer is golden as far as science is concerned: the proof is in the pudding. At least, that is what we say in Australia. Skinner had shown many times that certain behaviors, which others had tried to explain in exotic—i.e., Humanistic—terms, can be explained much more simply in terms of standard principles of learning. Are you familiar with any of them? What do you have to say about such successes?"

Again, stung by her strong words, Harry struck back, imitating her sarcasm. "You yourself are making my point, Dr. Patrick. Many authors have criticized Skinner's so-called demonstrations of the unmasking of the learning mechanisms presumably underlying certain behaviors. They say that his examples are trivially simple. Of course, no one would argue that some behaviors are directly the result of identifiable earlier learning. Therefore, those demonstrations are irrelevant to the central issue between the Humanists and the Behaviorists. The Humanists argue that Skinner cannot unmask the causes of more complex categories of behaviors, and that means the ones that really matter in life. For example, Skinner cannot explain many of the phenomena of social loafing."

Patience responded disdainfully, "Like I know what social loafing is. Give me an example that I can relate to."

"Ah! Ha!" burst out Hawkey. "Bingo! You are again making my point. You Behaviorists are not actually interested in studying such complex behaviors. You just assume, and then blithely assert, that your research is relevant to such situations.

"Social loafing is the phenomenon in which people working in a group tend not to work as hard as when they are working alone. Again, no one doubts that the levels of actual rewards can be important for such group tasks. But, still, the experts agree that the major variables are related to more subjective variables. They are concerned with perceptions and cognitions of the individuals, particularly in relation to the protection of self-esteem and other such individual personal motivations. These are factors that Behaviorists deliberately ignore.

"But, let's try a more familiar hypothetical situation—the one posed by Arthur Koestler. Suppose a robber points a gun at you, and demands your wallet or your life. Although this is the very first occasion that such a thing has happened to you, you know exactly what to do under a large number of different circumstances. For example, if you are alone in a dark alley, you will be likely to comply. If you are surrounded by policemen, you will not be likely to comply, and so forth."

"That is no problem," said Patience. "The mechanisms of generalization from related experience can account for prompt performance in novel situations. The mediations from verbal habits can account for all such so-called novel responses."

"Right!" said Hawkey. "That is just the point. You can account for all behaviors by glibly proposing just the right intersection of old habits and generalizations from old habits. Scientifically, such an interpretation is untestable. That meets the definition of a myth, in which the only evidence for a phenomenon is the very fact that it is derived to explain. Like the concept of instinct, a proposed explanation that explains everything actually therefore explains nothing.

"My point is that such a circular argument certainly does not constitute proof of the theoretical approach. The real question involves how far the theory must be stretched or strained to accommodate the facts. A theory is ordinarily not tested by crucial experiments. Instead, it is evaluated by the number of long stretches that it must make to cover embarrassing facts."

"I agree," said Rudy. "We need to break the circularity by some converging operations if we wish to talk about proof."

Harry smiled at him gratefully, and continued: "My main point is simply this: We can do a much better job of predicting human performance by surmising what a reasonable person will do under the circumstances than by trying to describe the particular interactions of inscrutable habit gradients. The common-sense approach would simply ask what a reasonable person would choose to do."

"That is wooly-headed and unscientific," said Patience. "You are setting the science of psychology back one hundred years. You act like the first laboratory in psychology had never been founded."

"Perhaps not that far," demurred Harry. "But I surely would like to set it back beyond the modern fixation on Behaviorism. Behaviorism wisely moved us away from a purely subjective approach to psychology. That was good. But now the pendulum of science needs to swing back to a middle ground, to a composite, an integrated view."

"Well," said Patience, "we cannot agree on that. So, let's try a new approach to the issue before us now.

"You want to talk practicalities, then let's talk practicalities. I think that the Behavioristic ideas have proven their value in terms of successful technologies. Let us look at the possibilities as suggested by Skinner in his *Walden Two*. In that book he described many improvements of an architectural and ecological nature that would be possible in an engineered society. You cannot argue that those ideas are not valuable, and unquestionably of benefit to any society."

"I surely do not deny it," said Harry. "In fact, I commend these ideas. I also support the aggressive use of all improvements in behavioral or other technologies that would make our lives better. Only some odd extremist would deny the usefulness of the technologies that the human brain has devised. Certainly such a denial is not in the credo of the Humanists.

"But, let us consider in a broader prospective some specific examples from *Walden Two*. Many—perhaps most—of the innovations that Skinner proposed were concerned with simple engineering: architecture, water sanitation, household items. For example, the improvement in the design of buildings and implements could go forth under any assumptions about psychological or metaphysical theory. Certainly, the Humanists would be entirely in favor of improved methods for ensuring clean water. I would say in fact that the great majority of suggestions for improvements in living conditions in *Walden Two* were of the nature of better engineering design. They were nice, but they did not make a case for the Behavioristic approach to a better society."

"Wrong!" said Patience. "It is true that the Humanistic approach *permits* the use of technology, but it produces a mind set that is counter to the acceptance of new technologies. Many Humanists consider that science is in itself de-humanizing. I agree that their resistance is unnecessary and irrational. But, it is nevertheless there. And that is the point that Skinner was trying to make."

"You have a point, Patience," agreed Hawkey. "But, it is a small one. The answer is education. We must teach the citizens of the new society that technology is not incompatible with humanistic thinking and attitudes. In fact, I think that Skinner himself helped to manufacture this whole dilemma. He was the one who harped on the alleged incompatibility of science with humanistic ideas. If the citizens buy into his metaphysical system, then his arguments make sense. But, if the citizens buy into the Humanistic way of thinking, then his argument is specious."

Patience clearly did not agree. She said with impatience, "There you go, assuming what you cannot prove. Who says that the acceptance of the concepts of human freedom and dignity will not interfere with the adoption of beneficial technologies?"

"You are right," said Harry. "We do not have the data to resolve this issue. But we do have data from Kipua that shows that a society that is based rigorously on the concepts of Behaviorism has become a nightmare."

"That is your interpretation, Bwana," she said sarcastically. "We do not have to agree with it."

There was a break in the discussion. No one seemed to know quite what to say. There seemed to be little point in continuing the same argument that had taken place so many times before in other places with other debaters, without resolution.

Finally, Patience said it: "Oh, well! This is getting us nowhere. We are not going to agree until we see and analyze the data on Kipua. That is why we have come. We might as well give it up for now."

"I agree," said Harry. "This is where these so-called theoretical debates always end. That is because they are metaphysical, and not truly theoretical. But, we do agree that the proof is in the pudding. We will have to see empirically which pudding is more palatable. You said it right: that is what the experiment on Kipua was trying to find out. We will just have to see what the data on Kipua tells us."

"You're on!" said Patience. The debate ended with a handshake. On impulse, Harry also gave Patience a little hug. He did not know whether he was consoling her in defeat, or if there was some other motive. She did not seem too happy about the familiarity, but she smiled and she did not pull away.

FOURTEEN

T HE *CORNUCOPIA* was slowly easing its way through the opening in the reef, reaching at last the smooth water that Harry had craved for twenty-four hours. It was truly a gorgeous day, with air so empty that he could see clearly the welcoming party on the dock ahead. It looked to him like an inordinately large group of people had come out to meet the CRASH team. That was a rather ominous sign. It tended to put a cloud on his psychological horizon. He tried to put it out of his mind so that he could take in all of the scene before him.

The broad white beach stretched out to the north and south to distant points where it met and mingled with the reef at the extreme ends of the island. The dark green of the forest behind the beach made a scene that would cause artists to grab for the tools of their trade. The only words that came to Harry's mind were trite: paradise and peace.

Those words might well describe the combination of the water, beach, sky and forest. They did not seem to describe the look of the folk on the pier. As the *Cornucopia* pulled closer, Harry could see that there indeed were many people there, and the atmosphere did not seem as happy as a genuine welcoming throng ought to exhibit. In fact, this particular throng seemed rather agitated and tense.

"Oh, God," he thought, "say it isn't so! Has the island already exploded with the awful social bomb that I fear? Will these people attack the team? Will they take the team members prisoner when the ship reaches the pier?" Any one of these behaviors seemed a real possibility at the moment.

The group at the near end of the pier appeared to be a welcoming committee, right enough. The group of men behind them were different. They were heavily armed with rifles and shotguns, as well as sidearms. They acted as though they were fully prepared to use the weapons.

Harry was worried about the armed men. He wondered if they were a militia, or a mob. From the distance, they did not appear to be angry and hostile, though. There was something foreboding in their manner, however. "Fear?" Harry thought, "Maybe it is fear. That is definitely what I do not need more of right now."

Yes, the dominant emotion on the dock seemed to be fear. The armed men kept looking back along the dock toward the buildings flanking its entrance on the shore. They seemed to be on guard for some kind of trouble. They were surrounding the welcoming party, some with their backs to the group of welcomers, forming a tight protective semi-circle. They were also making sure that the other persons crowding the dock did not get too close. Harry's stomach began to generate the familiar burning, sinking feeling. He felt like he wanted to put on a steel helmet, bullet-proof vest and asbestos suit before joining the group on the dock.

The small gray-haired lady at the end of the dock seemed to be the leader of the party. Harry guessed that she must be the mayor, Florence Gorsuch. She looked friendly enough, but apprehensive and frightened. Harry presumed that his landing party did not look anything like a triumphant platoon of marines storming the beach in a glorious rescue. The team members had not brought along any weapons with them, of course. The leaders had thought of it. Then, they decided that the lack of tactical and technical skills among the team members would only produce liabilities if they were armed. First, the group really could not use such weapons effectively. Second, the presence of weapons could insult and further incite the dissidents on the island.

Perhaps, the avoidance of weaponry was a serious mistake. Harry truly did not think so. That very dilemma—whether to fight or not to fight—was a good example of one of the truly tough problems of behavioral science. It was difficult to avoid being drawn into an armed conflict with a foe who would stop at nothing.

Harry judged that the big guy standing behind Florence must be Dan Crow. The man was a ruggedly handsome fellow, dark complexion, with coal-black hair in a very military haircut. His hair and bearing were consistent with the camouflage military fatigues that he was wearing. In sum, Crow was a splendid physical example of a Native American.

An even more striking individual was standing next to Crow. "She must be the famous Monika Luthsaar," thought Harry. "What a beauty indeed!" Monika was tall, blond—almost translucent hair—with a body and complexion that made her look like a walking milk commercial. She absolutely and finally destroyed the stereotype that good looks and brains were not found in the same bodies. Maybe Rudy was not guessing about Harry's motives for wanting to work with her!

Harry thought that the short man in the white shirt and slacks must be dePuy. He was pacing up and down. "Must be the nervous type. Too bad!" Then he thought, "Actually, that assessment is not fair. I would be nervous too if my life's work were in jeopardy. Is it not just his work, but his very life itself, that he is nervous about?"

dePuy had his arm around a pretty young girl, about college age. Harry though that she must be dePuy's daughter. She was standing next to a suitcase. Harry again got a now-very-familiar twitch in the pit of his stomach. The presence of the suitcase was foreboding. It was obvious that the girl was planning to take the boat off the island. This desire of the islanders to leave was surely no surprise. Several other people seemed equally well prepared to depart.

One outstanding individual in the group, a tall dark man, was in some sort of uniform. He seemed to be in charge of the armed men. That was probably Constable Gupta. One of the armed group of men was also in uniform. He was probably a deputy.

"Hello, Dr. Hawkey!" Florence Gorsuch even managed a smile, as the *Cornucopia* closed with the dock. She was a pleasant lady.

"Hello," Harry said. "Mayor Gorsuch, I presume?" thinking that maybe a little humor would help break the ice.

She nodded, still smiling, a bit more genuine this time.

"Call me Harry. Most people do. I am glad to meet you. Thank you for coming to meet us."

When the old ship nudged the pier, a few lines were quickly made fast. The team said pleasant good-byes to the ship's crew. The crew had been understanding and solicitous. Harry did remember the good tip for Palu.

As the team carefully negotiated the old gangway onto the dock, it was with mixed emotions, in Harry's case at least. He was glad to be free of the undulating deck, but apprehensive about their future on the shore. As the group proceeded with the introductions, Harry discovered that the short fellow in white was indeed dePuy, and the young girl was indeed his daughter, Rene. She seemed extremely nervous. She was also bruised at numerous visible points on her body. Harry could guess at the reasons. She was obviously there to take the boat away from the island. Harry had a huge surge of guilt at the thought.

He was also right about Crow. The closer view confirmed his earlier assessment of the man.

The officer in charge was in fact Constable Gupta. His name and dark complexion confirmed what Harry had read in the Schoonover file—that Gupta was of Indian ancestry.

Gupta's deputy was an attractive native boy named Kani whom everyone affectionately called Kenny. Kenny was wearing a uniform khaki shirt and shorts, but sandals on his feet and a Braves baseball cap on his head. His ready smile made him liked instantly.

The blond vision was of course Monika—not that Harry could have any doubts about it. There could not have been two like her. Her smile was like the rest of her—flawless. She smiled with her whole face, eyes narrowing and showing lots of perfect teeth. Her greeting was cordial and her handshake was strong. Harry thought, "What can a fellow say? She is truly a goddess!" He was suddenly just a little short of breath.

Patience whispered in his ear, "Down, Boy." Harry guessed that he must have been staring, open-mouthed, like a teenager on prom night. Obviously, Monika was used to it.

Harry was brought back to attention on business when Florence said that there is a light buffet lunch prepared for them at the Crow's Nest. Gupta's men would bring along the luggage to their rooms. It was just a short walk because the Nest was the first building at the foot of the dock.

dePuy, Rene and the other would-be travelers were understandably distraught that the *Cornucopia* would not take passengers back to Saipan. There was an agonizing scene which sorely tested the team's resolve to keep everyone on the island. Rene was particularly upset. Actually, she was frantic. They were told by dePuy that she was already on medication, because of her multiple traumas. Now, her medications would have to be increased. She would have to stay under guard at the plantation compound until the island was made safe. The CRASH team would share the responsibility for public safety, along with the island government.

Once the panicked islanders understood that the CRASH team was firm in its decision, they resigned themselves to staying. dePuy made sure that the employees of Schoonover understood their liability, if further violence were to erupt on the island.

It was agreed that the *Cornucopia* would sail again as soon as it was unloaded. That would take about an hour. Meanwhile, Constable Gupta stationed some men to ensure that there would be no communication between the islanders and the crew of the *Cornucopia*, and that no one could sneak aboard. Otherwise, the ship would have to be impounded to keep the news of Kipua from spreading beyond its shores.

Then, several of the armed men grabbed at the team's luggage and threw it into an ancient automobile of some mysterious make. The words "JAKE'S TAXI" hand-lettered on the doors advertised its ownership and its function. The letters were so weathered that they were barely readable. The "Jake" in the sign apparently referred to the driver. He was a man in his middle fifties with gray hair and a gray stubble that might have been mistaken for a beard. Despite an obvious attempt to look disheveled and disreputable, he had an air about him that suggested class and wealth. It showed when he came forward in a courtly manner to help Kate with her luggage.

Harry learned later that Jake Blankenship had retreated to Kipua after a tragic head injury in an industrial accident. He had come to be near Flo Gorsuch, who was his sister. He lived primarily off worker compensation payments and poker winnings. Consequently, he rarely bothered with running his taxi service. There really was not much business for a taxi on the island anyway. Most travel was on foot or bicycle. In fact, Jake now described himself chiefly as a professional beachcomber.

The taxi itself looked like an old touring car. It must have been very expensive in its day. Its grandeur was somewhat spoiled by the apparent use of miscellaneous parts from several different makes of cars for repairs. The car reminded Harry that there can be ugliness in paradise. Not that he needed reminding.

The radio transmitter had been placed in a foot locker that was included as part of Harry's luggage. Harry's reasoning was that keeping the transmitter hidden was a safer plan than advertising its presence by extra measures of security. In truth, they did not have adequate means for maintaining the security of the radio against strong attempts to seize or to damage it. The other members of the team agreed with his plan and vowed not to mention that they had brought along a radio.

Kenny went first with the police jeep loaded with three armed men, sitting with legs draped over the chassis. The other armed men followed along on foot behind the official party. They looked ugly, yet also frightened, with their rifles and shotguns at the ready. Harry wondered what they are looking for and what was frightening them. He guessed that he would discover the cause soon enough.

Flo anticipated his question: "We are sorry for the weapons. We don't want to alarm you, but we have been having some problems lately. We do want to be careful. Some gangs have been roaming about, and extorting cash from the shopkeepers. They have even roughed up some citizens. We have been having more than the usual numbers of muggings and sexual assaults, too. We fear that the tiny moral thread still holding back the population may snap at any moment. Anything can happen after that."

"Who are those men with the guns?" asked Harry. They worried him.

"These are guards. Most of them are plantation workers on loan from Pierre. They have been deputized by Constable Gupta. So, you see, they are not really a mob, although they may look like one. They have patrolled the streets of the village day and night to protect the shops since Professor Burnhouse disappeared. Thank God for them. They have probably saved many lives at the risk of their own.

"Incidentally, we have officially requested a platoon of marines from Saipan. The officials there say that the situation here doesn't warrant that level of intervention yet. They should know better. But, in fairness, they also fear that the presence of the marines will undermine local authority. That does make sense, of course. But I fear that they are going to wait for the thread to snap and someone is killed before they send the marines." She spoke with, Harry thought, a little bitterness. Then, she added, with obvious frustration, "The ugly, horrible situation here is all caused by your psychologist friend and his crazy ideas."

She paused. She seemed about to say more, but stopped. Then, she said, in a happier tone, "We will talk about that after we have had some lunch. Mary Murphy at the Crow Bar has been working very hard to fix up something nice for you. We eat a lot of fruit here. How does that sound to you?"

Flo obviously regretted her outburst. She seemed genuinely eager to get the relationship between the team and the islanders off to a good start. That was fine with Harry.

The team members individually indicated approval of the fare for lunch. Actually, Harry lied a little bit. He was really a meat-and-potatoes man. But, he did not want to be trouble. And he certainly did want to gain the confidence and good will of the islanders.

Harry decided not to take exception to the charge against Skull Burnhouse. Flo was understandably upset. And, obviously, she did not want to start an argument this early in the ballgame. There would be time enough for argument, if the evidence showed that the current situation, which obviously was bad, was none of Burnhouse's doing. Her remarks were very disturbing, nevertheless. She had been here on the scene from the beginning. Harry remembered that she had originally supported Burnhouse.

As the group came to the end of the dock, Harry looked quickly about the lone street of the small village. "Quaint" was the word that came to his mind. The character of the town was exemplified by the appearance of the two saloons on the street. The Bar Belle was most striking, possibly because the title figure was such an outrageous caricature. The Crow Bar was identified, of course, by the sign and the huge replica of the title tool hanging from it. There was really no evidence in the outward appearance of the village that there was trouble, except that there was a bit of trash littered about.

On the inside, the Crow Bar was indeed something of wonder! It looked like a last-century scene out of a Jack London novel. It reminded Harry of the First and Last Chance Saloon in San Francisco. Jack London used to hang out in that saloon when he was in town.

Harry's group actually pushed through swinging doors into a dark room. Other than the light coming through the door, the only light in the room came from a few candles burning in old wine bottles. Harry knew that Lottie would have thought that it was wonderful. Except for the cobwebs and dust. She definitely would not have liked the housekeeping. But, under the circumstances, a good housecleaning was not truly possible, by Lottie's standards. There were dusty memorabilia everywhere in the bar area in the front: photos, fish nets, spears, buoys, you name it. There was a large mirror behind the bar. Over it a sign proclaimed, "CROW BAR." Harry liked a man with a sense of humor, one who did not take himself too seriously. Score one for Dan Crow.

Never missing a chance at a bit of humor, Rudy edged over beside Harry, and whispered, "This place is really nothing to crow about." Harry painfully tried to smother a giggle, and motioned him to be quiet. But, then, he could not resist a whisper of his own: "You may have to eat crow for saying that."

Kate glared at the two of them, and said, "You kids behave yourselves!"

"Don't frown, Kate," Harry said. "It gives you crow's feet about the eyes."

Her double-strength glare of double-barreled disdain convinced Rudy and Harry that their little game must be stifled. Nevertheless, Harry was elated that he had defeated Rudy by a score of two to one in their little contest. Such a victory did not occur very often.

Lottie would not have liked to have lunch with all of the cobwebs hanging over her food though. "Oh, well," thought Harry, "It is all in your frame of mind. I will just pretend that I am camping." On camping trips you would always eat mysterious stuff under conditions that you absolutely would not tolerate at home.

"Watch out, Harry!" he told himself. "Harry Junior would say that such a thought is patronizing. And he would be right. Get rid of any such thinking right now!"

The bar at the front on the left was separated from several small tables on the right by a well-worn dance floor. Harry presumed that they had to make their own fun out here. The bar was closed in honor of the welcoming lunch. On the back wall, there was a door to the kitchen toward the left, and a door to what appeared to be a gaming room on the right.

Several tables in the back of the room had been covered with red and white checkered tablecloths. In addition to the several candles and a wave of pretty flowers, the tables had been filled abundantly with an array of delicious-looking fruit.

"That is what they call a light lunch in paradise," Harry whispered to Rudy.

Rudy said, "And the condemned ate a hearty meal." For once, Harry did not appreciate Rudy's humor.

Standing beside the food tables was a pretty woman in jeans and a peasant blouse. The blouse had been embroidered in a pleasant floral design. The wearer was a woman in, perhaps, the late forties or early fifties of age. Obviously, this was Mary Murphy. She was smiling proudly over the fruity feast that she had prepared.

"I'm Mary Murphy. The john is over there," she said, pointing to a small door at the left. "You can dig in on the food as soon as you get washed up. You must be really starved for something to eat other than Palu's fish. If you need anything, just let me know."

"They obviously do not stand on ceremony here," Harry thought. "I like that."

Mary surely looked like someone who would tell it like it was—or, at least, the way that she saw it. Harry was sure that they would be able to get plenty of information out of her. Everyone said that hairdressers and bartenders always knew what is going on. Mary surely seemed to be approachable. Harry wondered whether it was his professional-self talking, or the would-be macho male that he would like to be.

The fruit was delicious. Characteristically, Harry ate only what he could identify. Because he was not venturesome, the amount was not very much. Some of the exotic tropical stuff did not appeal to him, because of its very unfamiliarity.

Everyone in the party seemed pleasant. They had, to Harry's mind, an enjoyable meal. Nevertheless, Harry had the feeling that their hosts were holding back something that they thought would upset the newcomers. The idea that there was something more upsetting than armed men guarding the little luncheon gathering seemed unsettling enough to Harry.

Naturally, the conversation focused on the problems at hand. Everyone was particularly concerned about the disappearance of Burnhouse. Flo was almost convinced that the professor had succumbed to a climbing accident. Her late husband, who had worked at the plantation as a supervisor, had also been an avid rock climber. He had taken on more and more difficult climbs until he finally decided to attempt the west face of Mt. Kipuana all of the way to the summit.

It was a foolish decision that turned out to be a fatal one. Because the rock face came right down to the water, the climber had to start from a boat in the waves crashing against the rocks. Some prospective climbers never even made it out of the boats onto the rock face.

Flo told them that the smooth side of the mountain at that point offered few footholds and handholds. The only good holds occurred where the trail to the summit passed across the face of the cliff. The climbers could legitimately use the momentary convenience and safety of the trail on a climb straight upward, but it was a matter of pride for them not to use the trail more than that. Only novices and slackers followed along the trail to the summit once its lowest level was reached. Florence said, "Paul would never 'pull trail' like that, of course. And he died for it. I begged him not to try that climb. He was too old, although he was very experienced. The people in the boat saw him climb above the waves, and then they left, as was the custom. The descent usually stopped at the level of the last crossing of the trail. The climber then followed the trail around to the east face for the last part of the downward climb.

"We never knew what happened to Paul. We assume that he fell into the ocean. No trace of him was ever found. Not a shoe, or a knapsack, or anything. It may be the same for Professor Burnhouse."

"I am very sorry for your loss," Harry mumbled, awkwardly. He was indeed sorry. He had taken an immediate strong liking for Flo.

"Thank you," she said, with a friendly smile. "It was a long time ago. But, the memories are still fresh. I still catch myself expecting him to walk through the front door.

"Anyway, I think that the same thing could have happened to Skull. He was a kind of loner, except for Monika. He could have paid one of the natives to handle the boat for him. But, to tell you the truth, I cannot think why the native would not have come forward with such information. Having a canoe, perhaps the native has already fled the island."

Dan Crow interjected, "It is really not surprising that a native would not come forth with distressing information. He might think that someone would blame him. Or, perhaps he was playing hookey from his job, and did not want to be discovered."

"This is all quite true," Harry said. "And we have had such a possibility on our list from the beginning."

Dan added: "Dr. van Loon, the physician over at the plantation, thinks that Burnhouse just simply lost it because of all of the troubles that he was having with his program. He may have deliberately jumped in the ocean. Or, he could have wandered out of his head off into the jungle. If so, he will never be found. The jungle wipes out traces very quickly.

"Personally, I think that some of the natives killed him. It could have been rogue natives who resented his attempts to control them. Or it could have been concerned natives who thought that he was going to ruin their island."

Mary broke in with her idea. "I think that Burnhouse simply ran off, because he was humiliated by the turn of events here. He was really stressed out. He could have stolen a boat. It would not have taken much to bribe a native to take him to the next island."

Harry glanced at Patience to see how she was taking this idea a second time. She seemed to have made her peace with it. Harry let his breath out in relief.

The team decided that after lunch the members should rest a bit before they started on the serious business that brought them here. After resting, each person would study his or her briefing material, getting himself or herself prepared for a meeting after dinner. The team would meet back at the Bar for dinner at 6:00. Then, Flo would give them a full report on the situation.

Harry asked Flo and Constable Gupta if they could meet briefly after lunch to give him an up-date on the situation on Kipua. They quickly agreed. They seemed eager to share the burden of saving the population of the island. Harry could not find it in his heart to blame them.

After the others had finally gone to their rooms, Flo, Gupta and Harry sat down with fresh cups of coffee at a table in the corner. The room was now just a bar again. Other customers came in from time to time. The three were so engrossed in their task that they did not notice the paying customers.

The situation on the island was indeed bad. Ill-assorted bands of people from all socio-economic and professional classes had begun to roam the island—looting, extorting, robbing and raping. This had totally overwhelmed the efforts of the constable and his deputies. The only remaining civil order was provided by poorly organized, basically untrained quasi-vigilante groups. The barely-legitimate group outside the bar was an example of what they could rely on. Unless some positive actions were taken soon, the island government would have to put out a desperate call for the U. S. Marines to come immediately.

Harry informed Flo and Gupta that the CRASH team would take hold of the situation. It would do what it could to help. Harry said that he knew that his team could find a solution. He displayed more confidence than he actually felt. If he were lying, Harry reassured himself, it was for a good cause.

Harry advised the mayor and police chief that nevertheless it was important for them to remain in charge of the island government. They must keep up at least the appearance of trying to maintain law and order. The CRASH team would help with that when it was able, but there was not much help that it could give in that regard.

Gupta said that all of his training and experience were in paramilitary police work. In contrast, Dan Crow had been a sergeant in the U.S. Marine Corps. Actually, he had been in some kind of elite commando group. Also, several of the men in the group outside had military experience. Harry urged them both to seek advice from those with better qualifications in given areas. But nevertheless they must still maintain their personal roles of leadership, constantly trying to create an air of competence and confidence. They must always exude confidence, even if they did not feel it. Harry emphasized how it was important not to suggest in any way that there was indecision or weakness in the government. Especially, they must convince the mobster leaders who wished to exploit the selfish motives of the mob at no cost to themselves.

Harry suggested that he would like to begin his job by speaking to the population of the island about what was happening. He would explain the possible consequences of these events. So, he asked Flo and Gupta to arrange a general town meeting after dinner. At that time, the CRASH team could have an open discussion with anyone on the island who cared to come. They would specifically invite dePuy, the clergy and Chief Launo, as well as the leaders of the gangs, if any of them could be identified. Flo and Gupta agreed that an emergency meeting could be set up and advertised for 7:30 that evening at the largest auditorium available. On Kipua, that would be the sanctuary of the Catholic church.

Harry decided that nothing more could be done for now. He thanked Flo and Gupta for their leadership and help, and headed off for a brief nap. He did not know whether or not he could sleep. As much as he needed a nap, could he sleep now? As a safety measure, he asked Dan to call him in an hour, as he headed up to his room.

There was a sign on the stairwell that said, "Crow's Nest." The Nest itself consisted of a row of four rooms off a hallway running almost the length of the building. There was a community bathroom at the end of the hallway. According to the information given the team by Dan Crow over lunch, the first room had been Burnhouse's. It was now sealed by some duct tape. An attached notice by Gupta said that anyone wishing to examine the room must check with him first. The next room was Monika's; then the one to be shared by Posh and Rudy; and finally Harry's.

Harry closed the door, and checked to see that his luggage was there. Then, he took off his shirt, pulled off his shoes, and flopped on the bed. Nothing else made a particle of sense right then.

After just an hour of rest, Harry knew that he would have to get to work. His thoughts were of Lottie. He thought, "I miss you, Lottie, but I do not know whether or not to wish you were here. This thing that I have gotten myself into may not be too pleasant before it is over. Lottie, you are my strength." He concentrated on his mental image of her face. She was smiling encouragement, as always. His mental image turned into a wonderful dream.

* * * * * *

Someone was shaking Harry on the shoulders, hard. His first thought was that the Nest was under some kind of brutal all-out attack. Abruptly, he sat up in bed, fists clenched at the ready, in defensive position. He had expected this, and had been prepared for it from the very beginning. Nice concerns for psychological issues did not matter now. He would fight with the fervor of a cornered Norway rat. His fighting spirit would make up for his lack of skill and experience in combat.

"What is happening? Where am I?" he yelled in panic. Harry was still in a somnambulistic state of confusion. Deep sleep and strange surroundings had disoriented him completely. He fought to shake the cloud from his brain. He tried to loosen the grip on the muscular arms that pinned his arms to his side.

But, there was no danger. It was only Dan Crow. Crow had been energetically doing his innkeeping duty, serving as a human alarm clock. In the process, he was completely unmindful of his imposing strength.

Crow was apologetic when he saw Harry's sorry state. "Please excuse the rough stuff, Doc," he said. "You were really out cold. Grab a sock. It is seventeen hours—that's five o'clock to you. The dining room is open any time that you can make it down."

Harry could hardly believe that it had really been a full hour since he had flopped on the bed. He could only mumble his thanks, and wave his arms pointlessly in the air.

Harry was profoundly embarrassed by his uncharacteristic bellicose display. He always hated to appear ridiculous, particularly in front of strangers. Crow's broad grin made him feel like a tenderfoot among men.

Finally gaining his wits, Harry rolled out of the bed on to the floor, supporting himself on hands and knees. He felt exhausted and weak. He was not even sure at first that his impotent legs would bear his weight. He could barely whisper to Crow, "I just need a shower and some clothes on my back, and I am out of here. Give me a couple of minutes, and I will be okay."

"Right!" replied Crow, still grinning at Harry's discomfiture. Tossing a cursory salute in Harry's direction, like a good soldier, he hurried off like he had something important to do. His smooth gait made him seem to be a creature of the forest. He moved effortlessly and quietly in his leather moccasins and camouflaged/fatigue uniform, like a cat stalking nervous prey. Harry thought that he would not want to be stalked by Crow. Obviously, no one on the island would want to tangle with Crow.

Efficient. Strong. Those were excellent words to describe Dan Crow. Harry decided again that Crow was a good man. One could count on the bar owner in a crisis, he was sure. Harry made a mental note of it, because he was sure that Crow's strength and character would be needed desperately in the days to come.

Harry decided to unpack later. The other members of the team were probably waiting for him. Patience would be waiting impatiently, he was sure of that.

Harry showered and dressed as quickly as his stiff muscles would permit. He had to force his aching, aging body slowly down the stairs to where the others were waiting. He straightened up and tried to look a bit professorial before he appeared in their view.

But, Patience was not kind. "My God," she said, "what happened to you? I've seen better looking road-kill!"

Harry forced a half-grin. "Patience, some day it will be your turn. Besides, I feel great!"

Patience merely snorted in disbelief and distain.

The members of the team were indeed already gathered in the dining area. They were sitting down to a nice dinner of roast pork. Harry gathered that pork was considered to be quite a treat on the island. Their group was obviously being honored by the town council, he thought incidentally. But, Harry was already concentrating on the task ahead. He was not paying much attention to the quality of the cuisine.

Over dessert, which was some sort of banana pudding, garnished by cinnamon, Harry explained to the group the purposes of the evening meeting. He outlined the approach that he planned, "My intention is to explain that the team is primarily on the island to find Burnhouse. The assessment of the results of the scientific experiment is secondary. I want to make it clear that we are not on the island to place blame on anyone, or to punish anyone. They should know that we do not want to make any trouble for anybody."

Harry could not help but notice Mary Murphy. That would have been virtually impossible under the circumstances. She looked very pretty in her peasant outfit and red-and-white checkered apron. She had some kind of large white flower in her hair. Her ready smile was even more radiant than the flowers. Her up-beat beauty was very welcome, given the serious business to be conducted after dinner. Harry felt a connection with her that he could not form easily with everyone, especially with women. She was different for sure. A strange thought suddenly occurred to Harry. Perhaps, he was now ready to move on with his life without Lottie.

His admiration must have shown on his face. He noticed that Dan Crow was staring at him with a stoic expression. For a Native American, that was probably not a good omen. It now occurred to Harry that perhaps Crow had an eye for Mary. He would have to find out, if indeed that were true. Crow was needed as a friend and ally on the mission. Also, Crow would surely be a very difficult adversary if he were alienated. Harry had already decided that fact. But Harry would like to be his friend, in any case. So, he decided that he had better make a much better effort to stop staring at Mary Murphy.

Coming back to the present business, Harry continued, "We must listen and learn as much as we can. We must gain confidences on an individual-to-individual basis. We must get the people to talk to us. So, make friends. Convince them to trust that you will maintain confidence in your sources. And really earn that trust. Be genuine. Don't just try to fake it.

"That's about it. Any comments or suggestions before we leave?"

Hearing none, Harry declared, "Okay. Let's go to work. And good luck to us all."

FIFTEEN

HARRY NOTED WITH SATISFACTION that word of the meeting had spread effectively to all segments of the population. The sanctuary of the church was filled beyond capacity. The extra chairs lining the aisles were all occupied. Also, people were standing in the open space at the back. The old wooden building creaked and moaned as it withstood the extra weight of the overflowing crowd.

The furnishings in the room were rather spare. Of course, there was the usual abundance of crucifixes, dominated by the large one at the front. The single stained-glass window at the front provided a worshipful atmosphere. The reverence of the scene was augmented by a plentiful array of lighted candles, which painted dancing lights on the walls and ceilings. Harry guessed that the multiple candles were standard fare, even for scientific gatherings such as this was intended to be.

Harry tried to assess the mood of the crowd. He decided that the best description was "despondent and anxious." Apparently, there was not a lot of hope left in them. He would have a mammoth task in restoring trust on the island. But he did not sense general hostility toward him and the CRASH team.

By some miracle of determination and organization, Mary had managed to put together a table of fruit and a punch bowl. She was a most remarkable woman indeed. Harry took time to notice, out of the corner of his eye, that she looked very pretty with now a fresh pink flower in her hair. Apparently, the abundance of flowers on the island provided whimsical changes for each particular occasion.

As he secured a cup of punch, Harry thanked Mary for the thoughtfulness. "It should help to keep the tenor of the meeting at a less confrontational level," he said.

Mary smiled, and gave a brief curtsy. "Thanks, Doc," she murmured in a most friendly way. Harry felt a slight twinge in a long dormant segment of his heart.

Crow was still staring at Harry from a corner of the room. He did not look happy. Harry prayed that it was not a very hostile look.

The audience was a mixture of types, to say the least. There were townsfolk, natives, gang members, members of the city council and, of course, the police. Harry was extremely pleased that all of the different groups could still come together in the same room without open warfare. He hoped that he could keep it that way at least. Even if he could not establish positive harmony, he would settle for an uneasy truce.

Chief Gupta was trying to look inconspicuous. He was not having much success at it. Somehow a badge and gun seemed to draw attention to the wearer, whatever the circumstances. Gupta had put his gun away for a while, but subsequently found it necessary to strap it on again.

Several gang members were viciously taunting Gupta. But, he was resolutely keeping his actions in check, if not his mood. Harry admired his restraint. It was part of Gupta's obvious attempt to keep the crowd from becoming more aroused than they already were by the appearance of armed authority. The situation was very nervous. A wrong word from anyone would be disastrous. He prayed that he would not be the one to say that word.

Flo Gorsuch came quickly forward, and took Harry warmly by the hand. She said, "Harry, I would like to introduce you to several people that you should know. These are influential people on the island. Or, at least they were. They might be able to help you."

Harry thought, "If she were only a few years younger, or I were a few months older. Either way, something good could happen."

Flo, noticing his gaze, smiled knowingly. She obviously felt the same way. Then, she nodded toward an ebullient young man who was wearing a Roman collar, and carrying a Bible in his right hand. He kept the Bible with him so that he could always fill a few minutes with reading when he had the chance.

Harry had already noticed how the young priest bounced about the room, greeting everyone with the same genuine warmth and interest. His cheerful nature was revealed by the perpetual broad smile on his face, even when he was alone. He explained that God was always with him. So, it definitely was not a phony, fixed smile, but a real one.

"This man will be a peach of an ally," thought Harry immediately. "He will be a strong force to help us do some good things."

"This is Father Jacques Schindler," said Flo. "Watch out, or he will give you a job to do in his church."

Jack gave her a fake frown, and then broadened again to his usual smile. Harry could feel the affection between the priest and the schoolmarm.

"Jack, this is Professor Harry Hawkey. He is a real professor, but he likes to be called Harry by his friends."

"Glad to meet you, Harry," said the priest. "I am sure that we will be friends. Call me Jack. The kids call me Freré Jacques. I got my strange mixed name because my mother was French Canadian, and my father was a German immigrant to Canada. I tell you that in case you were wondering. Everybody does, you know."

Jack Schindler talked like he was going to run out of breath before he was finished. Now he talked even faster because he was concerned.

"I am sorry for the circumstances of your coming," he said. "If there is anything that I or my church can do for you, just give a shout. I can hear you from anywhere on the island."

"That means that he has spies everywhere, so be careful," interjected Flo, with a smile. "Nobody in his church can be trusted."

Jack gave her another fake frown. Such banter seemed to be a familiar routine between them. Harry could tell that Father Jack surely must be greatly beloved by all of the decent people on the island.

"Thanks," said Harry. "You have already helped us out with this place for a meeting. Now, just keep praying for us."

"You got it," said Jack with a wink, and another slight broadening of his usual broad smile. "See you," he said, as he moved on to greet some new arrivals.

Flo then placed her hand on the shoulder of a pleasant-looking, middle-aged black man who also was wearing a Roman collar. "This is the Baptist minister, Calvin Prescott. He and Jack have a friendly battle for the souls of the sinners on the island. They seem to think that there are not enough of us to go around." Everybody laughed. Flo was good at getting people to relax and feel comfortable.

"That will be the day," said Cal, with mock sarcasm. "Hey!" he said to Harry, and reached out his hand. His grip on Harry's hand was firm with sincerity.

Harry had recognized the name of the cleric from having read the mountain of briefing papers that earlier he had stuffed into his briefcase. Everything that he had read was positive.

"And this is Cal's wife, Minnie. This lovely girl here is their daughter, Calia," Flo reported with a smile. Turning to the trio, she continued with the introductions: "I would like you to meet Professor Harry Hawkey who is leading the investigative team to find out what has happened to Professor Burnhouse. He also came to evaluate the TECHland experiment. He hopes that his team can restore peace and harmony to the island."

"With your help, I hope," said Harry. "I am very pleased to meet you."

Minnie Prescott was attractive and well dressed. Like the rest of her family, she presented the appearance of a totally likeable person. She was the daughter of a prominent Baptist clergyman in Atlanta. She had met Cal Prescott at Tuskegee Institute, and married him as soon as they graduated. She had worked as a secretary in a dean's office while Cal had been in seminary. Soon after Calia was born, she herself began attending seminary. She did not finish the seminary training, because it had been too difficult with the baby, and with helping Cal get started in his first church. Nevertheless, she had become a deacon in the Baptist church. She was recognized by everyone as Cal's unofficial assistant on the island.

She was also the director of the Baptist church choir. Minnie was always one of the first persons called when anyone needed a favor or had a special need.

The Prescott daughter, Calia, had just returned to the island after graduating from Stanford. She had been a college roommate of Rene dePuy. The two girls had been devoted friends for most of their lives.

Calia was stunningly beautiful. Her perfect teeth flashed in harmonious contrast against a flawless light chocolate skin. She had inherited the good looks of each parent in a most advantageous way. While her parents were both attractive in appearance, she optimally combined their best features to produce a perfect result. In addition, Calia was remarkably self-assured for one her age. She was almost aggressively friendly.

As he shook hands in turn with the other two members of the family, Harry noted that he had taken an immediate liking to this family group. "Call me Harry, please," he said with all of the charm that he could summon. He truly hoped that these people would like him.

"Great, Harry," the minister responded. "Call me Cal. Everyone else does. We are rather informal here, as you have probably noticed. Just feel free to call on me at any time, if you need anything. Father Jack is the energizing, perpetual-motion machine. I am the plodding mule. We are a strange team, but we complement each other very well."

"Sometimes you are just an unmentionable part of a mule," Minnie informed him, laughing and giving him a hug. Cal laughed heartily, and gave her a return hug.

"Aren't we all?" said Harry, joining in the laughter. "Anyway, thanks for the offer. You can count on my request for help when it is needed. I am sure that it will be. For now, just keep praying."

"Of course. Always," Cal assured him. "And that includes the prayers of all of my family and congregation."

Just then, Posh entered the room. When he saw Calia, his eyes lit up like a marine beacon on a clear night. He practically sprinted across the room to introduce himself to the young woman. Harry thought briefly about a moth attracted to a flame. Posh was done for. That was obvious. He had finally cashed in all of his chips as a bachelor. It had happened in a flash.

In this case, it was a good flame. Harry decided that the flame in Calia was entirely illuminating and warming. From what he saw, it was not at all destructive. Posh was rushing to life, not death. Harry's snap judgment was that Posh, great as he was, could not do better. For that matter, neither could Calia. That indeed seemed to be her own reaction. No one could resist the broadside of feminine charm that she aimed his way. Posh's total surrender was obvious to all. No contest.

This match could be a union made in heaven. The smiles on the faces of both Prescott parents indicated that they thought so too. Posh was the answer to a parent's prayer.

"Go for it, Posh," Harry cheered silently, but nevertheless fervently.

Excusing himself from the Prescotts, Harry began looking over his notes, and glancing at the audience. Reluctantly returning his thoughts to grim business, he was both distressed and pleased to see a great many club jackets of gangs in the crowd. He was disheartened to see that there were so many gang members. But, he was happy that they had come to the meeting.

Harry could make out at least four different color combinations. He moved over to Constable Gupta in order to find out more about this possible threat. "Constable," he said, "tell me about the gangs."

Gupta began, "It is very bad, Harry. As you might expect, the gang memberships are determined along ethnic lines. The gangs have always been here. Unfortunately, the arrival of the TECH-land experiment gave vicious new life to them. They are stronger now, and prone to much greater excesses than before.

"Unfortunately, the memberships of the gangs now includes girls as well as boys. The girls seem to be even more vicious, probably because they want to prove their equality. Some paradox! This debacle should not provide the physical setting for the first full elimination of gender barriers."

"Amen to that!" said Harry, with conviction. "I favor equality, but hope that the equality will concern things that benefit society, or at least not be harmful to society."

"Right on," said the police chief. Then, he identified the various groups of jackets. "The colors of the jackets identify the gangs, of course. We have the Makos who are wearing the gray jackets. It is shark gray, as you can guess. They are mostly natives whose fathers make their living as fishermen, and for whom sharks are a constant threat. That is the statement that they hope to make. They want to dominate the island inside the reefs the same way that the real sharks dominate the sea outside the reefs.

"The bitter rivals of the Makos are the Tigers, the ones in the yellow and black striped jackets. These are mostly native boys whose fathers work on the plantation. Because they belong to the same ethnic group, the competition with the Makos is especially fierce. These two gangs really hate one another. It is ironic that the biggest hatred is within the same ethnic group."

Gupta said it with great sadness. Obviously, it was a topic that disturbed him greatly.

With a deep breath, he plunged ahead. "The Dragons in the red jackets are the kids of the Japanese minority. Like everyone else, they feel that they have to fight for status. They cut off the end of a little finger to prove their courage when they join the gang. They say that it is to be bitten by the dragon. So, as you might expect, it is impossible to intimidate them. Particularly, no legal methods will work with them. They pride themselves on the courage and dedication of the Samurai. I think that they are absolutely immune to pain. Just imagine an animal that cannot be controlled by even the most aversive methods. So, even if the particular society were willing to use such methods of control, they cannot be controlled by aversive means. They fear nothing, except to reveal fear in their behaviors. Because of it, I cannot control them."

Harry was stunned. "This is amazing," he said. "When you take away punishment—indeed any aversive methods—you are taking away the usual stopper among the methods to control poor behaviors. The only thing stronger, in my view, is the power of love. How can we show them love?"

"Good luck," intoned the chief of police. Then, going back to his descriptions, he said, "It doesn't get much better. The last group consists of the kids in the brown jackets with the letters JYD. They call themselves the Junkyard Dogs. The brown symbolizes dirt and feces. They are the kids that have been closed out of the other gangs for one reason or another. They are probably the worst of the lot. They feel that they are outcasts, treated like dirt underfoot, and therefore they have more to prove than the others. They are a mixed group ethnically. There are mostly blacks and Chinese and various mixed races, and a few individuals who are members from each of the other ethnic groups, but rejected by them for a variety of reasons.

"They have the crazy courage of cornered rats, and the frenzy of persons without goals or hope. Their weakness is that each member places his or her own self-interests before those of the group. But that also means that it is extremely difficult to control them as individuals or as a group."

"Maybe the key to helping them is to help them find a basis for self-esteem. We might start with a leader, if they have one," suggested Harry.

"Yes," said Gupta, "Worst luck! They do have a recognized leader. His name is Percy Hernandez. Do not let the fancy first name fool you. He is indeed the worst of the worst. Watch out for Percy. He is bright enough to be really dangerous in a lot of ways. His father is in jail in the States for bank robbery and felonious assault. His mother is living in sin, as they say, with one of the laborers on a plantation in Hawaii.

"Percy exerts control by intimidation and force when he cannot control in devious indirect ways. He is intelligent enough to be devious, and ruthless enough to be intimidating. That is why he is so dangerous. Do not trust anything that he says, and always watch your back."

"Thanks for the information," said Harry. "It is just as bad as I feared. This is surely going to be a tough audience. I will try to appear as optimistic as I can, though."

"Right on," agreed Gupta. "Remember that there are a lot of good people here too. And my deputy, my volunteers and I are here to back you up. If you need us, just give me a signal."

Harry nodded his agreement. "Right," he said. "But that should not be necessary. I will cut off the presentation if things seem to be getting out of hand."

Harry looked about for Mary Murphy. He would chat with her a bit before the presentation, if she were not too engrossed in something. Alas, she was engrossed. Crow had her surrounded, so to speak. Crow had dug an impenetrable social moat about Mary that would require a legion of troops to cross.

So, Harry decided to make as many friends as possible before his trial began. He moved about the room, trying to be charming.

Harry checked his watch. Because it was exactly 7:29, he ascended to the pulpit. He called firmly for attention. When he had it, he began. "Ladies and gentlemen, thank you for your attention. I will be brief in introducing the members of our team. Then, I will describe our mission here. After that, I will open the floor for comments and questions."

Each introduction was greeted with polite applause, and no enthusiasm. Apparently, the team would have to earn acceptance from the people on the island. The islanders were obviously afraid to trust.

Harry then described the mission of the team as honestly as he could. He wanted to give hope, and to instill determination. But he was determined to be realistic about what the team could reasonably accomplish.

The question and answer period was quite lively and informative. Most townspeople and plantation workers were rather supportive of the rescue mission, whether or not they had originally supported the behavioristic experiment.

One of the loudest critics among the adults was obviously some sort of supervisor at the copra plantation. Flo Gorsuch leaned over to say that this was Sam Conaway, the chief overseer at the plantation. Then, she added, "This is a real bad dude. Watch out for him."

Conaway had been a strong supporter of Burnhouse, and still supported the experiment. The TECHland experiment had actually given him the opportunity to gain more power. Conaway's main point of argument was that the authorities should let the experiment run its course without outside influence from the big money people in New York City. Harry was sorry to meet such opposition. Conaway carried a lot of influence among the native workers.

Harry explained that all of the experts, and most of the island-ers, agreed that the results of the experiment were already clear. Those results were completely disastrous. There was no need to let the situation get worse. Their first concern was containment and rescue. The task of the CRASH team would then be to evalu-ate the execution of the experiment to determine if it was a fair test of the underlying theory.

This explanation was accepted by most of those present. That number did not, of course, include the members of the gangs and the leaders of the junta. Their shouts of derision and dissent almost ended the meeting right then. Conaway was not about to concede anything. He obviously wanted to strengthen his hold on the leadership of the TECHland supporters.

Despite the opposition, Harry and Flo were finally able to quiet the crowd enough for the meeting to continue. But, the criticisms were not over.

Another particularly mean-looking individual was also out-spoken and harsh in his criticism of the rescue team. He was truly a giant of a man. Flo Gorsuch whispered to Harry, "His name is Mulik Efraim. He is the village blacksmith."

Harry whispered, in awe, "I believe you. Of course, he is."

Harry could not help but think of Goliath taunting the Isra-elites. This was truly a daunting adversary. His sheer physical presence, with ugly scowl, sucked the very marrow from your backbone. Obviously, he was feared by everyone in the room. As Harry looked about the room for a likely hero with a behav-ioral slingshot, he was sorely disappointed. No one appeared to be a good candidate to be a champion against the man. That situation was acceptable for now. The team was, in fact, not prepared for a serious confrontation at this time. Forceful confrontation was not in Harry's best interest at this stage of the game. Nevertheless, Harry resolved to keep looking for a

David with a giant-killing slingshot. The need was sure to come for a hero on his side.

Flo said that Efraim owned a fix-it shop down the street from the Crow Bar. Most of his work was done for the plantation. That fact meant that often he had to work with Sam Conaway. Nevertheless, Efraim did not like the overseer, despite their similar views on the TECHland experiment.

Efraim's strength was legendary in the town. No one wanted a confrontation with him, for obvious reasons. It would be difficult to even imagine surviving a fair fight with him. He was the only shopkeeper who could get away with refusing to pay a tribute to the junta. Presumably, they did not want to risk even an unfair fight with such a collosus.

Mulik Efraim was indeed a fearsome presence. The first sight of him was always dominated by impressions of immense size and brute power. He was huge—about six-foot-five tall—and broad as a purebred Hereford bull across the mighty, sloping shoulders. He was as thick and muscular as his blacksmith profession could make a person. Common tales in the village told of his strength. Once, to win a bet, he actually lifted the iron anvil in his shop, without even bothering to detach it from the heavy wooden block to which it was mounted.

The second part of the frightening image of the behemoth blacksmith was his personal demeanor. Efraim always looked fierce. He never smiled. In fact, he had a perpetual scowl fixed on his face. People walked on egg shells around him, for fear of provoking him. His rages were legendary when someone inadvertently touched a personal nerve of his being. An inadvertent offense against his person could happen, despite the care exercised by everyone, because no one knew much about him. No one knew anything about his life before he came to Kipua. He volunteered little information about himself, and actually deepened his ugly scowl if anyone seemed inclined to pry. It was never proved that he deliberately hurt anyone, however, even when he was provoked.

Efraim was born a Kurd in the hills of northern Iraq. All of his life before coming to Kipua, he had been victimized by the Iraqi majority in his Kurdish homeland. In fact, he had been reared on suffering. When, finally, the rest of his immediate family had been murdered by the Iraqi for some imagined offense, an uncle helped him get out of the country by hiding him in a large camel train. Only in a large train would his size remain unnoticed enough for him to avoid detection. Because he was a stowaway, there was no water ration for him. He remained alive, barely, because his uncle shared his meager water supply. The awful experience left him with terrible fears of personal danger. When he and his uncle eventually arrived in Istanbul, Efraim was able to become apprenticed to a blacksmith. That profession was a natural for him because of his formidable size. Therefore, his physical stature was his ticket to the job. In fact, his size and strength was the touchstone to most of the events in his life.

The culture of the Middle East was a constant reminder to Efraim of his tragic past. So, one day he answered an ad in a trade paper for a blacksmith position on Kipua. He was hired because of his strength and skill, despite his fierce demeanor. No one worried about his personal characteristics. He was glad that he had made the move. Life was better, but still he could not make himself happy.

He sought peace in the Catholic church because there was no Muslim mosque on the island. Father Jack had been understanding, and tried to be helpful. But Efraim still could not control the rage in his soul, despite his strong efforts.

Harry was greatly disturbed by one verbal exchange with Efraim. In response to Harry's question of how the people understood the basic principles of TECHland, Efraim said, "Might makes right!"

Harry was thrown into a difficult dilemma by these words. He knew that the Behaviorists would not accept such an interpretation of their credo. Indeed, even he himself could not agree with Efraim's conception of it. On the other hand, he could easily see how that conception was possible under the assumptions of Behaviorism. In fact, it explained precisely the reason that he himself opposed the Behavioristic plan.

Nevertheless, he decided quickly that the theoretical issue was just too complicated to tackle in this public forum. He would just combat the principle as stated, rather than get into the issue of whether or not that was the core of the TECHland plan. Harry knew that he would have problems with the CRASH team members, especially Patience, if he tried to push his own fundamental opposition to Skinner's plan.

"Friends," he said, "Mulik Efraim has raised a most fundamental point that must be addressed. It shows that he has misunderstood what Professor Burnhouse was saying. The TECHland model proposes that the values of the society be determined by the scientific research itself, and not by the edicts of some ruling powers, or by tradition. The empirical research tells the leaders what procedures and beliefs work best to ensure the benefit of the total group of people in the society. Therefore, the best way to run a society is the way that benefits everyone the most. It should not just benefit the few who have been given the power by the people to govern the society, or who may have seized such power by force.

"As you can see, this idea is therefore totally at odds with the idea that might makes right. The idea that 'might-makes-right' means that a few despots decide what is best for everyone, or perhaps just for themselves. Then, on their own, they cause that event to happen. In any case, they choose the goals on whatever basis they want. In contrast, the leaders of a Behavioristic society, such as TECHland, are constrained to expedite the goals that behavioral research has shown will be best for the overall society. Therefore, the goals of such a society do not take into consideration the immediate happiness of the rulers, but rather the long-time happiness of the society as a whole."

Efraim just snorted in frustration. "Words. Words. You play with words," he growled, with an even more ferocious scowl than usual. "In the last analysis, the rules for the society are made by the people with the power. It does not matter how they actually go about making them—with science, with Ouija boards or crystal balls. They have the power to make them the way they want. They just tell you some other reason."

"No, no," exploded Harry. "You have it wrong. The persons with power do not control the recommendations of science. Ideally, science is objective. It doesn't matter what the scientist wants.

"The TECHland model is very different from a 'might-makes-right' philosophy. In contrast, the goals of the TECHland society seek the happiness of everyone in the society, based on the objective recommendations of science. That is supposedly guaranteed by the fact that the procedures of government are determined by the results of research. The goals are definitely *not* determined by the wishes of the mighty."

Monika backed Harry: "Professor Hawkey is absolutely right. He says what Professor Burnhouse and I have said consistently from the beginning. The TECHland community does not provide for some people to satisfy their desires and needs at the expense of others. Good practices are those that work for the good of all. On that point all of the members of the CRASH team agree with the TECHland model."

With that she looked about her to the various members of the team. The team members all nodded vigorously. Patience said, with studied sincerity, "She is absolutely correct. I assure you of that as an avowed Behaviorist. That means that I am an ardent supporter of the basic plan."

Harry continued, "I should tell you that I am *not* a supporter of the TECHland model, precisely because it can be subverted by non-professionals and vested interests into the might-makes-right philosophy. That has obviously happened here on Kipua. I believe that empirical research will show that a society will progress and prosper if it accepts certain human values such as the ideas that all persons have freedom of choice in selection of their behaviors, and that moreover all persons have an intrinsic dignity that does not have to be earned by any actions on their parts.

"My friends, I just cannot emphasize enough the importance of this issue. If there was ever a clear-cut issue between good and evil, this is it. The way to salvation of the human species is through love and concern for each other as people of worth. All the rest are just tools of the trade in the service of ideas about the nature of human beings."

"Camel dung," roared Mulik Efraim, dangerously near to one of his rages. "Your words have no connection to the real world. I have not seen this alleged love and concern among my fellow citizens, except for Father Jack and Cal Prescott and his family. But, they are also paid to be that way. It is not the same. You are talking about beautiful mirages. I have often seen mirages in the desert. They are but wishful thinking."

Harry was intimidated, but knew that he could not show it. "The truths of these ideas are difficult to prove by laboratory experiments, or even field experiments, in science," he blurted out. "But, nevertheless there is plenty of observational evidence to support the view. For example, look at your own examples: the Prescotts and Father Jack. Can you truly think that all they have done for you is for money? I will never think so. If you cannot see the difference, there is no need to argue over it.

"So, let's look elsewhere. Let's look at the successful social programs in the inner cities of the United States of America. These programs provide our best evidence. They show that the most successful ones are based on a spiritual element. The spiritual element is not necessarily religious, but it has some of the important ingredients of a religious approach. The critical element is a genuine caring for the welfare of people. A person responds in a positive way to the belief that another person sincerely cares about his or her well-being, and is not just trying to bring him or her into line for the ease and convenience of someone else, or because it is a part of a paying job."

"Okay, okay," said Efraim, somewhat mollified. "I must agree with you about the Prescotts and Father Jack. But they are not the usual types. They are the oddballs. They are the exception that proves the rule. About the other evidence, I don't know. I have not seen it. I don't know about the success of spirituality in social programs. How can you say that with any confidence? Prove it."

"Well, as I said," Harry responded, "I cannot cite formal research studies, but I can say that most social observers have reached the same conclusion. Just think of how Cal Prescott and Father Jack would deal with problem kids. There are others who would do the exact same thing.

"But, there is other strong evidence of the opposite sort right here on this island. I refer to the obvious failure of the TECHland experiment on this island. You have seen it. You have seen that the attempt to build a society through scientifically-based technology, blocking out human feelings, has not worked in this case."

Some in the crowd were responding favorably to Harry's words, nodding in agreement. But others gave thumbs-down signals, and Bronx cheers. Some of the gang members shouted that they liked things just the way they were on Kipua right now. Harry feared a major conflict, if he did not discontinue the presentation.

"Friends, because we obviously cannot agree on this issue tonight, let's drop it for this evening. We have another more immediate problem to face. I think that we can all agree on this one. We are worried about the location and welfare of Professor Burnhouse. Regardless of our feelings about the TECHland experiment, we must all agree, I think, that Burnhouse sincerely wanted to develop and test a social model that he thought would be of benefit to all. We need your help in finding Professor Burnhouse, or at least in discovering what happened to him. We ask you to volunteer any information that you have that might help, and to volunteer for search parties that may be necessary. The search effort will be organized and coordinated by Constable Gupta. See him or Kenny, if you wish to help.

"It is probably best if we do not continue further discussion at this time. Thank you for coming. Good night."

Most of those present agreed that they should launch an all-out effort to find Burnhouse. Most of the islanders offered to help in the search. But there was a vocal minority that was openly hostile and oppositional. This group appeared to be composed primarily of members of the various gangs that they had been warned about. These gangs did not care about Burnhouse. They did not want to waste time and energy in trying to find him, or in finding out what happened to him.

The meeting made it clear to Harry that the CRASH team would surely have strong opposition to any real attempt to evaluate the TECHland model on Kipua. Obviously, most of the people saw the plan as a license to behave as they wished without interference from the government, or indeed by any group.

Surprisingly, the native chief, Launo, did not want to join in the search for Burnhouse, although he seemed to be an opponent of the TECHland plan. He argued that Burnhouse had decided to run off and abandon the project. Or, perhaps, the god of the mountain had punished him for his ideas, causing him to have some catastrophic accident. So, Launo argued strongly that the team should not interfere with the will of the gods.

As their group walked slowly back to the Crow Bar, anxious and depressed, the inevitable post-mortem began. Posh said, "Holy cow! Have we got problems!"—to which a chorus answered, "Amen!" The overall mood of the crowd indeed did not seem to promise much help. The best the CRASH team could hope for was that no one would decide to oppose the team with any degree of effort and coordination.

Harry noticed that Kate Okanarski hung back a little to chat with Jake Blankenship. The two had gotten very friendly. Harry fervently hoped that Kate had not gotten involved in a situation that she would regret. Jake seemed to be firmly fixed to a relatively aimless life. From what he knew of Kate, she would never be content to be unproductive for any extended period of time.

Back at the Bar, the team gathered around the largest table. They spread out many documents for study. The main goal at this stage was to identify the main pockets of potential opposition. Unfortunately, each potential group had a leader. In the town, the leader was Mulik Efraim. He obviously could not be intimidated. Whether or not he could be persuaded remained to be seen. Harry was not optimistic about that prospect, however.

Harry proposed that they check out his opinion of Mulik Efraim. This onerous task fell within the assignment that had been given to Patience. Accordingly, Patience was commissioned to talk to the blacksmith. She would try to discover whether or not he was irrevocably committed to the TECHland model, or if he could be considered an important person to try to gain as an ally in changing the opinions of the townspeople. Flo assured them that Efraim would not harm Patience, but he might, if riled, harm any male who accompanied her.

The leader of the opposition at the plantation was obviously Sam Conaway. He was another tough cookie. It appeared that he also could be neither intimidated nor reasoned with. They all agreed that there was no point in trying to reason with Conaway.

Finally, among the natives was the witch doctor, Malevi. Blinded by hate for the outsiders, there was no way that he could be reached or controlled. He would be the most feared adversary, because it appeared that he had even lost control of himself. He also was to be watched carefully, and not included in any plans for peace.

With Constable Gupta's permission, Kenny agreed to take the team on a tour of the island in order to give the members some perspective on the problems of searching for Skull. Perhaps, the team could even discover some clues to Skull's disappearance and present location. The first thing after breakfast the team would tour the beach north of town, then stop at the native village to meet with Chief Launo. Next, it would stop by the plantation house to have dinner with Mr. dePuy.

Finally, some of the group would strike off through the jungle toward the base of Mt. Kipuana; they would take a close look at some of the caves at its base.

They would also try to get a glimpse of the path up to the summit of the mountain. Kenny said that during World War II there had been a U. S. Navy weather station on the summit. It was now abandoned, and virtually inaccessible because the lowest portion of the path had been blown up by the Navy. The commanding officer of the naval station had tired of disciplining his sailors for unauthorized trips down the mountain. The lure of the town was more powerful than any punishment by Navy regulations. The sailors would crowd the bars in the town to enjoy the refreshments and the refreshing company of the native girls. There had been several serious injuries in falls and in bar fights before the officer finally ordered the demolition of the lower ridges of the path.

Now, some of the more adventurous lads of the island would occasionally risk life and limb by climbing the rock face to the lowest accessible portion of the path, and then following the path to the ruins of the station. Such bravery was a mark of distinction on the island. It was rumored that the display of a souvenir from the weather station was a tremendous advantage in the fierce competition for the scarce supply of single women on the island.

It was indeed possible that Burnhouse had succumbed to the lure of the challenge of the mountain. His motivation would presumably not be for the possibility of romantic conquests. What woman on the island could compete with Monika? The sheer boost to his macho self-image would have been a sufficient incentive. He could have found the sheer challenge irresistible. So, that was another possible fate for the man. Perhaps the team would find his lifeless body, with massive scrapes and broken bones, at the base of the mountain, or wedged in a craggy outcrop. Some natives should be sent to scour the side of the mountain in case his body was lodged in a crevice, or caught on a ridge somewhere higher up. If he had fallen into the sea on the west side of the mountain, his body would never be found.

When Harry arrived back at his room in the Nest he saw immediately that it had been ransacked. The motive appeared to be robbery. As best Harry could remember, a few items of personal jewelry were missing, along with his electric razor. The thief obviously did not take anything that could be easily identified by the owner, except for one thing: the radio transmitter. Only the radio really mattered, because it was an item of safety, rather than having great emotional or cash value.

As Harry straightened the room, and prepared for bed, he wondered if the radio was stolen for its re-sale value, or as a tactic to thwart the rescue of the island. But, it really did not matter; what mattered was that the radio was gone. Now, it would take possibly days to secure help from Saipan, instead of a few hours.

SIXTEEN

THERE IT WAS, the great mound of rocky rubble. It was formed from the remains of the base of the trail up the mountain. Whoever did the blasting job surely knew what he was doing. The rock had been blown away from the mountain such that nothing much remained except the sheer scarred face of the mountain wall. The face of the mountain could not be climbed to reach the path, some ten stories up, except perhaps by a brave and expert rock climber.

They could see up toward the left where the narrow ledge still etched across the rocky wall. But, the cliff itself was virtually perpendicular, with no evidence of cracks or ridges for handholds that could be seen from below. The trail rose at a steep incline up the side of the mountain. Occasionally, it disappeared into vertical fissures, and re-appeared at a much higher level on the other side of the fissure. According to Kenny, the trail wound around the mountain several times until it opened onto a rather flat summit. The weather station was perched on the edge of the seaward side of the summit area.

The team could surely keep this scary climb on the list of hazards that Burnhouse might have encountered. The actual list of potential fatal mishaps seemed, in fact, to remain quite long.

Having seen all that was necessary of the mountain, the team turned toward the native village. Chief Launo was expecting them for lunch. Harry suspected that the chief also craved a chance to discuss the evils of the TECHland experiment.

The village did not present anything out of the ordinary. There were the usual thatched native huts, and cooking fires. As would be expected, there were also many signs of modern conveniences, particularly pertaining to the preparation of food. Most of the natives had long since adopted western clothing.

Over lunch, there was not much serious discussion. Mostly, Chief Launo expounded on the problems that the TECHland experiment had posed for his leadership of the natives. Many of his young people had succumbed to the message of an easy, happy life. They now were beginning to blame the elders for all of the vicissitudes of life. The ultimate conclusion of the story was the same that the team had heard before: the situation was rapidly becoming worse.

Harry tried to reassure Launo that the team would get the situation in hand. When the current crisis was over, they would launch an educational program to teach the value of cooperative work and the assumption of personal responsibility. The chief was somewhat mollified. Harry could see that Launo was not completely satisfied with his assurances.

The lunch itself was more like a feast. In addition to the sumptuous array of fruits, there was the kingly offering of roast pork. After the talk turned away from the social problems of the island, the meal was quite pleasant. In fact, Harry felt that Patience was actually rather nice to him for a change.

Several times during the meal, Harry was distracted by a reflection of light into his eyes. There seemed to be sunlight reflected off some shiny surface at the top of Mt. Kipuana. It was intermittent, as if a window pane were shifting positions in the wind, occasionally catching the sun. Launo explained, with no small irritation, that the natives had complained about the annoyance. The problem was rather recent. Apparently, a window had broken loose in a high wind. The federal authorities had not seen fit, as yet, to remove either the weather station or even the offending pane of glass.

It seemed to Harry that Launo was rather reluctant to discuss the weather station. The problem with the glare from the sun off the glass could be solved easily by a warrior with a hammer on one of the glory trips to the summit. That would entail very little risk, because no one would really care if a pane of glass were broken. And, even if they did, who could discover the culprit? The chief had thought of simply smashing the glass, but that was a federal crime, as Launo said he had been warned. He himself would be charged, if the panel suddenly disintegrated. So, the pane would be smashed if and when the government decided to smash it. They all agreed that this was indeed the way that governments typically operate. In any case, of late, it had not been at the top of their list of worries.

Harry began to work on some hypothesis to explain the strange reactions of Launo. Perhaps the reflection of light came from someone stationed with binoculars on top of the peak for the purposes of spying on the activities of the team. He concluded, however, that such an idea really did not make a lot of sense. So, Harry decided that he must be becoming paranoid after just a few hours of stress on the fearful island.

They all rested briefly after the big lunch. Then, the team members decided to head over toward the plantation house. It was plain that Kenny had an agenda for the evening that had something to do with Launini. No one was inclined to delay him because he was such a nice kid. And they all agreed that Launini was an outstandingly beautiful and wholesome girl. The two young people seemed to be very much in love. Everyone happily approved of the match.

Harry had a moment of concern when he learned that Kenny intended to go back to the village alone. But he put aside his fears. After all, Kenny was armed, and trained to take care of himself. Besides it would be virtually inconceivable for anyone to want to harm Kenny. The only person in particular that Kenny should fear would be Sam Conaway, who also had an erotic eye for Launini, but zero expectation for a return.

* * * * * *

After dinner the group had gathered on the veranda of the plantation house. Harry had arranged for Patience to give a report on her interview with Mulik Efraim.

Patience began: "Mates, the situation does not look good for any help from Efraim. In fact, we may need protection from him. He is apparently bitter about some treatment that his family got in the old country, and seems ripe for revenge on something or somebody. That is a large part of his opposition to saving Burnhouse. He is full of rage, and the current situation gives a ready outlet for that. We can count on no help from him. We must be careful, or we will evoke a formidable enemy in him."

"Too bad," said Harry. "Patience, would you say that most, or many, of the trouble makers are simply latching onto the anti-TECHland bandwagon just to grind their own axes of discontent? That is a very interesting idea."

"Right," said Patience. "I think that we have some people on Kipua who just were unhappy with the status quo. These people would subvert any plan just to vent their anger."

"What do the rest of you think?" asked Harry.

The rest were inclined to agree. Rudy said, "It surely is a real possibility, at least. We will have to give that interpretation a thorough consideration, if we ever get to writing a report of this investigation."

Harry nodded. "In any case, for the moment, it appears that we can write off Efraim as a possible ally. That seems to be the sad truth."

As Harry looked about the group, there seemed to be a general agreement. So, he said, "Okay, I guess that we agree about Mulik Efraim. Kate, let that go on the record.

"Also, note that we should discuss in our final report that the TECHland experiment may have failed because of pre-existing revengeful motivations within the population. We should also discuss whether or not such a situation is indeed characteristic of all societies.

"Now let's move on to a different topic. Patience has some general theoretical issues that she wants to discuss. Now is a good time for it."

"Right, Harry," smiled Patience "I have wanted for some time to discuss the value of the Skinnerian approach to the foundation of a superior society. I think that the theory behind TECHland has been given a really bad rap. Especially by you, Harry Hawkey. It is my contention that the theory of behavioral technology is valid, even though the practitioners have often failed in making proper applications of it."

Harry also smiled, and said, "I surely am happy to discuss this topic. Personally, I am sick of hearing the determinists say how beneficial their view is to society. I think that Skinner's strict views are actually detrimental to society. In the first place, the deterministic view would wipe out much of psychotherapy. Some of the insight therapies, for example, depend upon the concept of a viable human will. With insight therapy based on the humanistic conception of people, the person is empowered to make difficult decisions so that he or she can choose those behaviors that will be beneficial to his or her well being."

Patience scoffed: "In the first place, who says that such so-called insight therapies work anyway. The evidence is not strong. Some researchers have even concluded that there is no compelling empirical evidence to support the contention that therapies based on the concept of personal choice even work. In fact, Skinner argued that a learning approach works better. You surely cannot deny that there is such a thing as learning, and that behavioral problems can be solved by learning. The learning approach is based on empirical science. Anything else is merely the speculations and opinions of people with vested interests."

Harry was annoyed. He shot back, "In the first place, who says that Skinner has a lock on science. You Behaviorists seem to think that Skinner's view is the only one based on science. I say that Skinner's views are not necessary for science. I say in fact that his views on Utopias are not based on science. He did not present empirical evidence to show that the concepts of freedom and dignity actually interfered with the progress of science in developing a superior culture. Moreover, he proposed that scientists should disregard certain categories of evidence because he himself considered those categories to be unscientific. Why should we believe him over others? The Humanists argue in fact that the evidence from casual observation should be incorporated by scientists, even if it is based on observations made by non-scientists."

Patience was shocked. "How could you be so wrong about science? You are wrong, wrong, wrong!"

This outburst was followed by an awkward silence. Finally, Patience spoke again: "Look, this line of argument is not getting us anywhere. Let's come at the problem another way. Let's look at the available data. Everyone says that is what scientists should do.

"Take Skinner's *Walden Two*, for example. In that book he describes many ways in which scientific and behavioral technology made life more comfortable in that fictional society. Consider the example of the swinging tea pot. The suspended tea pot that could swing from one hand was a vast improvement over the conventional design of tea pots and tea sets of cups and saucers. Then, there is the example in *Walden II* of the lake with pure water, constructed and maintained with modern engineering techniques. Can you doubt that such things are possible, if we will simply use the methods that have been developed to improve our environment? His book is full of such innovations—rammed earth, architectural designs for effective use of space—all based on scientific knowledge. What is your problem with such use of technologies? As Skinner once said, 'What is eating these people?'"

Harry was equally forceful. "What is eating me is that you Behaviorists are so selective about what evidence you will bless. Skinner continually denigrated the evidence in what he called the literature of freedom and dignity. Now you cite his fictional fantasies as evidence for the technologist's view. I think that is dirty pool.

"But that is really beside the point here. In fact, I concede that Skinner's descriptions of technological advances make sense. What I object to is that you Behaviorists continue to claim that only your view permits the use of such scientific innovations. To be sure, probably any Humanist would approve of such use. For example, why would a Humanist not approve of the use of our best technologies for improving water quality? If you value the dignity of people, would you not prefer that they drink pure water? Would a Humanist not desire a better tea pot? Get serious! A major advantage of the Humanist position is that it is liberal, it is enabling. Thus, it actually permits a wider range of possible technologies. Of course, it embraces the advances made by the physical sciences. But it does so only as long as they are not used to supplant human characteristics and possibilities. But that was exactly what Skinner tried to do. He was wrong. The physical sciences supplement or complement other human methods for coping with life. The down side comes when people such as you and Skinner try to use such arguments to eliminate the human spirit from our world. When you do that, you are fighting a strong force for human progress."

Patience was a bit calmer now. "Okay, okay," she said. "I agree that the environmental engineering examples do not distinguish the Behaviorist view from the Humanist view.

"But what about the real issue of controlling behavior? Let's get into the behavioral arena. That is really where the relevant issues are found. Whereas the Behaviorists have demonstrated that they know how to shape and control behavior, the evidence for such control must be absent for the Humanists because the notion of free will literally means that the behavior is controlled only by some whimsical notion of some ephemeral spirit."

"Not so," said Harry. "Again, the Humanists are enablers. We believe in the power of learning as strongly as you do. We just do not believe that the effects of environments are as complete as you think.

"Of course, we do not believe in a completely free will. The denial that behavior is caused by genetic and environmental events is not only unreasonable, it is admittedly incompatible with a science of psychology. If behavior were not connected with events in the environment and genetic factors, we would have no basis for understanding, predicting or controlling behavior. So, we absolutely, undeniably must believe in some level of circumstantial influence on behavior. Why do you Behaviorists not give us credit for that? Why do you insist on contending that we deny the effects of heredity and environment on behavior?

"We Humanists just believe that there is also some other force to be considered in the predictive equation. That force is a human will that can on occasion transcend the effects of the environment."

"But you do not have any scientific evidence for it," interrupted Patience.

"Any more than you have scientific evidence that it does not exist," shot back Harry. He was becoming increasingly annoyed.

Calming himself down a bit, Harry continued, "All this means is that the issue must be settled as a practical matter, not a philosophical one. What I am saying is that a belief in some freedom of will provides an optimism that is not found in the deterministic position of the Behaviorists. If you firmly believe the aphorism that 'what will be, will be,' you cannot logically believe that you can do anything to change the outcome. That's so fatalistic. That is depressing and defeatist. If you believe it, the next question then is to ask for a reason for trying to change anything. There is no justification in that case for any attempt to change. You see, whatever is attempting to effect a change was itself constrained by outside forces to make that particular attempt.

"So, how can the Behaviorists be creative in solving social problems, if they, like everyone else, are forced by past reward contingencies to take a particular course of action. They could not truly intervene. They could only hope that their training was specific to the specific problem."

The serious discussion was interrupted at that point by a commotion at the front gate of the compound. They could hear pistol shots and shouts of alarm. One of the native servants rushed in yelling that Constable Gupta was racing toward the compound at a high rate of speed. The party on the veranda ran around the house to the front driveway in time to see Gupta driving his jeep at a dangerous rate of speed down the road towards the compound. He was shouting excitably, but Harry could not make out the words.

Apparently, Gupta had found something important. Perhaps it had to do with the native man in the jeep behind him. The man was holding some bloodied rags.

Then, Harry was finally able to make out what Gupta was yelling. The police chief was saying, "We have found out what happened to Burnhouse. He was attacked, and apparently eaten, by sharks. Some remnants of his clothes were found by Kono here caught on some coral outside the reef. God only knows what Burnhouse was doing outside the reef.

"Kono says that he recognizes the clothes as belonging to Burnhouse. But the real proof is provided by the stencil on the neckband. The word "house" is clearly visible, even though the first part was ripped off. So, now we know the fate of Skull Burnhouse."

"That certainly seems to be true," agreed Harry. "But surely not all of this commotion is about the sad fate of Burnhouse, tragic as that is. What is it all of this disturbance about?"

Gupta nodded. "You are right, Professor. There is more bad news, but it is not about Burnhouse. Monika Luthsaar has disappeared. She disappeared just like Burnhouse—without a trace. For some reason, she was poking around the native village. I guess she was looking for clues about Burnhouse. She spent the night with Launo and his family. At least, she started to spend the night there. This morning she was gone. Her hiking clothes are missing, so presumably she was dressed. Everything else is left at the village—even her toothbrush.

"No one has seen her since last night—or at least no one will admit to seeing her. No one seems to have any information about where she has gone. I guess we had better search beyond the reef where we found Burnhouse's clothes. We went to tell her we had found them, but she had already gone. Maybe she went to that place for the same reason he did. But why she would do that is a mystery to me."

They agreed that the search should begin at first light in the morning. In order to organize his posse, Gupta would accompany them back to town. He would gather his deputies during the night. They would meet in front of the Crow Bar at dawn.

It was late when they returned to the Bar. Because there was nothing more to do until morning, they all decided to retire immediately in preparation for the next day.

Harry's mind was too agitated for sleep, however. He tried to think of Lottie, but Patience's angry stare kept intruding. He felt hugely annoyed, and anxious. The reason for his unrest was another mystery for him to ponder, but on another day.

* * * * * *

Kenny and Launini were tragically unaware that they were being followed. They would have been more attentive to the world about them if they had realized that their tracker was the worst of the characters that ran with the Junkyard Dogs. The enchanted lovers were being followed by the lowest member of the Dogs, a particularly reprehensible creature called Dregs. Dregs had earned his name from creepy acts that had caused even his fellow gangsters to recognize that he was at the bottom on the scale of depravity. He represented the very nadir on any vertical measure of righteousness.

Dreg's total wealth was constituted by the array of golden earrings in his left ear. His cast-off attire indicated that he had no money to spend for clothes. His long hair was stuffed into a bandana tied at the back of his head. He wore no shirt. His formerly white canvas trousers were cut off just below the knees. His sandals were crudely fashioned from old automobile tires.

Dregs survived by taking care of the Dog's headquarters building for free rent and a cot in the back, and by performing some small jobs about the island for food money. On days when he could not capture the jobs, he would simply steal or extort a helpless islander for what he needed. He always managed to be absolutely penniless by the time he went to bed each night.

Dregs had been visiting one of the professional native girls. He never paid the girls, of course, finding that simple threats of personal harm were usually sufficient to get what he wanted. He had left before sunlight could illuminate his deeds, in order to get back to an early morning meeting with the gang. As he was leaving in the dawning hours, he noticed Launini and Kenny quietly climbing into the taxi. Seeing a good opportunity for bad deeds, he decided to follow them. This, he thought, was at last a good chance to make the rest of the gang happy with him.

The situation for Launini and Kenny was all the more dangerous because of their innocence. They formed a blissful world of a single dyad. They were enjoying their blinding love too much to be concerned about the physical surroundings. With their picnic lunch and their swim suits in their knapsacks, they were happily oblivious to the danger of private picnics on the isolated beaches of Kipua these days. Deepest love, and a chance to be alone together, had preempted their attention and basic good sense.

It was Kenny's day off. He had borrowed the taxi from Jake Blankenship for the entire day, foolishly expecting that it would be a day of peace and love. He had said to Launini, "This will be a day to be remembered to the end of all our days." He was absolutely correct, but in a horribly tragic sense. The memories would indeed last to the end of his days. But, the reason for remembrance would be radically different from his optimistic vision.

Because the carefree couple had slipped away from the village in the early morning hours, before most the villagers were awake and stirring about, they were sure that no one would be aware of their departure, or indeed their absence for some hours. Kenny knew of a remote area of the northern beach that he thought would be safe from invading eyes. It was on the ocean side of the stretch of the island that formed the northern arm of the lagoon. It was sufficiently far toward the west to be hidden by a fringe of the forest.

It would be a glorious day all to themselves. They would be safely cocooned together for a little while, away from the pressing ambient fear now ravaging the island.

But love this day had blunted Kenny's professional training and instincts. His thinking had reverted to the optimistic days on the island before the advent of Burnhouse. It was not a time for blind love on Kipua.

Kenny and Launini were in no hurry. In any case, the top speed of the taxi was only about twenty miles per hour over the dirt roads. Dregs was able to keep them in sight by pedaling furiously on his bicycle. Fortunately for him, it was a ten-speed bike, and fairly new, the best one the gang possessed. He had been afraid that he would get in trouble for taking it. Still, in order to keep the couple in sight, he had to take short cuts through the forest and coconut trees when the road took sharp bends.

Dregs followed the young lovers long enough to get an accurate idea of where they were headed. Then, he rushed back toward town with thoughts of the evil opportunities to be seized from this chance encounter.

The Dogs were scheduled to meet to plan some new action. It had been a while since they had something exciting to do. They were restless and therefore they would be most eager to pursue this chance to let off some steam. Dregs would get a hero's welcome from the whole gang. Among the Dogs, the vilest member, the one with the most heinous scheme, was the one most admired.

Dregs pedaled as fast as he could, sometimes slowing down a bit to catch his breath. Nevertheless, it was about 9:30 by the time he reached the gang headquarters. Totally exhausted, he managed to gasp out his hateful news.

He was not wrong about the Dogs. His news was greeted with whoops of hilarity and shouts of pleasure. The leader of the pack, Percy Hernandez, dispatched several members of the gang to rush to the beach on their motorized bikes in order to catch Kenny and Launini in case they attempted to leave. This advance force would hold the lovers until the other Dogs were able to pedal to the spot on their bicycles. The mood of the gang was like the tenor of youthful schoolboys off on a holiday, anticipating the joys to come.

* * * * * *

Percival Fothergill Hernandez had all of the necessary attributes for leading a rat pack, or any other subterranean pestilence of vermin. If one could imagine a group even worse than the Junkyard Dogs, Percy could lead it. In fact, the textbook description of a Norway rat fitted him exactly: vicious, predatory, cunning, selfish, relentless. Thus, truthfully, he was far more vicious than even the mean junkyard dog which was his namesake. He truly demeaned the image of the dog.

Percy never had a family. He had been given up to social agencies by his unwed mother soon after his birth. His mother had not even wanted to see him, and indeed never had. The only thing that she gave him was his name.

Actually, she provided a dozen names of men who could have been his father. A social worker had selected three names for Percy from the list. The Hispanic surname was artfully selected with good intentions by the well-meaning social worker. He reasoned that the name might be an advantage for the boy later in some affirmative action program. It was a poor gamble, however, because the minority surname turned out to be a disadvantage in many other contexts. Therefore, Percy suffered about every social disadvantage that it was possible for a boy to experience.

Percy was shuffled among different foster families, until he was finally assigned to the juvenile detention authorities at the age of nine. By that time, he had been in trouble with the law for three years. When he had managed, all in the span of one week, to set fire to a cat, molest a neighbor girl and viciously beat up on a former friend with a bamboo rod, the judge decided that it was time for him to reside full-time in a correctional facility.

Upon his release from the juvenile facility at the age of seventeen, Percy immediately was jailed for car theft. After serving the full sentence, he was released, but soon again appeared before the judge on a charge of selling drugs. The judge suspended the sentence as a result of a plea bargain by which Percy agreed to leave the state. He knocked about several Pacific islands before he eventually landed on Kipua, like a germ that was an advance guard for a deadly plague.

No one was actually sure how Percy supported himself. He had jobs as handyman, janitor and sometimes bouncer at the Bar Belle saloon. In exchange for his work, he was allowed to stay in a back room of the bar. He obviously contributed something to his financial support by playing poker at the saloon. He was particularly good at bluffing opponents: some said it was really more like a form of extortion. It was rumored that anyone who beat Percy at poker was likely to experience some major mishap on the way home.

Because Percy had absolutely no conscience or pity within him, he was feared by everyone. There was no such thing as a fair fight with Percy Hernandez.

Most people on the island thought that Percy was at least a little bit crazy. In fact, there was no such thing as a fair encounter with Percy, whatever the occasion.

Nevertheless, Percy had been wise enough to see the opportunities in the TECHland experiment for persons like him. He surely did understand the general idea of aversive consequences. Positive reinforcement for him meant simply that he took what he wanted.

* * * * * *

The CRASH team was just finishing lunch when the shout came from the militia guarding the Bar. Someone yelled that Kenny had been badly hurt. He had somehow driven the old taxi out of the jungle, and down Main Street. Then, he collapsed in the middle of the street in front of the Crow Bar. He was bleeding freely from multiple wounds. Already, he was near death.

Several deputies of the island guard picked him up carefully and carried him into the Bar. They gently placed him on the nearest table. A cyclist was sent off to the plantation to fetch the doctor and some additional medical supplies.

Mary Murphy took immediate charge. Her credentials for nursing came from her extensive experience as a first-aid specialist in the aftermaths of many barroom brawls. Nevertheless, she gasped in terror and despair when she saw the extent of Kenny's wounds.

"Good Lord," she said. "What manner of beasts did this to you?" There was no single wound that would be immediately lethal. But there were many serious, potentially mortal, ones. Together they could produce a fatal result. That result was likely.

Kenny aroused enough to whisper through his agony, "Save Launini. The Junkyard Dogs have taken her. Into the jungle. They say that they are going to do terrible things to her. She was screaming. It was awful. They were hurting her.

"They cut me many times, and beat me. Kicked me. Left me for dead. I wish I were dead. I can't bear what they will do to Launini."

He had no strength to speak further. He subsided into quiet moans. The sounds wrenched pity and anguish from the circle of friends around him. Each wound in his flesh was draining some of the precious blood from his body. From all of the wounds together, the cumulative loss of blood was massive, probably too great for survival. Kenny was quickly losing strength.

Mary grasped him firmly by the shoulder with one hand while she attempted with to stop the flow of blood from a deep avulsion in his chest by stuffing a bar towel into the wound. They would have time to worry about infections only later, if he were actually to live.

"Kenny," she said urgently. "Kenny, can you hear me? Stay awake! Stay with us!

"You must tell us where you were. We cannot save Launini, unless we know where you were when she was captured. Where were you? What direction did the Dogs take?"

Kenny tried to answer. No sound came from his dry, smashed and swollen lips. His eyes were wide with exertion and pain. But he could not speak.

In her anxiety, Mary was shouting. "Please, Kenny. You must tell us where? Was it the picnic area of the plantation?

Still, no answer.

"Water! Water! Somebody bring some water for him," Mary suddenly demanded.

Some wise person had already fetched a glass of water. Mary was able to get a little of it down his throat. It was difficult for him to swallow.

Revived somewhat by the water, Kenny tried again to speak. With utmost effort, his lips formed the words: "Not the planta- tion."

"Was it the beach?"

Kenny gave an almost imperceptible nod.

"Which beach? Kenny, you must tell us which beach. Was it on the lagoon side?" As she spoke, Mary was now desperately applying pressure to each of the two largest wounds in Kenny's chest, one with each hand. She called for Patience to put pressure on another deep cut on his arm. There was an abrasion and lump over his right eye. The eye was swollen shut.

Kenny frowned, wincing at the pain it caused. The answer was an almost inaudible, "No."

"Was it the north beach?" asked Mary frantically. "Was it on the north, Kenny?"

Kenny struggled to answer. He was progressively getting weaker. The best efforts of Mary and Patience could only slow, never stop, the steady flow of blood. His life was seeping out around the rags and towels that they had stuffed into his deep cuts. They were not able to put an end to the slow, always unyielding, seepage of the vital essence from Kenny's body.

It had obviously been a heroic effort for Kenny even to have reached the old taxi and driven it back to town. The effort and the elapsed time had simply cost him too much blood.

Finally, he whispered with his last strength, "Northwest," and collapsed into unconsciousness. Courageously, he had told them what they needed.

Then, almost immediately, Kenny was dead. The effort and the anguish were over.

Mary slowly and gently pulled a checkered tablecloth over his face. As she lovingly performed this act of respect, there were moans and anguished cries all about the room. Then, after a moment, the group fell into shocked silence. All were simply stunned with amazement and pain.

Kenny had been much loved and respected by all of them. Despite the general anguish of the past weeks, they could all feel a new, deep sense of personal bereavement over Kenny. The communal suffering was genuine and intense.

But, after the moment of shock, fear for Launini took over and activated their minds to useful purpose. Gupta yelled, "Some of you men with guns, tie some bicycles to the roof of the taxi. As many of you as possible, get into the taxi. But, leave plenty of room for me to drive fast."

Then he said to the others: "We are going to look for Launini. Saving her must now be our first concern. After that, we will look for those scum. Then, we will deal with them. They probably took her for a short distance straight into the jungle."

As he was rushing out to the old car, he continued his instructions. Pointing to two young men, he said, "You two grab your bikes and alert the people of the native village. Also, tell the people at the plantation. We must get all available men and women to form search parties. For safety's sake, keep at least ten people in each group. That should prevent attack on the search parties by the Dogs. Above all, keep in close contact with one another.

"Let's get going. Let's all pray to God that we are not too late to save her."

Gupta was sobbing without shame as he jumped into the taxi. He was totally unmindful of the puddles of Kenny's blood. Caked and still drying on the seat, it drenched his clothes. Then, he rammed the accelerator of the old vehicle to the floor, and, with wheels spinning, he roared off toward the north beach.

The street was a mass of furious haste. The people were scrambling for guns, knives, any weapon. They all knew that it would be too late to save Launini from the deprecations of the gang, of course. But perhaps they could yet save her life. They knew that the Dogs were not known for following exactly the mandates of the junta. So, the gang could not be expected to use judgment in their treatment of Launini. Nor would they feel the slightest compassion for her. Clearly, Launini's life was in the direst danger.

Harry knew that the thin thread of restraint that had held the island back from total ruin had now been broken. From now on there would be total lawlessness and virtual social chaos on the island. In great distress, he said to Dan Crow, who was standing next to him, and weeping openly, "This is it! This is the end. The remaining social order on the island has been vulnerable to any aggressive action on either side.

"After this, neither side will be the same. Even if there were no attempt at retaliation by Kenny's friends, attitudes have changed. The gangs now have shown that no actions, no matter how despicable, will be out of bounds for them. We must now call for the marines to save us. I will send a native in a canoe to the next island to issue the call from there."

Dan readily agreed. "Go ahead," he said in a shaking voice, "Do not wait for advice and approval from the island council. I will take that responsibility."

* * * * * *

Dr. Pieter van Loon was born of Dutch parents in Antwerp, Belgium. Because his father was a physician, it was always assumed that he too would go to medical school. He focused his life on that goal, always taking the appropriate and difficult courses that would help him fulfill that purpose. Consequently, he was well-prepared to enter the medical school at the University of

Amsterdam when World War II broke out. His father immediately immigrated to Canada, and saw to it that Pieter was enrolled in the medical school at McGill University.

Van Loon performed so well that he was sought by several teaching medical schools to be on their faculties. But, he loved the real hands-on practice of medicine, and thus decided to become a general practitioner. He became associated with a general practice in a small Minnesota town, and took over the entire practice when the owner retired.

So it was that van Loon aged in the dedicated practice of medicine. He had retired from the large practice in rural Minnesota. He felt that he could no longer tolerate the rigors of the winters on the upper plains, and the demands of the paperwork imposed on physicians in the continental United States. So, he retired from his practice at the age of seventy, and moved to Florida. On paper, therefore, the move had looked wise. But, it really was a foolish move. His wife, Anna, had died many years before, and he had no children, indeed no family at all.

Van Loon had not counted on missing his friends, along with the challenges and personal rewards of his medical practice. The vicissitudes of the shuffleboard court and golf links did not satisfy his lust for life. He was bored, and rapidly becoming fat as well.

His life was saved when he saw the ad in a medical journal for a general practitioner on Kipua. The position sounded like it was made to order for him. Undoubtedly, the weather was warm. He would be provided with a nice home, with all utilities paid, and with someone else to provide the maintenance and yard work. He would be on salary, so there would be minimal paper work. And, he would be able to practice all kinds of medicine as the need arose. Best of all, he would not have to pay licensing fees or malpractice insurance.

DePuy had been so happy to have van Loon accept the job, that he agreed to hire a temporary replacement for one year while van Loon took a residency in general surgery at McGill. The Dutch physician felt that he needed the extra surgical skills because of the relative isolation of his new job from medical consultants.

The island adventure had paid off handsomely for van Loon. So far, he had made many good friends, and enjoyed the life on the island. He had been able to treat illnesses and diseases that he had only read about before. When he was stuck on a diagnosis or option for treatment, he could immediately contact the excellent staff at the Army medical hospital on Saipan. In emergencies, he could summon a rescue helicopter from the Coast Guard on Saipan.

Van Loon was an extraordinarily talented and versatile physician. He was able to supplement his broad base of experience with an adequate medical library at the plantation compound. DePuy would purchase any medical text that he requested, so that he could keep abreast of the latest in diagnostic methods and treatments. Truly, however, only about 20% of his cases involved anything in the way of specialized knowledge or treatment. So far, he had encountered no problems that he could not handle. Indeed, it had been a great life for him on the island for seven years.

Now, all of that was changing. There would be a need for his surgical skills on trauma victims that was far greater than anything that he might have imagined when he began the surgical residency.

SEVENTEEN

KNOWING THE GENERAL LOCATION of the attack on Kenny and Launini, Gupta easily backtracked to the area. Once there, he ordered his men to spread out along the beach to look for signs to help him locate the exact spot of the outrage.

The location was not difficult to find. Kenny's dark knapsack and the sobering remnants of the picnic stood out clearly on the otherwise clean, unspoiled white beach. The sand was greatly disturbed about the picnic area. Ominously, the area was heavily sprinkled with blood. There was a distinct trail of trampled sand leading toward the jungle, and disappearing into it.

Gupta motioned for quiet. Crouching low, he cautiously preceded the group into the tangle of trees and vines. Every gun was at the ready. Fingers were tense on the triggers. Surely, on that day, the posse—every single man in it—would shoot any member of the Dogs on sight.

The group did not have far to go. A few yards into the jungle they found a small clearing that had been the point of tragedy. A few torn articles of Launini's clothing, some blood, some beer cans and some trampled underbrush were about all that was left to tell the awful story. That story was as bad as they could have imagined, if they had dared to imagine.

The Dogs had gone. There was no sign that Launini was still there. She may have been taken away with them. Or, left to die, she may have crawled off into the jungle after they were done with her.

Gupta called her name, first softly and then louder. There was no response. Only jungle noises. He instructed the men to search the immediate area. He said, "Do not go far from this spot. It is

296

dangerous. Besides, if she crawled away on her own, she could not have gone far."

The men obeyed, fanning out from the spot, shouting Launini's name. Soon, they all had returned. Each had shaken his head sadly to indicate a failure of the search.

So, Gupta had to give up the search in this place, "All right, men," he said. "We must assume, and hope, that some of the Dogs took her to a place where she could get medical help when the gang was through with her. That would be to Doc van Loon over at the plantation compound. Get in the taxi quickly. We will look there first."

Gupta drove as fast as was rationally possible with the ancient taxi over the rough roads. They soon arrived at the plantation compound. To their delight they found that Gupta had been entirely correct.

But, the other news was very bad. As they expected, Launini was badly hurt.

The servants told them, in outrage and anxiety, that a couple of the Dogs had propped Launini's partially nude and unconscious body against the compound wall, near the gate. For some unfathomable reason, they had wrapped the remnants of her clothing about her. After ringing the bell outside the gate, they had wisely disappeared. Servants answering the bell discovered Launini. They went after Dr. van Loon immediately. He had already started for the village after the message for help for Kenny. But, he had started back toward the plantation after a message soon after informed him of Kenny's death. He had surmised correctly that Launini might be brought to him at the plantation house. Van Loon quickly instructed that she be taken to the plantation infirmary. At once, he instituted desperate procedures to resuscitate her.

By the time Gupta and his men arrived at the infirmary, Launini was partially conscious. Van Loon reluctantly permitted the constable to speak to her briefly, so that he might possibly learn the location of the Dogs. They both knew that it might be Gupta's only chance to talk to her. The odds were strong that she would not survive. She had been skipping back and forth between awareness and unconsciousness since her arrival at the plantation compound.

Gupta gasped in pity and despair when he saw her battered condition. She had apparently been subdued by repeated brutal blows to the face, chest and stomach. Her eyes were swollen closed. She was as still as the atmosphere of death in the room, except for the horrible grating, ripping sounds from deep in her chest. The sounds were wrenching mixtures of moans and sobs.

The fetid odor from her body gave crushing evidence of the evils perpetrated on it.

The spirit of life had gone out of her. It seemed to Gupta that the very force of life might follow at any time.

"Launini," he said, gently. "Launini, can you hear me?"

There was no answer. Gupta was now sobbing, desperate for some contact. He feared that there would never be an answer. He raised his voice slightly with deepening despair, and begged, "Launini, Honey, speak to me! Can you hear me? Please, answer me if you can."

Again, there was no answer. The silence was oppressive and growing more frightening moment by moment. The brutalized girl tried valiantly. But, she could not open her eyes. Still, her brave attempts revealed to them that she was still alive.

Then, with eyes still closed, Launini slowly and painfully formed the word: "Yes." There were gasps of joy about the room.

Then, there was another sound. It was a poignant question: "Kenny?"

Gupta let out another exclamation of relief and joy. He spoke slowly, taking care to form each word clearly. "We know that it was the Junkyard Dogs who did this to you. They are not likely to come back to town for a while. Do you know where they were going? Did anyone say where they intended to hide out?"

Again, the answer was slow in coming, produced with great difficulty, and severe pain. "Camping in jungle." There was a pause, and then again: "Kenny?"

"Thanks," said Gupta. "Now get some rest. We love you. Don't worry about Kenny. He is resting. Your mom and dad have been told about what happened to you. They will be here soon. Don't worry. Doc van Loon will fix you up." He spoke with more confidence than he felt.

Launini tried to smile when she heard the reassurance about Kenny. Painfully, she said, "Told ... not .... fight." Then, with a small moan, she passed again into unconsciousness. Launini would speak no more to them that day.

Gupta had wanted to know the location of the Dog pack so that he could pass the information on to Chief Launo. It would be up to Launo to obtain justice. Gupta's small posse might be able to locate the gang, but it could not possibly capture and hold all of its members. Even if that were possible, the other gangs would not let him keep the gang in custody. The various gangs all were bound by the common bond of opposition to law and order. So, at the moment, by himself, he was helpless. His only viable course of action as a police officer was to stay alive and to remain relatively independent. Perhaps, later, the conditions would be right for him to re-assert his rights and responsibilities as the chief of police.

In all probability, word of the attack had already reached Launo. His rage would be terrible. Gupta commissioned one of his men to go to Launo. He would ask for twenty of Launo's best and most loyal warriors to form a posse to find and arrest the perpetrators of the attack. He emphasized to the messenger that the posse would be appropriately deputized and under civil control.

Gupta's couriers would lead Launo's men to the site of the attack. Then, the warriors could follow the trail of the Dogs from there into the jungle. Gupta's posse would immediately enter the jungle from the town on a direct westerly course. After an hour, the natives would begin firing a rifle every ten minutes so that Gupta would be able to locate and to join forces with them. Together, they should be able to overpower the Dogs and hold them at a secret place in the jungle under joint guard until a trial and justice could be arranged.

* * * * * *

The CRASH team had gathered at the plantation house to wait for word of Launini's condition. Chief Launo, his wife, Kari, and the rest of his family, except for the sons who were chasing the Junkyard Dogs, had come from the village.

Dr. van Loon was not optimistic about the chances for Launini's recovery. He had not told her about Kenny, of course. She was already depressed enough to have it lessen her chances for recovery.

Jack Schindler and Cal Prescott stayed to pray quietly by her bed, and talk gently to her. At times, one of them would speak encouraging words to her in a low voice, hoping that she could somehow hear and respond, even while locked deeply into a comatose state.

The entire place was a dreary morass of misery and dread. People spoke in quiet groups. Spontaneous hugs of encouragement were frequent. Minnie and Calia Prescott were everywhere, bringing solace as best they could. Mary Murphy and Kate Okanarski kept a pot of coffee hot and ready.

After a short while, they could hear the distant sounds of rifle shots at the designated intervals. The sounds soon faded away, because the leaves in the jungle acted as excellent acoustical barriers. If later there were a full battle, they would not be able to hear it at the compound.

Jake Blankenship kept repeating that the whole tragedy would not have happened if he had not lent his taxi to Kenny. Kate assured him that it was not his fault. So did everyone else. But Jake was determined not to be consoled. He progressively went around to each person, agonizingly admitting to guilt. He thus added to the distress of everyone. Flo kept a watchful eye on him, fearful that the stress might bring on a seizure.

So, they waited through the afternoon and evening, and then into the night. A few of them found spare beds for sleeping, and others simply dozed on the overstuffed furniture, or outside in the veranda chairs. Some listlessly played cards, checkers or dominoes. Launo and Kari just sat, looking blankly into space. They were clutching each other tightly in their desperation. No one wanted to look into their faces for long. Most would stop by for a loving pat on the back or quick hug.

Everyone knew that the night would be long. So, they tried to sleep. Exhausted as they were, no one at first could sleep for very long at a time. Occasionally, someone would creep quietly to check on Launini's condition, and report back to anyone who was awake.

There was no change in Launini, but the reports indicated that she was still fighting and holding on. The continuous bubbling of percolating coffee mingled with the soft sobs and sighs of the bereaved.

There was no relief from the oppressive need to wait. A person could not refuse to wait, of course. But, waiting was impossible.

Finally, just before dawn, van Loon came quietly into the room, haggard and totally exhausted. Through a fog of weariness he said that Launini's vital signs had stabilized at last. He was confident that she would live. He could not be sure that there would not be residual effects of her injuries, however. Despite his absolute exhaustion, it was evident that he was proud of his accomplishment. They all gathered around to congratulate him. But, he was already asleep in the nearest chair.

The celebration was joyous, but subdued in order not to disturb Launini, or the doctor. There were hugs and smiles, and tears everywhere. The people from opposite sides of the world shared a bond of caring. Harry whispered to himself, "It's about time we got some good news!"

But those days on Kipua, good news could not be enjoyed for long. More bad news was to arrive to spoil the joy of Launini's survival.

In fact, the glad celebration was untimely interrupted just then by the arrival of Gupta. His stern, anguished look, and the blood on his clothing, indicated more bad news indeed.

Gupta flopped exhausted in a chair. He was barely able to say hoarsely, "There are wounded men in the jeep. The natives are bringing some others on litters."

He paused in an attempt to fill his lungs with air, and to deal with his shock. Finally, he could say, "God, it was awful! I had no idea that this would happen when I recruited the natives to capture the Dogs. I didn't know that it would come to this!"

Rudy brought him a drink of water. Then Gupta was able to gasp out the rest of his story. "We came upon the Dogs as they were eating dinner by the campfire. I called for them to surrender. I told them that they were surrounded and outnumbered. I told them that resistance was useless. Believe me, I told them that there was no escape, I swear that. So, I told them there was no reason for them to fight. I just wanted to capture and hold them for a trial later when we have retained some order on the island. I really didn't want to see them hurt this way. I told them that they would not be hurt, if they just surrendered peacefully."

He could not go on. He was too physically exhausted, and emotionally expended. He just attempted huge gasps for air, to try to get his breath and strength back. Also, he was destroyed by grief and remorse. It was obviously difficult for him to encompass with his mind what had happened. He seemed to be telling himself the story repeatedly in his mind, so that he himself could believe it.

Finally, Gupta was able to continue. "They absolutely would not come peacefully. I guess that they did not believe me. They thought that we were going to kill them. So, they tried to fight their way out. At first, the natives were just trying to subdue them. The warriors were just trying to keep them from getting away, as I instructed. But, when the Dogs drew first blood on Launo's youngest son, Kipu, inflicting a terrible wound, the natives went wild. They became just as crazy as the Dogs. Not only did all of the natives love Launini, they were insulted at the savage treatment of the daughter of their chief. Then, the wounding of Kipu was more than they could bear."

Gupta was so overcome with grief and horror that again he could not continue. But, the others had to know the end of the story. Harry tried to be re-assuring. "It's okay, old man. Everything will be all right. Take a deep breath. But, we do have to know what happened. You must tell us what happened next."

Gupta fought with difficulty to regain control of himself. Finally, he was able to continue. "Soon, no one on either side was giving any quarter. Each side acted like it was a pack of predatory animals, fighting an enemy of other such animals. The Dogs were using guns and knives, and the natives were using spears, clubs and those awful shark-toothed paddles. Blood was everywhere.

"Some were killed. I do not know how many. There were many. I am afraid to guess."

By that time, an awakened Dr. van Loon was able to give him a sedative which took effect almost immediately. Gupta lapsed into a troubled sleep, his body grotesquely twitching. Surely, the savage fight was continuing unabated in his dreams. The experience must have been nearly unbearable.

Patience was slowly stroking his head. She kept repeating the gentle strokes until his body finally relaxed, and his breathing seemed more peaceful. She carefully tucked a quilt about his shoulders, and gently patted his head. He had done his duty as best he could, with consummate sense and compassion. The carnage was not his fault.

Everyone had been called to hospital duty under the direction of van Loon, who had been shaken awake. He sent for Mary Murphy and Dan Crow to be his primary assistants, because they were the most experienced in dealing with traumas. But everyone had work to do.

Suddenly, it seemed like the wounded were everywhere. In the middle of the mass confusion, it occurred to Harry that the wounded members of the Junkyard Dogs should be protected from the wrath of Chief Launo, who already had been in unbelievable, uncontrollable anguish. Now the chief also had to worry about the welfare of those of his sons who had been in the native posse. As a precautionary move, at Harry's insistence, dePuy reluctantly placed armed guards around the wounded Dogs. To be sure, everyone was under suspicion as potential assailants against the hated Dogs.

A member of Gupta's posse reported that five of the Junkyard Dogs had been killed. All of the nine remaining perpetrators had been wounded. Dregs was among the dead. Percy Hernandez had been slightly wounded. Of the natives, two had been killed and five wounded. Launo's oldest son, Niko, was among the dead. His other two sons had been severely wounded. All three of his sons were reported to have shown total disregard for their own safety in the fight, thus inflicting horrible destruction on their enemies. In the end, Niko had forgotten his college ways, and had regained his ancient heritage. He died wearing the arm band of the son of a chief.

Now, Chief Launo was finally persuaded to return to the native village in order to organize the native women into health teams. He had to go because, without direct orders from the chief, the women would not help the members of the Dogs. But, they would, of course, be eager to minister to the wounded warriors.

At last, Dr. van Loon announced that relief personnel could handle the medical chores. Those who had been there at the beginning could get some rest. Finally, van Loon could nap in a chair near his most critical patients.

Each person found a loved one, or trusted companion, to hug and to sit beside. Kate was still trying to console Jake. Posh and Calia were inseparable, as usual. Dan Crow had come to take Mary back to town. As they walked arm-in-arm to Crow's tandem bicycle, Harry was truly glad that Mary had finally fully recognized the devotion and good qualities that were offered by her boss. He envied them both.

Gratefully, Harry found an empty veranda chair, and eased himself limply into it. Patience appeared from nowhere, and handed him a mug of hot coffee. He thought that he must really look pitiful.

The coffee tasted good, extraordinarily good. It was a brief delicious moment of satisfaction from having exhausted himself in good works. He felt warmly positive toward Patience for her unexpected kindness. He was strangely happy to spend a quiet moment alone with her. In fact, strangely he was very happy amidst the tragedies.

After a few sips of the brew, Harry was sufficiently revived to notice that Patience had something on her mind. She seemed to want to discuss it with him, but was having an uncharacteristic difficulty in finding the words to begin.

Harry was jump-started to attention. He stared at Patience with a quizzical expression, and said, "What?"

Patience still seemed a bit uncomfortable, still having trouble finding words. For her, that was truly unusual.

"Out with it," commanded Harry. He was too tired, and too intrigued, to be patient.

"Well, Harry," she began, "I know that you are tired. I guess it could wait, but I am disturbed. I'm going bonkers. I am having somewhat of a bloody mental crisis here. I don't know what to think anymore."

"That's a good start," encouraged Harry. "Keep going. What's your problem?"

"The problem is that Burnhouse's experiment has led to disaster after disaster. How could the most golden psychological principle of positive reinforcement, the most solid of psychological laws, have failed us in this way?"

Harry was now as fully alert as was possible under the circumstances. He said, "I will give you two quick answers to that. First, the law of effect has not failed. It is intact. But, it has been improperly applied. Burnhouse inadvertently removed the sanctions on punishments for bad behaviors, which were far more powerful than the positive rewards that he offered for good behavior. Second, and related, he refused to use other psychological principles that would foster good behaviors."

"That has been your story all along," said Patience. "So, now are you going to blame these disastrous behaviors here in Kipua on the free choices of despicable behaviors by the Junkyard Dogs and the free choice by the natives that were out for revenge? Where is the gain in that?"

"The gain is that we can hold them responsible for their actions. It means that we cannot simply say that they did wrong because their mothers, fathers, government or whatever, did wrong by them, and therefore they did bad things. That could be partly true, of course, and it probably is. But, it cannot be the whole story. All of these factors could contribute to the blame, along with Burnhouse himself, but we must assume—we must believe, we must assert—that it was in the power of the perpetrators to have done otherwise.

"Examine your own feelings. If you blame the Dogs and the natives for this situation, then you are a closet Humanist, because then you believe in personal responsibility."

"Okay! Okay!" Patience protested. "I see your point. But I will think more about that later. Right now I am scared. How does the idea of a voluntary human will save us from the terrible mess that we are in now? That is the true bottom-line question on all of our minds at the moment. What do you say to that, Big Bwana?"

She usually used that name for him in at least a slightly sarcastic tone. Now, it was more in the tone of a little child asking her father for comfort and reassurance.

"I am too tired to give you the full lecture on the wonders of Humanism right now, Little Sister," said Harry, gently. "But, I will do just that in the morning. Now, all that I will say is that a voluntary human will is not the only relevant concept. Only the Behaviorists feel that they need to rely on a single explanatory concept.

"The main point is that the viable will is possessed by a personal agent that feels, thinks and selects responses on the basis of personal characteristics of the individual. So, with the concept of a viable will there is always hope, because that personal will is in the service of human character. Now, in my view, the most important human characteristic is the capacity to love. That conclusion is based on my Christianity, and not on Humanistic psychology alone. It is nevertheless compatible with Humanistic psychology. The closest concept in Humanistic Psychology is the Rogerian concept of unconditional positive regard. But, I think, the concept of Christian love is stronger. So, Christian love is the key to solving all crises, including the one that now faces us."

"Whoa, there, Cowboy! You have just lost me." Patience was genuinely perplexed. "Are you really trying to tell me that the answer to the mayhem and misery that we have just witnessed is simply for us all to love one another? Get real! What planet were you raised and educated on? Can you really see love now between the Dogs and the natives on this particular island? Besides, love is just another term for positive reinforcement. And we have seen what a reliance on positive reinforcement alone has done to this island."

"Whoa, there, yourself, Miss Aussie Britches," responded Harry, with some fervor. "Just because your Behavioristic colleagues consider love to be nothing more than positive reinforcement, do not think that you have sole right to make a definition, or to pre-empt the concept. In fact, I say that anyone who thinks that love is merely another word for positive reinforcement does not really know what love is.

"Sure, that definition is okay for some kinds of love; but there are many different kinds of love. Some kinds of love go far beyond the concept of positive reinforcement. For example, the kind of love that Lottie and I had went far beyond the fact that we routinely reinforced each other with gifts and services and whatever else was rewarding. But there was more. Something deep inside of us was tapped, and graciously added to the feelings of secondary rewards. This need for attachment is the same one that parents feel for their young. It comes from a part of human nature lodged in the limbic system of our midbrains, which supports the rational processes lodged in our forebrains. It cannot be evoked by external manipulations; it must be freely given as an act of grace from one person to another. It involves a selfless commitment independent of any thoughts of reward. I truly hope that you can experience it some day, Patsy."

Patience scoffed. "That is the most wooly-headed, unsubstantiated nonsense that I have ever heard. I personally have been in love several times. And, I can tell you that, without a doubt, the concept of positive reinforcement does very nicely, thank you, for describing it.

"And don't call me Patsy. Only my father called me Patsy."

Harry was now very serious. "Okay, Patience, but all that I can say to that flat pronouncement on love is that you have apparently never experienced the kind of love that I am talking about. You must experience it to know it. It does not permit objective proof.

"But, again, there is nothing to be gained by arguing about the nature of love any more. The argument could go on forever. So, let's get back to your other question about whether or not I can foresee love between the Dogs and the natives."

"Right! How can you turn their feelings and attitudes around without differential positive reinforcement?" Patience thought that she had played an unanswerable trump card that she herself did not like.

"In the first place," said Harry, "I do not have to forego positive reinforcement. Nothing in my system rules out rewards. That, as I said, would be foolish. But, I have other tools as well in my model for controlling behaviors.

"Surely, it will not be easy. So, the answer to your question is as follows: Surely we cannot bring about such love tonight, and very probably not tomorrow, or even next month. To bring about such love will require a lot of hard effort and disappointments, of course. But we must adopt it as an ultimate goal, if this society, or any society on earth, is to survive. There really is no choice in this, you know. You have seen the result when the leaders attempt to discard virtues and values such as love."

"What you are saying does make sense," agreed Patience, "but we need salvation today—right now. If you cannot instill love today, how can we be saved today? I am still scared. Tell me that I do not have to be scared."

Harry nodded in sadness. "You are right," he said. "I can only give you hope, not positive assurance for today. Today, we may have to use emergency measures in order to survive. If we do not at least survive, there will be no chance for the long-term measures to take effect. Today, unfortunately, we must use force, in the form of knives, guns and bullets. They will be used courageously on your behalf by people who care about you—people who will risk their lives to save you. I will be one of them, believe it or not. We will give our best to save you. But, there is no guarantee.

"My only true assurance is for the long term—for the unknown future. It may be that love will not catch up today or tomorrow in time to prevent total destruction for you and me. We must accept that possibility. But I also believe that there is still love on this island, despite Burnhouse's efforts. It might not have saved him, and it might not save us from this present evil, but it will triumph eventually."

"God, you are an aging male Pollyanna," Patience said, more in pity than anger.

"If you say so," Harry wearily agreed. "But, nevertheless, we simply must think more positively. Let us do our part for love by trying to love the people on this island, while hating the terrible acts that some of them have done. There may be only a trace of good in some of them, but there is a lot of good in many others. There is a lot of good in us, in you and I, and we will do all that we can to help the others. I think that we can do it. We are instruments of God's love for His people. We can make it work. I don't know how, but I believe that we can do it. You must believe that.

"Now, let's stop worrying, and get some sleep. Tomorrow is another day, Pats."

"Also the master of the cliché," mumbled Patience, the look of lingering sadness on her face betraying the woe in her heart. But, her cynical words did not mask the fact that she and Harry had connected in a new way, at a new level. Somehow, Harry could feel it. It felt good.

Harry suddenly thought of Patience as a vulnerable baby, far from home, lonely and frightened. He laid her gently down on the sofa, and tucked the blanket about her shoulders. Then, he gave those suddenly fragile shoulders a fatherly hug, and kissed her tenderly on the forehead. Patience smiled faintly as she passed from exhaustion into a peaceful sleep.

Harry flopped heavily back on his veranda chair. In the morning he would regret giving up so easily on his intimate moment with Patience. Life was full of surprises these days. She would undoubtedly return to her hostility to him in the morning when she had time to think about it.

Now, merciful sleep battled to overcame Harry's racing, anxious thoughts. When it came, it was a deep, but restless, sleep. He had not been quite so confident of their survival on Kipua as he had led Patience to believe.

* * * * *

After Harry had fallen asleep, Patience had gone to check one more time on Launini. She still could not sleep. She decided that it would please Launini if she went to get a nightgown and some toilet articles for her from the village. So, Patience had slipped away with a group of natives to go back to the village to get a few things that Launini would enjoy when she was awake.

Patience had slept like a doped dingo in Launini's bed for what was left of the night, and for an hour into the daylight. Actually, this morning she felt rather refreshed. Her restful sleep could have been caused by the mysterious potion that Tari, Launini's aunt, had her drink before retiring. If they could do something about the taste, that elixir would go over as a big seller in the large American cities.

Patience stuffed a nightgown, some underwear, a blouse, socks and a pair of jeans in her knapsack. She topped it off with a double handful of toilet articles. Granted, all of those things could have been borrowed at the plantation. But, Patience knew that somehow a girl feels better having her own stuff about her, particularly the toilet articles. She was sure that Launini needed something to lift her spirits.

Tari did not like Patience's plan to return to the plantation alone. The young men had been stirred up by the fight. Malevi had taken advantage of their aroused state to goad them into marching on the plantation. His tune of hate was that the people within the plantation compound were both historically and currently the cause of all problems and torments on the island. It was, of course, the classic ploy of the dictator, to focus the anger of the masses on a convenient scapegoat. Therefore, it would not be prudent for a young woman to be caught alone on the trail.

Characteristically, Patience would not listen to the wise counsel of the older woman. She had always been proud that she could take care of herself.

After breakfast, bidding Tari a cheerful goodbye, Patience set off along the trail toward the plantation house. The mists had not yet completely burned off over the palm trees, but she could tell that the day was going to be hot and clear. She walked slowly along, enjoying the sounds of the animals and birds along the trail, mostly hidden by the dense foliage. She tried hard to concentrate on the sights and sounds of nature, in order to block out the memories of the night before. She could not quite expunge the cries of the wounded, and the sight and smell of their blood.

Today, the pleasant sights and sounds along the trail seemed light years away from the horror of last night at the plantation.

Fortunately, when a party of natives was about to overtake her on the trail, she could hear their loud talking and rattling of weapons while they were still far enough away that she could hide in the jungle off the trail. She could make herself invisible to persons on the trail when she was just a few feet into the thick foliage. No one traveling along the trail this day was looking for her, because they were concentrating on their own agendas. No one would have seen her in hiding anyway.

She felt that her leisurely pace, and tuned ears, would protect her from the raucous packs of natives. She tried to concentrate on possible present dangers, in order to distract her mind from the carnage of the previous evening. Nevertheless, she did have one narrow escape when one of the native groups was uncharacteristically quieter than most of the other groups. Only their full preoccupation with their own agenda prevented them from seeing her scurry into the underbrush.

* * * * * *

It was late when Harry finally woke, well after sunrise. Others around him were still sleeping. Some others were moving about performing various chores, cleaning up and eating breakfast. A breakfast table had been set up on the veranda, piled with a plentiful supply of various fruits, breads and several large coffee urns. It was strangely calm within the manor house, like the paradox of the still, quiet eye of a tornado, surrounded by violent agitation.

Harry helped himself clumsily to a glass of orange juice, several chunks of pineapple and a banana. After slowly munching the fruit, he filled a huge mug with coffee, and dropped limply back into the closest chair.

Posh appeared, and eased himself in the next chair. "It looks like a war zone around here, Chief," he said, in a matter-of-fact way.

Harry nodded, "That is because it really is one, Chum. I have imagined some pretty terrible things, but never anything like this and I hope never again."

"You said it," agreed Posh.

They sat without talking for a while. Neither could seem to find anything appropriate to say under the circumstances. The scene spoke for itself. Their friendship needed no words for communication at the moment.

Then, Constable Gupta limped painfully from inside the house. He had been wounded in the leg during the skirmish with the Dogs, struck on the thigh by an errant swing of a war club. A well-aimed blow would have broken his leg. Although the skin had not been seriously torn, there was a large, swollen bruise forming a large knot in the muscle. The injury made it very difficult and uncomfortable for him to walk.

Gupta whispered to Harry and Posh that one of his informants in the native village had reported some interesting activities by a group of the young men of the village the last several weeks. Quite often on moonlit nights the villagers had headed off into the jungle with loaded knapsacks. Before morning they returned with empty sacks, looking exhausted, as though they had been laboring all night. Gupta was sure that the information was important.

Gupta had criticized the man for not coming forward with the information before. Apparently, at first the man had wanted to solve the mystery himself, hoping for some kind of reward. He was sure that the authorities would be interested in the information.

The man had tried to follow the native bearers, but always lost them in the confusing tangle of jungle trails. It was not possible to know where they were going, because each time the native bearers had taken different paths. Nevertheless, the people with the knapsacks had always seemed to be heading toward the same point deep in the jungle.

The informant had used a map of the island to mark the approximate location of the points at which he had lost sight of the natives on their mysterious errands. The six points marked on the map were sufficiently close together that they surely indicated a single destination. The variations apparently represented attempts to foil discovery of the exact location of that specific goal. That inference added to the interest. Without a doubt, there was on the island some continuing clandestine activity that was known only to a few natives.

Harry agreed that this information absolutely demanded further investigation. To be sure, the strange behavior of the natives might have nothing at all to do with the disappearance of Monika Luthsaar. But, this like all other possibilities, must be checked out. Because the CRASH team had so little evidence to work with, it needed to find out if this secret behavior pertained in any way to its mission, especially the disappearance of Monika. The team needed to know if these activities represented something illegal, and, if so, whether or not the particular acts were an actual consequence of the TECHland experiment. It was a lead at least. Even if these men were simply stealing copra, or smuggling pearls from the lagoon, for example, Gupta, at least, needed to know what was happening.

Gupta's map showed that the cluster of points produced an oval shape about midway between the village and the base of Mt. Kipuana. Harry observed that, in fact, a straight line drawn from the center of the native village through the center of the cluster of six points actually passed close to the long axis of the oval of points. This coincidence suggested to him that the destination of the natives lay somewhere along the straight extension of that line beyond the oval. He proposed that the team track along that extended line. They just might discover at the end of the line the destination of the natives, and also what they were doing there.

Gupta proposed that they set out immediately after he had grabbed a little breakfast. Harry disagreed. He said, "Look, Chief, you have shown that you have guts aplenty. But, it is crazy for you to even consider a long hike with your leg in that shape. Besides, you are needed here.

"Anyway, this may be a wild goose chase. Rudy and Posh can go with me. One of us can run back, if we find anything, or need help."

Gupta did not like it, but he had to acquiesce to Harry's logic. The leg was indeed painful. He could barely walk on it. He would probably become a burden to them. But, he strongly insisted that Posh take his police pistol for their protection in an emergency.

Harry and Posh begged some supplies from the plantation cook for lunch. They recruited Rudy to go along with them in case they needed someone to come back for help. Harry reasoned that, in any case, they might need some help in the form of extra hands, or maybe even extra brain power in solving any puzzles that they might encounter.

As they were about to leave, Florence Gorsuch rushed up to say that last night Patience had gone with a group of natives to get some things for Launini at the native village. She had not yet returned. Even though she was not yet truly overdue, her absence gave rise to some horrible thoughts. That much could be seen in the face of each man. The disappearance of any woman on the island, no matter how brief, had come to portend dire events. Patience was probably in serious danger. Harry felt another, now-familiar, twist in his guts.

From the looks of the belligerent mob that had started to gather in front of the barred plantation gates, it was obvious that things could turn extremely ugly at any moment. From the angry shouts, Harry could tell that the mob planned to overrun the plantation house as soon as they thought that such an attack could succeed. The three men decided that they must try to intercept Patience if she were on her way back to the compound on the dePuy plantation. The result would be unthinkable if she walked unsuspectingly into the middle of a nasty scene when she returned to the plantation.

Harry could see on the faces of the other two men that they also feared that she may not even be heading back. She may have met the same uncertain fate of Monika Luthsaar, or the known fates of Burnhouse and many unfortunate women on the island. Harry could feel his stomach quiver and sink at the thought.

The three searchers were lowered by rope out of a second-story back window of a house whose west wall formed a part of the wall surrounding the compound. The foliage of the forest was close to the wall at that point. Because the mob was too disinterested, or too unorganized, to care whether or not anyone left the compound, Harry's party was able to slip away unnoticed. First, they circled in the jungle deep enough to avoid any stragglers from the mob. Then, they started off along the trail in the direction of the native village. They began looking for signs of Patience as they went. There was no sign of her, and no evidence of anything like a struggle along the main trail to the village. The lack of evidence of foul play carried little reassurance because a body could be dumped a few feet off the trail in the thick growth and it would never be discovered.

The trio did observe several bands of natives making their way toward the plantation house. Because they had decided that it would not make sense to confront the natives at this point, they hid off the trail when they heard a group of natives approaching. The demeanor of each small band indicated that there really was no hope of dissuading them from their attack on the plantation house. The immediate goal of the searchers was to find Patience, and to save her, and not to confront groups of natives.

After traveling about half way to the village, they did find Patience. She was walking slowly down the main wagon path from the village, pensive and apparently depressed at all of the evil that she had recently seen. She was more concerned about what might be behind her on the trail, than any possible danger that might be ahead of her.

Harry was irritated at what he perceived as the egg-headed lack of concern for the very real danger that confronted everyone, particularly attractive women, on the island. He found it difficult to believe that she had been traveling alone. It was even more amazing that she was nevertheless apparently unharmed.

"Patience, you blockhead," he screamed at her in uncontrolled distress. "Don't you realize that we have been worried out of our heads about your safety? You picked a bad time to go off by yourself without telling us!"

"Forget it, Daddy," said Patience, sarcastically. "You do not have to know my every move. There was no need to worry. I could hear the gangs of natives a mile away. I can take care of myself, thank you. Chill out."

Harry was still grossly upset, but forced himself to speak in a calmer tone. "It is just that we have been worried crazy about you. We had a lead on the whereabouts of Monika, and were planning to check it out. Now, your little excursion has delayed us in our search. Now, it will take at least an hour to get you back to the plantation."

"We had a report of some strange activities of some natives," Rudy continued. "They have been lugging something at night out into the jungle in the general direction of Mt. Kipuana. We thought it might have something to do with the disappearance of Monika. It seemed like a good lead. We are on our way to investigate it now."

"Do not bother to take me back. I am dressed for walking in the jungle," said Patience, with her usual set-jaw determination. "I would like to help find her myself, if she is still alive."

Harry muttered grimly, "You didn't have to add that last little part, did you?"

Patience answered defensively: "I just want to face reality. We must accept all possibilities. You said that yourself, if you remember, Fearless Leader." The last part entailed a familiar touch of sarcasm.

"Okay. Okay," said Harry, quickly, in a placating manner. He knew that he could never get anywhere arguing with Patience. So, he simply said, "We do not have time to argue. Let's get on with it."

It was difficult for Harry to act like a competent leader when Patience was around. She always seemed to be a mental step ahead of him. And, it seemed that she was always expecting him to do something stupid, and was rarely disappointed.

Despite his impatience with her cavalier attitude about her own safety and their concerns about it, he was truly glad to see her safe. He wondered for a moment or two about the unexpected depth of his anger and concern. Beside the concerns of a team leader, who wanted no more problems to deal with, he also cared about the welfare of a friend. But, what was it about Patience that vexed him so? His male mind was, as usual, unable to understand the functioning of the female mind, particularly hers. Was it because her mind was a strange mixture of bold femininity and scientific professionalism, or because they lived continents apart in different cultures?

Harry did note how Patience was dressed. He needed to determine whether or not her outfit was suitable for hiking, of course. As usual, her attire was remarkable. She was wearing one of her signature floppy hats, an embroidered cowboy shirt, blue jeans and—of all things—cowboy boots. Harry noticed, rather inconsequentially for the occasion, that the jeans were form-fitting, and that the form in the jeans was actually very pleasing.

Patience, noticing his surprise and fascination, said, "What?"

Harry's face must have been showing unusual interest. He felt like a school kid caught peeping in a neighbor's bathroom window. Once more, he was on the defensive with Patience. This time, an honest confession of the absolute truth was out of the question.

Never one to handle an awkward situation well, Harry stammered, "Nice boots." He was afraid to mention the fit of the jeans for fear of unleashing a strong local and vocal version of the women's lib movement. That type of explosion could indeed be expected from Patience.

She simply sneered, "What's the matter, you dunce? Don't you know that we have cows in Australia? Besides, these boots are excellent for hiking."

Harry wondered why she did not like him all of a sudden. They used to get along very well before this mess happened. At least, he thought so. Perhaps the worry about Burnhouse and Monika had gotten to her also. Perhaps, she was jealous of Monika over Burnhouse. Who could figure her out? Teamwork was supposed to draw people together, not intensify their differences.

They followed the main trail almost to the village, and then cut through the jungle until they reached the trail taken by the native bearers. Then, they carefully followed that trail toward the points on the map which indicated where the trail of the bearers had been lost.

As their party moved down the trail, Posh was in the lead, alternately consulting his map and compass. He was followed by Rudy, then Patience, with Harry acting as a sort of rear guard. They saw nothing suspicious. Occasionally, there were signs of previous passage through the jungle, but certainly there was no single clear trail to follow. They were guided primarily by the map and compass. There were occasional signs of previous human activity. That was not noteworthy, of course, because the islanders were known frequently to take picnics and to camp out in the jungle. Because the natives with the knapsacks had taken different paths through the jungle, there was no clear correct path to follow. It was still reasonable to assume, however, that they were always going to the same destination. Harry's party just had to keep moving and be prepared for any outcome.

EIGHTEEN

THE SEARCH PARTY followed the line on the map for over an hour, and could see that they were about to run out of space on the forest floor. Actually, they were nearly to the dead-end wall of the mountain.

At last, the group came to the base of the mountain. It was a disappointing dead end. Had they missed a side trail? What native tricks for avoiding pursuit could have thrown them off? There had been absolutely nothing unusual that they could find along the line of march to solve the problem of the disappearing night hikers. The mystery was complete. They could not imagine what these people were doing, or where they were going. The searchers also could not imagine how they had been thrown off the trail.

It did not make any sense at all to assume that the natives were performing to no purpose, or that their purpose was merely to confuse the CRASH team. The natives must have emptied their knapsacks to good purpose somewhere between the village and the mountain. The searchers could only look at each other in amazement and disappointment. Then they shrugged in resignation, almost in unison.

Then, Patience breathed a long "Oh!" and called excitedly for the map. After a few minutes of intense examination of the map, and the terrain ahead, looking back and forth, she exclaimed excitedly, "Oh, ho, you fine scientists and woodsmen have missed something. I see it."

As the group gathered about the map, she pointed out that the line they had drawn did not actually lead up to the solid face of the rock wall. Actually, it pointed directly toward one of the vertical fissures in the wall. Many of these fissures ran all the way from the floor of the jungle nearly to the summit of the mountain. In fact, the narrow trail angling upward along the face of the mountain would disappear into a vertical fissure and then re-appear higher up the mountain on the other side of the cleft, indicating a substantial horizontal depth of the cleft.

Patience proposed that they run the string out. They should go ahead along the line on the map directly into the crack in the wall of the mountain, and follow it until they absolutely could not go farther.

Posh said, "It works for me. It is either that, or give up and go home."

Rudy nodded agreement, also. So, Harry exclaimed, "Let's go for it!"

The trees and underbrush were very thick at the base of the mountain because a little more sun could peek through there. They pushed their way through with difficulty. Some kind of tropical briars tore at their clothes and skin. It was not pleasant, but they knew that they must see it through. They could see no sign of prior human passage, but knew that the availability of sunlight at the spot would have permitted any damaged foliage to repair itself quickly. Presumably, also the packers knew very well how to cover their trail, if indeed they had passed this way.

In fact, no one in Harry's party was sufficiently experienced as a tracker to know for sure whether or not the natives with the knapsacks had passed that way. Occasionally, there was a broken twig, but that could have been done by a creature of the forest. One could not even say with assurance that there was a discernible path. Nevertheless, skilled natives could have hidden a path, if they so desired.

Patience was having a bit of a hard time. But, she was not complaining. She forged resolutely ahead. She was obviously determined to keep up with the pace set by the men.

For some reason—perhaps it was the uncomfortable progress—Harry suddenly felt a little mean. He said to Patience, "You are going to scratch your fine boots, Honey."

Patience snapped back: "That's none of your business, you airhead. And don't call me Honey. I wouldn't be the honey of a classic male chauvinist pig."

The hostility in her response rocked Harry back a bit. He felt deflated, humiliated and surprisingly depressed. All he could say was an involuntary, "Ouch". It was another point scored by Patience, with no opposition, and no reason or hope for a counterattack.

"Take that, Bwana," said Posh, grinning. "You deserved it. So, lighten up. Give her a break!"

"Sorry, guys and doll," said Harry, in exaggerated contrition. He actually felt, however, that Patience had gotten the better of the exchange. He really did feel bad for teasing her, especially because the going was so rough. Why did he do such things when he had been trying so hard to get along with Patience?

Suddenly, his thoughts were interrupted by a surprising event. Posh parted the underbrush, and there it was! They collectively let out astonished gasps of amazement. At first, they could only stare mutely. Each was shocked and dumbfounded by the new discovery.

There was one of Monika's bandanas! They all recognized the red and white scarf. Harry remembered vividly seeing it tied about her white head, framing to perfection that perfect face.

Harry gasped, "Monika!"

Posh grinned, "Yep!"

It surely belonged to Monika. It even had a slight aroma of her distinct perfume, lingering yet. Harry thought that he could recognize it. Rudy confirmed it. "Monika's perfume," he said.

The presence of the scarf was significant. They all knew that it had a lot of sentimental value to her. She would not have dropped it carelessly. And she would not have given it up easily. But, if she were in distress, she could have dropped it as a marker for rescuers. Or it could have been wrestled from her head as she engaged in a fierce struggle for survival.

In any case, its appearance was ominous, even though it suggested that they were on the right track to find her. It meant that, wherever she was, she was in serious trouble.

Even more amazing was the fact that the scarf was lying across a branch beneath the rungs of a crude ladder. The ladder was fabricated by short bamboo rungs lashed by marine cord to join two long bamboo poles. The ladder appeared to be strong enough in fact to hold a grown man carrying a loaded knapsack. The significance of this fact was not lost on any member of the search party.

As they looked up the fissure in the face of the cliff, they saw a series of about a dozen such ladders criss-crossing the fissure until a final one reached the lowest narrow ledge of the trail to the summit, perhaps ten stories up. The whole system of ladders was not visible from the edge of the jungle because of a bend in the fissure.

"Yahoo!" Harry heard himself yelling exultantly. "I don't know for sure what it is, but we have found something. It absolutely for sure must lead to Monika!"

"Stop drooling," sneered Patience. Harry wondered why she was not as pleased as the men to have found a clue to the fate of Monika. Perhaps she was jealous that all of the men appreciated the charms of Monika so much.

Rudy, in a serious analytical tone, said the obvious, "I bet that this has something to do with Monika and TECHland. It doesn't seem likely that thieves or smugglers would go to this much trouble just to provide access to the summit. I can think of no good reason for them to want access to the top. Maybe they could signal somebody from the top, but that does not seem likely. And it would not seem necessary to carry any contraband loads all of the way to the summit."

Posh nodded agreement. He observed, "Anyway, the rungs of the ladders are tied with new rope and the whole thing looks recent. This was obviously put here after Burnhouse came on the island. Let's go on up, Lads and Lassie, and see what happens."

"Arf! Arf!" complained Patience, in mock seriousness. "What am I, a dog?" Then, with typical enthusiasm, and a return of her good nature, she proposed, "Let's bloody well go for it! Time could be a vital factor in life or death."

While Rudy and Harry agreed on the need for haste, they were much more conservative than the other two. Rudy suggested extreme caution, "We do not know whether or not any of the men with knapsacks are still up there, and what they are about. They could be armed and extremely dangerous, especially if cornered. There may be explosives in the knapsacks. I propose that Posh goes back to get some men in case there is trouble, while Hawkey, Patience and I climb up to see what is there. If it concerns Monika, time may be truly of the essence. We cannot afford to wait.

"Posh can try to get some help if he can, but they may have their hands full back at the plantation. In any case, they at least need to know where we are.

"Maybe we can find something here that will help to calm and secure the island. If Monika has run away or been kidnaped, she may know something that will help."

"Like what?" said Posh.

"I don't know, but we have to do something," Harry countered, helplessly.

Posh did not like the idea of being the one to seek help, and made a counter proposal to Rudy: "You are not experienced at climbing, and not in such good physical shape at that, if you will pardon my saying so. And you are the best one to go back. You should be the one to go for help. Meanwhile, we will do the climbing. I will take the pistol just in case. I know how to use it."

Rudy reluctantly agreed. In case of trouble, Posh would be the better man. It turned out to be a fateful decision. They could not have known or anticipated its vital significance at the time.

Posh carefully unloaded the pistol and put it and the bullets in his backpack. Hopefully, if he needed the weapon, there would be time to re-load it. That seemed to be a good gamble. Surely, an accident with a loaded gun was much more likely than the pressing need for a gun without the time to load it.

Harry, for one, did not like the idea of the artillery. But, he had to admit at this point that no one could have made a strong case against the potential need for a weapon. They would keep it out of sight, and hope for the best.

Rudy took the knapsack with the personal articles for Launini from Patience. With a final nod and words of good wishes and encouragement, he started back along the floor of the crevice. As they silently watched him disappear around the bend, Harry said a quick prayer for his safety. Then, he said one for their own.

There was no doubt that the prayer was necessary. So, there was little conversation as the search party concentrated on the serious business of making its way upward. Part of the reason for silence was that everyone, except Posh, was saving breath for the climb. Partly, also, no one wished to hazard a guess about what they would find at the top of the mountain. They absolutely had to find out if there were anything on the top of the mountain. But, nevertheless, they dreaded what the answer might be. No one wanted to risk a guess.

Posh was leading the way, because he was judged to be the best able to cope with a dangerous physical emergency. Presumably, also any rung of a ladder or rock ledge that would carry his weight would also support each of the other two. Patience was following Posh, always careful to stay on the next ladder below him. Harry again served as the rear guard, also always staying one ladder below Patience.

Harry was grateful that the ropes holding the rungs of the ladders were new, and made of marine nylon instead of some kind of jungle vine. The knots were expertly tied, and very secure. But, there was still danger. The ladders rested very precariously on sometimes tiny niches and crannies in the rock wall. Thus, the ascent was a dangerous enterprise, as they all well understood. They had to climb without bouncing or swaying the ladder any more than was absolutely necessary.

It was indeed frightening to climb a swaying hand-made ladder across the crevice from the face of one wall to the distant opposite wall. At the midpoint of a crossing, the climber was suspended many feet above the craggy, rocky floor of the crevice. Death was almost inevitable for anyone who fell on the sharp stones below. The spring in the bamboo poles of the ladders necessarily produced a terrifying bounce and sway, despite the slow, deliberate upward crawling motions of the particular climber.

Harry, for one, was aware that it was indeed a long way down to the base of the first ladder. He continually reminded himself that a fall to the rock floor below would be fatal. That same probability was impressed on the mind of each of the others as they cautiously crept up each ladder. In case of a mishap, eight to ten feet of agonizing, but futile, stretching would be required to reach the dubious safety of either wall.

Some of the ladders rested on narrow natural ledges along the rock face. Others fit into notches chipped with some kind of chisel or rock hammer into the very face of the cliff. These notches left no room to spare for the ladder pole. Indeed, the butts of the poles had also, in some cases, been tapered to fit into the narrow supporting grooves. Those precarious tapered slots for the supporting ladders were the ones that really worried Harry.

Patience was obviously frightened, although she tried to hide it. Harry noticed her fear, and wondered, "Why hide it? Maybe she does not think that fear is consistent with her image as a woman who can do anything a man can do, but better." In his own case, he decided that the superior attitude for each person would actually consist of being more afraid than less afraid. Under the circumstances, fear was a very sensible response. It would undoubtedly prompt greater attention to safety. Harry was reassured that there was one situation in which a professor's ability to concentrate on one task would be extremely useful indeed.

The thought also occurred to Harry that maybe Patience just did not want them to worry about her. Because she had practically forced her way into the search party, she would not want to be a burden to them. In fairness, that would be a reasonable assumption.

Thought Harry: "I have to admire her spunk. As a matter of fact, I have to admire her altogether. She does look quite attractive as she moves slowly up the ladders, with total childlike concentration, like a nervous cat cautiously stalking its prey. For an academic," he thought, "she does move quite well."

Harry abruptly interrupted his thoughts. He amazed himself at his irrelevant thoughts under the circumstances. Despite his well-documented, and fully acknowledged, penchant for single-minded concentration on important matters, his mind was idly wandering at a most inappropriate time. How could that be?

So, Harry had to admit to himself that he was somehow fascinated by Patience. She puzzled him. She could be at once an objective scientist, and then an ardent feminist. And then later she could be altogether feminine. He recognized instantly that some would charge him with male chauvinistic thinking for such ideas. He assuaged his guilt by assuring himself that he did not mean it that way. He merely meant that science was neither a masculine nor a feminine pursuit. And, sometimes, Patience appeared to be rather masculine in her contempt for him. At other times, he even thought that her feminine side was attracted to him.

A slight misstep, and near disaster, on the rung of a ladder made Harry decide to put away such odd thoughts as inappropriate to their serious situation. At this point, it was better to concentrate on the climb than to admire the fit of any pair of blue jeans. Possibly, he could admire such things at length later, if indeed he were fortunate enough to live through this climb. Of course, he would also have to mend his fences with Patience. He wondered if she were too frightened to be still angry with him. Frightened or not, she nevertheless moved steadily upward on the swaying ladders.

The switch to a different ladder was especially difficult. Although it was near the comparative safety of a ledge in the wall, and a possible handhold, it still required a moment when one hand and one foot were simultaneously in motion, and thus without support for the body.

They had almost reached the trail when the rock ledge supporting one of the poles of the ladder under Patience suddenly gave way with a sickening sound. It was just a slight crunch, but the meaning was altogether terrible, and starkly clear to each of them. The ladder flipped quickly on its side, nearly throwing Patience uncontrollably into open space. Only the desperate grab of her left hand on the lower pole of the ladder prevented a fatal plunge down to the floor of the crevice. Fortunately, the other pole held fast, though precariously so. But, for this instant the entire ladder did not fall. It did not seem possible for it to remain in place for long, however.

Patience screamed wildly in terror. Harry called her name in agony. He could see at once that, if she panicked, she was lost. Uncontrolled panic would evoke violent gyrations of the body. That would surely shake the ladder loose. Fear was like a knife in his belly. It spread outward to take command of his entire body.

But Patience did not panic. Bless her! She kept sufficient control to grab the lower pole of the ladder with her other hand. Thus, she held on. She held doggedly on. Her legs were still swinging wildly in air as the ladder rocked, bounced and swayed back and forth. Surely, she could easily lose her grip on the bucking ladder at any second. Also, the combined forces from all sources could jostle the ladder loose from its meager support. That conclusion was obvious.

It did not appear that anything could save her. "Patsy, hold on!," Harry shouted frantically. "Please hold on and hold still. Don't let the ladder bounce." It was really a prayer, as well as desperate advice.

Himself panicked, he shouted, "Keep calm. Be as still as you can, so you won't shake the ladder loose. Save your strength until we can find a way to save you."

"Help! Help! For God's sake, help me!" she was screaming. "I can't hold on for long."

Patience herself was trying to cope. She was trying desperately to hook the heel of her right boot over the lower pole of the ladder. But, the heel of the boot was too smooth to provide much of a ridge to hold her weight. Harry silently cursed the boots. Regular shoes would have given her a better ridge to catch a pole. She did not have enough strength in her arms to pull her body up high enough to catch the boot heel. And the effort to do so was quickly exhausting her. She was failing by a greater margin with each attempt. And the ladder continued to sway dangerously with each attempt.

Harry called to Patience to save her strength. "Patience," he yelled, "stop trying to climb on the ladder. Save your strength for holding on. Don't jerk the ladder. We will save you. Just stay calm, and hold on." He tried to exude a confidence that he did not feel.

Harry had climbed quickly to the top of his ladder, but found that he could not help much. All that he could do was to clutch the one pole that was still in its niche, and try to keep it from slipping out. If it slipped just a mite, Patience would surely be dead.

Unfortunately, the pole that was still holding in place was the one that had been the farthest from Harry. He could not reach it well enough to apply much strength for holding or repositioning it.

Harry desperately tried to think of a way to save her. A rescue seemed totally impossible under the worst of conditions.

Posh had almost simultaneously reached the top of Patience's ladder. It had been only seconds since she fell. It seemed a lifetime—two lifetimes. Trying with all his strength, Posh could not twist the ladder back into position. Her weight on the lower pole of the ladder was too great. Any leverage that he could apply in that position was far less than enough. Because of the awkward position for lifting, the mechanical advantage was hopelessly against him.

Neither man could climb out to her without the absolute certainty of dislodging, or even breaking, the remaining pole that was supporting her. Surely, Harry would not be able to hold the one pole in place with the extra weight of Posh on the ladder. If he himself tried to reach Patience, without someone to hold the pole in place, it would surely work loose from the precarious niche in which it was lodged. Patience would have to make the climb or descent herself to either end of the ladder. But, she obviously did not have the arm strength to pull herself up enough to get a foothold on the ladder. So, to work up or down on the ladder using only her hands and arms with her body hanging free, was clearly impossible.

Both men could easily predict the tragic outcome. So could Patience. She would dangle until her strength was gone. The others could only watch. Harry could not help, even if he knew what to do.

All that they could do was to plead for Patience to hold on a little longer. Harry continued to call out encouraging words that he himself did not believe. Perhaps, by some miracle a rescue plan could be devised before she lost her grip on the ladder.

But, it would take a miracle. Neither of them had experience with aerial rescues. Harry thought irrelevantly, "I shouldn't even be here. This isn't what I do. I merely theorize and write about real life problems. I don't know how to cope with this real situation. We cannot save her. This is the end, the very final end. I can't bear it!"

Then, a cruel thought stabbed into his mind and twisted like a knife, "I am thinking like a Behaviorist. If Skinner is right, then we as academics and social activists will never be able to devise a way to save her. Neither Posh nor I are mountain climbers. Neither are we soldiers of fortune. We have no experience with this sort of thing. We never did anything like it. We have no firm habits that can help us. This is not like playing football, or giving a learned lecture. Our failure to save Patience will validate the idea that Skinner was right after all. Our failure now would be vindication for Skinner. That would be the bitter outcome. Apparently, Skinner was right. Only someone with the appropriate learned habits would have any chance to devise a plan to save her.

"But what does that matter now when Patience's life is on the line? This is life or death. It's not some academic interest in a psychological theory."

Harry thought again that Patience obviously did not have the strength in her arms to pull herself up on the ladder. Soon, her remaining strength would be exhausted. When that happened, she would lose her grip, without a doubt. Horror fully engulfed him. And still the terrible fear.

But, God had given him inspirations before. Harry pleaded: "Please, God, just give me one more!" He had never wanted anything more in his life. Not only was Patience's life at stake, so also was his belief in a creative mind of the human animal that could cope with novel situations.

Then, quickly, a desperate plan flashed into the veteran professor's mind. He called excitedly to Posh: "Can you get the footing to hold the combined weight of Patience and the ladder if we can release this end? If you can, the ladder would fall against the wall and then be in a vertical position. Then, Patsy should be able to climb up, because she can then use her feet to help."

The plan violated his strong desire to keep the ladder in place. He felt the almost uncontrollable urge to provide a stable platform for Patience. Indeed, he had been striving with all of his strength to keep the pole of the ladder safely in its niche. He hated the idea of releasing his grip on the ladder that was holding her safe. At this moment, it was the only thing supporting her life. How could he pry it loose?

Posh caught on to the plan quickly. "I will try, partner. It is the only chance that she has. We have to try it. God help us all."

Posh placed one foot on the base of his ladder and searched for a foothold on the rock face. He found just a rough spot on the wall. It was not good enough. It would have to do. He braced himself against the wall, then nodded that he was ready.

"Oh, God help him," Harry prayed. "Patsy, did you hear the plan?" he shouted.

"Yes," she said. "Let's do it fast, for God's sake. My hold is slipping!"

"Okay, Pats," yelled Harry. "Hold very tight, and hold still. If you move, you can jerk the ladder out of Posh's hands, and maybe dislodge us all. Here we go!"

Together Posh and Harry eased the fixed pole of the ladder from its notch in the wall. Then, the ladder swung free. It arched swiftly downward, ominously gaining speed. It would literally crash against the opposite wall. That was sure. Could Posh and Patience both hold on when the impact came? Posh groaned with the strain. His bulging muscles bulged even more.

This would be a supreme test for Posh, mental as well as physical. The multiple push-ups in football training camps could pay off handsomely, at last. Or, perhaps not. Perhaps, they would not be enough.

Harry wondered, "Does Posh have the sheer brute physical strength and agility, and the personal guts, to hang on? Few men would be able to do it. If any man can do this, Posh can. For the love of God, Posh, do it for me!"

Then, too quickly, there came the crash of ladder against stone wall. It was harder, louder, more fearsome than Harry had expected. He feared the worst. He doubted that any man on earth could accomplish what he had asked of Posh.

But, mercifully, Posh held on. His face was a contorted mask of strain and agony, from both the mental and the physical test. Somehow, this strong, brave, wonderful man had managed to cling to the virtually smooth wall, and to hold on to the precious cargo at the same time. It was indeed miraculous! It was the superhuman strength given to a man who received tremendous emotional energy from an extreme motivation.

Patience had landed between the ladder and the face of the rock. She groaned when she hit the wall, and again when the ladder mashed her against the rock face. Both times she almost lost her grip. But, she had been able to grasp the ladder with her other hand as it fell toward the wall. The dual impacts knocked the breath out of her, but she hung on with the tenacity of a person facing death. So, she held on.

The two men gave exultant shouts in unison when they saw that she was still clinging to the ladder after the crash. They gave another joyful shout when they saw that she could get a foot on a rung, and was starting to climb.

Despite her exhaustion, Patience was able quickly to accomplish the now relatively easy climb to Posh. Then, she clung to him totally spent.

Posh fell back against the cliff wall, also limp and powerless. The ladder slipped out of his unnerved, powerless hand. It dropped heavily into the crevice below. They heard it bounce along the mountain walls, and finally smash into small pieces on the rocky floor below.

Now they all could collapse in total exhaustion. Harry was almost too weak to hold on to his ledge. It was in fact many minutes before anyone could even speak.

Patience finally broke the silence: "Thanks, Mates." They knew it came from her heart.

"You are both beauts. Posh, you are the bloody greatest." Her death grip on him now became a grateful hug.

"No problem," shrugged Posh, with a proud grin. He was still in pain. The combined weight of Patience and the ladder had practically pulled his arms from the sockets, especially during the impact with the stone wall.

Harry could scarcely believe that the tiny footholds had held. That had been one of the necessary miracles.

"We got accustomed to your face," said Harry, still below them by a length of one ladder. "We didn't want to have to find ourselves another team member. And we didn't want to explain to the others what happened to you while we were looking after you." He could joke about it now that the immediate danger was over.

Patience seemed to be okay. She would recover from the bruises and sore muscles before she would get over the fright of her ordeal. Indeed, it would be many years before the nightmares of the mountain experience would subside.

Harry himself was definitely not okay. He really had been scared for Patience. He was still so shaken that he could barely move. He knew that he must follow the two of them up the ladders to the path to the summit. He did not want to admit how the experience had drained him emotionally. His legs seemed to be rubbery things that would not respond to his attempts at control. He needed a minute to will some strength into them.

As a psychologist, he marveled at the sudden appearance of a successful plan. He had been panicked, and therefore was not in a good state for logical thinking. But the inspiration, when it came, was immediate. Obviously, it had worked. He thanked God for it, because he was certain that he could not have achieved it by himself. He also believed that Posh definitely had a third hand on the ladder, and an extra foot on the smooth wall of the mountain.

So, now the worm of psychological theory had turned. Prof. Skinner was definitely refuted that day on Mt. Kipuana. A failure to find a plan to save Patience would have supported Skinner's notion of only fixed non-creative habits. The success of Harry's plan now showed that Skinner's view was wrong. The plan had required something more than a twist of old habits. The human spirit could transcend the ordinary limitations of personal habits, and usual capacities. The human will could prevail after all, despite such formidable obstacles. Harry's body was weak, but his spirits had risen as high as the mountain.

After a few minutes of rest, Harry was then able to pull himself together well enough to reach the other two by following the trail the long way around, back into the crevice. It was tedious, but not very difficult. When he reached the other two at the ladders, they continued together to climb them very carefully. Thus, at last they all reached the relative safety of the trail higher up the cliff.

It had been important for them to continue the climb before their anxiety had time to incubate to an unmanageable level.

Still, it took great courage for Patience to attempt the ladders again.

The natural trail proved to be wide enough to walk on relatively easily. Although the trail was ordinarily wide enough to walk on comfortably, a step off to the sky side would be a rather tall one. Therefore, the vast open space on one side made the proposed ascent horribly intimidating, especially after the fright that they had experienced. That fact was especially true when they reached the sea side of the mountain, although logically the danger was no greater.

"This ascent will definitely not be a walk in the park," Harry said to himself more than to the other climbers. Patience gasped and nodded, and Posh said simply, "Yeah."

After one circle of the mountain, Harry called for a brief rest before continuing. The others did not put up much resistance to the idea. A rest was wise, although they all were eager to see what the end of the trail ahead would reveal to them. The impulse to keep following the trail was almost irresistible. But they were truly not ready for the attempt without some rest. Because it was now somewhat after noon, Posh suggested that they have their lunch while they were resting. Moreover, they were not even sure if there would be a spot for resting before they reached the summit.

"Capital idea," said Patience. "I could use a spot of hot tea about now. Anybody have a fire handy?"

Harry smiled. "I know that it is against your principles, but you will have to be satisfied with tepid tea for now. Just be sure that you do not fall off the bloody trail."

"Kiss my bloody foot, you jerk," smiled Patience. Harry was greatly pleased, because this time she obviously did not mean what she said.

Harry was always truly delighted when Patience was decent to him. He said, in mock bitterness, "What a short memory you have, my dear."

The two men took out their prepared lunches from their knapsacks and shared them with Patience. There was plenty of food, because the plantation cooks had been generous. Moreover, the trio of climbers did not want to stuff themselves before continuing the ascent. In fact, it was not much of a meal, or rest either. Planting one's feet on the narrow trail, and leaning back against the mountain wall was not a desirable way to eat a meal.

After the brief lunch, and the debris was returned to their knapsacks, the trio prepared for the continuation of their climb up the mountain. They could not tarry long, because it would be deadly for them to be caught on the narrow trail after nightfall, given their lack of familiarity with it.

Perhaps the end of this trail would provide the answers to questions that they had been pondering for months. Monika must surely be there. And, she must therefore have many of the answers that they had been seeking. Barring further accidents, hopefully the team would know in a few hours.

NINETEEN

THEY HAD BEEN CLIMBING for three arduous hours. They could see that they now were near the summit. Each time they had circled the mountain they were about 100 feet higher than the stretch of trail below. Patience suggested several times that they climb straight up to save time. The others thought that the absence of reliable handholds and footholds made such a venture too risky.

The passage along the trail itself was really not extremely dangerous, if one were careful to hug the wall closely. Each of them most assuredly did that. Especially Harry. He noticed how the long drop on one side made the trail itself seem fearfully narrow. Actually, the trail did become slightly narrower as they approached the top. But, it was really not more dangerous because the wall of the mountain progressively sloped more inward as they climbed higher. It was not quite so scary because they could lean in against the rock face, and away from the precipice. They carefully tested each step before they put their full weight on it. Occasionally, they were reminded of the wisdom of this practice when a foothold gave way, launching a rocky missile to the forest floor below.

Still, they sometimes had to take baby steps cautiously along the trail with their faces and bodies pressed flat against the stone. The tactual feel of the hard face of the mountain was somehow extremely comforting. It was really not too frightening as long as they could feel the bright, warm sun on their backs when they reached the sunny side of the mountain.

The view off the mountain was absolutely marvelous whenever they had the courage to look. Harry could not often muster sufficient bravery to look, though. They could see far beyond the reefs out to sea, and the backs of the sea birds as they flew about below them. The sun was exactly at the right height to glimmer on the waves. At times, the entire expanse of the flat part of the island lay clearly visible before them. It seemed like they were some god-like creatures beholding a model of one part of Eden.

Harry was brought back down to the reality of the present situation by the thought that the fate of all the human beings down there could rest upon what the search party accomplished on the mountain. So, he again concentrated on the climb. He did not want to slow the group. It was too bad that they had things other than beauty to think about at the moment.

The climbers kept moving cautiously and slowly forward. The rate of ascent had steadily increased as they got closer to the summit. Nevertheless, the progress seemed painfully slow to Harry. Posh and Patience seemed unconcerned, however. Harry had to agree that there was no point in hurrying, given the possible catastrophic consequences of excessive haste.

Finally, they rounded a bulge in the rock wall and saw a rough wooden door, barred from the outside by a heavy plank. The door seemed entirely out of place on the mountain. It was set in an opening in a poured-concrete wall, about 6 feet high, which circled the rim of the mountain top. The wall was crowned by a mixture of old rusty wire, and new barbed wire. The latter strongly indicated recent repair. The wall and door completely covered the trail such that no one on the other side could possibly remove the barrier or climb over it. The absence of weathering on some of the wooden planks indicated that they had not been in place for long.

Patience said tremulously to the others, "I think we have found Monika. I think that she must still be alive. Otherwise the door would not be barred."

"Yes," agreed Harry, "I think you are correct. I pray that you are correct." Words seemed inadequate for expressing his fervent hopes.

Posh softly murmured, "Amen."

Patience was crying. Harry marveled at the fact. She had always seemed so aloof, so dispassionate. All of this, he suddenly realized, had been extremely hard on her.

Quickly, Posh removed the bar and pushed against the heavy door. It slowly swung inward with a low grating sound.

None of them were in any way prepared for what they saw.

Patience had been prepared, of course, to see some sort of Navy facility. Because she had never before seen a weather station, she did not know exactly what that would be like. She did hope, and expect, to see Monika Luthsaar.

There was a weather station, sure enough. But Patience barely noticed it at first. What she saw was incredible. She could barely believe it.

There stood Skull Burnhouse! The dazzling white background made Burnhouse, in his dark rumpled suit, look like an actor on the stage with bright backlighting. Their attention was fixed on him, drawn like iron filings to a magnet. His body was positioned much like an actor after the opening curtain, waiting for the applause to cease before continuing with Act 1.

Burnhouse obviously relished these dramatic situations on the attentional stage. He enjoyed the limelight even on a rough mountain top in the South Pacific.

So, Burnhouse was very much alive. And now he was quite interested in discovering the identity of his daytime visitors. His surprise at seeing the search party was nearly as great as theirs at discovering him.

Burnhouse looked entirely healthy. In fact, he looked remarkably tanned and fit. If Patience's recollection were correct, Burnhouse seemed even to have gained some weight since they last met. That actually looked good on him, because he had been rather sparse in physical frame as well as theoretical breadth.

Patience blurted out, "My God, Skull! We thought you were dead! They found your bloody clothes on the beach. How could you be alive?"

Despite his surprise and shock, Harry could not resist the opportunity for a little humor. In a faulty attempt at imitating Patience's Australian accent, he said, "Yes, and your bloody clothes had blood all over them."

Patience was not amused. But her mood was not spoiled. Nevertheless, she growled in fake exasperation, "Shut your bloody cake-hole, you jerk! This is no time for your wise cracks."

Then she turned to a still-puzzled Burnhouse. "Do not pay attention to this imbecile," she advised. "He is in over his head. The fact that you two are still alive is great news. It is no time for joking around. Please forgive him. I assume that Monika is with you."

Burnhouse very graciously said, with a smile, "I get it. No problem. Yes, Monika is here, and she is okay."

He was indeed very glad to see them. It showed in every aspect of his manner. "Patience! Harry Hawkey, is it really you?" he asked in a single breath. "My God, how did you two get up here? Patience, what a pleasure to see you! Man, am I glad to see you guys! I assume that you are part of a rescue team. How many are with you? I knew Schoonover would send one. Who else is with you? How did you find us?"

Stopping for breath, he seemed almost amused at their shock in seeing him. Then, Burnhouse noticing Posh, turned to him. "And who is this young man?"

Patience introduced Posh to Burnhouse. They shook hands warmly. It was impossible to know who was happier to see whom.

Burnhouse was so excited that he rambled on. "I know why you thought I was dead. My death was faked. Some natives actually dressed a pig in my clothes and dangled it on a chain just outside the reef. The sharks took care of the next part of the plot. Then, the natives scattered what was left of my bloody clothes on the beach. Chief Launo told me all about it. We all believed that the search for me would stop when you thought that I was dead." He said the word "bloody" with his own version of an Australian accent.

Harry was favorably impressed with the humor. "He was right," he admitted, smiling. "We were convinced that you were gone."

Patience was just about to ask about Monika when another, even more beautiful, sight appeared. It was Monika Luthsaar. She came running out of the station, and began embracing everyone.

Amid all of the communal hugs, she laughed, "It's good to see you. I wondered if you would find me. Thanks, thanks, thanks! How did you do it? You must have needed a miracle. Did you see my scarf?"

The three rescuers said, almost in chorus, "We were really worried about you." It was truly an emotional moment. They clasped hands and embraced, and then embraced again. The three rescuers were about as thoroughly overjoyed to see the two of them alive as the latter were to be rescued.

Monika said with assurance, "Actually, I do not think that I was ever really in any serious danger. I followed the natives to the ladder at the base of the cliff. I knew that was dangerous and stupid, but I saw them leaving the village quickly and did not have time to get someone to come with me, or to tell where I was going.

"I guess I am not a good detective, because they soon saw me. Catching me was no problem for them. Then they brought me up here. Did you find my scarf?" she asked again.

"We sure did," replied Harry. "It was very encouraging. We hoped that you had dropped it as a signal."

Then Patience briefly recounted how they had come to find the trail to the summit, emphasizing her own key role in the exploit. She told it with pride, because it had indeed taken substantial levels of reasoning, courage and persistence. She also briefly described the composition and mission of the CRASH team, and their brief history on the island.

Burnhouse rushed ahead with his own story: "There is so much to tell. I am here against my will, of course. Admittedly, the natives have treated me well, so far. But, to be honest, I fear that they may change their minds at any time. Besides, this is like prison. I want to get out of here."

Patience looked about the old weather station. Everything surrounding them was white, as dazzling in the sun as a cover girl's smile in a toothpaste ad. The buildings and floors were originally white, made from what Patience took to be pressed concrete. All surfaces were further whitewashed by the blessings of countless sea birds, and then bleached by the Pacific sun. The whole setting was from a story book. It looked like a penthouse for the gods, or a heavenly nest or villa high above the forests and beach.

Burnhouse continued his tirade against those who had incarcerated him on the summit. The heavenly villa was, after all, a prison for him.

Finally, Burnhouse said, "I am sorry to be carrying on like this over a few weeks in their prison. It really seemed longer to me. But, prison or not, it is essentially my present home. And you are my welcome guests. You must be tired and thirsty after your tough climb. Come into the observation room and rest while I get some iced lemonade. I had just made some when I heard you."

He noticed their amazed stares. "Yes, I do have ice. The U.S. Navy left a refrigerator which the natives fixed. It is usually powered by a generator run by a windmill on the roof. There is always wind up here!"

Once they had their drinks, Burnhouse began his story. There really was nothing remarkable about it.

The elders of the native village, led by Launo, had found the products of the TECHland community intolerable. They had called Burnhouse to some sort of tribal council meeting at the village to beg him to call off his project before more damage was done. Launo was particularly insistent that his young men not be exposed to such potentially dangerous ideas. He said that they could not handle the volatile mixture of the concept of warrior, and the opposing concept of equality for all, regardless of gender and strength and athleticism. The idea that the victor gets all of the spoils was a part of their heritage, inculcated in the young men of the village for centuries. The result of the TECHland experiment had been to unleash these aggressive tendencies. The result had surely not been in keeping with the traditional morality of the people on this island. It would undoubtedly result in long jail sentences for the young men when the experiment was finally over, and the regular authorities eventually regained control of the island government. So, he had begged Burnhouse to stop the experiment immediately, before more damage was done.

Burnhouse had adamantly refused, arguing that they could not say that the experiment had failed. He said that he could not stop it, because it had just begun. He said that it would take time to make all of the changes that must be made in order to make the plan work. He asked for just a few more weeks, at least, of trial.

But, Launo had been deadly serious about stopping the study. He warned Burnhouse that the tribal council had decided that the experiment must be stopped at any cost. He said that they absolutely could not abide a continuation of the situation as it had become. The very future of the young people was at stake, he said. He asked one last time for Burnhouse to stop the experiment.

Burnhouse had told Luano that he could not stop the study now on his own, even if he wanted to. There was too much of an investment by too many people simply to stop. He said that he was sorry if the chief believed that the result was adversely affecting his people. But, his decision was final. He had said that they would have to kill him to stop him.

Launo had been outraged by his words. He warned Burnhouse not to be fooled about the villagers' intentions. He reminded Burnhouse that the natives had the means, and the natural courage, to kill him if they wished. They had the means to kill him so that no one would ever know. He would just disappear.

Launo told him that they were going to keep him in the village under guard until they could decide what to do about him. The village council would decide. Launo promised to tell him of their decision the next dawn.

The deliberations had taken most of the night. Some of the elders actually wanted to kill him on the spot, and throw his body to the sharks. They feared the authorities, if they were found to have imprisoned him. But Launo, who had been baptized in the Christian church, would not hear of such barbaric behavior.

As the council argued on through the night about what to do with him, Burnhouse could not know, of course, the tenor of the meeting. He recalled that he had experienced it as a very long night.

When he was led in to the council chamber at dawn, he had looked about the faces in the room to discover the nature of his fate. He could gather no clue, however, from the stoic native countenances. Launo had announced with obvious relief that one wise elder had suggested that they simply incarcerate him in the weather station at the top of the mountain. That would work for their purpose, if they could arrange a passage to it that was not too dangerous for Burnhouse to manage, or for the young men who would have to take him supplies. So, they had locked him in

a storage shed for a few days until they could make the arrangements. They had to construct the ladder bridge to the path to the
summit, check the safety of the path and prepare an entrance door
to keep him in the station. They had been able to fix everything
in about four days of hard work.

Burnhouse had been there on the mountain since, healthy
and well-provisioned. He was really in no immediate danger. But
he had not been at all happy with his incarceration. Mainly, he had
been worried about the fate of his research project. After all of the
time and money spent on the project, how could they now reach
any valid conclusions about it, one way or the other? The work
was not completed. It could not be completed without him.

Having completed his story, Burnhouse glanced about his
temporary lofty dwelling. Grudgingly, he said, "Actually, the natives have done an amazing job of getting this place ready. Everything has been provided for me. If there is anything that I need,
they do their best to supply it. Potable water is collected from large
pans on the roof that are protected from the birds by electrically
charged wires surrounding them. After a few jolts, the birds learn
to avoid the roof, and so did I. I feel very comfortable elsewhere
about the station—sometimes, I think, too comfortable.

"The electricity is provided by wind power, as I said. Two
large windmills and generators were left by the Navy. Because
the wind is always blowing up here, there is plenty of power for
cooking, heating water, running the refrigerator and so forth. The
sea breezes keep the temperature nice and cool during the day. It
gets a bit cool during the night, but I have plenty of sweaters and
blankets, plus some electric heaters if it really gets too cold."

"And the natives with knapsacks bring up supplies on a regular basis," prompted Posh.

"Yes," said Burnhouse. "The natives come up twice a week or
so to bring supplies. They bring canned goods, an occasional pork
chop, fresh fruits and the like. They even brought up some carp to
stock the carp pool. Now, I can have fresh fish whenever I want,
or when bad weather prevents the supply trips. They also rigged
up this net with springs so that when I release a lever it pivots up
to snare birds that happen to be flying by. I catch a lot of sea gulls
that way. I release them, of course. There are also some fat quail-

like birds that are really delicious. I really think that these people could make this place entirely self-sufficient for an indefinite period. Apparently, that is what they intended to work toward. That does not make me feel very happy, I can tell you.

"It was a bit lonesome here, but they tried to find things to keep me busy. You can see the satellite dish over there that provides a decent number of television channels. God knows where they got it. It took a bunch of them all night to get it up here."

"I'm afraid that I do know where they got it," Harry said. "It came from the mayor's house. I think the kind term for the acquisition process was `midnight requisition'. Skull, my friend, you are a receiver of stolen goods."

Burnhouse shrugged, and smiled slightly. "I've done worse," he admitted.

Burnhouse continued: "There truly is about everything one needs here. There are terrace gardens for fresh fruits and vegetables. There are the carp pools for fresh fish, and hydroponic pools of both salt water for seaweed and fresh water for some vegetables. A septic system has been set up to provide several stages of processing that ends with a germ-free fertilizer for the terrace gardens. So, the needs for nourishment have been provided for an indefinitely long period.

"Besides the library and the TV, there is an old piano and sheet music for my entertainment. There is a stationary bicycle for exercise. It can be hooked up to the generator, if the wind were suddenly to stop for a while.

"They seem to have thought of everything. They even have emergency signals if I need something before the next scheduled re-supply. In the daylight, I can signal to the village with a heliograph that was left here by the Navy. It is pointed at the chief's hut. I just flash a few times, and someone is here within twenty-four hours. If there were an emergency, I point the beam without flashing it."

Harry nodded. "Yes, I saw the flashing beam of light the other day while we were having lunch with the chief. I could not imagine that you were responsible for it. All of this is truly amazing."

Harry then decided to risk a little teasing of Burnhouse. Devilishly, he asked, "Doesn't this place remind you a little bit of

Skinner's air crib? It looks like you have everything to keep you happy with very little effort on your part. What a wonderful life!" Skinner had invented an air-conditioned crib for his daughter. It contained all of the physical necessities of life, and was a safe, comfortable environment for the child.

Burnhouse was not amused by the analogy. "No way!" he said angrily. "I want out of this place. It is still like a prison. The air crib seems perfect for a young child, but for an adult like me, it is unbearable. I want to be free to go where I please."

"Don't we all," said Harry. He mused about Burnhouse's words reflecting his desire to be free to go where he pleased. Harry really could not accept the Behavioristic argument that such use of words represented mere short cuts of speech in expressing Behavioristic interpretations of the overt behaviors. He was sure that, at the human core, a Behaviorist feels about personal freedom like everyone else.

Harry thought that Burnhouse's attitude was amazing. He was amazed because the Behaviorists could blow off negative information about their philosophy without qualms. It seemed impossible to him that anyone could not see that Burnhouse's contempt for his personal 'air crib' was a devastating blow to the Behavioristic position.

But he decided that there was no advantage to confronting Burnhouse further about it at that particular time. So, he concluded that it was expedient to let the matter drop. Posh winked knowingly at him. And grinned. Patience simply looked pensive and uncomfortable. She definitely got the message.

Actually, Burnhouse did too. For a moment, it appeared as though the animosity between the two men was going to flare into open conflict. Harry braced himself. He was in no mood to listen to garbage from Burnhouse.

Then, Burnhouse decided not to fight from such a disadvantageous position. He abruptly changed the subject back to the task at hand. He asked, "So, what is happening down below? Things were not looking too good when they brought me up here. I have asked repeatedly, but Launo has been very close-mouthed about the news on the island. Nevertheless, he talks freely about everything else. That worries me a lot. I suspect that things are not going well."

"Skull, it is bad—very, very bad," Harry began, for the moment content to skip the conflict. "That is the reason that we must hurry. We must grab a bit of supper and start back as soon as possible. You can fill us in on your complete story as soon as we get the situation down there under control, if indeed we can. Malevi's native thugs have joined with Mulik Efraim and Sam Conaway, and his men, and Percy Hernandez and the gangs to form a formidable mob of thugs and hooligans.

"They are still raping the people and the island, without any limits on what they will do. They have no sense of fairness or decency or any other human virtue, it seems. We need you to talk to them, to try to convince them that this sort of behavior is not what your TECHland plan is all about. But you have let loose a monster. They have perverted your ideals."

"Oh, my God," gasped Burnhouse. "Of course, I never dreamed such things could happen. It absolutely is not a part of the plan. How could they think so? How can we convince them to stop?"

Harry was firm. "You are the one that must stop them. You are our only hope now. The radio transmitters are destroyed or stolen, so we cannot reach help in Saipan soon enough. We must use our own resources.

"Our group has joined with some others to barricade themselves inside the plantation house. I think that they will be okay tonight, while the mobsters work up their courage. But we must get back before dark tomorrow night, because I think that the mob will surely be large enough and brave enough to attack by then. They will have enough people to attack, as things looked when we were there. The defenders will never be able to see their attackers without the daylight. They will be overwhelmed in the dark. There is no telling what manner of evil will happen then."

Burnhouse was quite distressed at the news. "Of course, I will do what I can to stop their nonsense. I never imagined that these people would so misunderstand what TECHland is all about."

Harry was eager for a quick resolution to the Kipua situation. "Okay," he said, "let's grab a bite and get rolling."

The other four all objected, in concert. Patience said, wisely, "We must get some good food in our stomachs, and some real rest, before we start back. Otherwise, we will probably fall off the trail. And, even if we make it, there is no benefit in arriving back there totally exhausted. Considering what we will face, and what we might have to do, we need our best edge. If we leave here in the early morning, we can easily get to the compound by dark tomorrow."

Burnhouse also was absolutely against the idea of attempting a descent in the dark. He warned that, even with flashlights, the trail was too treacherous. Also, their psychological states of fatigue and anxiety were not conducive to safe travel down the mountain.

"Stay the night," he said. "You can have plenty of food and rest. We will start back early in the morning. I hate to be unilateral about this thing, but I myself will absolutely not try to negotiate the trail in the dark. We are quite willing to follow you as leader of the rescue team. But please do not ask us to start back today, and end up on the side of the mountain in the dark. Do not make me defy an order. What do you say?"

The others all agreed on the wisdom of Burnhouse's suggestion. So, Harry decided to be wise. "You are right. We will rest for the night, and start down the trail early in the morning," agreed Harry. "It will be much safer. You are right in saying that we will be in better shape when we arrive to cope with whatever we have to deal with."

Monika brought out some fruit and bread and cheese for them to snack on while Patience and Burnhouse prepared dinner. Harry had not realized how welcome the chance to rest would be.

As they chatted through dinner, Burnhouse talked about his capture. "You know," he said, "Launo really felt bad about keeping me here, but he didn't know any alternative. He has seen to it that one of his people got some of my books and papers for me to read and work on, so I wouldn't be too bored. And he comes up once a week to talk and to play chess. He even offered to bring up his widowed sister so that I could have a little feminine company, if I wanted it. All I had to do was ask. A few more weeks of the loneliness before Monika arrived, and I probably would have taken him up on his most thoughtful offer."

Patience snorted, "That's sexist and disgusting. You ought to be ashamed!"

Burnhouse, like everyone else, retreated from her fury. "Take it easy," he said. "I only said I would think about it. But, still, it is a part of a happy life for most of us, you have to admit."

"Okay, okay," Harry said. "Let's not get side-tracked on such academic issues right now. I must say, Patience, that I am surprised at your moral outrage at a little romance."

"Romance, schmo-mance!" she snapped. "What do you know about it? If you think that what he is talking about is romance, you are a male-chauvinist dodo bird."

Then, she abruptly changed the subject, "But I do agree that we must concentrate on saving lives and property right now. Let's try to map out a strategy that might work. Skull, it is really your baby. What approach will you try?"

Harry agreed to change the subject. "This romance thing is surely interesting, and we will talk more about it later, if we live long enough. Right now, I agree that we must try to make a plan to save us all."

Burnhouse was alarmed: "You mean things are that bad down there? My God, what can we do? Can't we send for outside help, the Marines or somebody?"

Harry saw no reason to show false optimism. "We must do what we ourselves can do here now. We have sent natives in canoes to the next island to radio for help. Gupta's radio and the radio at the plantation house have been destroyed, and mine has been stolen. I fear that the situation will be over one way or another before outside help can get here."

Patience picked up the story. "Our earlier plan was to find Monika, and hope that then she could convince the mob that this behavior is not consistent with the TECHland program. But, Skull, as the leader of the TECHland experiment, you have a better chance. Did you have a contingency plan in case the experiment went sour—as it apparently has?"

Burnhouse shook his head despairingly. "We have no power to control the mob. Their leaders hold all the cards. TECHland requires total control by the leaders. So, truly, that much is as it should be in TECHland."

"Just my major criticism of the plan," said Harry, because he could not resist saying it. Then, he moved on. "But my way gives us some hope. It is a matter of frame of mind. You must talk to them, try to convince them there is no room in the TECHland program for the use of force and other aversive tactics. Will you do it?"

Burnhouse replied, "I have no confidence in such a strategy. It will not work."

Harry was practically screaming, pleading, by now, "But there is no other plan. We must at least try something. We must at least *try* to save the women and children. None of them deserves what the leaders of the mob are likely to do to them! I will help you as much as I can. But you are the key. Think of Monika! Think of Patience!"

"All right! All right!" said Burnhouse. "I'll do it." He was not really a bad person. Ultimately, he truly did care about people. Harry really had never doubted it. Too bad that such caring was not a part of Burnhouse's social plan, and a larger part of his personality.

"Thanks," Harry said, somewhat calmed. Then: "Okay, let's get some sleep. Big day tomorrow."

There were plenty of bunks for them in the old Navy installation. Burnhouse plugged in some electric heaters, so the room was relatively comfortable. Harry and Posh had packed sweaters, so they were warm. Burnhouse had enough blankets for each of the women to have one. The travelers, tired from their climb, fell asleep immediately. Monika and Burnhouse talked quietly for awhile before turning into their bunks.

* * * * * *

After breakfast of fruit, toast, eggs and coffee, the group was ready for the dangerous trip down the mountain. As they started

off cautiously down the thin winding trail, there was little conversation. They all had accurate ideas of what fearful prospects
waited for them below. The thought occurred to each of them
that they might have a chance to save themselves if they just hid
in the jungle below until help arrived. Each one in turn quickly
dismissed such a shameful idea, without mentioning it. Each felt
shame for even entertaining the idea for an instant.

Truly, such a cowardly action seemed to be the only real hope
for their individual survival. Only a miracle could save them now.
If Burnhouse were not successful in stopping the mob, they did
not have a fall-back plan. Indeed, his chances of success were not
good. In fact, they each privately had to admit that they would not
wager on his success, if they had a choice. The mob had shown
that it would not listen to reason. Therefore, there were no strong
reasons to believe that the attempt would be successful.

Perhaps by explaining that TECHland was not supposed to
work by might and violence, Burnhouse could persuade enough
of them to back off in order to save the island. He just must do it!
He really was the last hope against the gangs.

Thus, they all entertained the same thoughts as they edged
their way down the mountain. Harry was silently reciting every
prayer that he could remember. The rest of them were trying their
own methods for achieving peace.

* * * * * *

They had negotiated the trail successfully and were approaching the last ladder. It had been tedious, but not difficult, to by-pass
the missing ladder by replacing it with the one above, and repeating the process as they progressed downward. Posh was leading
the way, followed by Monika and Patience, and then Harry. They
were making good time. They should be at the plantation compound by mid-afternoon.

At last, Posh reached the floor of the crevice. As he turned to
help Monika, but before he could grab her, she jumped off the
last ring with a triumphant cry, to celebrate the end of the ordeal.
It was a near-tragic mistake. Her left foot landed on a rock and

twisted to one side, causing her to land heavily on her left knee. Screaming in pain, she rolled onto her side, grasping her ankle with both hands.

Posh pried her hands loose, and examined the boot and leg. He was joined quickly by Harry and Patience. They could see that the knee seemed sound, except that there was a large bruise forming just below the kneecap. They could not tell much about the ankle because Monika was wearing high hiking boots. Nothing in the leg seemed out of place, however. Monika was able, despite the pain, to move the foot. Together, they decided that the injury was merely a painful sprain. The leg and ankle did not seem to be broken.

Under the circumstances, she would have to try to walk on it. They would have to watch the swelling to be sure that the boot did not cut off the circulation of blood to the foot. Each one of the others would have to take turns helping her to keep as much weight off of the foot as possible. Tragically, it was going to be slow going at a time when the need for speed was great.

They managed rather well to move through the jungle, because there was a semblance of a trail. The plan of rotating helpers for Monika seemed to be working. The changing of helpers about every fifteen minutes enabled all of them to remain relatively fresh. Monika was obviously in great pain, but she realized the need for haste. So, she did not complain.

As they approached the main trail from the native village to the plantation house, near the end of their trek, a major problem confronted them. Groups of natives heading toward the plantation appeared at intervals on the trail. Posh motioned for their party to stay concealed in the jungle until he could discover whether or not the natives were likely to harm them. He reported, unfortunately, that the tenor of the conversations along the trail indicated that the natives were upset with the leaders of the island government, and were planning to join the assault on the plantation manor.

Posh whispered that they would have to continue off the trail in order to avoid detection. It would slow them down even more. But, it was better to arrive later, they decided, than to risk a confrontation with the isolated bands of natives.

Now the progress was very slow and torturous. They were all in extreme discomfort, especially Monika, although she still did not complain. Harry was distressed at his own surprise at Monika's fortitude. He guessed that he must be some kind of male chauvinist after all.

In any case, he still marveled at the human spirit. Here were five intelligent adult human beings punishing their bodies to get to a place of possible total destruction for them all. Was there some important psychological principle involved? Or was this just mass disordered thinking brought about by the inordinate level of stress that they all had been exercising? "No," decided Harry, mostly to himself, "all of us are not crazy. We are heroes."

TWENTY

MALEVI HAD SENT A GROUP of his followers on ahead to the plantation to make sure that none of the inhabitants escaped the consequences of resisting the forces of the junta. He had made sure that his warriors were well armed. His physical revenge would be complete. He knew that he could trust his minions to keep the passions of the mob inflamed so that the entire mass of warriors and townsfolk would be ready for deadly conflict when he arrived.

As he adorned his body with the full regalia of his office, Malevi contemplated his tactics when he would arrive at the plantation. First, he would complete the arousal of the animosities of the natives against the dePuy family and their guests. To his mind, he had endured many snubs and insults from the plantation owners. Now, he would be able to avenge these affronts in full.

Also, he hated, almost as much, the new arrivals from the prestigious universities. He thought how they had come here to tell the inhabitants how to run the island. His ancestors had been on the island for centuries. They had been part of the ruling order for generations. And, now, the first of these outsiders had come with the idea of using them, and a second group had come with the idea of protecting them from the first group. His ancestors had died exploring the seas. They had fought in many wars to preserve the freedom of the island. The ancestors of these mainland dogs had then been farmers and sheepherders.

Malevi fiercely clutched his great polished war club, making small involuntary movements, as if to bring it down on some hated object. He imagined, with consummate joy, smashing the swelled head of that dung heap of a professor from some foreign school who had come with his fancy group of egg-heads to rescue them from him.

352

When he had completed his preparations, Malevi started off for the plantation at an easy lope. He would arrive just before dark. When darkness fell, he would be ready to lead the mob in the final rape and destruction of the plantation.

* * * * * *

It was late when the weary and battered travelers drew near the plantation house. The sun was just about to dive below the horizon. The leaves and trunks of the coconut palm trees splashed elongated shadows against white walls, glistening bodies and flashing metal blades. The orange-tinted light presented the aura of an animated tableau, somehow unreal in tone, but ominously real in portent. The individual shouts from the crowd blended into a masking white noise that blanked out even the thoughts of individual minds.

Patience was stunned and numbed by the potential horror in the explosive scene before her. It was obviously about to erupt into a gigantic burst of kinetic energy. Time, she knew, was short. The rumbling, roaring mob before the gates was held back tenuously by the dwindling authority of Constable Gupta, backed resolutely by Dan Crow. The two friends were trying desperately to hold back and disperse the crowd. They pushed against the front rows with their shotguns. Flo Gorsuch was standing beside the partially-opened gate, pleading with the crowd. She joined Crow and Gupta in yelling out the names of those who would not disperse, trying to develop individual consciences.

It was evident to everyone that just two courageous men with shotguns, and a brave lady, armed only with her wits and courage, were not enough. The beseiged trio could not long restrain the mob that was already nearly out of control. The angry mass of men was too narrowly focused and rigidly fixed on its own awful agenda.

Blood would be spilled this night. That fearsome fact was immediately obvious to the new arrivals. The plan that did not seem promising on the top of the mountain now seemed totally worthless in the face of this throbbing mob of reptilian characters.

The only choices were either to press on, or to run. Instinctively, without thinking, each of them knew that they must move ahead, whatever the cost. Retreat would be defeat, and complete ruin for everyone and everything on the island, not to say the scientific community.

The raucous crowd did not see the newcomers at first. Consequently, the would-be rescue party was able to bluff brazenly through to Gupta and Crow without serious opposition. The frightened defenders within the compound cautiously opened the gate just wide enough for one person at a time to squeeze inside. Posh hurriedly ushered Florence, Monika and Patience to safety through the small opening in the gate. He succeeded despite surprisingly strong protests from the latter two. Apparently, for some strange reason, neither Monika nor Patience wanted to enter the temporary safety of the compound. Having completed the difficult chore of getting them securely inside the walls, Posh then quickly followed them into the relative safety of the provisional fortress.

The reasons for the protests of the two women were a mystery to Harry, given the serious danger outside the gates, and their obvious fear. The relative safety inside the walls of the compound was ample reason for them to covet fervently the other side of the gates.

Monika's actions were easier to explain. Presumably, she was in love with Burnhouse, and wanted to be at his side. At least, everyone thought that there was love between them. That surely would give her some reason to be outside.

Patience's behavior was unfathomable, even to Harry, the so-called expert in human psychology, who thought that he knew her well.

Once again, Harry was amazed at the complexity of the causation of human behavior. Perhaps Patience's strange response had something to do with the feminist movement. Did she want to show that she could die as well as men? Or, could it be that she thought that she could succeed where the men had failed? Perhaps, it was just a perverted version of a mother-hen instinct.

That would be a peculiar instinct indeed. Harry decided that he would worry about how to understand such behavior later when—and if—he had the time. He wondered what habits anyone would have that would apply to this situation well enough to save them.

As Harry and Burnhouse turned to face the mob, both of them knew that the rioters were not at all intimidated by them, any more than they had been cowed by Gupta's and Crow's weapons. The mob was instead actually inflamed by the apparent unified show of resistance. The mobsters were apparently offended by any attempt by the legal leaders to exercise their due authority, or to impose any restraints on the actions of the mob. The members of the angry crowd surely showed no regard for the theory behind TECHland. Under the circumstances, such a realization was rather irrelevant to the defenders at the moment.

Patience could see that Harry was about to die and with him her dreams of a technical Utopia. Through an emotional haze, she could only understand clearly that Harry, barring some miracle, was going to die. Only that mattered now.

Suddenly, Patience found herself outside the gate and beside Harry. She intended to make a valiant effort to protect him in some way, in whatever way she could.

Harry panicked instantly when he saw her. What was with her? What perversity was this? He wanted to spank her like a spoiled child. He could not handle her being outside the gate. He realized now that he would find it unbearable, if something were to happen to her. Again, the basic psychologist in his very nature wondered how to interpret these strange reactions. He wondered what was driving such a normally sane and logical person to perform such illogical behaviors.

Patience was looking at him with an expression that he had never before seen on her face. It baffled him. It was not the aloof and disdainful look that was so familiar between them. There was determination in her look, but also something else. What was it, he wondered?

"Now, what?" he said. He feared some entirely new problem of the female mind that he would not be able to solve.

"'What' is that I am staying here with you. I may not get another chance to tell you that I love you," she yelled through her tears. Then, she wrapped her arms tightly about him, and clung to him as a terrified baby clings to its mother.

Joy at once drove away Harry's fear, allowing a brief moment of respite. His disbelief of the meaning of her words was dispelled by the earnest look that she had shown on her gorgeous face. Was it true?

It was true! She really meant it! Her desperate grip told it all. The glad realization rushed over him like hot lava from a volcano, firing his emotions, dominating his consciousness. It was totally overwhelming, masking all else at the moment with its enormity.

For a while, for Harry, there was no one else in the world. Only the two of them, embracing as if it were to be their last embrace, their last kiss. It was a wonder! It was a joy! Here was deep and lasting love amid the massive mountains of hate flooding the world immediately around them. For an excruciating instant, the ambient mood of hate at the jungle's edge could not penetrate Harry's joyous personal space.

The private mood of joy was shattered when the crowd erupted in derisive cries. The reptiles were in no mood for tender feelings. Such attitudes would simply blunt their resolve to crush the opposition of the defenders, and to humiliate them. Someone shouted, "Go make love somewhere else, or share it with us."

Harry could now sense that the crowd was pressing forward. The end would not be delayed for long.

Night had fallen. The glow of the torches reflected in Patience's honey-colored hair, turning it into a bright halo. The flicking light softened the lines of her face. It created for Harry an image of an angel. Harry was entranced, dumbfounded by her ultimate beauty in that frozen moment of crystal splendor.

To be sure, he had never been happier. There was no place for the ugly crowd in his mind. He could hardly speak.

Finally, Harry heard a husky voice from deep inside his personal core say, with conviction, "Wonderful. I love you, too." It was his voice. He used it again. "I have loved you for years. I know it now."

Patience smiled when she heard the words. Her smile had become his favorite sight in the world. Harry thought again that he had never seen a vision so exquisite! It was truly a thing of sublime beauty amid the ugliness about them.

Strange, he never before realized his love for her. The cues had surely been there. He should have read them. But he had been so pre-occupied, or so stupid, that he could not identify them. Perhaps, he had been blind because he was afraid of rejection. Maybe, he had been fixed on lingering ties of loyalty to Lottie. Or perhaps he was just a stupid jerk, as Patience had so often accused him of being.

Now, all of Harry's reservations and doubts were expunged in a wave of boundless love. So, holding her tightly, Harry kissed his love again briefly, but nicely, satisfactorily, superbly. They both knew that they must quickly break apart. Neither could make the first move.

Then, Harry took control. The instinct of the male chauvinist within him had to be asserted in this time of crisis. His love was watching. He must not disappoint her. He knew that now he had a new powerful reason for his mission to succeed. He must save the thing that he now cared for beyond all else. It made him strong.

Coming reluctantly back to the other reality, he said, softly, lovingly, "Now, get inside quickly, you goof. We have work to do out here. With all due respect, you will just get in the way." He was trying to re-establish logical thinking.

Patience was too distraught to respond. She knew that he was right at this particular time. Still, she did not want to go. Love still overpowered the logic. She continued to cling like a baby monkey clings to its mother.

Now, Harry pushed her gently, but firmly, back toward the safety of the gate. Other hands pulled her protesting, tearfully inside, pleading that she wanted to be at his side. This was truly a different Patience than he had seen before. It was wonderful! It was indeed a welcome improvement to a package that he had not thought could be improved.

He was absolutely sure that their loves were genuine. To be sure, the love was entirely wonderful. Their's was a prototypical manifestation of love, a very definition of love. Strange that it had lain dormant and still, unrecognized, until it was roused by the horror of this madding moment.

Harry still snatched a sweet second to marvel at the omnipotent nature of love. Genuine love superseded all other motives—even for personal safety. It was more powerful than any drive that could be manipulated by any social planner. It could not be produced by any known behavioral technology. It was possible only for dispassionate technology to produce weak imitations. Such love could never be reduced to simple impersonal positive reinforcement.

True love was shown when, with full understanding of the possible excruciating consequences, Patience still wanted unconditionally, without hesitation, to be in danger at his side. He knew that he, too, would willingly die to protect her. That was the magnificent wonder of it all! It was truly beyond rational understanding, and thus beyond the reach of any known behavioral technology. It was an omnipotent wonder that had been tragically omitted from the cursed TECHland plan.

Then, Harry was drawn by duty back to the pending tragedy before him. Still shaken and confused by the unexpected event, he yelled to Gupta and Dan Crow, "You have done your best, but the crowd is not responding well to your show of authority, especially an armed authority. It is best if you go back inside. The sight of you inflames the crowd.

"Our plan now is to have Burnhouse try to reason with them. He will argue from the scientific viewpoint of the TECHland experiment that their behavior is not in keeping with the TECHland ideal. It is our last chance."

Gupta agreed readily, and hurriedly pushed on the gate for admittance. When the gate was opened a bit more, he jumped quickly inside. Harry could not blame him. None of this was Gupta's doing. Nevertheless, he had indeed been sublimely faithful to his job as long as he had a chance for success. Further effort on his part now would simply be foolish.

Crow obviously wanted to remain outside. He was thinking of Mary, of course. Harry merely gave him a stern look which meant that the barkeep must be out of his mind. "You can protect Mary better from inside," he yelled. "Do it! Be smart!"

Crow stared a piercing stare which penetrated into Harry's heart. After a brief moment of hesitation, he completely yielded to Harry's logic. Placing his hands in a defensive position, he nodded an acquiescence. Crow could not be forced to do anything, but he could be persuaded. Harry had guessed correctly that Crow's first priority was to save lives, and not to prove anything about himself, particularly his courage.

Crow then raised his fist at Harry in a salute and show of support. There was a lifetime of communication in the meaningful looks that they exchanged. A bond of eternal friendship and transcendental understanding had been sealed in an instant. Then, without another spoken word, Crow quickly squeezed his large body back into the temporary safety of the compound. He would serve where he would be most effective.

Harry then insisted nervously to Skull Burnhouse, "Okay, man. It's your turn, your ball game. Do your stuff. The longer you can talk, the better the chances for our side. Get them to talk out their anger, if you can. Remember, time itself is on our side."

Obligingly, Burnhouse raised his arms in a placating gesture to the crowd. "Friends," he said, "what you are doing is not what TECHland is supposed to be about. Confrontation and violence will not improve anything."

The rumbling restlessness in the mob increased. Burnhouse was not reaching them. He could not hold them off for long. Both Harry and Burnhouse understood that.

Nevertheless, Burnhouse continued to try valiantly: "What you are doing is in no way consistent with the ideals and proposals of the behavioristic plan. Actions like the murder of Kenny and the vicious rapes of Launini and the others are not a part of the scientific way, or any other way, to a better world. The right way is exactly the opposite. Can't you see that? The goal of TECHland is happiness and improved welfare for *all* people. It is not just for the strong who can take what they want.

"In fact, the strong are supposed to dedicate their work and their lives for the good of all. What you are doing now actually departs and detracts from the TECHland ideal. Actually, your behavior shows that something has gone terribly wrong with our plan, in order for it to allow such importations of evil."

Burnhouse realized as he was talking that he, himself, had temporarily abandoned the TECHland model. He was appealing to human values and human decency to save them. At the moment, it did not seem to matter.

Harry tried to support Burnhouse. "Dr. Burnhouse is right. We both agree on this, absolutely without question. I admit that I have never been an admirer of his overall plan. But, I do agree with him that the experiment was not supposed to turn out this way. Aversive methods are definitely not a part of the plan—they are not a part of anyone's plan, except apparently your own. But, really, you are not following any reasonable plan. You are merely pursuing your own selfish goals. That approach is not a plan. It will not solve any problems. There should not be winners and losers at a TECHland, if the plan is followed exactly. A valid Utopian society could not have either victors or victims, winners or losers."

Malevi shouted out viciously, "The Western scientists are lying. They are just trying to save their own possessions and privileges. We have understood the plan very well. The plan argues that fake moral arguments just get in the way of happiness. These are the very same fake moral arguments that they are dredging up now, when it suits their purposes. We know that the experimenters were following the plan. We understand sharing the wealth well enough. The TECHland plan is for us to behave as we feel natural, to do what we wish, to be happy."

Then, he shouted even louder, "I will be happy to lie with one of the women behind these walls, the younger the better."

Others called out their agreement in obscene ways. They wanted satisfaction for all of their denied pleasures. They wanted it now. Or else, they wanted blood.

Now Sam Conaway joined in against Burnhouse: "You and others like you have helped to shape us to be the way we are. You and the politicians have been in control. We have let you be in control. You and the others like you. You cannot change by your words now anything that has happened, just because now *we* have the power. You cannot change the principles of behavior whenever it suits you, in some last-ditch effort to save yourselves. Now, we finally see that you will say anything to save yourself, to save your privileges, your money and your women. It's only now that you try to make us feel that we have choices, that we should consider right and wrong. But, your claims are simply another desperate attempt to control us.

"Burnhouse, the fake savior, cannot just pull some fancy psychobabble arguments out of the hat now to confuse us. Those are actually the very same arguments that he has denied for weeks. We do what we have been shaped, molded by circumstances, to do. That's all there is to it. You cannot change that basic fact, which you preached to us for weeks. Your pretty words now cannot change anything!"

"No, listen to me, please," pleaded Burnhouse. "I am saying what I have always said. You have misunderstood me. You misunderstand me now. What you are doing is not justified by the TECHland model. Neither is it supported by any other reputable psychological theory."

"Shut up, and get out of the way," warned Conaway. "We will hear no more. We do what we will do. Nothing has changed. We have no choice, just like you said. Don't try to tell us now that we have a choice. We will play out the game tonight. We will run the string all of the way to the end. And there is not a thing that you can do to change our minds, or to change us. You cannot stop us. We cannot stop ourselves. That is exactly what you had been saying before. We believed you."

There was more shouted approval from the mob. They obviously had exhausted their patience. They began moving ominously toward Harry and Burnhouse, surging forward like a relentless and deadly tide of wanton emotion. The blood lust was upon them. It clung to them like an evil spell of a witch. Now, they really did not desire cooperation. They did not even want capitulation. In fact, they actually preferred resistance and conflict. Such was their mood. So, violence was imminent. And it would bring its own rewards.

In a menacing attitude, Malevi advanced toward the embattled academics, brandishing his dreaded war club. He ordered Burnhouse and Harry to step aside. He ordered them to instruct the guards inside the compound to open the gates. As of one accord, the two academics, now turned defensive warriors, shook their heads slowly and defiantly, despite their fears. Their bravery was great, because their fears were great.

Harry wondered what it would feel like to have his skull crushed. He hoped that the first blow would render him instantly unconscious.

Malevi seemed to read his mind. He threatened, "Do not think that I am going to kill you with one blow. Assuredly, I could do so, if I desired. But you do not deserve it. You have angered me. So, you will die slowly, in gradual stages, as an evil intruder. First, I will break your arms and legs, and then your ribs. But, be assured, the final killing blow to your head will come while you are still conscious enough to know it."

His words terrified Harry. But, he knew that his terror must not show. So, he tried to sound brave. "Perhaps you can. But, it will not get you what you want. We are prepared to fight, if necessary. And, if we lose, the American marines will punish you when they arrive."

Malevi still snarled, "But all of that is not necessary. You can stop such pain. Bloodshed does not need to happen. Just give us what we want, and my anger will dissolve in my mindless passion. I would rather writhe with women than smash bones. I promise that then no one will be hurt. It will be your own fault if you, or they, are hurt."

"And just what is it that you want," Harry asked, fearful of the obvious answer, but still stalling for time. "We need to know what you want, so that we can make an informed decision."

He had no intention of giving in to Malevi, of course. Mostly, he wanted to gain time for a miracle to materialize from thin air. Perhaps, given enough time, some members of the crowd would come to their senses. He himself would not bet on it, but there was no choice.

He had not fooled Malevi.

"You heard me. Everything," Malevi screamed. "We want money, food, wine, young women—all of the things that you have had for so many years and would not share with us. You were happy, but we were not happy. It is all about sharing and letting each person have what he wants. I want what will make me happy tonight. What will make me happy is to have your haughty Australian professor on a bed of palm leaves. You must watch. I want to show her, and you, that the new plan of life has no place for haughty women, or for arrogant professors. Then, I will bash in the skull of that snooty old woman who runs the school, and thinks that she owns the island."

His manner and his words brought panic to Harry. He felt his backbone turn to ice. He was sick to his stomach. His heart thudded at a scary pace. He knew that he could never let Malevi have his way. He thought, "Patience, my love, this thing must not happen to you!" His only plan was to die there in front of the gate, hoping that his murder would quench the blood thirst of the crowd.

He managed to shout a defiant deterrent, still trying to project a courage that he did not really possess. The kind of courage that he possessed was the ability to overcome fear, not to preclude fear. But, he knew that now he must not show his fear. "You know that is impossible," he yelled. "We will never agree to such unthinkable terms. We have seen what you have done to the women that you have raped. You have hurt them without mercy.

"But let me tell you that whatever you might succeed in accomplishing tonight will be at a great personal cost to you. It will not be so easy this time. We have weapons, too. Many of you will be hurt or killed, also. Just ask the Junk Yard Dogs. We will do what we have to do. Be sure of it. So just go on home tonight. We will talk about any grievances you have in the morning when we are all sober and have quieted down. We can work things out, if you just give us a chance."

Sam Conaway screamed: "Enough of this talk. You just want to talk to buy more time. It means nothing! And there is no one to save you. Now get out of the way. Now! Right now! Or suffer what we do not want. But, be sure of this: We will do what we have to do to get satisfaction tonight. Move aside, or be hurt. It is as simple as that. It is your choice."

"So, now we have a choice, and you do not," Harry shot back. "Think about what you are saying, man. I say that we *all* do have choices. Make a decent one! We are not moving from here. We have made our choice. Now each of you must make his or her own choice, and suffer or savor the consequences."

"Right! No way," said Burnhouse, defiantly. "We will not yield without a fight."

"The snob does have courage," thought Harry.

But their show of courage was not enough to divert the will of the mob. Some particularly vicious members of the mob began throwing rocks. Others began poking the defenders with sticks and spears. It was just a matter of time before someone used a club, or gun, or a knife, with catastrophic effect. Strangely, Malevi held back. Apparently, he was hoping that the horror and fear of the defenders would grow further to his advantage.

Harry knew that finally, it was truly hopeless. Harry could see in Burnhouse's face that he thought so, too. His own face must be an exact replica of the despair on the face of Burnhouse. Surely, the members of the mob could see it too. The furious crowd surged forward toward the kill, more quickly now.

Harry now had no new plan to save them. Obviously, his present plan was decidedly not working. For the second straight day, he combed, sifted and massaged his brain. He searched to discover some little-used habit, or a new response, one that might possibly work. He needed an answer to a seemingly impossible question. He was searching his scorched and numbed brain for some clue to a strategy that might carry some hope of success. But, this time, nothing would come. The only possible answer for him now was a noble, painful death.

That could hardly be considered a plan. So, valiant death was the only so-called plan. He decided that is was not even worthy of being called a plan, really. As a professor, he himself would give it a weak D- grade for its very lack of creativity.

No one in the crowd had been at all moved by either their pleas, arguments or threats. To give the mob what it wanted was unthinkable. The thought of what they would do to Mary, Patience and the other women and young girls was unbearable.

The Marines would never arrive in time. Realistically, any effective resistance from within the compound, despite the best efforts of Gupta and Dan Crow, would be shattered in a matter of minutes. The first wave of pillage and rape would be over within another ten minutes. So, in about a quarter of an hour from now the worst fears of the scientists would be realized.

"God help us!" prayed Harry.

Harry's tortured mind recognized only a slim glimmer of hope. It was all that he could devise to save them. The only hope for survival now was a desperate fight to his death. Perhaps, if he and the rest of the defenders in the compound inflicted enough pain on the leaders, they would induce the rest of the mob to quit. It might save just a few of the innocents behind the walls. Unfortunately, that was his best plan. He did not think that it would work. It was at least something to try.

"Skull, we must get to our weapons—fight fire with fire," he called out to Burnhouse. "Let's get inside. Get some weapons. Save ourselves for a fight. This is no good here. Maybe we can make the cost of their intentions too high for them to want to pay."

Burnhouse nodded in total despair. "I agree that it is no good out here in the open. We need the cover of the walls."

Then, they began backing slowly toward the gates, still facing down the mob. Burnhouse was in tears. His tears were not from fear of personal bodily injury, Harry thought. The breakdown was from the massive disappointment, the gnawing frustration and the unrelenting remorse for the horrible danger that he had brought upon them all.

The growling mob marched slowly forward by baby steps, with unlimited ugly intent, obviously gloating. They were savoring the anticipation of a crushing victory. The individual members of the mob obviously felt no need to hurry, because the desired outcome was inevitable. It was the end! The puny defensive force in the compound could not put a dent in the mob's intentions. Now, Harry had finally given up all expectation of survival. "No power on earth can save us now," he thought.

But there was other power!

The gate opened narrowly. Before Harry and Burnhouse could slip inside, Cal Prescott and Jack Schindler pushed quickly out, and actually rushed out in front of the mob. They placed themselves resolutely between the two retreating men and the relentless crowd. They locked their arms together to make a single united barrier. They looked defiantly at the mob, but without malice.

"What do they intend?" wondered Harry.

Skull Burnhouse was obviously also perplexed. His face was a picture of amazement. Then, when full realization come upon him, his face became solemn. He said, "They intend to die for us, if necessary." His voice was shaking, but utterly convincing.

Harry knew that it was so. He felt both sad and joyful. He was flooded with a shower of emotions. It was both beautiful and tragic.

With their free hands Cal and Jack clutched crucifix and cross. Harry had seen in their determined faces, as they brushed by him, that they were not going to give in to the mob. They could not fight and would not cooperate. The mobsters seemed to sense it too. Briefly, perceptibly, the reptiles slowed their forward movement. The obvious intent of the two friends instilled awe even in the lowest of the robbers and rapists in the crowd.

The two men were widely mismatched on most points of comparison. One was Catholic; one was Protestant. One was a native of Canada, and the other was a product of the rural south in the United States. One was dark-skinned and aging; the other was white, rosy and youthful. One was tall and spare; the other was short and well-fleshed. One was typically calm and dignified; the other, fidgety, usually full of useless motions. Indeed, they probably had only one significant point in common: their striving for oneness with God. They were committed to the Great Commandment to love God with their whole being, and to accord an unconditional and encompassing love for their neighbors.

It was a rare kind of love that only a few can fully understand. Their love embraced even those who had committed heinous atrocities, and were about to commit new ones. These two clerics who were so mismatched in other ways had both managed to fill their hearts so full of love that there was no room for hate in them.

They showed a sublime model for human order that trivialized all other plans for the survival of human cultures.

Father Schindler spoke out resolutely to the crowd, "Friends, we have loved and served you. We now call upon you to go back to your homes. You owe us better than this. We know that this wantonness is really not your nature. You are confused and upset, we know. Do not demean yourselves further by continuing this madness. Do what is right. Call upon the love of God that we know is truly in your hearts, but temporarily drowned out by this insanity that has taken hold of you."

Cal added his strong voice: "Neighbors, you know what Father Jack says is true. Just think about it! We have served you with love. We love you, and we also love the people behind these gates. All of you are children of God. We are prepared to die for you both, to prove our love for you, as did our Savior to prove His love for all peoples.

"Come to your senses. We are here to protect you from yourselves, to save you from yourselves. We are also here to protect from you the people behind these gates. You must not be allowed to ruin their lives, and your lives also, if you harm them in any way. By doing harm to these people, you will also be destroying yourselves. You will be destroying what Father Jack and I have worked for these many years."

The priest joined again in the plea. "We have shown you love. We still show you love. We call for love. Do not give us hatred."

The brief hesitation of the mob continued for a moment, and then it abruptly ended. The reptilian minds were still closed and set, and the hearts were too hardened to human sentiment. The growls and the ominous forward movement returned.

Malevi snarled the response of the mob: "We will not listen to your stinking lies. You just want to keep us down. We will kill you like the sniveling dogs you are."

Then, he hurled a large rock that had been in his hand, hidden behind his back. It hit Jack Schindler directly on the breastbone. The priest reeled back, but then painfully recovered. Resolutely, he moved ahead to stand his ground beside Cal.

Others in the crowd now followed Malevi's vicious example. They threw more and more rocks, with horrible intent, striking both men with abominable effect.

Through now swollen and bleeding lips, Cal still called to the crowd: "Choose love while you yet can. It is not too late. Think of a God who loves you and wants what is truly best for you. Think of us, His servants, who love you. Come join us in a song of love and praise."

Cal began to sing the old hymn, *Oh, love that will not let me go,* in a weak wavering voice that grew a little stronger as Jack joined in.

Harry tried to sing, too, with little success. His emotion was too strong to permit much of a sound above the malevolent noises of the crowd. Burnhouse just stood in front of the gate, dazed.

Soon, Cal and Jack were bloodied and drooping, still clinging to one another, now just even to stand. The effects of the blows on their bodies was increasingly damaging, now inevitably lethal. But they still endeavored to protect Harry and Burnhouse and the rest. All the while, they continued to sing with fervor, with happy smiles on their faces. There was no bitterness, no hate in them.

Harry marveled again at such love. It matched, or exceeded, the strength of the love that he felt for Patience, but for people who were simply neighbors. But, the clerics' kind of love was different, and somehow better, too. It was total love even for those about them who were nominally strangers. Even as he witnessed it, Harry could not really understand such a love that had no limit. He stood fixed, unable to move, afraid to move, as if movement would somehow destroy the respectful awe that he felt.

More, now complete, madness took over the crowd. The chaotic emotion was like a feeding frenzy in sharks. All control was gone. Humanity disappeared. Knives and spears and rocks pounded and thumped and dug into the bodies of the two clerics. Scattered blood covered everyone outside the gate.

Now, the two clerics were forced to cling together more tightly, even to be able to stand. Their attempts at smiles remained. But they were now too weak and battered about the mouth to sing.

Then, finally, they sagged slowly and silently, sickeningly, to the bloody ground, still clinging together. The last of their physical strength was seeping out of their bodies through many wounds. Then, they collapsed together, and lay before the gate, twisted and despairingly motionless.

There was a pause in the depredations, as the mob contemplated its vile work. A few of the more responsive members began crying in horror. But the general bloodthirsty mood of the mob was still unchanged.

Harry was completely overcome by the total sacrifice that he had witnessed. With cracking voice, he called out: "Stop! Stop, for the love of God!" He was crying, too. But he himself did not have the raw courage that it would take to step out again in front of the murderous rocks and spears.

No matter. He would not be safe from the mob. Now, the attack was suddenly renewed and redirected. Some rocks began to slam anew against his body. More rocks crashed into Burnhouse also. The crowd was now turning its fury on them. Harry felt pain, much pain. He crouched and raised his arms in a protective stance, to protect his face. Burnhouse was also putting up his hands to ward off the blows.

In addition to the physical pain, there was pain of the soul for both men. They were experiencing the nadir of human existence. They were beaten. The forces of evil had triumphed, even over the personification of Christian agapé. The excruciating psychological pain matched the excruciating level of physical pain.

Patience called out from the still partially opened gate: "You brave idiots. Come inside. You can do no good by dying out there. If it didn't work for Cal and Jack, it won't work for you. Save yourselves now for a last-ditch effort to protect the children. God help them, if these beasts get their hands on them."

Despite the panic in her voice, there was reason in it also.

They both quickly understood that she was right.

Harry backed toward the gate, slowly, like a cornered rat. He was motivated by a mixture of fear and the firm realization that Patience was right about the children.

Burnhouse followed woodenly, limping grotesquely from his many wounds. He too was totally devastated and defeated.

"Act brave," Harry whispered to Burnhouse, "like a hero to be reckoned with. Don't panic, or they will be all over us in a flash. We must not act defeated. Look them in the eye. Prolong the game as long as we can."

As he stumbled dejectedly inside the compound gate, Harry knew that they had failed. Both of them. All of them had failed. Social order itself had failed. Humanity had failed. Psychological technology had not only failed, it itself had created the necessary conditions for that very failure.

There was a pounding of heavy objects on the gates. All sorts of instruments of destruction were taking their toll on the heavy timbers. Obviously, stout as they were, the gates could not withstand such abuse for long.

Sadness, indescribable in completeness and depth, took over the very soul of Harry. He could hardly move, unable even to breathe without effort. He could not speak. Patience was there, trying desperately to comfort. She wrapped her arms tightly around him as if to bandage his emotional wounds also. The newly declared lovers thus clasped each other in desolate silence. They would fight when they needed to, but now they responded to a different need.

But neither of them could be fully comforted, even by one another. They shared a misery that could not be truly shared, even with a loved one. They knew that they would die together in defeat. They would not die as Cal and Jack had triumphed in victory of the spirit. Harry thought that death would not be so bad if it were in her arms. But life with her would have been perfect.

Then, Harry heard Burnhouse gasp as he looked out at the mob through a porthole in the gate. Monika was clinging desperately to him. What new terror was there now? Indeed, incredibly, there was yet a new threat.

Harry looked through another porthole. He could see that, swiftly, Mulik Efraim was marching resolutely toward the gate with a heavy smith's hammer resting across his powerful sloping shoulder. It was a sixteen-pound sledge hammer. When placed in the hands of a powerful man, it was capable of pulverizing concrete and splintering the hardest of woods. The gate was doomed! They were doomed!

Efraim's face was set with determination. He was the very image of irresistible power. No man would be able to withstand him. Neither could a stout wooden gate turn back his wrath. His appearance demolished any small flicker of any vestigial hope that might somehow have remained.

Harry had not seen him tonight until now. Perhaps Efraim had been saving himself for the final blows against the defenders of the compound. As the blacksmith reached the two fallen men, Harry broke free of Patience's desperate grasp, and struggled to open the gate. Efraim must not be allowed to desecrate the sacred sacrifice of the two martyrs.

But, to Harry's total amazement, Efraim quickly turned on the mob in fury, putting his back to the gate. He cried out, in anguish. "Stop! Stop! See what you have done! Just *think* what you have done. I should have stopped you. Cal and Jack loved you; they served every one of you. Every one of you! I saw it all! They brought you food; they sat with you when you were sick. They prayed with you. They were there for you whenever you needed them. They asked for nothing in return. Never before now!

"But now you have repaid their many kindness by brutally murdering them. How could you? No plan for a better world would approve of such barbaric behavior. None. Never! But, in the end they showed you the right way. They did it many times before, and now finally once more tonight. Even through to the end. I see now that love such as they have shown for you wicked, undeserving ones is truly the way to a better world. I see that clearly now. At last, I see it. You can see it. You *have* seen it! Just think! Put your minds on it, and you will see it too."

He raised his hammer in a threatening stance. It caused his matchless muscles to bulk up even more. His complete demeanor, his stern face muscles, frozen in anger, showed convincingly that he was committed to what he said. The members of the mob shrank from his anger, most from sheer habit.

Then, in a somewhat more moderate tone, Efraim said, "It is over. Go on home. Leave here immediately. Otherwise you will have to kill me, too. And that will not be easy, I promise you. I will not let you harm anyone else here tonight while I am yet alive. Go home, and pray to your private gods for forgiveness for what you have already done."

The mob suddenly quieted as if responding to a compelling universal signal. The enormity of their heinous crime seemed finally to reach their consciousness. Most of them were normally reasonable people. They had been confused, misled and transformed by the inciters of inflamed emotions. Finally, at last, Efraim had reached through to the hidden, deep, decent core of many of them. He had succeeded in opening their hearts to this most recent wonderful message of the heroic clerics. The crowd had finally listened with its heart. The inflamed blood in their veins was cooled and calmed by the final appreciation of love.

Harry stepped forward through the partially opened gate, not really knowing what he was doing. Some outside force seemed to have control of his body. He felt that he must get to Cal and Jack and Efraim. He put his arm around Efraim to give him a gentle, heartfelt hug and a smile of thanks.

"Thank you, Mulik. And God bless you," he said, warmly and sincerely.

Efraim's face was a mixture of a faint smile and tears. He nodded to Harry, squeezed his arm, and said, "Finally, I understand. It is I who should thank you."

Then, Harry turned to the former mob. "You have tried to kill love. But the evil in you failed, as it will always fail against love. They loved you until the end. You had no control over that. They gave their lives for you, without conditions. That is the greatest love. That is what can save the world. It is the only thing that can bring happiness. That is what truly makes sense. We join Mulik in love. Look into your hearts and find love. That is more powerful than any TECHland philosophy."

He then began anew the lines of the old hymn: "Oh, love that will not let me go, I hide my weary soul in Thee. To give Thee back the life I owe. So that life can richer, fuller be."

Some of the former members of the mob began to join in the song. Some of them dropped to their knees and folded their hands in prayer. Many of them were crying. Miraculously, there were wounded Junk Yard Dogs among the group. And soon Makos. Tigers and Dragons were kneeling among the Makos. Harry felt exhilarated and humbled. He himself had not anticipated the full power of unconditional love. It shamed him.

Then, at first a few members of the former mob started to drift slowly away. Then others followed. The sounds of flowing tears and moans could be heard in the darkness. It was over. For tonight, it was over.

Constable Gupta rushed out of the compound with several armed deputies. He was determined to hunt down Malevi and Conaway, and place them under arrest for murder. The two thugs had disappeared into the darkness. Harry was sure that they would not find a secure hiding place on the island tonight.

Mourners hurried tearfully out of the compound, and from the former mob, to minister to Cal and Jack.

It was too late.

Cal lay dead, with the smile still on his face. Amazing, but not so amazing. Everyone was sobbing. Father Jack, barely alive, struggled to kiss his crucifix. Patience gently lifted his hand toward his lips. Painfully, with heroic effort, he pressed his lips to the cross. And, thus, he died, still smiling also, that same peaceful smile.

How could they smile? They smiled while everyone else was crying. It was terribly sad, but, yet, somehow an uplifting moment. For one brief beautiful moment all hearts were filled with love. The fear and hate had been driven out, lifted like an odorous cloud. There was still some pain, but mostly joy. That was undoubtedly the way that Cal and Jack wanted it.

This sacrifice was a peerlessly beautiful model of Christian agapé, the like of which Harry had never personally witnessed before. He said reverently so that overwhelming awe was evident in his voice: "Thank you, Cal and Jack, not just for saving our bodies, but for rescuing all of our souls as well. You have lifted our spirits, vitalized our faiths. You have modeled the way. I have never before in my life felt a stronger presence of God. Truly, this night we have seen His instruments. We have come as close to seeing His face as is possible for human beings."

About him there was a universal, "Amen." For some it was a ringing shout of affirmation. For others, it was a committed murmur. Some were kneeling, and others were standing with their arms upraised toward Heaven. Each person celebrated in his or her own way.

Harry knew that he had failed to devise a successful plan. But his prayer had worked. He was awed by the enormity of the idea.

Then, with one accord, Patience and Harry leaped quickly to clasp one another. It was a brief embrace of both comfort and joy, with a promise of more to follow later.

Breaking away, Patience followed the men carrying the bodies of Cal and Jack into the compound. Her arms were tightly locked around the sobbing frames of Calia and Minnie.

And so the experiment and the rebellion ended. The frenzy had not been stopped by armed troops or militia with assault rifles and bayonets, but by simple men with the overwhelming power of gentle love. Thus, the Kipua experiment yielded a powerful scientific conclusion through serendipity. That conclusion is that a love-controlled world is safe, and thus permits all of those human joys that depend upon safety.

TWENTY-ONE

I T WAS A WHILE before Harry could turn his thoughts back to Patience. He had many duties to perform as leader of the CRASH team, and as a friend to the frightened and injured. He saw that Dr. van Loon took care of Burnhouse's wounds. They were a bit more serious than Harry's, but not life-threatening. Harry's wounds were indeed extremely painful. But they also were serious enough to be distracting, not debilitating.

Harry interviewed Flo Gorsuch about the events at the plantation house while he was on the mountain. Then, he put down some notes of his own experiences, both on the mountain, and during the tragic evening at the plantation compound.

Once he was sure that the records were complete, Harry turned to love. It was a different kind of love than that shown by the clerics. It was the kind of love that Harry thought that he deserved. This was the type of love that was easier for Harry to understand. And it was nearly as strong.

But, expression of that love was to be delayed, painfully. Patience had disappeared. Where was she? Harry looked about the compound, but did not see her. Seemingly, no one knew where she had gone. Harry again felt the familiar sour wrenching in his guts.

Harry rushed frantically about the plantation compound, and then began searching the house. Surely, no one could have kidnapped her out of the compound. He did not think it at all likely that she could have been spirited past him out into the jungle. Had she been hurt somehow? She had not been injured the last time he saw her. And the battles were over. Or were they? Could Patience be hiding from him? He could not imagine why Patience would be hiding from him. But he thought that she must be deliberately staying out of his sight. Otherwise, he would have been able to find her. After what they had been through, he needed her in his arms. Surely, her need for him must be equally great. Had she been playing some kind of merciful game with him, and was now ashamed of it?

In his agitated state, Harry could only think, "What a woman! She lays what she did on me, and then takes off! What a woman indeed."

* * * * * *

Patience had indeed surprised herself at the gate. She did not often act so impulsively. The terror and urgency of the moment indeed caused her to feel a strong emotion that to then had been only an unidentifiable tickle or twinge. An unfamiliar burst of some overpowering urge had taken over her person. Suddenly, she had felt that she absolutely could not let Harry die. At least, he could not die without her. A subterranean mental force had compelled her to rush to Harry's side. Some lower level of consciousness took over her being. It shamelessly committed deeds with her body that were entirely out of character for her. Her conscious mind was completely pre-empted. Her behavior became irrational, instinctive. And the result was bloody pleasant. Later, she was still in the sub-conscious state. She acted like a baby without a brain. She hated to be like that. She craved to be in control, especially of herself. She felt like a silly schoolgirl. Harry and the others must not see her embarrassment.

* * * * * *

Harry too had been surprised, but nevertheless delighted at the precipitous breakdown of rational control for both of them. It was good, though, when other indicators were favorable. Despite the differences in homelands, he and Patience had many good things going for them. Without the love, all of that amounted to nothing, of course. But, with the fullness of love, everything was perfect.

Harry had been overwhelmed, stunned, by Patience's revelation. He realized that he had loved her for a long time. But, he had not dared to admit it even to himself, because he had no hope at all that she would fall in love with him. He was glad that in this he could not predict the female mind. Because, undoubtedly she had fallen in love with him. He was sure of it.

Harry only knew that it felt good. It was a feeling beyond the scope and capability of any behavioral technology. Indeed, it felt very good!

Harry finally found Patience in the study of the plantation house. She was curled up on a sofa, facing away from the door. She was moodily drinking a cup of coffee. Harry noted again that, as usual, he was mystified by the female mind. A mere male, psychologist or not, he thought, could not figure out what a woman was thinking. Particularly, this woman. A man was, of course, stuck with a mere male mind.

Patience had one of her stupid hats pulled way down over her forehead, and an afghan pulled around her shoulders, hiding the lower half of her face. Her eyes were barely visible between the brim of the hat and the afghan. They were like a mask, hiding her face. "At least that makes sense," Harry thought, "if she wants to disappear."

Thoroughly agitated, Harry burst out in exasperation: "Where did you go? Why did you go? Did you mean what you said?" He managed to blurt out all of the important questions on his mind at the moment.

Patience merely looked at him, defensively. Her answer was curt: "Here; that's my business; not by a damn site. That takes care of your questions, not that I have to answer them. So, don't get your knickers in knots, cowboy. I just got carried away for a few minutes. Trying to get us through it. I was giddy and foolish. Must have been the fear and excitement of the bloody moment.

"Afterwards, I felt that we both needed some comforting. It was fair dinkum then. A girl needs a man once in a while. Any man. But the need for such comforts is over now. You look okay, and I am jolly good now, as we say down under. That is where I live, you know."

Harry was shocked, rocked back on his heels. His only thought was that she had put out the light in his life forever. He could only stammer in confusion, "But, I thought...."

Patience interrupted seriously and firmly, but not unkindly: "Forget that other stuff ever happened, Harry. It was just the crazy situation. It worked for us when it had to, to get us through the craziness. What happened was not really us. It really had nothing to do with you and me personally. We were just there, available to one another, convenient to fill an immediate need. It was a safe haven in a storm. That is all that it meant."

Harry finally understood her well enough not to believe her. He smiled his broadest smile, and chuckled. "Oh, no you don't. I believed you, Pats. I still believe that you meant what you said at the gate. And you made me realize that I love you, too. So, you opened the gates of love. You can't just back off from it. We are both absolutely stuck with it. So, tell me about it again in detail, and with conviction."

With that, he slowly took her cup, placed it carefully on the coffee table. Then, he carefully removed her hat. Finally, he pressed himself down against her, and drew her up against his body. Her body stiffened. Harry's heart sank. Had he again been so awfully wrong about her?

Then, she yielded. All at once she yielded! Joyfully, he could tell that she had been telling the truth at the gate. He slowly pulled her even closer. They kissed for a long, long time. It occurred to Harry that he had been wondering for years what it would be like to kiss Patience. Now he knew. As he expected, Patience did everything well. "What a beautiful bunch of woman," he thought gleefully. He felt like a child at Christmas with exactly the present he had wanted.

The need for a personal connection was deep inside each of them. So, they closely clung to one another as children cling to mothers in the night, drawing comfort from one another. The tactual comfort of a warm female body fulfilled a gnawing need that Harry had felt for many years since Lottie's death. Renewed strength and assurance passed back and forth through the bond of love between them. Neither of them wanted to stop the savoring.

Harry ruined it by striving for even more. Never one to miss an apparent golden opportunity, he foolishly asserted, "We will have to get married. And, we will live happily ever after."

Patience abruptly stiffened. Her body no longer pliant. The sublime moment was over. Harry quickly realized with dismay that he had somehow destroyed the rapture. Had he mis-read the signs? Had he been too presumptuous? How could a proposal of marriage be offensive?

He silently berated himself: "Another idiotic move, Harry! I don't know why, but it was idiotic."

Patience merely said, "Yeah, like where?"

"In my house, in North Carolina."

She whispered, "I thought so. But, we'll talk about it in the morning. Right now, kiss me again, you dodo bird." Again, she clung to him. The rapture returned. How could she call him a dodo when he was flying?

But the rapture now encompassed a point of concern. She had aroused a worry. For a moment, something had been wrong. Harry thought, "Patience, will you live in the states? Is that it? Will you give up your job and your family to be with me? I desperately hope so. But it is a worry. My darling, you never answered my question."

* * * * * *

The next few days, Harry plunged into the rest of the job for which he had come to the island. Burnhouse had been rescued, and the later events at the plantation gates had placed the team a good distance along the way toward restoring peace and order to the island. Most of the islanders now saw the need for an effective civil government, based on mutual concern for law and order, and were willing to cooperate with it, even fight for it. Mulik Efraim was a major force in both planning and enforcing the peace. His transformation was a religious conversion. In fact, he indicated a desire to convert formally to the Catholic faith. He worked tirelessly in the church to try to fill the void left by Father Jack's death. He was now entirely gentle, loving and helpful. At last, Mulik had found the personal peace that he had sought for so long.

The new peace was being enforced also by the arrival of a company of U.S. Marines. They were young, but they were a fit, well-trained, disciplined bunch. Their presence provided a sense of security that extended beyond their weapons and physical strength. They represented order and dedication, a commitment to a cause. They were a reminder of what the real world could be like when there was a respect for human dignity.

The marines were scrupulously courteous to everyone, to the men as well as to the women. Harry knew that it was the result of the way that they had been trained. But, it was nice to experience it anyway. The trainers, at least, had good intentions for the people.

With peace restored, the immediate job now was to begin the evaluation process. So, Harry went to work gathering evidence from the rest of his team. He assigned parts of the dreadful evening at the compound for each member to record. He wanted to record not only the verbatim transcription of the words of the players, as closely as possible, but also interpretations to be drawn from their vocal inflections and gestures.

The CRASH Team spent three days meeting with Burnhouse and Monika working on a report for the Schoonover Foundation. The two groups had no difficulty in agreeing on the basic facts concerning the disaster on Kipua. Nevertheless, the different groups had developed quite different interpretations of these facts.

Today, Harry and Skull Burnhouse had been glaring at each other for many minutes across the dinner/conference table in the dining area of the Crow Bar. Each was incredulous at the perceived theoretical blindness of the other. Neither man was stupid, to be sure. They each understood that. But, each of them was stubbornly refusing to acknowledge the sense of the other's views in the case of the experiment on Kipua.

Except for Patience, the CRASH team believed that the TECH-land experiment indicated a clear failure for the deterministic model. They argued that Burnhouse had carefully selected the population and conditions for a fair test of the Skinner model. The outcome of the experiment was undeniably a social nightmare.

Patience believed that the TECHland model was basically sound, but that Skull's style of implementation, stemming from his peculiar authoritarian and chauvinistic personality, involved extraneous variables that perverted the model. She contended that his assertive and confrontational style produced resistance and blocking responses in the population. Thus, the islanders had reacted to his impersonal and confrontational style rather than to his behavioristic message. In her view, the TECHland experiment would work only if the founders were more responsive to the initial humanistic beliefs of the target population. In other words, they needed a more accurate assessment of the original starting point for the program in terms of the attitudes of the population.

In marked contrast, Burnhouse and Monika Luthsaar believed that the results were simply inconclusive. Although Burnhouse and Monika did agree that the result in Kipua was disastrous, and that it would have been worse except for the ultimate sacrifice of Cal and Jack, they argued that certain inappropriate contextual conditions did not permit a fair test of the TECHland model. In fact, they attributed the disaster to the benign living conditions on a tropical island such as Kipua. They argued that these conditions had developed unusual hereditary predispositions and learned attitudes among the islanders. The islanders were accustomed to favorable living conditions without working for them. Therefore, the benefits of TECHland living were not particularly desirable to them. Such an unusual living situation, they argued, was thus not appropriate to the Skinnerian model.

Burnhouse had already begun looking for a new sponsor to finance another test of the TECHland model in a different locale which would entail different conditions. He proposed to do the study again in harsher climates, thus with more taxing physical conditions in the environment. He was considering Tierra del Fuego in South America, or the Orkney Islands of Great Britain, as possible sites for the future tests.

The others on the CRASH team were dumbfounded by Burnhouse's interpretation. The basic premise of science was that the researcher made a prediction on the basis of a theory about what would happen in a specified given situation. If he or she were successful in the prediction, the theory that had been the basis for the successful prediction would be considered as supported. By the same logic, if the prediction failed, the foundational theory under test was weakened—perhaps even refuted, if the evidence could not be discounted in any way.

To be sure, each member of the team understood that it is not likely that any empirical research is perfect in every way. Therefore, there is usually some basis, no matter how tiny, for criticizing any empirical evidence. Therefore, there is frequently some element of doubt in interpreting the results of any empirical research as a test of theory. That is an academic truth. The real question is whether or not any identifiable flaw is great enough to invalidate the conclusion.

Each member of the team, other than Patience, was personally convinced that Burnhouse was the victim of Maier's tongue-in-cheek law: *Discard the facts, if they do not fit the theory.* That law was a satirical commentary on those scientists who, inappropriately, reverse the usual scientific dictum that the facts must rule. For science to work, theories must yield to facts. Maier's point was that it is totally disastrous for the scientist to become so committed to a theoretical point of view that he or she cannot accept pertinent data that tend to refute his or her favorite theory. Indeed, under such a circumstance, the person really ceased to be a scientist, becoming merely a dedicated advocate for a theory.

Even Patience was disappointed with Burnhouse's reaction to his failure to gain support for the TECHland model. She was now willing to concede that there should at least be a place for a *belief* in personal freedom in the behavioral plan. The plan must acknowledge the citizens' commitment to beliefs in personal freedom and dignity. And it also must include in the plan some way for dealing with these beliefs. Nevertheless, Patience still could not bring herself to commit personally to such a belief.

Actually, without saying so in open meetings, Harry was inclined to think that there was a kind of poetic justice in Burnhouse's incarceration in a real-life air crib. Interestingly enough, however, Burnhouse apparently still did not view his personal indignation at this assault on his personhood as related in any way to the weakness of the Behavioristic theory and the resulting social model. The relationship did seem rather obvious, however, to the other members of the CRASH team. It seemed to be a modified form of the actor-observer effect: The actor in a scenario emphasizes the importance of controlling conditions that are not fully appreciated by his audience. In this case, Burnhouse was confident in principle that all people are controlled by their environment, and that the concept of freedom was only an illusion brought about by the complexities of interacting causes of behaviors. Nevertheless, he was chagrined at what he perceived to be an infringement on his own personal freedom. Harry was personally rather disgusted by such dissociative thinking.

Finally, shaking his reverie, Harry broke the depressing silence. "This is getting us nowhere. We are never going to agree on why the TECHland experiment failed. Let me propose that each of our three partisan groups work together to prepare a common report of the facts of the case. Then, each different group can submit a separate report of their own group's conclusions from the study. In this way, other scientists at the foundation will be able to decide for themselves which conclusion is most believable. Good science dictates that the views of any reputable scientist should be considered. With my proposal, all three views will be fairly presented."

Burnhouse quickly nodded in agreement, apparently relieved. He looked quizzically at Monika. She also seemed relieved, smiled back, and nodded her head in assent.

They all looked hopefully at Patience. She nodded agreement as well. She seemed satisfied.

"It's a deal, then," promised Burnhouse.

There was a general explosion of happy exclamations at the final agreement. Everyone wanted to finish the job, and begin the journey home.

In the end, the contention of Harry's committee was that people were basically the same everywhere with respect to the variables that were important to the foundation of a Utopian society. The CRASH team concluded that three related factors produced the failure of the TECHland model: 1) the lack of sensitivity of Burnhouse to the prevailing attitudes of the populace; 2) the insistence of the people on keeping their cherished beliefs in personal freedom and dignity, thus resisting the very keystone argument of the Behavioristic plan; and 3) the overall anti-evolutionary nature of the plan itself, which attempted to negate the beneficial effects of evolution on human beings. Another factor was not a cause of the failure, but it tended to exacerbate the effects of the causal factors. It represented the personal history of some members of the population who had experienced abuse, neglect and humiliation. Such persons are likely to seize the opportunity of a permissive environment to vent their feelings of anger and frustration. Thus, any flaws in the social system become magnified in their effects by such people.

Harry's final argument prevailed as the report of the CRASH team was prepared:

> Getting to the crux of the issue before us, the question is whether or not the elimination of the humanistic concepts of personal freedom and dignity is the first step toward a better society. That was Skinner's argument, and that was the fundamental idea tested in the TECHland experiment. Skinner himself proposed that the ultimate test of his notion was its worth for the survival of human society.
>
> It seems to us that evolution itself had already answered the question. The process of natural selection has indicated the special value of the brain for human survival. We survive because we possess a big brain, and not because we possess a big tooth. Specifically, the human animal has the largest brain with respect to body size of all land animals. Moreover, the largest part of this overall larger brain consists of the forebrain. This is the part of the brain that is primarily concerned with learning, individual feelings and thinking. Accordingly, this forebrain of the human animal has gained the capacity to control the lower centers of the brain which, if left uncontrolled, impel the animal to seek survival by selfish, brutish means.
>
> Modern human beings survive, and indeed dominate, the animal kingdom by virtue of this excellent forebrain. This is indeed proof that the functions of the forebrain are valuable to survival of human beings. Skinner was correct in saying that this forebrain has enabled us to develop technologies that are valuable to our survival. But he forgot one important fact: the forebrain *also* has developed the capacity to think distinctively human thoughts. We submit that it is these very thoughts that have been primarily responsible for the human successes, more so than even the fruits of technological thinking.

To eliminate these thoughts from the human repertoire is to eliminate the function of the human brain that has developed for centuries, and therefore has proven effective in an evolutionary sense. With it removed, we will return to the cave-man mentality. We would be on a par socially and morally with the alligators, cold-blooded creatures who have developed relatively little forebrains. The improved technology that is possible with the present human forebrain would be blunted, vitiated and perverted if it were not guided by the humanistic intelligence of a morally-developed forebrain. Indeed, such technology without moral and spiritual guidance will hasten the decline of human civilization because they will be directed toward the achievement of personal power and privilege, rather than the welfare of the group.

Therefore, we conclude that the TECHland experiment failed precisely because it attempted systematically to exclude moral and spiritual values from the plan of governance. Psychologists' ability to control human motivations by behavioral technology has not advanced far enough to be effective without the supplement from humanistic thought. Indeed, we speculate that it never will.

The CRASH group did concede that some other experimental societies have indeed enjoyed success in the past, but not because of the formal technological plan. The report concluded, as follows:

Those societies succeeded only to the extent to which they included subtle, unacknowledged importations of humanistic thinking. In such cases, humanistic thinking may not have been a part of the social plan itself. It sneaked, or was inserted, into the actual treatment of the citizens because it was virtually impossible for the decent, caring psychological technologists to eliminate it from their thoughts and behaviors. It was a humanistic throw-in, an unknown, unacknowledged and unappreciated importation that was not part of the formal plan.

Such humanistic concerns could be revealed to the citizens in the experimental society by very subtle minimal cues. Therefore, often the important role of humanistic values for the success of the community was not recognized. Consequently, their vital importance was not rightfully acknowledged in the interpretation of the data from a successful program.

So, the theoretical and scientific problem of TECHland was solved to Harry's satisfaction. He was sure that his interpretation was consistent with the evidence, and not just a superficial confirmation of *his* own biases. Such unknown bias was surely always a danger. But, he was as satisfied as a scientist could be about the nature of his objective proof and the logical deductions from it.

Patience ultimately agreed to sign the report, because it did not get into the issue of whether or not behavior is completely determined by heredity and environment. She agreed that some belief in free will and human moral values were necessary to prevent tragedies such as the events on Kipua. She did not agree that such beliefs represented objective reality.

Harry was privately convinced that Patience's view was not entirely consistent. He believed that Patience would soon recognize that fact, and shift to a humanistic point of view. Thus, this issue between them was, therefore, resolved for a while, at least.

* * * * * * * *

Harry was on his way to meet Patience on the north beach of the island. The place had bad associations in memory. But, it was the most secluded spot on the island, an excellent location for the important private conversation that must be held between them.

Harry had borrowed a bicycle from Dan Crow. He was laboring on the bike along the dirt road at a pace that was deliberately calculated to get him there sometime in the afternoon. Hopefully, he would still be in a reasonable state of breath to carry on the necessary conversation.

A pre-final draft of the CRASH team report was being typed and collated under the capable supervision of Kate Okanarski. She would make a sufficient number of these draft copies for the team, plus others for Burnhouse, Monika and the island council. After everyone had a chance to comment on the draft, Harry would prepare a finished copy for Schoonover. They could then duplicate and bind as many copies as they saw fit.

So, Harry felt a surge of elation, satisfaction and relief. The team, under his leadership, had accomplished all of its objectives.

The life of Burnhouse had been saved, along with many other lives, maybe very many. There had been a cost, because some precious lives had been lost. The TECHland results had been clearly described and accurately recorded in a scientific report. But the lives that were lost could not have been saved by any actions of his team. He was absolutely sure of that.

Harry had succeeded in securing the cooperation and funding from Schoonover for Rudy and Patience to stay on the island to help with the sequelae of the experiment. To their credit, the Schoonover board members recognized the severity of the damage done to the people of Kipua from the ideas that had been impressed and imposed on them. The Schoonover Board also understood the responsibility of the Foundation to set it right.

The problems for Schoonover were exacerbated by the fact that several of the islanders, led by dePuy and Chief Launo, were investigating the possibility of law suits for damages. Harry had agreed to testify for them. The foundation should have to pay for its mistakes on Kipua that had caused such torment and hardship for the islanders.

Harry was glad to be done with his basic mission. He felt at the same time a deep sense of accomplishment and a total exhaustion. It was finally over.

Still, he felt incomplete, an unrest in spirit. The source was obvious. It surged to the forefront of his consciousness now that the scientific issue had been laid aside. The worrisome problem with Patience was still out there.

The problem with Patience was even worse than Harry had feared. Patience would agree to marry him. Nevertheless, she absolutely refused to live with him in the States. To Harry, that seemed like an unworkable arrangement. As reasons for her refusal to move to the States, she cited her job, her family, her friends and her national pride.

Harry accepted that they all were good and sufficient reasons, to be sure. Reluctantly, he had to agree with that.

Actually, he had the same reasons for proposing that they live in North Carolina. But, Harry also knew that he needed her and wanted her with him. He knew also that he could never survive in

Australia. "They have Christmas in the summer, if you can believe it," he thought to himself, rather pointlessly.

He tried to think of arguments that could work to convince her that she should move to North Carolina to live with him. But, he could not think of any that he had not tried before. She had already rejected all of them.

As his bike crested a hillock of sand, and slowed in the deep sand of the beach, he saw her. A huge, floppy hat covered her head and shoulders, and a giant muu muu covered the rest of her body from the burning sun. She was just gazing off over the lagoon, occasionally stopping to watch some boys cast their nets for fish along the shoreline. Harry could not detect any body language to give him a clue as to how the meeting would go this afternoon.

She turned when she heard him coming. Her dark sun glasses obscured enough of her face, the part left visible by the hat, that Harry could not discern an attitude. "Hi," he said, as cheerfully as he was able, given his forebodings.

"Hi, yourself, Mate," she replied, matching his cheerfulness. He could see that the fraction of visible face was smiling. So far, the signs were good. He knew enough by now to know that when an Australian called you "mate," that it was indeed a very good sign.

Harry sat beside her. He timidly gave her a brotherly kiss on the cheek.

"What's with the flaming kiss on the cheek, you jerk? Can't you manage better than that this afternoon?" She was not angry. Harry was now sure of that.

He kissed her again. This time it was a Hollywood kiss, surely adequate to satisfy the most demanding of film directors. Patience, too, was apparently fully satisfied.

Then, they sat quietly looking out to sea. After a moment of the stillness, Patience said, "Okay, Luv, out with it. What did you want to discuss that was so bloody important?" Her manner indicated that she already knew the answer to her question, and her response to his answer.

* * * * * *

As the *Corncucopia's* crew made the usual busy noises associated with preparing to get under way, Harry's sadness deepened. Complete happiness had been close. But there had been no brass ring. And that was what really counted. It was probably over for him and Patience. That seemed certain for now, anyway. He wondered who wrote that nonsense about it being better to have loved and lost than never to have loved at all. There is too much pain in the loss when the love is very great.

Patience had refused for an uncountable number of times to change her mind. Harry had reluctantly resolved to leave the island without her. He felt that he must go back to his university responsibilities, to his family and to his secure environment. Nevertheless, he would have stayed in the Pacific and persevered if he thought that there were any chance for changing Patience's mind.

Patience had called him a male chauvinist pig for insisting that she come with him, rather than the reverse. He knew that she was right. But, old habits die hard, especially in old male animals. Harry wished that he were truly a male chauvinist pig so that he could grab her by the hair and drag her along with him back to the States. It was a silly male chauvinist idea, of course, but he could not help thinking it.

Of course, Patience was right. But, he had been born and bred an American male. He could not shake the star-spangled notion that the U.S. of A. was the best place in the world to live, and the chauvinist pig idea that a wife should follow her husband.

In any case, he surely had a wretched feeling all over. His professional success on the island was now overshadowed by his overwhelming personal disappointment. He understood that there were some conditions in life that personal desire and dedication could not overcome. He decided there was nothing that he could do to change these conditions. Sometimes the will just cannot make the way.

Posh had a similar problem with Calia. She would not leave her mother in such a time of bereavement. She felt that her mother would not be able to manage life on the island without Cal. As a responsible daughter, she must stay with her mother, at least for a while.

Jake would not leave the renewed tranquility of the island for an uncertain go at life in the fast lane. Because Kate was wedded to her job in New York City, they had to agree that they really had no future together. It was a difficult decision for each of them, but they had to accept the compelling truth out of respect for one another.

Well, Harry was glad anyway that things worked out for Dan Crow and Mary Murphy. One happy couple out of four was not too bad a batting average for baseball, or for romance either, he decided. Such positive thinking was small consolation to the losers though. The six losers were totally miserable. Harry, Posh and Kate had come disconsolately on board the *Cornucopia* for the voyage back to Saipan. Patience, Calia and Jake were still somewhere in similar deep states of depression on Kipua.

Harry really did not blame Patience for her decision. After all, he did not want to try to make a life in Australia. And he reminded himself that she had family and friends there, as well as a good job. "So," he said to himself, "Harry, unpack your bags. Get on with the rest of your life, miserable as it will be. It is too much to ask, even to hope that she could love you that much."

Posh obviously felt exactly the same as Harry. He said, more to himself than to Harry, "I do not blame Calia. Actually, I even admire her decision to stay with her mother. The irony is that Calia's choice makes me love her even more, if that were possible. It separates us, but it reminds me of the things that caused me to fall in love with her in the first place."

They plodded ahead with the business of unpacking, slowly, listlessly, morosely. They could feel that the ship was now floating free of the dock. Feeling the motion of the ship, Harry petulantly complained to no one in particular: "Why couldn't they have loved us more?"

There was a silence. The gloom of despair clouded their minds as they contemplated the implications of the question that had no answer. It was in fact even the wrong question.

Then, Posh said quietly: "Why couldn't *we* have loved *them* more?"

The two confused and dejected men just looked at each other intently for a long moment. The right answers to the right questions suddenly became clear to them both. They were no longer confused. And, surely, there was no need for delay.

In concert, as if by some mutual signal, the two men frantically threw their clothes back in the suitcases. After snapping them shut, they raced in a frenzy of haste toward the topside. They hoped that the boat was not already too far away from the dock for them to disembark. They could clearly feel the movement of the old boat away from their hopes for the future.

As they emerged into the sunlight, Posh gasped in amazement. Harry did also when he saw the reason for Posh's reaction. There was a wonderful vision on the dock. It was Calia, tears cascading down her cheeks, running toward the boat as if chased by the devil. When she saw the men and luggage, she paused, still with an anguished look. Now, suddenly hopeful, she called out, "Posh." It was a plea, a question, an affirmation, all in one.

An inspired Posh easily cleared the distance to the dock, luggage and all. Harry followed. He barely made it to the dock, and without the luggage. No matter. He was not going to miss another shot at being with Patsy.

At once, Posh and Calia became entwined like two indistinguishable honeysuckle bushes by the roadside. Calia blurted out between smothered kisses that her mother threatened to disown her if she did not immediately follow Posh to the ends of the earth.

"Smart woman!" thought Harry. "And brave and caring."

The two young people were obviously as happy as two reunited lovers could be—which seemed entirely natural given the circumstances. The sight of them made Harry ache even more for Patience.

Calia disengaged her lips long enough to gasp, "Patsy is in the Crow Bar." And then she returned to pressing business.

Harry did not know that his old professor's legs could move as fast as he compelled them at his best version of a sprint down the dock. He felt like he was flying, but yet somehow his progress seemed so terribly, agonizingly slow. It seemed to him like a dream when you feel like some force is holding you back. He was not slow. Only his impatience made it seem so. It was just that he was in such a panic to get to the Crow Bar.

392 E. Rae Harcum

Finally, completely out of breath, he crashed through the swinging front door. It didn't swing quite fast enough. Undoubtedly, he had inflicted some irreparable damage to the door. "I will have to square the damages with Dan Crow," he thought, inconsequentially.

But there was no need for him to have hurried. Patience was sitting patiently—Harry could hardly believe it—on a large suitcase facing the door. Incredibly, she was surrounded by luggage and other assorted belongings. And, as always, she was wearing a ridiculous hat. This one had the usual floppy brim, with flowers and feathers stuck in the hat band. The designer of this hat was surely not paying attention to normal business.

Harry could hardly believe what he then perceived: *She was actually patiently waiting for him!* When she saw him, she smiled the most gorgeous smile that a gorgeous, happy face can create. The last time he had seen such a smile was a few moments ago, twins on the faces of Posh and Calia. He was sure that his own face must be like that right now, if it even began to show a little bit of the joy that engulfed him.

Harry blurted out, joyously: "Australia, here I come. I can live anywhere as long as I am with you, Pats."

"So kiss me, you fool," she commanded, dashing toward him. Obligingly, as always, Harry rushed to her open arms and willingly obeyed, knocking her hat to the floor. His surrender was as complete as hers. It was mutual surrender. So, both of them were victorious.

Harry was happy beyond his ability to express it, even to himself. He was consumed with love in a way that he thought could never happen to him again. He had thought that such feelings were buried forever with Lottie. He could bless this place after all!

Suddenly alert to his surroundings, Harry whispered between kisses, "What's with the luggage? Did you change your mind? I thought you were staying."

Patience replied, seriously, "I didn't change my mind, you bloody jerk. I always wanted to come with you. But, if I came at first, I would always resent that I was the one to make the sacrifice. I had to know what was really in your heart. Was I just a little positive reinforcement, a nifty little squeeze for you, when you were far away from home and desperate? Was I just a little part of an interlude for comfort? Or, do you love me with something like the selfless love that you had for Lottie?

"I have that kind of full love for you. I needed to know that your love was worthy of that kind of love from me. All I needed was to know that you were willing to make hard sacrifices, too. Now it is all right! It is enough to know that you love me more than your bloody male role model and Yankee pride. I can live anywhere with you, as long as I am free to visit my family whenever I want."

"You got it," the astonished professor promised. He would have promised anything at the moment. "But what about finishing your job here on Kipua?"

"Oh, Rudy said that he can handle it alone, if you want. I am sure he can," she answered. "So, I am all yours. Together, we can help Rudy, and also have a small vacation while we are waiting for the next boat. We will have to wait now for the next boat because you didn't get smart soon enough to get to me in time to catch this one. Surely, by the time the boat returns, Rudy will be able to handle things very well by himself."

Harry could only say, "Yeah! But you will have to buy me a toothbrush because mine is either on the way to Saipan or at the bottom of the lagoon."

"No problem," said Patience. "They have toothbrushes all over."

Joy filled Harry to overflowing like he had felt only a few times before. He could tell from Patience's trembling body that she, too, was consumed by joy.

Harry was sure that, somewhere in Heaven, Lottie was sharing their happiness. He decided that the feeling was good, very good.

* * * * * *

So, at this time, in this very island paradise, love had triumphed, undeniably, completely, joyfully. It had been discovered to have two faces: the face of transcendental love for all human beings, shown by the two clerics; and of personal love between man and woman, shown by three pairs of lovers. Both faces of love were beautiful and miraculous, worthy of more than spare descriptions as positive reinforcement.

If such loves could work under the tragic conditions on Kipua, they could succeed everywhere, every time. So, the answer to the question of Utopia came through the process of serendipity. Obviously, a true answer was found. But it was not the answer that was envisioned by the authors of the TECHland experiment. The answer was that the Kipua experiement was based on a blueprint for Hell.

Burnhouse found an answer that he was not looking for, and could not accept. In trying to prove the weakness of particular human emotions and beliefs as a basis for social organization, Burnhouse actually set the stage for proof of the very opposite. The experience at Kipua told human society that love is likely to prevail. It spoke a message to the whole world—not just the scientific community. Simple incentives of power, sex, cash, all personal gain, given without love, no matter in what amounts, were doomed to fail.

As the song says! "Love is the answer." It is the open gate to Utopia, and to Heaven, available to everyone, in all societies. That is the true lesson, the ultimate blessing, of the Kipua experiment. A passionate commitment to that simple conviction will surely save us from the evils of a technocratic world.

About the author

E. Rae Harcum was born on March 1, 1927. He completed high school in 1945, and volunteered for the U.S. Navy in January, 1946. He was honor man in his recruit company, and first in his class in quartermaster school. He was discharged from the Navy in June, 1947, as a Quartermaster Third Class.

He enrolled at the College of William and Mary in 1947, and graduated Phi Beta Kappa in February, 1950. He served as director of the Wesley Foundation at William and Mary until matriculating in graduate school at the Johns Hopkins University in September, 1950. He received a Master of Arts degree in psychology in June, 1952.

Harcum continued graduate study at the University of Michigan in Fall, 1952, and received a Ph.D. in 1955. He worked in the vision laboratory at Michigan until September, 1958, doing applied research in visual perception.

He taught at William and Mary from September, 1958, until retiring in June, 1992, as professor. During his tenure at William and Mary, he served as department chair for six years. He also served six years on the Virginia Licensing Board for Psychologists, two as Chair. He spent one year as a Visiting Scholar at the University of California, Berkeley, and other leaves on COSIP

395

and other grants. He was elected as Fellow by the American Psychological Association, the American Psychological Society and the American Association for the Advancement of Science. He holds memberships in Sigma Xi (honorary research society), Psi Chi (undergraduate honor society in psychology) and Pi Tau Chi (honorary religious society).

Harcum has published numerous articles and chapters and five books in psychology. He has published two books on religion.

He was married in August, 1952, to Phoebe Carroll Martin. They have two children and three grandchildren.